This Large Print Book carries the
Seal of Approval of N.A.V.H.

THE QUEEN'S LADY

THE QUEEN'S LADY

SHANNON DRAKE

THORNDIKE PRESS

A part of Gale, Cengage Learning

GALE
CENGAGE Learning

Detroit • New York • San Francisco • New Haven, Conn • Waterville, Maine • London

GALE
CENGAGE Learning™

Thorndike Press® Large Print Romance.
The text of this Large Print edition is unabridged.
Other aspects of the book may vary from the original edition.
Set in 16 pt. Plantin.
Printed on permanent paper.

LIBRARY OF CONGRESS CATALOGING-IN-PUBLICATION DATA

Drake, Shannon.
  The queen's lady / by Shannon Drake.
    p. cm. — (Thorndike Press large print romance)
    ISBN-13: 978-1-4104-0759-7 (alk. paper)
    ISBN-10: 1-4104-0759-4 (alk. paper)
    1. Large type books. I. Title.
  PS3557.R198Q44 2008
  813'.54—dc22   2008010458

Published in 2008 by arrangement with Harlequin Books S.A.

Printed in the United States of America
1 2 3 4 5 6 7 12 11 10 09 08

JUL 0 2 2008

For Joan Hammond, Judy DeWitt
and Kristi and Brian Ahlers, with love
and thanks for always
being so wonderfully supportive

PROLOGUE

Before the fire

Gwenyth heard the sound of footsteps and the clang of metal, and knew the guards were on their way to her cell.

Her time had come.

Despite knowing since the beginning that she was doomed, despite her determination to die defiant, scornful and with dignity, she felt her blood grow cold and congeal in her veins. Easy to be brave before the time, but now, faced with the reality of the moment, she was terrified.

She closed her eyes, seeking strength.

At least she could stand on her own two feet. She would not have to be dragged out to the pyre like so many pathetic souls who had been "led" into confession. Those who had seen the evil of their ways through the thumbscrews, the rack or any of the other methods used to encourage a prisoner to talk, could rarely walk on their own. She had given her interrogators what they had wanted from the beginning, standing tall and, she hoped, making a mockery of her judges through her sarcastic confession. She had saved the Crown a great deal of money, since the monsters who tortured prisoners to draw out the truth had to be paid for their heinous work.

And she had saved herself the ignominy of being dragged — broken, bleeding and disfigured — to the stake.

Another clank of metal, and footsteps drawing closer.

Breathe, she commanded herself. She could and would die with dignity. She was whole, and she had to be grateful that she could walk to her execution, having seen what they were capable of doing. But the terror. . . .

She stood as straight as a ramrod, not from pride but because she had grown so cold it was as if she were made of ice, unable to bend. Not for long, though, she mocked herself. The flames would quickly thaw her with their deep and deadly caress. Instead of adding to the agony of the punishment, further torturing the doomed and broken souls delivered to their kiss, the flames were meant to see that such damned creatures were destroyed completely, ashes to ashes, dust to dust. Before the flames were ignited, the condemned was usually strangled. Usually.

But when the judges were infuriated, the flames might be lit too quickly, without allowing the executioner time to hasten the end and lessen the agony. She had made enemies. She had spoken up for others; she had fought for herself. Her death was unlikely to be quick.

She'd made too many enemies, and that had led to her conviction and impending death. It had been easy to put the pieces together — after her arrest.

There were many who believed in the devil, believed that witchcraft was the source of all evil in the world — including the queen Gwenyth had served with such loyalty. They believed that mankind was weak, that Satan came in the night, that pacts were signed in blood, and curses and spells cast upon the innocent. They thought confession could save the eternal soul, that excruciating torture and death were the only way back into the arms of the Almighty. In fact, they were in the majority, for now; in Scotland and most of Europe, the practice of witchcraft was a capital crime.

She was not guilty of witchcraft, and her judges knew it. Her crime was one of

9

loyalty, of love for a queen who, with her reckless passions, had damned them all.

Not that the cause mattered, nor the sham of a trial and the cruelty of the judgment against her. She was about to die. That was the only thing that mattered now.

Would she falter? What would happen when she felt the scorching touch of the first flames? Would she scream? Of course she would; she would be in agony.

She had been right and righteous.

Little good that did now.

And beyond the fear of death and pain, she was sorry. She hadn't realized how much she had traded away in adhering to her ideals. The pain of what she was leaving behind had become a ragged, bleeding wound in her heart, burning as if salt had been poured on the tender flesh. Nothing they were about to do to her body could be as heinous as the agony tearing at her soul. For once she was gone. . . .

What would happen to Daniel?

Nothing, surely. God could not be so cruel. The trial, the execution . . . they were meant to silence her and her alone. Daniel was safe. He was with those who loved him, and surely his father would allow no harm to befall him. No matter what she had done or how she had defied him.

The footsteps came closer, stopped just outside her cell. For a moment she was blinded by the light of the lantern they had brought with them into the darkness of the dungeon. She could tell there were three of them, but nothing more. Then her vision cleared and for a moment her heart took flight.

He was there.

Surely he could not mean for her life to end this way. Despite his anger, his warnings, his threats, he couldn't have intended *this*. He had told her often enough — accurately, she had to admit — that she was far too like the queen she had served, rashly speaking her mind and blind to the dangers inherent in such honesty. But still, could he really be a part of this charade, this spectacle of political injustice and machination? He had held her in his arms, given her a brief, shimmering glimpse of how the heart could rule the mind, how passion could destroy sanity, how love could sweep away all sense.

They had shared so much. *Too* much.

And yet . . .

Men could betray one another as quickly as the wind shifted. For their own lives, for the sake of position and wealth, property and prosperity. Was he indeed a part of this travesty? For she had not been mistaken.

Rowan was here in all his grandeur. His wheaten hair was golden in the flickering torchlight, and he epitomized nobility in every way — kilted in his colors, a sweeping, fur-trimmed cape adding to the breadth of his swordsman's shoulders. He stood before her now, flanked by her judge and her executioner, chiseled features grim and condemning, eyes as dark as coal, cold and disdainful. Long fingers of ice reached up and gripped her heart. How foolish she had been to believe he had come to her rescue.

He had not come to help her but to further condemn her. He was not immune to the political machinations of the day. Like so many of the nobility, with skills honed through years of bloodshed, he was adept at straddling a wall, then landing on the winning side in battle, whether on the field or in the halls of government.

She stared at him without moving, the other men invisible to her. She forced herself to ignore her own filthy and disheveled state — clothing torn and damp, crusted with the dirt and mold of her dungeon cell. She refused to allow herself to falter beneath his stare. Despite the rags that clung to her now, she remained still and regal, determined to end her life with grace. He watched her, his scorching blue eyes so dark with condemnation that they appeared to her like stygian pits, a glimpse into the hell into which she would find herself cast once she had breathed her last in this life and endured the final agony of the fire.

She met his look with scorn, barely aware that the judge was reading the accusation and the sentence, informing her that the time had come.

"Burned at the stake until dead . . . ashes cast to the wind . . ."

She didn't move, didn't blink, simply stood quite still, with her head held high. She realized that Reverend Martin had come up behind the others. She was almost amused to see that they had sent their esteemed lapdog to try to force her into abject terror and a renewed confession, even at the stake. After all, if she were to assure the crowd that she was indeed the devil's pawn, guilty of all manner of horrors, then the whispers that she was innocent, a victim of a political struggle, would not rise to become shouts that stirred resistance the length and breadth of the country.

"Lady Gwenyth MacLeod, you must confess before the crowds, and your death will go easy," the rector said. "Confess and pray now, for with your deepest repentance, our great Father in Heaven may well see fit to keep you from an eternity in the very bowels of hell."

She couldn't tear her eyes from Rowan, who appeared so tall and indomitable among the others, though he was still watching her with such loathing. She prayed that her own disgust outshone the fear in her eyes.

"Take care, reverend," she said softly. "I stand condemned, and if I speak now before the crowd, I will say that I am guilty of nothing. I will not confess to a lie before the crowd, else my Father in Heaven would abandon me. I go to my death, and on to Heaven, because the good Lord knows I am innocent, and that you are using His name to rid yourselves of a political enemy. It is *you,* I fear, who will long rot in hell."

"Blasphemy!"

She was stunned, for it was Rowan who shouted out the word.

The barred door of her cell was flung wide with terrible violence. Before she knew it, he had seized hold of her, the fingers of one hand threaded cruelly through her hair, forcing her to stare up into his eyes, power-less to escape the touch of his other hand against her cheek.

"She must not be allowed to speak before

any crowd. She knows her soul is bound for hell, and she will try only to drag others down into Satan's rancid hole along with her," Rowan said, his voice rough with hatred and conviction. "Trust me, for I know too well the witchery of her enchantment."

How could such words fall from his lips? Once he had sworn to love her forever. Before God, he had vowed his love.

Her heart shattered at the thought that he had come not only to bear witness to her agony but to be a part of it.

His hand was large, his fingers long and strangely gentle, despite the fact that he was so accustomed to wielding a sword. She recalled with renewed pain how those fingers had once reached for her only to stroke with the greatest tenderness. And his eyes . . . eyes that had gazed at her with such delight, such amusement, even anger at times, but most of all with a deep, shattering passion that touched her soul as she could never be touched in the flesh.

Now they were nothing but dark, brutal.

As he stared at her, held her defenseless, he moved, and she realized that he was holding something. It was, she saw, a small glass vial, and he held it to her lips as he bent closer and whispered for her ears alone, "Drink this. Now."

She stared at him blankly, knowing that she had no choice, and almost smiled, because she saw the flicker of . . . something in those eyes that were so blue a color that they defied both sea and sky. She saw desperation and something more. Suddenly she recognized what it was. He was playing a part. He had not forgotten her.

"For the love of God, drink this now," he said.

She closed her eyes and drank.

In an instant, the room began to spin, and she realized that there had been mercy in him, after all, some memory of the sweeping passions they had shared, for he had given her poison to spare her the searing agony of the flames devouring her flesh, roaring until she was nothing but ash cast into the wind.

"She's Satan's bitch! She seeks to make a mockery of us all." Rowan growled as she felt his hands tighten around her throat.

He wanted them to think that he had strangled her not as an act of mercy, but to keep her silent before the crowd.

Darkness began to encroach upon her vision, and a numbness invaded her limbs. She could no longer stand, and she sank against him, grateful that she would be dead before she was consumed by the fire.

And yet, in those last moments, she raged against the agonizing truth that the man she had once trusted, had loved above life itself, with whom she had shared ecstasy, known paradise, should be the one to take her life.

She saw his eyes again, bright like blue flame, and wondered if those fiery beacons would follow her even unto death.

Her lips moved. "Bastard," she told him.

"I shall meet you in hell, lady," he replied, his voice a whisper, and yet, like the fire in his eyes they would surely follow her into eternity.

Was there a smile curving his lips? Was he mocking her, even as she died? Her vision fading, she looked into his eyes for confirmation and saw both sorrow and something more, as if he were trying to convey something to her, something the others must not see.

For as long as she could, she continued to meet his eyes, trying to see all that was in them and to convey her own message to him.

Daniel . . .

She wanted to say his name, but she dared not. She knew — *knew* — that he would love their son, that Daniel would never want for anything. Rowan would see to that. Unlike her, he would never fall prey to the vicissitudes of power. He had always been a statesman; his enemies never underestimated his strength — or his popularity.

The darkness closed in more fully around her, yet she felt no pain, wishing she had learned the lessons of statesmanship more fully.

That the queen had learned them, as well.

She wondered if she, like Mary, had given way too often to passion and her own convictions, her own definitions of right and wrong. Had there been a better way to stand her ground, to help the woman who even now knew she was in grave peril? The queen, too, might well lose her life; she had already been forced to abandon everything that made life worth living.

How could she have known? How could any of them have known? It had begun with such power and grandeur, such a beautiful and glorious dream. Even as the light faded, she remembered how it had shone once, so long ago.

■ ■ ■ ■

Part I
Homecoming

■ ■ ■ ■

CHAPTER ONE

August 19, Year of Our Lord 1561
"Who is that?" one of the maids whispered, hovering behind Queen Mary as they arrived, earlier than expected, at Leith. Gwenyth wasn't sure who had spoken; Mary, Queen of Scots, had left her native land as a child with four ladies-in-waiting, all of them also named Mary: Mary Seton, Mary Fleming, Mary Livingstone and Mary Beaton. Gwenyth liked them all very much. They were all charming and sweet. Each had her individual personality traits, but they were known collectively as "the Marys" or "the queen's Marys," and sometimes it seemed as if they had become one collective person, as now, when Gwenyth wasn't sure who had spoken.

They were all — including the queen — watching the shore, their eyes on the contingent awaiting them. The queen's beautiful dark eyes seemed, to Gwenyth, as misty as the day itself.

Gwenyth didn't think the queen had heard the question, until suddenly she replied. "Rowan. Rowan Graham, Lord of Lochraven. He visited France with my half brother, Lord James, some months ago."

Gwenyth had heard the name. Rowan Graham was considered to be one of the most powerful nobles in Scotland. She seemed to recall that there was some strange tragedy connected with him, but she didn't know what it was. She also knew that he had a reputation for speaking boldly and having the personal power and political strength to assure he was heard.

She sensed at that moment that this man was destined to haunt her life. He was impossible to miss, standing beside the queen's half brother and regent, Lord James Stewart. Mary herself was tall, at five feet and eleven inches, taller than most of the men who served her. James himself was not as tall, but even if he had been taller than the queen, the man by his side would have towered above him in the mist that shrouded the land. The light was thin, but what there was of it gilded his wheat-gold hair, turning him into a golden lord, a warrior knight, akin to the Viking raiders of long ago. He was clad in the colors of his clan, blues and greens and, despite the fashionable raiment of the group assembled to greet the returning queen, he was the man to whom eyes turned.

Lochraven, Gwenyth thought. A Highland holding. Even in Scotland, the Highlanders were considered a race unto themselves. Gwenyth knew Scotland better than her queen, and she knew that a Highland lord could be a dangerous man, for she was from the Highlands herself, and very aware of the fierce power of the clan thanes. Rowan Graham was a man to be watched.

Not that the queen had a reason to fear any man in Scotland. Mary had been asked to return home, but there were things Gwenyth knew that the queen did not. Just a year ago, Protestantism had become the official religion in Scotland, and with fanatical men — *persuasive* men — such as John Knox preaching in Edinburgh, the queen's devotion to the Catholic faith could place her in danger. The thought made Gwenyth angry; Mary's intent was to let people worship as they chose. Surely the same courtesy should be extended to the queen.

"Home. Scotland." Mary murmured the two words as if trying, in her own mind, to make them synonymous.

Gwenyth was startled from her own

thoughts and looked at her sovereign and friend worriedly. She herself was delighted to return home. Unlike many of the queen's ladies, she had been gone but a short time, only a year. Mary had left her home before the age of six. The Queen of Scotland was far more French than Scottish. When they had left France, Mary had stood at the rail of their ship for a long time, tears in her eyes, repeating, "*Adieu,* France."

For a moment Gwenyth felt a surge of resentment on behalf of Scotland. She loved her homeland. There was nothing as beautiful as the rocky coast, with its shades of gray, green and mauve in spring and summer turning to a fantasy of white come winter. And she loved her country's rugged castles, a match for the steep crags of the landscape. But perhaps she wasn't being fair to Mary. The queen had been away for a long time. It couldn't help that the French themselves considered Scotland a land where barbarians still roamed, possessed of nothing that could compare with the sophistication of their own country.

Mary was barely nineteen and a widow. No longer Queen of France but ruler of the country that was her birthright, a country she hardly knew.

The queen smiled at those around her.

"We have won through," she said with forced cheer.

"Yes," agreed Mary Seton. "Despite all those wretched threats from Elizabeth."

There had been a certain sense of nervousness when they had sailed, since Queen Elizabeth had not responded to their request for safe passage. Many in France and Scotland had feared that the English queen intended to waylay and capture her cousin. There had been a terrifying moment when they had been stopped on their journey by English ships. However, the English crews had merely saluted, and their vessels, other than those in Mary's immediate party, had been inspected for pirates. Lord Eglington had been detained, but he had been assured of safe conduct after interrogation. At Tynemouth, Mary's horses and mules had been confiscated, with promises of a safe return once proper documents were obtained.

"This is quite exciting," Mary Seton said, indicating the tall Scotsman.

The queen looked out at the shore again, staring at the man in question. "He is not for you," she said simply.

"Perhaps there are more like him," Mary Livingstone said lightly.

"There are many like him," Gwenyth said.

They all turned to stare at her, and she flushed. "Scotland is known for birthing some of the finest warriors in the world," she said, upset with herself for sounding so defensive.

"I vow we will have peace," Queen Mary said, her gaze still on the shore, then she shivered slightly.

It was not the cold, Gwenyth thought, that caused the shiver. She knew that Mary was thinking that France was a far grander country than Scotland, offering far more comfortable accommodations along with its warmer weather. Much of the known world, and certainly the French themselves, considered the country to be the epitome of art and learning and felt that Scotland had been blessed to be tied to such a great power by marriage. In France, Mary had known the finest of everything. Gwenyth feared that the queen would be disappointed by the amenities her homeland offered.

Cheers went up from the shore, as Mary offered a radiant smile. Despite their early arrival after five days at sea, a good-sized crowd had mustered. "Curiosity," Mary whispered to Gwenyth, a dry note in her voice.

"They've come to honor their queen,"

Gwenyth protested.

Mary merely smiled and waved; radiant, she stepped from the ship, to be greeted first by her half brother James and then the milling court around him. The people were shouting joyously. Perhaps they *had* come out of nothing more than curiosity, but they were impressed now, as well they should be. Mary had never forgotten her Scots tongue; she spoke it fluently, with no trace of an accent. Her voice was clear, and she was not only beautiful — tall, stately and slender — but she moved with an unmistakably regal grace.

Gwenyth stood slightly behind the queen and Lord James. The towering blond man, Lord Rowan, slipped past her, bending to whisper in Lord James's ear. "It's time to move on. She's done well. Let's not take a chance that the mood will turn."

When he moved to retreat, Gwenyth caught his eyes and she knew her own were indignant. He wasn't, however, cowed in the least by her fury; instead was amused. His lips twitched, and Gwenyth felt her anger deepen. Mary of Scotland was a caring queen. True, she was young, and she had grown up in France, but since the death of her young husband — not just the King and her marriage partner, but her dear friend since childhood — Mary had demonstrated a firm grasp of statesmanship. That this man should doubt her in any way was nothing less than infuriating. And, Gwenyth decided, traitorous.

Soon they were all mounted, ready to ride to Holyrood Palace, where they would dine while the queen's rooms were prepared. Gwenyth sighed softly. This homecoming would be a good thing. The people would continue to rally around Mary. Meanwhile, Gwenyth herself was content simply to revel in the familiarity of the truest home she had ever known. Though the day was a bit foggy, even what some might call dismal, the gray and mauve skies were as much a part of Scotland's wild beauty as the rugged landscape itself.

"At the least," one of the young Marys said, "it seems that Mary will be adored and honored here. Even if it isn't France," she added sadly.

Gwenyth was dismayed to feel a strange chill as they rode through Leith. There was nothing to cause her such discomfort, she assured herself. People were cheering the queen's passage with great enthusiasm. She had no reason for uneasiness.

"Why the frown?"

She turned, startled, to see that Rowan

Graham had moved up and was riding at her side — and regarding her with amusement.

"I am not frowning," she said.

"Really? And to think I had imagined you might have the intelligence to worry about the future despite the fanfare."

"Worry about the future?" she said indignantly. "Why should I worry that the concerns of the world might impose themselves upon a queen?"

He stared forward, a strange look of both amusement and distance in his eyes. "A Catholic queen has suddenly come home to rule a nation that has wholeheartedly embraced Protestantism in the last year." He turned back to her. "Surely that is cause for concern?"

"Queen Mary's half brother, the Lord James, has assured her that she may worship as she chooses," she said.

"Indeed," he said, and laughed aloud, which she thought quite rude.

"Would you deny the queen her right to worship God?" she inquired. "If so, perhaps you'd be best off returning to the Highlands, my lord," she said sweetly.

"Ah, such fierce loyalty."

"No more than you, too, owe your queen," she snapped.

"How long have you been gone, Lady Gwenyth?" he asked softly in return.

"A year."

"Then such pretense on your part is either foolish or you are sadly not as well-read or intelligent as I had imagined. You speak of loyalty, but surely you know loyalty is something to be earned. Perhaps your young queen does indeed deserve such a fierce defense, but she must prove herself to her people, having been gone so long. Have you been gone so long that you have forgotten how it is here? That there are parts of this land where the monarchy and government mean nothing, and devotion is given first and foremost to one's own clan? When there is no war to fight, we fight among ourselves. I am a loyal man, my lady. Fiercely loyal to Scotland. Young Mary is our queen, and as such, she has not just my loyalty but every shred of strength I can provide, both my sword arm and my life. But if she wishes to gain real control as a monarch, she will have to come to know her people and make them love her. For if they love her . . . no battle in her name will be too great. History has proven us reckless, far too ready to die for those with the passion to lead us into battle. Time will tell if Mary is one such."

Gwenyth stared at him, incredulous. It was a heroic speech, but she sensed something of a threat in it, as well. "You, my lord, haven't the manners of a Highland hound," she returned, fighting for control.

He didn't lose his temper, only shrugged. She was further irritated when once again he laughed out loud. "A year in France has made you quite high and mighty, has it not? Have you forgotten that your own father hailed from the Highlands?"

Was that a subtle rebuke? Her father had died on the battlefield with James V, though he'd not left such a great legacy as the king. He'd been Laird MacLeod of Islington Isle, but the tiny spit of land just off the high tors barely afforded a meager living for those who lived upon it. Riches had not sent her to France to serve Queen Mary; respect for her father's memory was all that had been left her.

"It's my understanding that my father was stalwart and brave, *and* courteous at all times," she informed him.

"Ah, how sharp that dagger," he murmured.

"What is the matter with you, Laird Rowan? This is a day of great joy. A young queen has returned to claim her birthright. Look around you. People are happy."

31

"Indeed," he agreed. "So far."

"Beware. Your words hold a hint of what might sound traitorous to other ears," she informed him coolly.

"My point," he said softly, "is that this Scotland is a far different place than the Scotland she left so long ago — indeed, even from the Scotland *you* left behind. But if you think I am less than pleased to see Mary here, you are mistaken. It is my entire aim to keep Mary on her throne. I, too, believe a man — or a woman — must worship God from the heart and as seems best, not turning upon details that have so torn apart the Catholic Church and the people of this country. Men of power write policy and interpret words on paper, yet it is the innocents who so often die because of that simple fact. I speak bluntly and boldly — that is my way. I will always be here to guard your Mary — even against herself, if need be. You, my dear, are young, with the idealistic perceptions of youth. May God guard *you,* as well."

"I hope He will start by helping me avoid the boors of my own country," she returned, her chin high.

"With one so charming and dedicated as yourself, dear Lady Gwenyth, how could our Maker not oblige?"

Kneeing her horse, she hurried forward, keeping her place within Mary's vanguard, but putting some distance between herself and the rough Laird Rowan. She heard his soft laughter follow her and shivered. He had managed to cast a pall over what should have been a day of unalloyed triumph. Why, she wondered, did she let his subtle byplay disturb her so deeply?

She turned her horse back toward him. Riding was one of her finer talents, and she wasn't averse to displaying her abilities as she swerved her mount, covered the distance she'd put between them, then swerved once again and rode up beside him.

"You know nothing," she informed him heatedly. "You do not know Mary. She was sent to France as a child and given a husband. And she was a friend, the best friend possible, to him. The poor king was sickly from the beginning, but Mary remained a dear and loyal friend — and wife. In the end, despite the wretched conditions of the sickroom, she never once wavered. She cared for him until his death, then mourned his loss with dignity. And as the world changed around her, she kept that dignity. As diplomats and courtiers from all over the world came with petitions and suggestions for her next marriage, she weighed her options, *including what was best for Scotland,* with deep concern and a full understanding of the statesmanship demanded by her position. How dare you doubt her?" she demanded.

This time, he didn't laugh. Instead, his eyes softened. "If she has the power to earn such passionate praise from one such as yourself, my lady, then there must be deep resources indeed beneath her lovely and noble appearance. May you always be so certain in all things," he said at last, softly.

"Why should not one be certain, sir?" she inquired.

"Because the wind is quick to change."

"And do you, like the wind, change so easily, Laird Rowan?"

He studied her for a moment, almost fondly, as if he had stumbled upon a curious child. "The wind will blow, and it will bend the great trees in the forest, whether I wish it were so or not," he said. "When there is a storm brewing, 'tis best to take heed. The bough that does not bend will break."

"That," she said, "is the problem with the Scots."

"You are a Scot," he reminded her.

"Yes. And I have seen far too often how easily great lords can be bribed to one point of view or another."

He looked ahead. Whether she liked him or not, the man had a fine profile: strong, clean-shaven chin; high, broad cheekbones; sharp eyes; and a wide brow. Perhaps it was his appearance that allowed him to be so patronizing without fear of reprisal.

"There are things I know, my lady, and things I know about my people. They are superstitious. They believe in evil. They believe in God — and they believe in the devil."

"Don't you?"

He looked at her again. "I believe in God, because it comforts me to do so. And if there is good, then truly there must be evil. Does it matter to a greater being — one so great as God — if a man believes in one interpretation of His word or another? I'm afraid He does not whisper His true wisdom into my ears."

"How amazing. From your behavior, one would assume He did," she retorted.

He smiled slightly. "I have seen a great deal of tragedy and misery — sad old women condemned to the flames as witches, great men meeting the same fate for their convictions. What do I believe in? Compromise. And compromise, I propose, is what the queen must do."

"Compromise — or bow down?" she

inquired, trying not to allow the heat she felt into her words.

"Compromise," he assured her.

Then it was he who moved on. Perhaps he had decided he was wasting his wisdom on a mere lady-in-waiting, that he no longer found her amusing. . . .

"I shall tell the queen about you," she murmured to herself, more worried than she cared to admit about the doubts he had planted in her mind. The barons here were indeed powerful men, men whose loyalty Mary needed to retain.

Lord Rowan, she convinced herself as the day wore on, was a man to be watched, to be wary of. There was no reason to expect anything but the best for both Scotland, and the queen. The nobles had come to greet her with full hearts, as had the common folk. The very air seemed alive with hope and happiness. And why not? Mary offered youth mixed with wisdom, an eagerness to be home and pleasure at the sight of her people — whether her heart was inwardly breaking or not.

Some things were true. Though Gwenyth did not believe her own beloved homeland was barbarous or uncouth, it could not be denied that the landscape was rough, wild and often dangerous. As could the Scottish nobles.

No, this was not France, but it was a land with much to offer its lovely queen.

As they continued along the road to Edinburgh, Rowan was pleased to see that prudence was evident in the populace's welcome to the queen. People lined the streets, many among them costumed and employed to both welcome and amuse. Fifty men were dressed as Moors, turbaned, wearing ballooned trousers of yellow taffeta, and bowing the procession along as if offering tremendous riches. Four young maidens representing the virtues greeted the queen from atop a hastily erected stage. A child walked up shyly to present Queen Mary with a Bible and Psalter.

There had been heated arguments before the queen's arrival, with several of the Protestant lords desirous of presenting an effigy of a burning priest for Mary's viewing. Many among their own number had furiously decried such an idea. There were some subtle hints as they rode past that this was no longer a Catholic country: burning effigies of biblical sons who had worshiped false idols, and a slight hint in the child's speech that the queen should embrace the religion of her country. But none of it was heavy-handed, allowing the new queen to ignore what she might not like. And the festive tenor of the day was real; people were ready and willing to welcome back such a beautiful monarch.

As Rowan carefully watched the activity surrounding the queen, he found his eyes frequently straying to her maid, the Lady Gwenyth, whose eyes were fixed upon the queen and those around her. The young woman was strikingly beautiful. In fact, all the queen's attendants were attractive — something, he mused, that the queen probably allowed because she herself was so regal and lovely, so she did not fear the glory of those around her. It was something that spoke well of her, Rowan thought.

But what was it about Lady Gwenyth that drew him so strongly? Certainly she was lovely, but the same could be said of many women. There was something, he realized, about her speech and her eyes that he found most provocative. A fire simmered within her, a fire to match the color of her hair — not really brown, not really blond, streaked with shades of red. And her eyes, a tempestuous mix of green, brown and gold. She wasn't as tall as the queen, but as even few men equaled Mary's height, it was not surprising that her maids were all diminutive in comparison. Still, Gwenyth was of a respectable height, perhaps five-foot-six. She gave her loyalty, and did so fiercely. She had shown herself ready and able to argue her point lucidly and with an effective command of language. She had a sharp wit. He smiled, thinking that when she disdained someone, she would do it with a cutting edge. When she hated someone, it would be with fervor. And when she loved, it would be with a passion and depth that could not be questioned or mistrusted.

A strange searing pain suddenly tore at his heart. Strange, for he had long ago accepted the tragedy of his own situation. He could not forget, would never truly heal. Yet he could not deny the carnal reality of his nature, though he allowed it free rein only when circumstances conspired to provide an acceptable mixture of time, place and partner. This girl in the queen's retinue was never to be taken lightly, and therefore . . .

Never to be taken at all.

He should keep his distance, yet he smiled as he recalled the joys of debating with her. She was far too amusing. Far too tempting.

Her eyes met his suddenly, and she didn't flush or look away. She gazed at him instead with defiance. Understandable, given that he had dared to express his wariness about this homecoming. A homecoming that, he was forced to admit, was going exceptionally well, at least so far. He was surprised to find himself the first to look away, and to cover his feelings, he rode forward, nearer to James Stewart. Nearer to Queen Mary. The people continued to boisterously cheer her, but. . . .

He would be the last to deny that there were fanatics in Scotland, and he was relieved when the queen's party at last reached Holyrood Palace.

Perhaps appearances could be trusted and the queen was going to be accepted and loved — maybe even revered and adored. He didn't understand the deep feeling of dread that had settled over him when the day dawned for the young queen to arrive. Lord James, her half brother and, in essence, ruler of Scotland, had seemed pleased enough that his sister had been bound for home. Having accompanied James to France, Rowan had met her briefly already. She had been everything a country could long for in a monarch — elegant, poised and tactful. She was also beautiful, and her unusual height simply added to the impressiveness of her appearance. He simply found it worrying that she had spent virtually her entire life in France.

He himself had nothing against the French. He found their nobles' more than occasional slurs against the Scots to be amusing — and almost complimentary. Yes, theirs was a remote and rugged landscape. Yes, there were those among the Highland lords who were not only rightfully proud but fierce. They were not a dandified people, were fighters more often than courtiers, but their hearts were strong and true. And he knew that when his people accepted a belief into their hearts, they did it without stinting. Such was the case now, with the Protestant cause.

And the queen was Catholic.

He laid no blame upon her for that; in fact, he admired her loyalty. She had spent her life living with the God of the Catholic Church. She was constant in her beliefs. Throughout the years of his own life, he had seen far too much brutality committed in the name of religion.

Elizabeth now held the throne of England, herself a Protestant monarch. But though the Queen of England was judicious, not one to order executions lightly, she was not afraid of doing what must be done. Against the odds, she had created a realm in which no one needed to die for choosing to worship in his own way.

But here in Scotland, it had been only a year since the fever of Protestantism had taken hold, and Rowan knew his people. What they embraced, they embraced with abandon. He could not help but dread what was to come.

When they at last arrived at Holyrood Palace, he felt some of his forebodings ease away. Holyrood was magnificent. Set outside the city walls of Edinburgh, it was surrounded by magnificent vistas and delightful forests. Holyrood had been established as a tower, but in the days of the queen's father, it had been extended and improved upon in the style of the Scottish Renaissance. French masons had been brought in to do much of the work. Rowan thought proudly that Holyrood rivaled many a continental palace. Both Holyrood itself and the neighboring abbey had been burnt seventeen years earlier by the English, but in the years since, everything had been lovingly restored.

He saw Queen Mary's face as they arrived, and was glad to see her obvious pleasure at the sight of her new home as Scotland's queen. She had been nothing since her arrival but tactful and diplomatic, but he himself had played the game of diplomacy for many a year, and he knew that her delight in seeing the palace was genuine.

Rowan noticed that Gwenyth was anxiously watching the queen, as well, and he diverted his attention from the monarch and directed it toward the maid.

The Lady Gwenyth was an enigma. It was evident in her words and manner that she did not take her position in the queen's court lightly; she seemed to feel something for Mary that was precious even among kings and queens: real friendship. And yet here she was clearly no fool. She had not been gone long from the country of her birth and, though she loved Scotland dearly, she could not help but be aware, as the queen who had been so long away could not be, of the dangers here, perhaps more aware than she was willing to admit, even to herself.

The steward and servants assembled in the courtyard as Queen Mary and her noble entourage arrived, activity tempered by awe as the household staff awaited a greeting from their queen and mistress. Mary did not fail them. Once again, Rowan had to admire her charisma and character, for she remained every inch a queen while offering courtesy and even affection. Lord James took charge of his half sister, leaving the others of lesser station to discover their quarters for themselves, leading to a state of some confusion. He heard several among the French escort muttering with relief that the palace seemed to offer surprisingly comfortable accommodation, while clearly lamenting the lack of art, music and poetry in this sadly uncultured land.

"Rowan?"

He heard his name familiarly spoken and turned. Laird James Stewart was at his sister's side, glancing Rowan's way in question. Rowan nodded, aware that the northwest tower had been chosen for the establishment of the royal apartments, and that his help was being requested.

"Ladies of the court, if you will . . ." he suggested.

With a nod to one of the housekeepers, he led Mary's ladies toward their apartments. There was a great deal of tittering and whispering in French as he walked ahead. He shook his head, amazed that they weren't knowledgeable enough to realize that many Scottish nobles were well-versed in the language. He was well aware that they were discussing his attire and his *derriere,* and speculating as to what might lie beneath the wool of his kilt.

He chafed a bit at their company, his interest lying far more in the manner with which Mary conducted herself with both staff and statesmen. He was unsure whether even James was aware of these first hours as the queen was duly greeted and settled in Holyrood.

As he showed the ladies the magnificence of the palace, and pointed out where the queen's quarters, as well as their own, would be, the Marys flirted with him. They were lovely and charming, cheerful and full of life — and yet, he knew, as chaste as their young mistress now was in her widowhood. One day these ladies would marry well, with the approval of their families, but for now they simply longed to have fun, as was natural at their age. He did his best to be gallant to them in turn.

There was, however, one among their group who did not laugh and certainly did not flirt. She simply followed and listened in silence. The Lady Gwenyth.

He knew she was watching him, and he had to secretly smile at that knowledge, even though he knew she was wary, that she did not trust him. He was quite certain she did not give a damn what might lie beneath his kilt. She disliked him intensely — or thought she did.

"Are you happy with your situation?" he asked her at last, having shown the women the way to their chambers. "Will you be able to discover your way?" The hallways were long, the layout complicated, though certainly nothing when compared with some of the grander palaces of France. Still, they were arriving in a new home and might feel some confusion.

"I believe we can manage just fine on our own," she assured him.

He had noticed that she seemed to hold herself slightly apart from the other women, which was, perhaps, natural. She hadn't left Scotland as a child, as so many sons and daughters of Scotland had, the bonds with France having been long established. Many noble sons of Scotland attended school in France. Trade between the two countries flourished.

She stared at him now through narrowed eyes, her expression deeply distrustful. And yet so beautiful, as well, he could not help but think. She was well-spoken, certainly well-read and, despite her words, he believed that she shared his concerns for the queen's safety. At the same time, despite her intelligence and dagger-sharp wit, there was an air of naiveté about her.

He stepped away from her now, nodding

curtly in acknowledgment of what amounted to a dismissal. Striding the length of the hall, anxious to return to James and the new queen, he found himself pausing to look out a window.

From his vantage point, he could see the great stone edifice of Edinburgh Castle. The sky was as gray as the castle's stone, the recent weather having been wet and cold, and mist, a common enough occurrence, had settled around the stark battlements. There was a tinge of mauve in the gray, lovely to one who knew this as home. Foreboding, perhaps, for those accustomed to blue skies. He shifted his gaze to the Royal Mile, a fine thoroughfare offering shops that sold goods from around the world. Holyrood was a fine palace, Edinburgh a fine city. Surely the queen would find much to love here and in her people, people who had cheered for her arrival.

Perhaps he was being too defensive, worrying for naught. And yet . . . He knew that many members of Queen Mary's French escort mocked this land. It was cold, they said. Hard, like the unyielding, rugged rock of Edinburgh Castle. French shops were finer, French palaces far more beautiful — even if French laborers had worked on Holyrood.

Rowan forced himself to look on his city as others might see it. In the gray, foreboding day, the castle rose like a bleak and terrible fortress. The people themselves were as rough and hard.

Rock versus marble. Wool versus silk.

He gritted his teeth. They simply needed time. Time would bring the changes the young queen and her entourage needed.

The ties Scotland had shared with France were long-lived and strong. And yet. . . .

No alliance was founded purely on friendship. Both the Scots and the French had fought the English, and that shared enmity had made them allies, even friends. But friendship was so often only on the surface, easily broken when more selfish needs intruded. And therein lay the dilemma.

What really simmered beneath the deeper waters of that alliance now that the French-raised queen had come home?

CHAPTER TWO

"I am exhausted," Mary sighed, throwing herself onto the bed in her chamber. She stared up at the ceiling and laughed softly, sounding for a moment like any young woman. "Actually, this is quite lovely," she said, surveying the room. She rolled to stare at Gwenyth, who was standing nearby. "It is, isn't it?" she whispered, and Gwenyth knew she was missing France.

"It is magnificent," Gwenyth assured her.

Mary leaned back on the bed again. "Crowns," she murmured. "They do weigh heavily."

"My queen —" Gwenyth began.

Mary rose to a sitting position, shaking her head. "For now, I beg of you, please drop the formality. We are alone, and I must trust in you. You've not been gone so long from here, and you're not after any reward, nor testing me, weighing me. Use my given name, as if we were nothing more than a pair of friends. For you truly *are* my friend, and that is what I need now."

"Mary, I believe your arrival here was a complete success. Your people are delighted to have their young and beautiful queen returned."

She shook her head. "These people seem so forbidding."

"They're . . ." Gwenyth paused, not sure what to say. She shrugged. "They're forbidding," she agreed. She hesitated, then went on. "It's due to John Knox and the way they have embraced their church."

"Right. They can't follow the English, heaven forbid, but they don't want to believe in the old religion, either, so they must have their own church." She sighed, then patted the side of the richly canopied bed to urge Gwenyth to join her. As soon as Gwenyth sat down, Mary gave her a fierce hug. "It's cold here, have you felt it?"

"There's a lovely fire burning," Gwenyth said.

"You're right. And it will be warming soon. This is so strange a place, though. In France, while my husband lived, there was such a marvelous sense of security in being queen. And here . . . it is as if I am being tested because I am queen."

"You must remember, your half brother,

Lord James, has been the power behind the throne since the death of your mother. Time has passed, and things have changed. But now, both lords and churchmen have gathered to welcome you home. You must remember that. Everything is going to be wonderful."

"Is it?"

Mary rose and walked toward the fire to warm her hands. For a moment she looked lost, even tragic. "If only . . ." Then she steeled her shoulders and swung around. "I have barely arrived, we're all dressed in the grays and blacks of our mourning, and do you know what was on the mind of those great and noble lords who greeted us and rode as our escort here to the palace?"

"What?"

"My remarriage."

Gwenyth smiled. "My dear queen —"

"Friends, we are friends here tonight."

"Mary, I'm sorry to say this, for I know your heart and know that you were deeply grieved by the death of your husband, but from the instant the king of France died, nobles and monarchs across our world were discussing your next marriage. You are a queen, and your alliances, both personal and political, can change the face of history. This is a sad truth to face when the soul is in pain, but it is the way of the world."

"I am a commodity," Mary said softly.

"You are a queen."

Again, Mary paced. "You are right, I know. I scarcely had time to bury my husband with the honor that was his due before I, too, realized my future had to be decided. Today, when we stepped ashore, I had to wonder if perhaps I made a grave error. There were offers, you know, offers from *Catholic* royal houses. There is no right step to take, I fear. Were I to marry into such a house, I would turn Scotland against me. But here, today, I learned the minds of these men. They want me to choose one of their number as consort, a man who honors all that is Scottish, who bleeds pure Scottish blood, who will compensate for what they consider the disadvantage of my upbringing. Oh, Gwen, what is the matter with the people? How can I be anything less than true to what I have been taught all my life, to what I have read, to God as I know Him?"

"No one expects that of you."

Mary shook her head in denial, and Gwenyth thought that, sadly, she was most likely right.

"They expect everything of me. But I am not an inconstant queen. I will honor and worship God as I see fit. But . . ." She turned away, lowering her head.

"But?" Gwenyth started to smile. She thought she had seen something in Mary's face.

"Well . . ." Mary inhaled deeply. "I loved him, but my late husband . . . he was never well."

"There was no romance," Gwenyth whispered.

Mary spun and rushed back to the bed. "Am I terrible? I have seen someone who . . . well, I was newly widowed when I saw him. He is a distant cousin, in fact." She looked at Gwenyth mischievously. "He is most handsome."

"Who is he?"

"Henry Stewart, Lord Darnley."

"Ah," Gwenyth murmured, looking away, thinking that Mary deserved some genuine happiness. She had spent her life doing what was expected of her, performing her duty. To hear that whisper of excitement in her voice was, Gwenyth thought, most gratifying.

Henry Stewart, Lord Darnley, was, like Mary, a grandchild of Margaret Tudor, the sister of the late English king, Henry VIII. Gwenyth did not know him so much as know *of* him. He was living in England currently, a so-called guest of Queen Elizabeth, due to what that monarch considered his Scottish father's sin in standing against her. His mother was an English peeress, however, so his stay could not properly be considered incarceration.

Gwenyth had met Lord Darnley only briefly, at the same time as the queen, when he had come to bring condolences on the death of King Francis. He was indeed handsome, as Mary had said, and he could be charming. Other nobles, she knew — especially many of the Highlanders — did not like him. He was fond of drinking, gambling and all manner of debauchery. He had Stewart blood, but he had English blood, as well. Then again, so did many of the Scottish nobility.

Gwenyth looked at Mary then with a definite sense of unease, though happily Mary did not take that look to mean personal dissatisfaction with the one man who seemed to appeal to her on a sensual level.

"Don't look at me like that! Why may I not enjoy the fact that I have seen a man who is both acceptable in the minds of many *and* appealing? Fear not, I have not lost my senses. I am in mourning, and despite everything, I did love Francis, dearly, though it was . . . it was perhaps more a deep and tender friendship than a passionate love. I remain in mourning, and I will not be rash in my decisions. I will be careful, and I will be listening to my advisors. No decision can be made for some time. I am still considering negotiations with Don Carlos of Spain and other foreign princes. My greatest strength lies in where I will cast my die. I shall not forget that for me, even more so than most, marriage is a matter political alliance, not love."

"Mary, I know you will do what is right, but you certainly must allow yourself to dream of what will make you happy, as well," Gwenyth said.

Mary, so tall and elegant in her robe trimmed with fur, looked at her with wide, beautiful dark eyes. "I am frightened," she whispered. "Frightened that no matter how hard I try to do the right thing, I cannot make my people happy."

"Oh, Mary! You must not feel so. It was a wonderful homecoming. And you're going to be a wonderful queen. You *are* a wonderful queen."

"It is so . . . so different here."

"These are your people. They love you."

"They're so . . ." Mary paused, then offered a smile. "So Scottish."

"True, this is not France. But, Mary, it is a wonderful country, filled with wonderful people. Who do outsiders look to when they seek military assistance? They offer rich rewards to entice Scotsmen to fight in their battles, because we are fierce and strong and loyal."

"But I seek peace."

"Of course. But peace is often obtained through strength."

"Not in Scotland."

"Ah, Mary. That's not true, not always. Think back. We are a country because of the determination and courage of men such as William Wallace and Robert the Bruce, your own ancestor. Scotsmen are also poets and scientists. They go to schools elsewhere, and they learn about the world. You have only to love the Scots and they will love you."

Mary let out a soft sigh. "I pray . . . yes, I pray. And I thank you — my friend. My four Marys are most dear to me, but they do not know this land as you know it. They, like me, have been away too long. Tonight I dearly needed your friendship and understanding, and you have not disappointed me."

"Mary, anyone who knows you is aware that you have a great heart, that you are both kind and wise. You don't need me. You need only to believe in yourself and to be willing to understand your own people."

"I intend to try. For I intend to be a great queen." Mary hesitated. "Greater, even," she said softly, "than my cousin who sits on the throne of England."

Achill snaked along Gwenyth's spine. Elizabeth was proving to be a very powerful monarch. She was ten years older than Mary and had been queen of England for several years now. And she was Mary's opponent in the political arena, for when Mary Tudor had died, the French royalty had declared Mary Stewart not just Queen of Scotland and of France, but Queen of England and Ireland, as well, considering Elizabeth to be Henry's bastard and therefore lacking the right to rule.

Politics could be a very dangerous game. Gwenyth knew Mary did not wish to oust her cousin from the throne, but she was loyal to her religion. It had become quite apparent that not only did the English not wish to have anyone other than their own Queen Bess, they wanted nothing to do with a Catholic monarch, and therein lay the seeds of potential — or perhaps inevitable — conflict.

Throughout the centuries, wars with England had torn Scotland apart. None wished to have more bloodshed to be forced upon them by the English, yet every alliance was like a dagger in the heart of some other nation. The English warily watched Scotland's friendship with the French, and the Spanish watched them all, so they watched the Spanish in turn. Such concerns would have a crucial impact on Mary's future marriage. She could bring an ally to their cause — and create a wellspring of enemies, as well.

As if reading Gwenyth's thoughts, Mary said softly, "I do believe it will be best if I marry within this realm in time. And he *is* good looking, isn't he?"

"Who?"

"Lord Darnley."

"Ah, yes."

Mary narrowed her eyes in amusement. "I gather you think someone else is also handsome? I believe I know of whom you speak."

"You do?"

"Laird Rowan."

Gwenyth started, and could feel her spine stiffening. "He is very rude."

"He's blunt, and as you're the one teaching me about my people, you should know that such a laird, well-versed in both battle and politics, will be blunt. He is the epitome of a perfect Scottish nobleman."

"In that case, why don't you have *your* eye

on Laird Rowan?"

"Now you are joking with me, are you not?"

Gwenyth frowned. "I'm not joking at all."

Mary laughed. "Well, then, I suppose rumor is not as rife as one would imagine."

"Mary, please, whatever are you talking about?"

"My father had thirteen recognized bastards, you know. Some of them lovely people, actually. Like my dear brother James," she said, and Gwenyth wondered if she heard a touch of bitterness in the queen's voice.

There had been talk at one time of having James Stewart legitimized, though it had come to nothing in the end.

Gwenyth's frown deepened. "He isn't one of your father's bastards, is he?" she asked incredulously.

Mary let out a small dry laugh. "No. Though he is the son of one of my father's bastards. His mother was the first issue of one of my father's first dalliances."

"Is this true — or rumor?" Gwenyth asked.

"Don't be so concerned, my dear friend, or you will furrow terrible wrinkles into your brow. Laird Rowan's lineage is considered quite acceptable, I assure you. However, to find one's nephew to be attractive is quite another. Besides, he is married."

"Oh," Gwenyth murmured.

"Quite sad, really. He is married to Lady Catherine of Brechman."

"The daughter of the Lord of Brechman — but . . . those are English lands," Gwenyth said, realizing that she was about to hear the truth about Laird Rowan's mysteriously tragic past.

"Yes. And how do I know all this and you do not?" Mary inquired, seemingly pleased to be able to share what she knew. "I suppose, in the last months, I have had quite a lot of communication with my brother James, and he has told me the story. It's terribly sad. They were madly in love, and Rowan boldly declared himself to the lady's father. They were granted permission for the union by both my brother, James, and Queen Elizabeth. She became with child immediately, but shortly before the babe was due to be born, she was in a coach accident on her father's lands. She was badly injured and fell into a raging fever. The child did not survive, and Lady Catherine has not been of sound mind since, nor has her health ever improved. She is now quite insane and lives in Laird Rowan's castle in the Highlands, where she is tended by a nurse and the Laird's steward, who is both kind and loyal. She is very frail and, most fear, soon for the grave."

Gwenyth simply stared.

Mary smiled sadly. "Close your mouth, my dear."

"I . . . I . . . how sad."

"Yes." Watching her carefully, Mary said, "Don't fall in love with him."

"Fall in love with him? He's a . . . wretched, uncouth boor!"

Mary smiled. "I see. Well, though this may be of no interest to you, I must tell you that he no longer cohabits with his wife, which would be pure cruelty, since she has the mind of a small child. And he has maintained a certain dignity in his situation."

"Dignity?"

"I know this only from James, of course, but they say that though Laird Rowan has not become celibate, what affairs he has are . . . discreet and with women who cannot be hurt. And I would never want to see you hurt, my dear friend," Mary said gravely.

"You needn't worry," Gwenyth assured her. "Ever. I've no intention of falling in love. It does nothing but make dangerous fools of any of us. And if I *were* to be idiot enough to fall in love, it would never be with a Highland savage such as Laird Rowan."

Mary looked at the fire, smiling distantly. "There, you see, is the difference between us. How I long to fall in love, to know such great passion. . . . Ah, well. Marriage for me is a matter of contracts. Still, to once know that kind of love . . ."

"Mary," Gwenyth murmured uneasily.

"Don't worry, dear friend. When I marry again, I shall not forget what I owe to my people. Still, even a queen may dream." She waved a hand dismissively in the air. "This has been a long, and difficult day, and there will be many more such to come."

Aware that the queen had clearly declared that it was time to sleep, Gwenyth hastily headed for the door. "Good night, then, my queen."

"Gwenyth . . ."

"I am on my way out. Now you are my queen."

"And you remain my friend," Mary said.

Gwenyth lowered her head, smiling, and departed, eager for her own bed in this great Scottish palace that would now be her home. As she hurried down the long hall toward her chambers, she heard voices and paused. She realized she was overhearing a conversation from one of the smaller chambers reserved for state occasions.

"There is nothing else to be done. You cannot go back on your word." The words were spoken in a deep, masculine — and recognizable — voice. Laird Rowan Graham.

"We are asking for trouble." She knew the second speaker's voice equally well. James Stewart. Was the queen's half brother really her friend? Or did he, in secret, covet the crown and believe it should have been set upon his own head?

"Perhaps, but there is no other option. We can only hope that the queen's determination to avoid religious persecutions will prevail."

"Then, as you have said, we must be prepared."

"Always."

Gwenyth was stunned when the door swung open and Laird Rowan exited, and she was caught standing, quite obviously eavesdropping, in the hall. She blinked and swallowed, as he eyed her gravely.

"I'm . . . lost," she managed.

"Are you?" he inquired skeptically.

"Indeed," she told him indignantly.

He offered a smile of grim amusement. "The ladies' chambers are there — you should have turned. If you were seeking your own bed, that is."

"And what else would I have been seeking?" she demanded.

"What else?" he repeated, then bowed mockingly but did not answer. He simply turned and left, and she was startled to feel a deep anger that he had dismissed her so easily.

Good God, why?

She disliked him intensely. True, she was sorry for the poor man's wife, but it did not sound as if he led a very Christian life, and he was rude and annoying and presumptuous and . . .

She was exhausted. She was going to bed, to get well-deserved sleep. And she would not think of him at all.

Her room was small, but it was all her own. Not that she cared so much. Traveling with the queen in France, she had sometimes had quarters of her own, and sometimes, she had shared a bed with one or more of the Marys. That had led to much laughter, for they loved to imitate the esteemed princes, nobles and diplomats they met. Like the queen, they loved to dance and also to gamble, and they deeply enjoyed music. They had been together so long that they were like a family, and they had kindly accepted her into it. Still, she would never entirely be one of them.

And here at Holyrood she would sleep alone, she thought, as she surveyed her new home. She had a tiny window and even a tiny fireplace. The glow from the fire lit the window, and though it was small, she saw that it was stained glass. The firelight played across the image of a dove alighting on a tree. Below it was the Stewart coat of arms, the colors beautiful in the muted light.

She decided that here, back home in Scotland, she was glad for her privacy. The Marys had forgotten too much about Scotland. She loved them and did not want to lose their friendship, but she did not want to hear the country constantly vilified in comparison to France.

If she grew angry with someone, she could come here and rant into her pillow.

If she needed to think, she could find solitude.

If she needed to hide. . . .

From whom would she need to hide? She mocked herself.

It didn't matter. This lovely little place was her personal sanctuary.

Her mattress was comfortable, her pillow plump. Next to the fireplace was a very narrow door. When she opened it, she discovered that she even had a private necessary room. Amazing.

All in all, it was lovely to be home.

She carefully discarded her travel clothing, storing everything in her trunk; the room was far too small for clutter. Clad in her soft woolen nightgown, she was warm and comfortable. And exhausted. Yet when she lay in her bed at last, cozy and comfortable, she lay awake.

Thinking about Laird Rowan.

Her disturbing thoughts were broken when a clatter arose from the courtyard.

She leapt out of bed as if she had been singed by the fire. Panic, dreadful fear for the queen, seized her, and heedless of shoes or robe, she burst out into the hallway, the din from below continuing. She heard an incoherent screeching sound, followed by voices.

Along with many others who had been roused by the noise, she raced down the hall toward Mary's rooms, where the door to the hall stood ajar. As Gwenyth and the ladies and guards rushed in, they found the queen awake and standing at one of the windows, looking down.

"It's quite all right," the queen assured them, lifting a hand and smiling at those who all but tumbled one over another in their headlong rush into her bedroom. "My subjects are greeting me. I am being serenaded," she called cheerfully. She appeared wan and very tired, and yet she kept her smile in place. "Listen."

"Mon Dieu!" cried Pierre de Brantome, one of Mary's French escorts. "That is not a serenade. That is a like the sound of a thousand cats being stepped on."

"Bagpipes," Gwenyth heard herself say irritably. "If you listen, the sound is quite beautiful."

"I have heard them before," Brantome said with a huff, and stared at her, his eyes narrowing, as if he had just remembered that she'd been raised in what he clearly considered a benighted backwater.

"They have a lovely quality," she assured him. "Which Mary, Queen of Scots, quite obviously appreciates." She had never been quite sure what Pierre de Brantome's role was in the household, though he considered himself a diplomat and courtier. Gwenyth wasn't fond of him; he was too mocking of everything for her taste. But he did love Mary Stewart, and so, Gwenyth decided, he must be tolerated.

"Oh, yes, I love the cry of the pipes," Mary said. "My dear Pierre, you must acquire a taste for this form of music."

"It's certainly loud," Brantome commented drily.

That much was true. It seemed as if a hundred of her people, at the very least, were outside, that the cry of the pipes was mixing with the efforts of an off-key chorus.

Mary looked strained, clearly weary, but she was ever the queen. "How lovely," she said simply.

And so they all listened until the impromptu concert ended, the French ministers muttering beneath their breath all the while, and then there was chatter and laughter as the household slowly returned to bed.

Gwenyth was the last to bid Mary goodnight, and this time she headed unerringly down the hall to her own chamber.

Back in her own bed once again, she slept, but in her dreams she pictured Laird Rowan's poor mad wife singing along to the plaintive call of a pipe, her laird, no longer her lover but her keeper, towering somewhere in the distance.

"Don't fall in love with him," Mary had warned.

How absurd.

If anything, she would have to fall out of loathing, if she could bring herself to do so.

CHAPTER THREE

In the first days that followed their arrival, Gwenyth began to feel with relief that the forebodings that had plagued her had been absurd. The Scots clearly loved their queen.

The Frenchmen among their party — and even those Scots who had lived so long in France that they seemed to think of themselves as French — began to cease their complaints. Holyrood was not just a beautiful palace but peopled with a household eager to serve the young queen, who was unceasingly kind to those around her. The forest surrounding the palace was thick and wild, and soon became a popular spot for the court to go riding, and there was always an impressive view of Edinburgh Castle, high upon its rocky tor.

The view of the stalwart stone fortress even had its effect on those who had been less than happy to leave France behind. Gwenyth had taken the Marys on an afternoon shopping expedition along the Mile, and they had commented on the very unique charm of the Scottish capital. Everything seemed to be going well.

Then came the first Sunday.

"This would not happen in France," one of the French retainers declared.

Though she was herself a Protestant, Gwenyth had vowed that she would attend Mass at the queen's side while they resided in Scotland, in support of her choice, and then observe her own rites, as well. The queen was now ready for church, having been assured by her half brother that she would be free to celebrate Mass just as she had in France.

Mary's French mother had been a devout Catholic, and when Mary had left as a child, the outcry against Catholicism had not yet begun.

Gwenyth had come to know enough about James Stewart, himself a son of the reformed Scottish church, to believe he intended to honor his vow to Mary. He was a dour and stalwart Scotsman by nature, but she had no cause to doubt his word. Perhaps he felt somewhere in his heart that he should wear the crown, but though he bowed to the Church of Scotland, he was like Mary in many ways. Like her, he abhorred the concept of violence over religious differences, and he proved it now.

A rumbling, threatening crowd had formed outside the small private chapel directly in front of the palace. The priest who was to say the Mass was shaking, afraid to walk forward to the altar. The servants carrying the candles were in terror, and their fear grew when some among the crowd laid hands upon them.

Shouts rose from the courtyard.

"Kill the priest!"

"Shall we suffer the worship of idols again?"

"Dear God," the priest prayed, eyes rolling.

Then James Stewart, with the imposingly tall and broad-shouldered Rowan Graham at his side, stared at those gathered in the courtyard and roared, "I have given my word."

"You will honor the promises given to your queen," Rowan announced.

"Ye're not of them. Ye're not Papists!" came a cry.

"Queen Mary had decreed that no one shall be persecuted for choices that lie between God and a man or woman," Rowan replied harshly. "Would you see the wretched fires burn here as they did in

England during the days when heresy was at the whim of the monarch?"

There was more muttering, but the crowd subsided, and, with James, Rowan and a troop of their trusted men as escort, the royal party entered into the chapel.

The priest shook throughout the Mass and spoke so quickly that the service was over in what seemed to Gwenyth like mere moments.

Mary was clearly shaken, but she managed to wave to the people and return to her apartments, and then James dispersed the crowd that had gathered in the court-yard.

Gwenyth had expected Mary to be deeply disturbed by what had occurred, but the queen was surprisingly resilient. "They'll understand soon enough," she told her ladies, as they all sat with her in her chambers, "I will not tolerate violence against Catholics — or those who have chosen any faith, including the Church of Scotland."

Though she loved embroidery, which was occupying her other ladies, Mary was also an avid reader. She was able to read in many languages; at the moment, she was reading the work of a Spanish poet. But she looked up suddenly, oblivious of the volume she held. "It's Knox!" she said vehemently, and stared at Gwenyth. "He is the very personification of fanaticism and violence."

There was silence in the room, and for a moment Gwenyth thought that the queen's eyes seemed almost to condemn her — as if, because she was more familiar with recent events in Scotland, she should somehow have been able to avert the morning's trouble.

Gwenyth drew a deep breath. She knew that Mary couldn't intend violence or even punishment against John Knox, for if she were to take such a position, not only would she be contradicting her own stance against religious persecution, she would be inviting her people to rebel. Gwenyth shook her head, a rueful smile curving her lips. Mary didn't want violence; she sought an understanding of the man. Gwenyth suddenly realized that the queen meant to debate him.

"My queen . . . John Knox is well-traveled and well-read. Despite that, he is of the opinion that women are inferior to men."

"Though they do need us, do they not?" Mary Livingstone said, a sweet grin upon her face as she looked around at the other Marys — Fleming, Seton and Beaton — and at Gwenyth.

Gwenyth offered a swift smile in return but looked back to the queen and spoke in

73

all seriousness. "Most men here believe women to be inferior, but they are willing to accept a queen as . . . a necessary evil, if you will. They also believe that an ill-suited ruler is best off removed. Or . . . dead. Knox is an excellent speaker, filled with fire, and though the new church took hold with the masses first, Knox swayed the nobles to accept it, and it was certainly his influence that caused the legal formation of the Church of Scotland just a year ago. He is an intelligent man, but a zealot. You must . . . you must beware of him."

"I must meet him," Mary said.

Gwenyth thought she should protest, but what could she say? If Mary was determined, she was the queen.

But Mary had never seen Knox speak. And Gwenyth had.

Rowan accompanied Laird James Stewart on the appointed day when John Knox was to have his audience with the queen. He was not surprised, when they greeted Knox and brought him into the reception hall to meet the queen, to find that she was with only one attendant, Lady Gwenyth MacLeod of Islington Island. Gwenyth, he gathered, had heard Knox speak at some time during her young life. And of all the queen's intimate circle, though her many ladies might be Scottish by birth, Gwenyth was the only one who knew at first hand about the recent mood of the country.

Rowan was afraid that this day would bring fireworks, because Knox was a very dangerous man. All fanatics were.

John Knox was in his late forties, and had a fevered and intense gaze. The minister of the great parish church in Edinburgh held tremendous sway among the people. He was, however, courteous enough, behaving with decorum and civility upon meeting the queen, who was cordial in return, indicating that they might speak privately, while her brother James, Rowan and Gwenyth took up chairs some distance away, closer to the fire, in attendance but not close enough to interfere with a private conversation.

"Foul weather, eh, lass?" Laird James said kindly to Gwenyth as they took their appointed positions.

"It does seem as if fall has come with a vengeance, my lord," Gwenyth replied.

James smiled, but Rowan didn't venture a word, only watched her intently. In truth, they were all attempting to listen to the queen's conversation, despite their pretense of holding private conversation of their own.

Things seemed to begin well. Knox was

courteous, if brusque, and Mary firmly stated that she had no intention of disturbing the Church of Scotland. Then Knox began offering his views. And they were blunt.

While Mary felt it was possible to allow people to choose their mode of worship, Knox vehemently believed there was but one true way. There was a constant danger, he insisted, that, as she was a Catholic monarch, Catholics would rise up in revolt and foreign princes and armies would attempt to stamp their own Catholic religion back on the surface of Scotland.

"One Mass," Knox informed her in righteous tones, "is far more frightening to me than ten-thousand armed enemies, madam."

Mary again tried to show reason. "I offer no threat to what is established. Do you not see that I was taught by great scholars, that I know the Bible, that I know my God?"

"You have been misled by misguided scholars."

"But many men, great in learning, do not see the word of God as you do," Mary protested.

And they began again to go around.

"It is right for men to rise up against a monarch who does not see the light of God," he said.

"That most certainly is not right. I am God's choice as your queen," Mary snapped in turn.

"It is not fitting that so frail a creature as a woman should sit upon a throne. It is a hazard of circumstance, and a true hazard indeed," Knox replied.

"My dear man, I am hardly frail. I tower over you," Mary retorted.

Their voices dropped again.

Rowan was startled to see that Gwenyth was smiling. He arched a brow to her in question.

"She is enjoying this," she said.

Even James appeared proud of his sister. "She is deeply intelligent and has the weapon of words at her disposal."

Rowan nodded, aware that Gwenyth was staring at him. "Aye, the queen holds her own. But Knox will not stop, and he will not bend."

Even as he spoke, they could hear Mary's voice rising again.

Gwenyth started to stand, alarmed. Rowan shook his head imperceptibly. To his amazement, she appeared uncertain and sat again.

Knox went on to tell Mary that, despite his misgivings, he would accept her, just as the apostle Paul had lived under Nero's rule. He lamented her lack of learning, for surely that was what kept her so stubborn. She assured him that she had read a great deal.

In the end, it was an impasse.

But when they all rose, Rowan was certain that Mary had discovered much about Knox — and that Knox had learned a new respect for the so-called lesser being who was his queen.

When Knox was gone, Mary spun to face them. "What a horrid little man."

"Your Grace, I tried to tell you —" Gwenyth began.

"I actually did enjoy sparring with him," Mary said. "Though he is stubborn as an ox, and misled. But, James," she said, addressing her brother, "doesn't he see I mean him no harm? I intend to rule with respect for my people, and I will honor the Church of Scotland."

James sighed, at a loss. Rowan stepped in. "Your Grace, men such as Knox are fanatics. There is but one way to salvation in his eyes, and you do not follow his way."

"Nor will I."

Rowan bowed his head in acknowledgment.

Mary looked at Gwenyth. "I did match him, argument for argument."

"You did."

Mary offered them a wide smile. "Now we must hunt."

"Hunt?" James said in dour confusion.

"My dear brother, there are times to work hard, and there are times to play."

James rolled his eyes.

"Do not be dour," Mary commanded. "If there were no hunts, how would we eat anything beyond mutton and beef? I long to ride today, to hunt."

"I will see that it is arranged," Gwenyth promised. "Shall I call your ladies and the noble French gentlemen of your retinue?"

"No, I would prefer a small hunt today. We will take a fine meal with us of meat and cheese and wine, and we will dine in the fresh air."

James was still staring at her. "Mary, there are grave matters to be dealt with. There is the matter of the treaty you have refused to sign with Elizabeth."

"There is the matter that Elizabeth still refuses to acknowledge me as her heir," Mary informed him, her tone slightly sharp. "There are indeed many serious matters ahead — and I will devote my full attention to every one of them. I will be the queen you wish to see upon the throne, brother. But not this afternoon. I will meet you in the courtyard in an hour. We must let no more of the day go by." When it looked as if James would protest once again, Mary continued quickly. "Why did God place this wondrous forest near the palace if it is not to be appreciated? Remember, brother, all men must eat. And we will also discuss an order of business . . . Laird Rowan."

James Stewart's bushy brows shot upward. He had been taken by surprise. Gwenyth, however, smiled, and Rowan was more aware than ever that she did indeed know her queen. What she didn't know, he realized as he looked at her more closely, was what the queen wanted with *him.*

Mary was an excellent rider and hunter; she had a fine kennel of sporting dogs, as well as the many smaller lapdogs she so loved. She had an exceptional air of happiness about her as they set off into the forest. She had been desirous that they go alone, though neither James nor Rowan was at ease with that, and Gwenyth understood why. They could not be comfortable, not when men such as Knox were preaching from the pulpit that a man had a right to remove a ruler who was ungodly. In his narrow mind, ungodly meant anything that did not precisely match his teachings, so the queen could well be in danger from religious zealots.

Mary could not believe that anyone would dare to harm a royal, so she chafed at their restrictions, but at last she agreed that guards could be posted around the section of forest where they would be hunting. And so, with the hounds baying around their horses' hooves, they began.

Scotland might not be as lush and rich as the continent, but the forest did have an almost eerie and beckoning beauty. It was barely fall, yet it seemed that under the green canopy, darkness came quickly. At first Mary rode ahead with James. Gwenyth, riding behind with Rowan, could not hear their conversation, though the two of them rode in silence, which seemed a strain to her.

Laird Rowan did not seem to notice, being caught up in his thoughts. Then, suddenly, he turned to her. "Will you go home soon to visit?" he inquired.

She stared blankly back at him. Amazingly, she had come here and not even thought about returning to her home on Islington Isle. She didn't answer with the first thought that came to her mind.

I am not wanted there.

"I . . . have not thought so far ahead."

81

"So far ahead? But you've known for some time that you would be returning to Scotland."

"I've been worried about the queen, I suppose." She found herself adding in a rush, "You don't understand. This has been a difficult time for her. She is, despite her rank, an extremely caring and kind woman. She nursed King Francis through terrible times. She was with him when he breathed his last. Suddenly, despite her youth, she was the *dowager* Queen of France, and there were so many problems to be faced, so many people to be seen. . . . She was in mourning, but there were emissaries, strangers, coming to offer messages of solace from royalty and nobility, all of whom had to be seen and greeted courteously. All the while, she had to decide on the best course of action for herself and others."

He was smiling as he watched her — sardonically, she thought.

"One would think that you, of all men, would not judge her but would have some understanding of what she felt," she snapped.

His smile faded slightly, and he looked ahead. "I was thinking again, Lady Gwenyth, that our good Queen Mary is lucky to have such a staunch friend as you."

She felt like a fool. "Thank you," she murmured stiffly, then talking to cover her confusion. "Those who know her well truly love her — *all* those who know her, not just me."

"Then she is very lucky indeed," he said softly.

"Are you coming?" Mary called back to them then.

As she spoke, something thrashed in the woods ahead of them.

"Boar," James said. "Let it be. We haven't the men to cope if the hunt goes badly."

But Mary never heard him; she was off. She was an excellent archer, and Gwenyth knew full well that she could make the kill. But James raced after her, concerned, and Rowan, muttering beneath his breath, followed.

Gwenyth kneed her mount, ready for the chase, as well, though she didn't particularly like the hunt. Once she had seen a hart die a slow death; she had watched the glow go out of the beautiful beast's eyes, and she had never desired to be part of the hunt again, though there were times, such as now, when she had no choice.

Ahead, the unfamiliar path twisted and veered. Gwenyth found herself alone and realized that the others had apparently taken a different turn. She wasn't concerned; she *did* love riding. But as she slowed her horse, wondering where she had gone astray, she heard a thrashing sound.

Her horse heard it, as well, and began to shy. She talked soothingly, her hands firm on the reins.

All her experience did her no good. The mare suddenly shot straight up in the air, then flipped over, snorting and screaming, a blood-curdling sound. The next thing Gwenyth knew, she was on the ground, lying several feet from the mare, which struggled to its feet and bolted.

"Wait! Traitor!" Gwenyth shouted.

She stumbled to her feet, testing her limbs for breaks. She was sore from head to foot, covered in dirt and forest bracken. At first she was aggravated with both the horse and herself; there had been no way to keep her seat, but she should have been up more quickly, soothing the animal, keeping it near her.

Then she heard the noise again, and the boar appeared.

Arrows stuck out from its left shoulder. Blood oozed down the maddened animal's side. It had been hit and badly wounded, and now it was staggering but still on its feet.

And it saw her.

It stared at her, and she stared into its tiny eyes in return. It was immense; she couldn't begin to imagine its weight.

Die, she thought. Oh, please, die.

But it wasn't ready to die. Not yet. It pawed the ground, staggered, snorted — and began to race toward her.

She screamed and ran, looking desperately for a clear trail — and a tree she could climb.

Was it the pounding of the creature's hooves she heard, or the rapid thunder of her own heart? If she could just keep ahead of it long enough, it would have to die, given that it was losing so much blood. It seemed as if she ran for eons, and still she could hear it coming behind her.

Then she stumbled on a tree root and went flying into the brush. Despite being certain she was dead, she rolled, desperately trying to jump to her feet and run again.

The boar was almost upon her.

Then she heard a new thundering drawing near and heard the whistle of an arrow cutting through the air.

The boar wasn't ten feet from her when the arrow caught the creature cleanly in the throat. It seemed to back up a step, then wavered and fell dead.

She inhaled deeply, hunched down on the forest floor, shaking like a leaf. She blinked, and was barely aware when strong arms came around her, lifting her to her feet. She had never thought of herself as a coward, yet her knees gave way. She barely registered that it was Laird Rowan who had come for her, who had so unerringly killed the boar with a fraction of a second to spare, and who now lifted her cleanly to her feet, holding her close, soothing her as gently as he might a child. "You're all right. It's over."

She clung to him, her arms around his neck, and as she leaned against the powerful bastion of his chest, she was all too aware that she was continuing to tremble.

"She should not have shot as she did," he muttered.

"She" was the queen, Gwenyth knew. He was criticizing the queen.

She felt her indignation grow and gained strength from that. Her trembling ceased, and she realized Laird Rowan was shaking, as well, and she almost kept silent, but in the end she had to speak. She stiffened in his arms and said, "The queen is an excellent shot. Laird James should not have raced after her. He no doubt distracted her."

"He was concerned for her life," Rowan retorted instantly. "Apparently he should also have been concerned with yours."

"Set me down, please, this instant," she demanded, offended that he so clearly saw her as a useless fool.

He did as she demanded, and she wavered, then fell against him again. She really *was* a fool, she thought. She had not realized that her limbs had remained as weak as jelly.

He steadied her, not allowing her to fall. She fought desperately for strength and finally found it. "Thank you," she enunciated, stepping back on her own at last. Of course, she must have made a sadly ridiculous picture, she thought, her riding hat gone, every pin lost from her hair, wild strands of it flying everywhere and filled with leaves and twigs. There was dirt on her face; she could feel it. Her riding costume was completely askew.

Embarrassed by her appearance, she knew she was defensive, and she even knew she had been wrong to take offense, when he had so clearly saved her life. As he stared at her, she felt the blood rush to her cheeks, and she wanted desperately to open her mouth and speak, yet something — pride? shame? — kept her from it.

She saw disappointment seep into his eyes as she remained silent, and that made it all the worse. Why did she care so much what he thought of her?

She managed to whisper words at last. "It wasn't the queen's fault," she said, but she knew those words were not enough. He'd saved her life. She needed to thank him.

It didn't help that he just kept staring at her.

At last she dredged up some dignity, as well as her manners. "Thank you," she said primly and quietly. "You saved my life."

He bowed low to her courteously, as if her words had not come shamefully late. "Perhaps you'll learn to ride with greater authority now that you are home," he said, and turned away, heading for his mount.

Naturally his horse had obediently awaited him.

She followed him, moving with swift and certain strides. "I ride quite well," she informed him.

"Oh?"

She flushed again. "My horse shied and fell," she told him.

"I see."

She could see that he didn't believe her. "She reared straight up, and then went over," she elaborated.

"Of course."

"You are impossible!" she exclaimed.

"I'm so sorry. Why is that?"

"You are not listening to me."

"Of course I am."

"You do not believe a word I say."

"Did I say any such thing?" he demanded.

She tried very hard not to grit her teeth as she gathered up her torn riding skirt so she would not trip. "Again, I thank you for saving my life," she said, and started down the path.

Unaware that he had followed her, she was startled when he grasped her arm. She spun around and stared up at him, her breath catching, her heart beating too quickly. Like him or not, he was imposingly tall and strong. He was also aggravating beyond redemption. But there was nothing repulsive about his touch.

"Where are you going?"

Where indeed?

"To find the queen."

"On foot?"

She exhaled. "My horse, as you may have noticed, is nowhere to be seen."

"Come." When she continued to stand stiffly, he smiled at last and said, "You don't need to be afraid of me."

"I'm not."

"Perhaps not, but you're wary."

"You haven't learned to love the queen. Maybe you will now," she informed him.

"I serve Queen Mary with all that is in me."

"But it's Scotland you love," she informed him.

His smile deepened. "If it's Scotland I love, she is the persona of Scotland, is she not? Now come along. Join me in the saddle, so we can find the others."

"You're horrible, and I don't think I can sit a horse with you."

He laughed out loud then. "I agree with you, and you attack me."

"You are not at all agreeing with me."

He reached out and touched her forehead, brushing a strand of leaf litter from her forehead. It was an oddly tender gesture. Suddenly she didn't want to argue with him, she wanted to . . .

Feel his fingers brush her flesh again.

She stepped back quickly. He had a wife. One he adored, though she was so gravely ill.

"Come," he said again, this time impatiently, then gave her no choice, picking her up easily and setting her atop the tall stallion before jumping up behind her. There was no help for it; his arms came around her as he managed the reins. She swallowed deeply, wondering how this person who could be so blunt and rude seemed to arouse something in her that she had never felt before.

It was absurd. And wrong.

Keeping her seat was not difficult. His horse was an immense ebony stallion, but completely under his control. The animal's gait was smooth, even and swift. Gwenyth leaned back in an uncomfortable combination of misery and arousal, more aware of a human touch than she had ever been in her life.

At last they returned to the copse where James and Mary awaited them. The queen cried out, upset, rushing over to Gwenyth and pulling her close the minute Rowan set her on the ground, hugging her fiercely, then withdrawing to search out her eyes and look for any injury upon her person.

"Are you hurt? My poor dear, it was my fault." She accepted the blame while casting an angry eye toward her brother. "What happened? You found the boar. No, obviously, the boar found you. Oh, dear God, to think of what might have happened . . ."

"The creature is dead at last. We'll send someone for it, Your Grace," Rowan said.

Mary cast him an appreciative glance, then looked back at Gwenyth. "You are all right?"

"My dignity is sadly shaken, but in all else,

I am fine," Gwenyth assured her, then drew a deep breath. "Laird Rowan arrived with miraculous timing. He —" Why, she wondered, did she hate so to say it? "He saved my life."

"Then we are beyond grateful to Laird Rowan," Mary said gravely.

He nodded in easy acknowledgment of her words. "Your Grace, I am pleased to serve in any way that I can."

James said gruffly, "Let's return to the palace. Lady Gwenyth needs care and rest."

"Your horse?" Mary asked Gwenyth.

"I dare say the mare has returned to the stables. I'm certain she knows the way," Rowan said. "Styx is broad and strong," he added, indicating his horse. "Lady Gwenyth and I will reach the stables as easily as we rode here."

To protest in the circumstances would be futile and she would merely look the fool, so Gwenyth acquiesced with no more than a murmur.

Later, when they returned, and stable-hands and servants ran about shouting and hurrying to assist in whatever ways they could, she heard Laird James speaking softly with Rowan. "If they are to prowl the forests seeking diversion, then they must learn to ride."

Gwenyth longed to turn and confront the man, but then, to her surprise, found she did not need to do so.

"James, I believe the lady rides as well as any woman, perhaps as well as any man. No one can stay atop a falling horse. If the horse is flat upon the ground, so shall the rider be."

Startled by Rowan's defense of her, Gwenyth was not prepared when one of the large, bulky guards came to take her arm and escort her within.

"I can stand on my own, please," she insisted. "I am not hurt, merely wearing much of the forest floor."

She was not released on her own say-so. The guard looked to Mary, who nodded, and only then was she allowed to stand on her own.

She fled to her apartments, anxious to escape being the object of so much concern.

Rowan watched Gwenyth go, surprised by the tugging she could so easily exert upon his heart. He didn't know if it was the look in her eyes, the passion in her voice, or even the ferocity of her manner combined with the innocence that lay beneath.

"Laird Rowan," Mary said.

"My queen?"

"I did wish to speak with you away from the palace, but the opportunity did not present itself. And so, if you will attend me in chambers . . . ?"

"Whatever your desire."

He realized that she and James must have spoken while he was rescuing Gwenyth, for the other man now clearly knew exactly what Mary intended to say to him. Indeed, James was the one to lead the way to the small reception chamber near the queen's apartments.

An exceptional French wine was brought for their pleasure. Rowan preferred good Scottish ale or whiskey, but he graciously complimented the queen on her choice. She did not sit in the regal high-backed chair she would be expected to take when receiving foreign ambassadors but rather chose one of the fine brocade upholstered chairs grouped before the fire.

James didn't sit. He stood by the mantel as Mary indicated that Rowan should join her, which he did, his curiosity growing by the second.

"I have it on good authority that you are on friendly terms with my cousin," Mary said.

He sat back, caught unprepared. "Queen Elizabeth?" He should not have been surprised, he chided himself. Mary had very able ministers who had served her for years.

"Yes."

"My wife's mother is distantly related to Queen Elizabeth's mother," he said.

"Relationships are a good thing, are they not?" she inquired. "We are taught to honor our fathers and our mothers, which makes it strange that, in matters of politics and crowns, so much evil may be done to those we should love. But that is not of import now. We are engaged in quite a complicated game, Elizabeth and I. I have never met my cousin. I know her only through her letters and the reports of others. Serious matters occupy us now. I have not ratified a treaty between our countries. And that is because she has not ratified her will."

This was something that he already knew. "I suppose," he replied carefully, "that Elizabeth still considers herself to be young and is not eager to contemplate what will happen upon her death."

Mary shook her head. "She must agree that I am the natural heir to her crown."

Rowan held silent. He was certain that Mary was aware of why Elizabeth was hesitant. England was staunchly Protestant now. If she were to recognize a Catholic heir to the crown, it could create a tremendous schism in her country. He knew the Protestant powers in England were not looking to the Catholic Queen of Scotland. Though the line of sucession would most probably recognize her claim, there were other grandchildren of Henry VIII, among them Catherine, the sister of poor Lady Jane Grey, known as the Nine Days Queen. The Protestant faction had set Jane upon the throne following the death of Henry VIII's one son, Edward. The forces behind another Mary, this one the daughter of Catherine of Aragon, a Catholic, had easily routed Jane's defenders, and in the end Jane had lost her head upon the scaffold. She had died not because her family had urged her toward the throne, but because she had refused to change her religion at Mary's demand. It had been Mary's legitimate right of succession to the throne that had won her so many followers, and it had been her order that so many Protestant leaders be executed that had earned her the title "Bloody Mary." At her death, when Elizabeth had ascended the throne of England, she had put an end to religious persecution, but the memory of blood was still rife in the hearts and minds of the English, and they wanted no Catholic ruler now.

"We all know why Elizabeth stalls," he said.

"But here is the thing. You know, Laird Rowan, that I have no intention of forcing my beliefs on my people, who are so set now in the ways of the Church of Scotland. If Elizabeth knew this, believed it as you do, I don't believe she would balk. You are on friendly terms with her. You can seek an audience to wish her good health, and during that audience, you can tell her what you have learned about me."

"Rowan, you're being sent to London," James said bluntly.

Rowan looked at James. The man was so often an enigma. He knew so much about the people of Scotland, having served as regent. He knew the law, and he had asked his sister to return, ceding the crown to her. And yet there must have been times when he thought that this country would be in a much better position had he been his father's only legal issue.

"Naturally I am willing to obey your every command." Rowan hesitated. "Though I was planning a trip to my estates," he said huskily. "There are matters to which I must, in good conscience, attend."

Mary set a hand on his arm. He saw the deep sympathy in her eyes, and he realized that one thing her supporters said of the queen was very true: she had an enormous heart. She was kind and cared deeply for those around her.

"You certainly have leave to travel home and to take whatever time you need there. But then I would have you journey westward as escort to Lady Gwenyth, then on to London."

"Escort to Lady Gwenyth?" he repeated questioningly.

"I have received a letter from Angus MacLeod, great uncle to and steward for Lady Gwenyth's estates. He is anxious that she return to visit, to greet her clansmen and allow herself to be seen. You will do me great service if you act as her escort, bringing her to Islington Isle before you yourself travel onward to England."

He was startled by the request, and dismayed, though he was not certain why. "Perhaps, as speed is of importance, I should simply ride to my estates and then on to England without even attendants of my own," he suggested.

Mary frowned slightly. "No, Laird Rowan. I think not. I would prefer that the Lady Gwenyth should travel the full journey with you, accompanying you to the English court once she has visited her own home. I shall have you serve as guardian for her, and it will be known that I sincerely wish for her, my dearest lady, to know more about the English way of things, that she may tutor me in understanding my close neighbors, in the interest of the continuing peace between our two countries."

Trapped.

There was little he could say or do. For how could a man tell the queen that she was asking him to be escort to far too great a temptation?

No. He would be expected to be the staunch guardian, whatever his thoughts or desires.

"Rowan, Mary asked my advice on this matter," James informed him. "I think your friendly visit to Elizabeth will mean much, and bringing Lady Gwenyth along will help matters. She attends Mary but remains Protestant herself. She loves Mary dearly, but her blood and her ways remain far more Scottish than French. Unofficially, she will serve as an ambassador for our queen's cause."

"Does Lady Gwenyth know about this?" Rowan inquired.

"Not yet," Mary said. "But she will understand perfectly what I want from her. I am newly here, though not newly queen, for that has been my title since I was but days old. My desire to bring only good to my country must be understood, as must my desire for peace. You, sir, are the man who can hold out the true hand of friendship in what is most important, an unofficial capacity. I will not be bound to words you exchange, while, if my ministers and ambassadors make foolish statements in the heat of the moment, I am held to them. You will bring Elizabeth some personal gifts from me, and I know that she will be enchanted by Gwenyth. I have yet to meet anyone, commoner or king, who has not found her to be charming and intelligent. Her nature will serve me well."

"When did you intend that I begin this journey?" Rowan asked.

"After the next Sabbath," the queen informed him gravely.

CHAPTER FOUR

Gwenyth was stunned.

She couldn't believe that Mary would send her away. Of course the queen had her ladies, her Marys, but Gwenyth had believed that Mary depended on her for her friendship. As well, they had just arrived. Surely Mary needed her for her knowledge of Scotland.

Though she realized she was being presumptuous, Gwenyth told her thoughts to the queen. "I can't leave you now. You need me with you."

At that, Mary smiled. "Please, Gwenyth, have you no faith in me? I have been away since childhood, but I am extremely well-read, and I am also fortunate to have my brother James to advise me in all things. I intend to move very slowly and carefully. I'll be journeying to many cities within the country soon, so I can meet more of my people. Gwenyth, I am not sending you away. I am placing the dearest desire of my heart in your hands."

That was a staggering thought.

Elizabeth was more than a decade older than Mary. She had taken the throne at the age of twenty-five, after bearing witness to turmoil, battle and death for many years. She had even been incarcerated — in royal conditions, it was true, but incarcerated nonetheless — because there had been times when her older half sister, Bloody Mary Tudor, had feared a Protestant uprising. In time, Mary had died a natural death and Elizabeth had duly taken the throne. She was neither young nor naive, and she had gained a reputation as a powerful and judicial monarch. Mary of Scotland still believed in the heart — in her emotions — in the belief that wishing could make things right.

"I fear you set a task before me that I may not be adequate to achieve," Gwenyth said.

"I ask of you what I can ask of no other person. Gwenyth, it will not be for so long. A few weeks in the Highlands, a few weeks journeying south, perhaps a month in London, and then you will return. You are perfect for what must be done. I am not expecting an official reply from Elizabeth. I am seeking merely to lay groundwork for the future, for all that the ministers and ambassadors hope to accomplish."

"What if I fail you?"

"You will not," Mary said, and that was that.

They were due to leave after services on Sunday.

Mary had already informed Laird Rowan of her intent, something that, Gwenyth was certain, sorely aggravated him, as well. Surely he could not welcome the task of being responsible for her safety. Her determination to attend two services, both the Catholic Mass and her own Protestant rite, was intended at least in part to irritate him, as it would no doubt make their departure later than he had intended.

However, her plans went immediately astray.

She had wisely known she mustn't attend the great kirk in Edinburgh where the fiery John Knox was the preacher, so she rode out with several other Protestant members of Mary's court to the smaller, very plain chapel that lay just a few miles to the southwest of the city.

The minister's name was David Donahue; he was a man of about fifty, and appeared to be soft spoken and gentle. But as he began his sermon, Gwenyth knew that she was in trouble. He was what the Marys laughingly called a pounder.

From the moment he began his vindictive tirade against the taint of Papists in the land, he was pounding his lectern. And he stared straight at Gwenyth as he did so. Then he pointed at her.

"Those who worship false idols are blasphemers! They live in blasphemy, and they are like a curse upon this land. They are akin to the witches who call upon dark evil and rancor and death."

Shocked at first, Gwenyth sat still. But as his words reverberated, she stood.

She pointed at him in return, seething with fury. Her mind seemed to be moving at a maddened pace; she wanted to choose her words carefully, but that proved impossible, for she was inwardly burning, as if she were about to combust.

"Those who believe that God is their friend, and their friend alone, who dare to think He whispers what is right and wrong in their ears alone, *they* are the taint upon this land. None of us knows for a fact what His divine purpose may be. Those who condemn others and see no fault in themselves, they are dangerous and evil. When a land is blessed with a monarch who sees clearly that no one will know God until called before Him, who wants to allow her people to see goodness as they will, then the inhabitants of that land should bow down and be grateful. Sometimes, I fear, it may well be a pity that she is so kind and wise that no blood will be spilled."

After she finished speaking, she stared at him for a moment longer, then swung around and stumbled over her neighbors in her haste to exit the pew.

The whole congregation reacted with shocked silence. She felt it keenly as she walked with as much dignity as she could muster down the aisle.

Just as she was about to exit the church, she froze, for fierce pounding was coming from the podium once again.

"Satan's witch!" the reverend bellowed.

She turned. "I'm very sorry you think so, reverend, for you have impressed me as being a servant of Satan yourself," she said with far more calm than she felt.

"This will stop now!"

Gwenyth was stunned when she saw Laird Rowan Graham rise from a pew toward the front of the church. He stared at the reverend, then at her. "There will no casting of vindictive accusations by any party within this house of God. Reverend Donahue, speak to our souls, but do not let the pulpit become your venue for personal attack or political arousal. Lady Gwenyth —"

"He attacked the queen!" she raged.

"And he will no longer do so," Rowan declared. He turned back to the reverend. "Our queen shows nothing but tolerance for other beliefs and encourages the Scottish Kirk. She has asked only to be left to cleave to the religion she has known since a child. She will never tell others what they must feel or believe in their hearts. Let us respect her mind and steadfastness, and worry about our own souls."

Gwenyth could only imagine how all the parishioners would be talking that evening. At the moment, however, they were all simply sitting, shocked and perhaps a bit excited, as they awaited the next lines of the scandalous scene unfolding before them.

But the show was over, Gwenyth thought with relief, as she virtually stumbled out into the day. Amazingly, the sun was shining.

She hurried along the broken stepping stones that led from the church and wound between the long rows of graves, both ancient and new. At the low wall that enclosed the churchyard, she paused, grasping the stone for support, gasping for breath.

The next thing she knew, brisk footsteps

were heading her way. She looked up and saw without surprise that Rowan had followed her from the church.

"What the hell were you doing in there?" he demanded heatedly.

"What was *I* doing?" she repeated incredulously. "Reverend Donahue was attacking your queen."

"And many ministers throughout the land will be doing so for some time to come. She is a Catholic. When Scots embrace something, they do so with a reckless abandon, and such is their feeling now for the church that bears their country's name. You are but adding flame to a fire that already burns far too high. You attend Mass with the queen, then come to this church."

"I have chosen the Protestant faith," she said indignantly. "I attend Mary when she goes to Mass because I am sworn to accompany her wherever she goes."

"She would understand if you did not."

"It would show a lack of support for her choice."

"You would show that you honor hers but have made your own."

"You're telling me every man, woman and child in this country is a Protestant?" she said. "So suddenly? It is but a year since the edict went through. What are we, then,

107

sheep? Does no one think for him or herself? This morning we honored the Church of Rome. Tonight we honor that of Scotland. Tomorrow, good God, will we begin worshiping the goat gods of the ancient past? You, Laird Rowan, did nothing to speak up in defense of the queen."

He folded his arms over his chest, staring down at her and shaking his head. "Do you think I have the power to force people to change their minds? Should I have demanded to meet an elderly white-haired preacher in the churchyard for a duel?"

"You should have spoken up."

"And added fuel to his fire? Don't you see? He wants a fight. If you ignore those who would degrade Queen Mary, you give them nothing with which to support their savage anger."

"He pointed at me," she said through clenched teeth.

"You should have listened quietly and pretended to find his words unworthy of response."

"I can't do that," she said flatly.

"Then it is good that we are leaving."

"Are you such a coward, then?" she asked, still seething as she looked up to meet his eyes.

She saw them narrow with a fury he

nevertheless controlled. "I am not young, and I am not reckless. I know the mood of the people. I know that trying to silence a minister at his pulpit will only make him cry the louder, and his cries will then enter into the souls of his congregation, for they will believe his words. Your outburst will be seen only as proof of what he said. There are others inside who would have spoken later, quietly and with thought. They — and I — would have said the queen is proving herself to be a font of kindness, justice and the deepest concern for her people. Our measured words would have echoed far more resoundingly and effectively than your angry retort."

She looked away. "He called me a witch. How dare he?"

Rowan sighed deeply. "If we can all rise above what is said by those who seek to disrupt the country with their own fanaticism, all will end as it should. The queen will not be swayed from her stance, I am certain. And, yes, there *are* other Catholics in the country — that is what angers men like the reverend. They fear there will be a revolt, an uprising." He hesitated. "Pray God, Mary does not continue her quest for a marriage with Don Carlos of Spain."

Gwenyth stared at him, deeply troubled.

She had thought Mary's contemplation of marriage to the Spanish heir was not known — even by James Stewart. She shook her head. "She has stated that she believes a union with a Protestant in her own country would be best."

"Let us pray, then, that such all alliance comes to pass. It will be best, however, if she establishes her own rule first. Now, there is your horse," he said, pointing. "Let us return to Holyrood, then depart for the Highlands."

He caught her hand and led her to her mare, Chloe — who had indeed headed back to the stables after the ill-fated hunt. She might have chosen another mount after what had happened, but Gwenyth was resolute that she and Chloe would become a team. She could hardly blame the horse for its fear; the boar had certainly given her cause for terror, as well.

She didn't need assistance to reach the saddle, but as he was determined to give it, she decided not to opt for another argument.

"You did not defend me *or* the queen," she accused him again, as he mounted and rode up beside her.

"I defended you both," he told her curtly. "I am responsible for you."

"You do not have to be responsible for me. I am quite capable of being responsible for myself."

She was surprised when he offered her an amused smile. "Really? In that case, I think perhaps you *are* a witch."

"Don't say that!"

He laughed. "It was intended as a compliment — of sorts. You have the ability to sway and enchant — and certainly to create a whirlwind."

He kneed his horse, moving ahead of her. She seethed, wishing she could drag the reverend out by his hair and tell him that he was small-minded and evil. She was equally angry at Rowan, and dismayed that she must now be in his company for days. Weeks.

Months.

"I think I should speak with Queen Mary once more before we depart," she said as they reached Holyrood.

"Oh?"

"We shall surely kill one another in the time that stretches before us. I must ask her again to release me from your company."

"Do your best," he told her. "It certainly slows me down to have you in tow."

It was true, and she knew it. It didn't matter. Something about the offhand way he spoke made her long to rip his hair out.

"You could speak to her, too," she reminded him.

"I tried."

"You didn't try hard enough."

"Lady Gwenyth, I have been on this earth several years longer than you. I know how to go to battle, with a sword — and with words. I have learned when it is best to retreat, so that battle may be waged again. I've studied the history of this country that I love so dearly. I am not reckless, and I know when to fight. I have lost my argument with the queen. You are free to take up arms again. I, however, wish to be gone within the hour," he told her.

Gwenyth tried. She found Mary in the small receiving chamber, where James was reporting to her about the sermon Knox had given that day. The man hadn't accepted her or her ideals, but he had admitted from his pulpit that she was keenly intelligent and clever — misguided, and therefore still a thorn in the country's side, but a ruler they must ever try to sway to the True Belief.

Mary seemed amused. And her smile deepened when she saw Gwenyth. "Ah, my fierce little hummingbird," she said laughing. "Ready to battle the entire Church of

Scotland in my defense."

Gwenyth stopped in the doorway, frowning. How had word gotten back so quickly?

Mary rose, setting her embroidery aside, and walked forward to hug Gwenyth. "I will miss you so dearly," she said, drawing away but still holding Gwenyth's hands.

"I needn't go," Gwenyth said.

"Yes, you must," Mary said. She flashed a glance at James. "Perhaps it is particularly important that you leave now."

"I but defended Your Grace," Gwenyth said.

"You are ever loyal, and I am grateful. I, too, am furious with the zealots who are so blind that they cannot see beyond their own narrow interests. But were I to forcibly silence them, I might well create an uprising, so I will just let them speak and hope to create a climate in which they are forced to silence themselves. Now, are you ready for your journey? Are you anxious to see your home?"

No, Gwenyth thought, she was not. She had neither father nor mother left to her, only a strict, dour uncle to whom duty meant everything in the world. Her home was a crude rock fortress virtually surrounded by the sea. The people there fished, eeled and tended a few rugged sheep for their livelihood, or eked out a living from the harsh, rocky earth. Usually they were happy. They had families, loved ones. In her uncle's eyes, however, she deserved no such frivolity; she had duty to occupy her. Angus MacLeod was surely loved by the fierce John Knox.

"I am anxious about you, Your Grace," she said.

Mary's smile deepened. "I am blessed, truly. You must go."

Gwenyth admitted to herself that she was not going to win the argument. Rowan had known it. Now she was going to have to hurry to be ready by his deadline. And she would not allow herself to be late, to give him any opportunity to wear that look of irritated, forced patience because of her.

"Then . . . *adieu.*"

"You'll return quickly," Mary assured her. "It seems long, but it will not really be so."

Gwenyth nodded. They hugged, and then she was startled when Laird James came over to say a warm farewell to her. He was not a man prone to easy displays of affection, she knew, and she was pleased when he awkwardly patted her shoulder. "Go with God, Lady Gwenyth. You will be missed."

She smiled and thanked him. Then she fled the chamber before the tears she felt welling up in her eyes could spill. This was life, she told herself brusquely. When Mary had been but a child, she had been sent overseas, without her mother, to meet the man she would wed whether she liked him or not. Women were sent from place to place constantly to honor marriage contracts — and often, it was as if they had been sold to horrid beasts.

Her heart froze for a moment. Customarily, despite the fact that her father's title was hers, her great-uncle Angus had the power to decide her future. She could only thank God that because of her position at court, Mary had to approve any plan for her life.

Mary would never force anything heinous upon her. Would she?

No. Even now, Mary had but sent her on a journey to feel out the chance for a friendship with her cousin, the powerful English queen. She had never forced her will on any of her ladies.

Except now. Then Gwenyth chided herself for the uncharitable, even traitorous, thought.

In her room, the little private chamber she so loved, she found a middle-aged, slightly stout woman awaiting her. She had cherubic cheeks, a warm smile and an ample bosom.

"My lady, I'm Annie, Annie MacLeod, actually, though any relationship is certainly quite distant." She grinned, a rosy and cheerful expression, and said, "I am to accompany you and serve you, if you will grant me the honor."

Gwenyth smiled. At last, here was someone who seemed to be nothing but cheerful and nice — and glad to be with her.

"I am delighted to have you, Annie."

"I've sent your trunk down to our small caravan. I am ready, my lady, when you are."

So this was it.

She had dressed for the long day's ride when she had headed to the kirk, expecting to leave feeling refreshed and blessed by the word of God. Instead . . . No matter, will it or nil it, she was ready.

"Annie, it is time. We need to be on our way."

She closed the door to her sanctuary within Holyrood. It was with a heavy heart that she hurried down the stone stairs and out to the courtyard where the packhorses, the small retinue of guards — and Laird Rowan — awaited.

At least the Lady Gwenyth was not an elderly or sickly ward, Rowan thought. On his own, he could easily make fifty miles in a day. If he'd had to move with a coach and a great deal of baggage, he would have been slowed almost to a stop. As it was, the Lady Gwenyth had shown herself pleasantly capable of packing lightly. The cheerful woman chosen to accompany her was far greater a burden, actually, albeit through no fault of her own. She was a decent enough horsewoman, comfortable on her placid mount, but as she had not spent endless hours in the saddle before, Rowan was forced to stop regularly so they might stretch their legs, sup and rest.

On his own, he might have made Stirling on that first day. With the women, he thought it best to spend his first night at Linlithgow Palace, which sat almost midway between Edinburgh and Stirling.

At the gates, he was greeted by an armed guard, recognized and welcomed. The castle steward, knowing Gwenyth's name and position, was both curious and charmed. Though they had arrived late, he and Gwenyth were ushered into the massive great hall, while their four-man escort was shown to berths above the stables, and Annie and his man were brought to the kitchen to eat and then given beds in the servants' quarters. He and Gwenyth stayed awake talking with the steward, Amos MacAlistair, for the robust fellow was fond of telling how Queen Mary had been born at the palace, though alas her father had died just six days later. Rowan watched Gwenyth as she listened, rapt, smiling, as the old man talked about Mary as an infant. Rowan decided the day had gone well — especially considering the morning. He and Gwenyth had kept a polite distance for the long ride, and he hoped they could keep moving on in similar harmony.

The next evening was equally fine, for they were greeted by the steward of Stirling Castle, and accorded equal consideration and respect. Gwenyth seemed to love Stirling, and, indeed, the castle was impressive and the town beautiful. People whispered about their arrival in the streets; Gwenyth smiled as she saw the townsfolk, calling out greetings. She was, he had to admit, a charming unofficial ambassador for her queen, even here.

It wasn't until the next afternoon, when they were on their way to the Highlands, that the journey took a foul turn.

They had come to the small village of Loch Grann, though the loch was really no more than a small pool. As they rode along, nearing the village, they could hear shouting.

Gwenyth, who had ridden abreast with Annie most of the way, trotted her mare forward to reach his side. "What is the commotion?" she asked.

He shook his head. "I don't know."

She kneed her horse and rode ahead of him.

"Will you wait?" he called in aggravation.

Following Gwenyth, he passed several charming cottages, a kirk and the unimpressive building that passed as the thane's manor here, and then reached the village center, where a narrow stream trickled through.

Gwenyth had reined in, horror evident on her face.

He immediately saw why. The shouting was coming from a mob of townspeople, urged on by what appeared to the local thane's men-at-arms. The object of their derision was a young woman bound to a stake, with faggots and branches piled at her feet. She was stripped down to a white gown of sheer linen; her long dark tresses were in sad tangles; and the look on her face was one of utter defeat and anguish.

"They are going to burn her!" Gwenyth exclaimed in horror.

"She has probably been convicted of witchcraft, or perhaps of heresy," Rowan informed her.

She looked at him, those immense golden eyes of her alive with indignation. "Do you believe in such ridiculousness?" she demanded.

"I believe that even your precious queen believes in it," he said softly.

"But . . . tried *here?*" she demanded. "Not in Edinburgh? By what law? *Whose* law?"

"Local, I daresay."

"Then you must stop them."

He had to wonder what he would have done had she not been with him. He was frequently appalled by the harshness of the Scottish laws. As a lad, he had seen a young man hanged at St. Giles in Edinburgh, his crime no greater than the theft of a leg of lamb. His father had told him sadly then that such was the law; he could not stop the execution.

He did not believe in superstition, or that certain women had the evil eye, and before God, he certainly did not believe it was possible to make a pact with the Devil. But there were laws. . . .

"Do something!" Gwenyth cried. "Please, Rowan, they are about to light the fires."

"Hold, and watch at the ready," he told Gavin, head of their escort.

She had never before called him by his

given name, Rowan realized, and in her eyes there was nothing but honest and sincere entreaty. Emotions, he thought; they become the downfall of us all.

He spurred his horse forward, a display of power as he raced through the townspeople to confront the churchmen. "What is this mockery of justice?" he demanded angrily. "What right have you to impose the sentence of execution?"

As he had hoped, the size and evident breeding of his horse and the colors he wore indicated his association with the royal house. Most of the crowd fell back in silence, but one black-clad minister stepped toward him. "I am reverend of the kirk here, my laird. She has been duly tried and found guilty."

"Duly tried? What manner of court do you have here? Is it authorized by the queen?" Rowan demanded.

"It was a local matter," the man protested.

He looked around. The crowd had remained silent. The only sound came from the young woman at the stake, who was sobbing softly.

"Release her," he said quietly.

"But . . . but she has been tried."

"By no proper court. In a matter of life and death, according to the dictates of both law and conscience, my good man, you surely know you should seek higher authority."

The pastor looked more closely at Rowan, noted his colors and the presence of his armed escort, and took a small step back. "You are Rowan Graham, Laird of the Far Isles?" he asked uneasily.

"Aye. Sworn to the Stewarts of Scotland."

The pastor arched a brow. "The *French* Stewart?"

"The Queen of Scotland. And I have long ridden at the side of James Stewart, Earl of Mar, the greatest law of our land, our regent following the death of the queen's mother."

A woman stepped forward. She was middle-aged and stout, and despite the set look of her jaw, he felt sorry for her. She was worn, looking to be a bitter woman whose life had held little joy.

"Ye do nae understand, great laird. She looked at me. Liza Duff looked at me and gave me her evil stare, and my pig died the next day," the woman said.

A man found courage and joined her. "My babe took sick with the cough after Liza Duff looked at me."

"Did no one else look at you?" he queried sharply. "Good people! Life is God's domain. Do you so easily feel it your right,

122

without seeking the highest authority in the land, to condemn any woman or man to so heinous a death because misfortune has befallen you?"

He reached into his sporran, seeking a few gold coins, which he cast down before the two who had spoken. "Buy more pigs," he said to the embittered matron. "And you," he told the man. "Perhaps there is some medicine that you can buy."

They scrambled for the gold coins, clutching them. The pastor stared at him.

Gwenyth rode forward, staring down at the pastor before turning to Rowan. "She cannot remain here," she said. "If she is so despised," she said softly, "they will take your gold, then try her again tomorrow, and we will only have delayed her execution."

She was right.

He looked down again at the pastor. "I will bring this woman, Liza Duff, to my homestead, where she may serve in my household. Should we find there is truth in your accusations, she will be brought to Edinburgh to stand trial before the proper authority."

He wasn't sure he needed to have added the last; his gold and status seemed to have turned the tide in their direction.

"That sounds a fair and solid proposition.

She will no longer be here to torment the tenants of this village," the churchman said.

"See her brought down," Rowan said. "Now."

"And," Gwenyth added quietly, "see that she is given a decent dress for traveling, and I believe we will need a horse."

Rowan stared at her, surprised but also amused.

The pastor began to protest. "We're to pay to see that a witch lives?"

"Laird Rowan has just cast before you a sum more than ample to purchase a horse and a few pieces of clothing," Gwenyth said pleasantly. "Even after purchasing many pigs and the services of a decent physician."

There was silence. Then the men nearest the pyre set about releasing the young woman from the stake.

As the ropes holding her upright were released, she started to fall. Gwenyth was instantly off her horse, racing forward. While the men might have handled her roughly, had they deigned to help her at all, Gwenyth showed an admirable strength mixed with gentleness, allowing the young woman to lean against her as she moved back to the horses. She looked up at Rowan. "She can't ride alone. And we need to be on our way, I believe."

Before someone changes his mind.

He could see the last in her eyes, though she did not speak the words aloud.

"A horse," he said firmly. "For when she regains her strength. And clothing."

A horse was brought, a bundle given to Gwenyth, and then the pastor and his flock all stepped back. Again Gwenyth looked at him, and Rowan could read her eyes. The girl would indeed need to regain her strength before she could ride on her own. They would lead the animal meant for her use until she could handle a horse on her own.

If she even knew how to ride.

If not . . . they would take the horse anyway.

He dismounted, took the young woman — who was looking at him with dazed and worshipful eyes — and set her upon his horse. He would have assisted Gwenyth to mount — as their guard of armed men continued to wait at a discreet distance at his command — but she was too quick, and was back on her mare before he could offer his help. "In future, take care what justice you decide to mete out on your own, pastor," he warned very quietly. "I will be back this way."

With that, he rode to Gwenyth's side, the

"witch" sitting before him like a limp rag doll.

They proceeded at a walk, lest any haste cause a change of heart and incur pursuit — something that he could see Gwenyth understood from the glance he cast her way — until they were well past the eyes of the villagers.

"Now let us put some distance between us," he ordered once they had passed the limits of the village and, as they hadn't yet reached the rocky tors of the true Highlands, they were able to make good time. Strange winds and early cold were bedeviling Scotland that year, but the wicked ice and snow had not yet fallen, and that too, helped them as they rode.

Finally he reined in near a copse of trees close by a small brook, lifting a hand to the others. The small party halted.

"Ooh, me aching bones," Annie protested.

Gavin dismounted, helping the ungainly woman from her perch.

"They'll nae be a pursuit, Laird Rowan," Gavin said, shaking his head, his disapproval for the village obvious.

"I agree, Gavin," Rowan told his man. "But it's always best to get a distance from the scene of any trouble."

After dismounting, he was careful to lift

126

the girl down slowly. Annie, clucking in concern, went to help her, as did Gwenyth.

"Some wine, please?" Gwenyth said, looking to the men.

"Aye, my lady, immediately," Dirk, one of the other guards, assured her.

Rowan set the woman on the soft pine-needle-covered floor of the copse, her back resting against a sturdy tree. She stared at Gwenyth, and Rowan thought his charge indeed looked like some angel of mercy come to earth, for in the dim light, with rays of sun arrowing through the canopy of branches and leaves, her hair was shimmering as if it were spun gold, and her eyes were alight with compassion. She had a leather skin of wine, and brought it to the young woman's lips.

"Sip slowly," Gwenyth said softly.

Liza did so, staring at her all the while. And when Gwenyth took the skin from her, lest she choke or become ill from too much too soon, she said, "God will bless you, for I am innocent, I swear it. Old Meg was not angry about her pig. She believed I cast a spell to seduce her wretched lout of a husband. I am innocent, before God, I am. And I owe you my life and my deepest loyalty forever," she vowed brokenly.

"Well, let's get you strong again . . . and

127

into some decent clothing. You may use those trees over there for privacy," Gwenyth said.

"I'll be helpin' the lass," Annie assured her, and the two of them walked deeper into the copse.

Gwenyth knew Rowan was staring at her, and she flushed. "I believe she is innocent," she murmured. "I find it ridiculous to believe that God has granted some people the powers to simply look upon another and cause evil."

He sighed. "Ah, lass. You'd be surprised what evil can exist merely in the mind."

"That woman is no witch." She paused, then said softly, "Thank you."

Would I have stopped such an obvious injustice had you not been with me? he wondered.

"I did as you wished today," he told her, "because I don't believe the trial was justly conducted or that the pastor had the right to condemn her to death. Such a grave penalty is held for the higher courts to dispense. But, my lady, I am sorry to say that people have often been put to death for the crime of witchcraft. Whether you believe in it or not, it is punishable by execution, for it goes hand in hand with heresy. And I will remind you again that the very queen you so adore believes in witchcraft, as does Lord James. As a rule, I believe the Stewart clan holds a belief in curses and hexes."

She smiled. "Laird Rowan, you are, I know, a well-read and learned man. I know, as you do, that there are some who believe themselves able to create dolls, prick them and draw blood from others. Those who think they can brew up herbs and make magical potions. But you surely know, as well as I, that most of those accused of such evil craft are nothing more than healers who know the potency of certain herbs and flowers. Evil has too often been done to those who would do their best to help others, all because of what men believe, rather than what is known."

"Be that as it may, if you brew a potion, you risk being accused of witchcraft, which means a pact with the devil. And heresy," he said wearily.

"It is such foolishness —"

"It is the law."

She nodded and said flatly, "Thank you. Our discussion has been most enlightening."

"To serve you in any way is merely my duty," he said lightly, bowing to her, a note of sarcasm in his voice. He wasn't sure why, but her chilly gratitude bothered him.

She was such an enigma, and he found himself fascinated by her. And there was no denying the beauty of her face and person, and her effect upon him because of that.

He was going home, he reminded himself.

His heart suddenly felt as heavy as if he'd been struck by a boulder. Once upon a time, he had been so deeply in love, ready to defy God, king and country.

And now . . .

He still loved his wife, but bitter circumstance had turned the passion he had once felt into the kind of love a man might feel for a wounded child or a failing elder.

"We need to ride," he said curtly. "Now." And he turned away, shouting for Annie to bring Liza Duff along and for his men to mount up once again.

As he lifted Liza upon his horse, he knew Gwenyth was still watching him, and he wondered what feelings now lay hidden behind her strange and haunting eyes.

Chapter Five

Though it was her home, Gwenyth had always thought of the Highlands as a wild place, peopled by a rugged, raw and nearly lawless people.

Perhaps lawless was not correct. There was law. It was just that the thanes, lairds and family heads were a law unto themselves. Her time in France had taught her a grievance against her own people. Scotland could do so much as a country if the great lairds and barons fought together as one, rather than continually feuding and striving to increase their fortunes and holdings at the expense of their neighbors. Far too often, dating back to the days when William Wallace fought so valiantly to keep Scotland a sovereign power, the barons were more worried about their personal estates and fortunes than they were the future of their country. It was understandable, perhaps, where there was intermarriage. Many a great Scottish laird had acquired lands in England through inheritance or marriage, lands that were sometimes more valuable than their Scottish holdings.

Too often, the lairds sat as if upon a fence, watching which way the winds of victory might blow, rather than gathering to become one daunting force.

In her concern with this problem, Gwenyth had forgotten the beauty of her homeland.

Their journey had become slow indeed, with the addition of Liza Duff. Though she had not been the victim of torture, she was weak and not a strong rider, though the horse the village had provided for her was calm enough. They needed to stop frequently to rest, particularly as they had entered that portion of the Highlands where the hills climbed steeply and roads were treacherous.

Eventually they turned onto a narrow, ill-hewn trail that climbed a glorious hill carpeted in mauve wildflowers, then arrived at a peak and looked down at a majestic valley lying below. There was fertile land in that valley. Gwenyth could see farmers laboring in their fields; it was the season to reap, before the harshness of fall and winter settled heavily upon them. Beyond the rich fields, rising upon an outcrop, was a fortress home. In the late afternoon glow of the setting sun, the masonry gleamed gold and silver. Asparkling brook meandered in front of the moat that surrounded the fortress. It was not as large and formidable a place as Edinburgh Castle, but like that fortress, it used the sheer power of its natural position to create a daunting defense. From their position atop this hill, Gwenyth could see that beyond the moat lay a walled courtyard; within it, tradesmen manned stalls stocked with goods of all kinds, and women moved about on various errands. She also saw a plethora of pigs and chickens in pens to one side of the enclosure.

She glanced at Rowan and saw that he, too, was looking toward the settlement, a strange, taut look on his face. It seemed to mingle pride and pain, and a deep and anguished thoughtfulness.

"Lochraven Castle?" she murmured.

He turned to her. "Nay, Lochraven Castle itself sits upon an isle north of Islington. But this land is part of Lochraven. The fortress here is called Castle Grey," he said. "It was named by an ancestor many generations ago who knew that the family name meant 'from the grey home.' "

"It is yours, as well?" she said.

"Aye. It is a gateway to the isles beyond, from which my family draws its title," he said.

"It's . . . glorious," she said.

She was dismayed when he murmured in return, "It is a sad and bitter home."

They had paused there for several moments; he was suddenly impatient. "Come, let's hurry onward."

Their approach was seen, of course, but the drawbridge did not have to be lowered, for it was already down, as she was certain it was most of the time. For the moment, the country was — as it all too often was not — at peace. The drawbridge allowed those who worked the fields to come and go, and those who lived on the outlying tenant farms to visit the marketplace within the walls, then leave again easily. Castle Grey was like a village unto itself, and it appeared to be thriving.

As they neared the estate, children came running out, strewing flowers and running ahead of a man in Rowan's own colors — a single rider who waited for them just outside the gates.

"Laird Rowan, Laird Rowan," the children chanted. One small girl made her way to his giant mount, and Rowan, smiling despite the stern visage he had worn earlier, reached down to raise her up to ride in front of him on the horse.

"M'laird!" the rider cried with pleasure as they reached him. "We'd word ye were on ye'r way."

"Tristan, my good man. All goes well?"

"A rich harvest, indeed," the man said. He was perhaps forty or so, a man who sat his saddle well, with broad shoulders, a full-bearded face and long, dark hair, just beginning to gray.

"Tristan, this is the Lady Gwenyth MacLeod. My lady, this is my steward, Tristan. We'll stay the night, Tristan, perhaps the next. Meanwhile, please see to it that a ferryman is ready to bring my lady, her company and their horses to Islington Isle."

"Aye, m'laird," Tristan said, bowing dutifully, then turning with a pleasant grin to Gwenyth and bowing again.

"How does my fair wife?" Rowan asked softly.

Tristan tried manfully to maintain his pleasant expression. "We care for her and love her as ever," he said quietly.

"And her health?" Rowan inquired, his features taut.

"She is weak," Tristan said.

"I will ride ahead. Tristan, will you see to the Lady Gwenyth's comfort and to suitable quarters for her women?"

Then he spurred his horse forward and didn't so much as glance back at Gwenyth as he rode on ahead.

Tristan and the milling children were left with their party. The steward lifted a hand in acknowledgment of the four guards, evidently all men he'd met before.

"I've heard from y'er uncle, m'lady," Tristan said, filling the silence that had ensued after Rowan left. "Ye'll be glad to hear that all is well on the isle."

"Thank you," she told him.

"Come, 'tis nae Edinburgh here, but I'll see tha' y'er comfort is assured. Ye'll enjoy y'er stay, I vow it, m'lady."

"I am certain," she said. But despite her words, she was no such thing. Despite the lushness of the fields and the obvious strength of the stone fortress, she felt an air of sadness, as if it had permeated the very rock of the estate, and she dreaded going forward. She dreaded seeing Rowan's wife.

Tristan provided a running commentary as they rode over the drawbridge and reached the courtyard, pointing out a paddock of sheep and explaining that the rocky tor upon which the castle itself had been built offered no sustenance for domestic animals, but that the lands beyond offered ample grazing opportunities.

"Castle Grey, small and poor as she might be next to the crown palaces of more recent years, has never been taken in battle, be it earthshaking or a mere Highland feud. No man attacks a Scotsman upon these rocks."

"It's quite impressive," she assured him.

"Come then, we'll have y'er horses stabled and see that ye have all ye need to be comfortable. Ye must be famished. We'll have a meal in the great hall soon."

They followed the steward through the immense walled courtyard. People stopped at their tasks, watching them, openly curious. They greeted her with smiles, men and women dipping low in acknowledgment of her position at the queen's court, and she smiled to all in return.

There was something fascinating about the workers, and after a moment she realized what it was. They all seemed happy, content with their lot in life.

"Welcome home, Lady Gwenyth. Welcome home to the Highlands," a man called to her.

"Deepest thanks," Gwenyth said in return.

"How lovely this place is," Annie whispered behind her.

Gwenyth had to agree, and yet she felt oddly guilty in coming here, and she didn't know why. She was a guest, nothing more. But this was Laird Rowan's homestead; it was where his beloved and gravely ill wife lived. Perhaps her guilt came from her knowledge that, had he been given the choice, he would not want her here, where he could not help but be reminded of his pain.

She rode closer to Tristan and spoke quietly. "Please forgive me for speaking freely, but I know that the lady here is ill. Please . . . don't let our arrival create any difficulty."

"We are pleased to serve, m'lady."

"You are kind, but please understand that I don't wish to distress the lady in any way."

He looked at her with kind eyes. "My lady is dying," he said quietly, "and has been doing so for some time. We watch her waste away. There is nothing anyone can do. The finest physicians have come and gone, powerless, so we make her life as easy as possible. We keep her from pain, and we tell her often that she is loved. Ye are nae a burden here, lass. Our burden is one we have borne for some time, and it is not affected by your coming. We are glad to have ye in the castle, and ye are welcome here ever. The Laird Rowan, no matter what the dictates were of God, queen or man, would nae have brought ye here did he not believe ye had a brave and gentle heart. And now . . . here we are. M'lady, if ye'll allow me . . . ?"

He dismounted before a massive stone stairway that led up to heavy doors one story above. These were the stables, she realized, and the horses were stabled on the first floor, while living quarters were located above. Had any enemy ever managed to enter the courtyard, the defenders here would have had the advantage when it came to battle. There were no windows to be seen on the face of the building, only slender arrow slits. Comfortable as it might prove to be, Castle Grey was a fortress built not for the niceties of life, but for defense.

She thanked the man for assisting her to the ground, while groomsmen helped Annie and Liza to dismount. Her women, she was told, were to be taken to the kitchen — apparently, it was assumed that Liza was a part of her company now. Before heading off with one of the cooks, Annie assured her that she would explore the lay of the castle, then quickly return to arrange Gwenyth's travel wardrobe and see to her comforts. Annie looked worn from the ride, Gwenyth saw, and Liza appeared nothing short of exhausted. She made a decision and turned to Tristan. "May my women be fed and shown to their sleeping quarters?" she asked.

"Nay, nay," Annie began to protest.

"Please, we'll all rest," Gwenyth said. "Tristan, please see that a meal is sent to my room. Laird Rowan has just returned, and I know will cherish his time with his wife, while I will be happiest if I know that I have created no conflict for him."

"As you wish," he assured her.

Still, there was a massive great hall to be traversed when they entered the castle, after passing through one doorway and then another, with nothing but sky overhead to allow the defenders in a battle to rain down arrows or pour boiling oil upon any attackers who might make it so far. This was an impressive holding, indeed, she thought.

Swords and shields, new and from ancient times, were hung the length of the great hall, adding to the impression of strength and permanence. Tristan led her along a seemingly endless corridor, until they finally arrived at a broad flight of stone steps leading to the floor above.

"The laird's home is immense," she said when they reached the top.

"Ah, m'lady, not so grand," Tristan said cheerfully. "Living quarters above, servants' quarters below. There is the main building, nae more. Ye'll learn y'er way easily enough. I'll have y'er women brought to the small chamber there, at the end of the hall, so they'll be near. The master's chambers are to the right, there, and I am ever in the wee room abutting his laird's, should ye need a thing."

He opened one of the many doors along the hallway, allowing her to pass before him into the room. Her travel bags had been brought and set against the wardrobe along the rear wall. These might have been guest quarters, but the room was quite grand to her eyes, far larger than her accommodations at Holyrood.

Water had already been brought that she might wash the travel dust from her person, and a tray with wine, bread and cheese had been left upon the fine dressing table. The bed was a massive four-poster, with sheets smelling of the fresh Highland air and a warm wool cover. There was nothing she could want.

"M'lady?" Tristan inquired.

"It is lovely, and I will be very comfortable," she assured him.

He paused for a moment longer.

"Thank you," she told him.

And still he hesitated.

"I don't wish to keep you from your other duties," she said.

Then he spoke at last. "If ye hear screams in the night, do nae fear. Lady Catherine . . . she wakes in the night sometimes, haunted by strange creatures in her mind. We have taken to sitting with the lady through the night, to soothe her quickly. But should ye hear a cry . . . it should not be a source of fear for you."

"The poor lady," Gwenyth said.

"Aye, poor lady, poor laird . . ." She was startled when Tristan suddenly grew indignant. "Pray God that the queen knows the mettle of the men who serve her," he said. "Oft, loyalty is naught but the wind, while m'Laird Rowan is ever constant in all that he honors." Then he seemed to realize that he had spoken too freely. "Forgive me. Rest well."

The last was said calmly, as if he had donned a mask to hide his true feelings once again.

He smiled and left her. She turned around, surveying her temporary domain more thoroughly. Some thoughtful soul had even left her a vase of wildflowers. She was lodged here as commanded by the queen, yet that strange sense of guilt remained. She still felt that she was intruding where she should not be. She had so loathed Rowan in the beginning, when he had not seemed supportive of Mary, when he had seemed to consider himself superior to the French attendants, who themselves felt superior to everyone here in Scotland. He was so quick to mock, and yet she knew now that the man was not shallow but instead hid his depths and his sorrow. He was merely wary, yet he was prepared to right whatever wrongs might arise.

He had twice come to her defense or bowed to her desires.

She was grateful, she told herself, no more.

Their journey had been long and hard; she was grateful for the opportunity to stay within this room, graciously accept the service offered her and await the time — which she fervently hoped would come soon — to leave.

And so she settled in, grateful for the water and soap — *French* soap, she noted with a smile — left for her pleasure. She bathed as best she could, and in time Annie arrived with her supper, assuring her that she had immediately put Liza to bed, and that in the morning, they would all feel much fresher.

Annie was delighted with their accommodations. "We've a room together, and it's lovely big," she said enthusiastically, then whispered, "I think we're in a room for a visiting laird and lady, just so we might be near you. What kindness we are finding here."

That was certainly true, Gwenyth thought, then quickly thanked Annie and sent her off to bed. Afterward, she dined, finding herself quite hungry after the long ride, then put on her nightgown and lay down to sleep.

But despite her exhaustion, she could not lose herself in slumber. The darkness of the strange castle plagued her. Her fire was burning low, and there were long shadows in the room.

She'd been warned that she might hear screams in the night, that the lady was plagued by demons, and she could not help but listen nervously, even as she told herself not to be afraid.

She didn't know him. His own wife didn't know him.

It was always the same, but each time it hurt afresh, and he felt as if his heart bled. Catherine was but a shell, so slim that she was like a child, as weak as a kitten, and she stared at him with empty eyes when her nurse cheerfully informed her that her laird and husband was home.

They were blue eyes, and they looked as huge as saucers in the skeletal thinness of her face. At least she did not fear him when he set a kiss upon her forehead, then sat by her side, taking her hand. It seemed she had been ill forever, and that his heart had lain in tatters just as long, as he realized he must still take responsibility for his own life, even as he watched hers slip away.

There were times when he loathed himself, for he had often felt relief that his duty to the Crown had taken him away from the suffering here, though Tristan had assured him that his lady did not suffer, did not feel pain.

But Tristan had informed him privately that in the last month or so, Catherine had taken a serious downturn. A late summer fever had taken its toll.

"My lady," Rowan said now, holding her delicate hand, the skin like parchment. "You are as beautiful as ever."

She blinked, looking at him in confusion.

"It's me, Catherine. Rowan," he told her.

Something seemed to register in the depths of her eyes, and he felt as if he were being stabbed through by an enemy broadsword. Leaning forward, he took her from the bed, then carried her over to the chair by the fire. She was as light as a child in his arms.

He cradled her to him, and remembered a lost time when she had been headstrong and filled with laughter, when her eyes had caught fire at the sight of him and the world had been filled with promise.

And now . . .

Now she sat limply in his arms. She did not fight him, but neither did she find any comfort in him. And still he sat there, holding her for hours, until she drifted to sleep in his arms. At last he rose, returning her to bed.

He called to her nurse, Agatha, so the woman would know Catherine was alone again, and he returned to his private quarters to bathe and dress anew, thinking he could not leave now, and yet he was duty and honor bound to see Gwenyth MacLeod safely home, and to travel on to England as quickly as possible. He pressed his head between his hands and, as he did so, he realized his exhaustion. He lay down, thinking he would rest for no more than a few minutes.

He felt numb, beyond pain. He *was* numb, and he despised himself for it.

At first it truly did sound as if demons had

descended upon the castle.

What she heard first was like the cry of the wind, the bitter lament of a storm sweeping through the valley. Gwenyth awoke instantly at the sound, and sat up in bed.

Then it came again, a low, plaintive tone of anguish.

Tristan had told her to not fear, that the lady heard demons in her mind and sometimes screamed in the night. But there was something about the desperate tone of those screams that tore at her heart, and she rose, feet bare upon the cold stone floor, and ventured to the door, opened it and looked out.

At the end of the hall, she could see a glow of light slipping out past an open door. The sounds that had roused her were emanating from that room.

She paused, torn. She was a guest here; she was not privy to the personal lives of those who lived here in the castle. But she could not remain as she was; the lady seemed to be crying out to her in pain.

She moved down the hall and looked past the open door. She saw no one within, though the cries were echoing more loudly now. She tentatively stepped inside.

The first thing that met her eyes was a giant bed in the far corner of the room. It seemed at first that there was nothing there other than a pile of sheets and finely embroidered covers. Then the mound of bed clothing moved, and Gwenyth heard a low, keening moan.

She couldn't bear the sound and hurried closer, asking tentatively, "My lady Catherine?"

The moaning continued. It was low now, yet it seemed to reverberate loudly in Gwenyth's soul. Should she seek help elsewhere in the castle?

Again, the heartrending moan.

She moved forward, unable to do anything else.

In the bed she saw a tiny ghost of a woman, tossing, her eyes wide, as if she saw something in the night. Her former beauty was evident in the vast pools of her eyes and the golden strands of hair tangled about the cadaverous sculpture of her face. She stared at Gwenyth suddenly.

"They come," Catherine whispered.

Gwenyth sat at her side, taking her hands. "No one comes, my lady."

Catherine stared at Gwenyth with an eerie glint in her eyes, but she had ceased to moan. Gwenyth smoothed back the tangled mass of her hair. "You are safe and well in your own home, loved and cherished."

"If I but knew that my God was with me," the woman murmured suddenly, and she seemed as lucid as anyone in that moment.

"My dear Lady Catherine, I assure you that God is with you always," Gwenyth said. She realized Catherine was clinging to her, that the bony hands within hers had found a sudden and terrible strength. "He is with you," Gwenyth went on, feeling at a terrible loss, not knowing what else to say or do. Then a song taught her long ago by one of her nurses when she was a child came to mind. She began to sing it softly.

God is in the Highland, God guarding on
   high,
Above the tor, within the night sky,
God is always with me,
At my side He doth lie.
Never fear the night,
Never mind the dark,
God is always light
A beacon 'gainst the dark.

"It's beautiful," Catherine whispered. "Please . . . sing more."

If there was more, Gwenyth didn't know it, so she was momentarily silent.

"I love that song," Catherine said, her grip

tightening further, her wide eyes childlike, trusting. "Please sing it again."

So Gwenyth sang it again, and then again.

To her amazement, the grip upon her hand eased as she repeated the only verse she remembered for the third time and watched as Catherine slowly closed her eyes. After a minute, when she seemed to be sleeping in peace, Gwenyth gently disengaged her hands and rose.

When she turned, she froze.

She was not alone in the room. The nurse was just a few feet away, standing in silence. Rowan was at the rear of the room, seemingly held there only by Tristan's hand upon his arm. They were all staring at her.

Rowan's thick wheaten hair was tousled, as if he'd just risen from bed, and he wore a look of undisguised anguish. It seemed to her that he was staring at her as if she were some sort of abomination. She was certain, from the way he stood, as tense as a bow string, he longed to step forward and wrest her away from his wife's bedside.

Ready to defend his wife in the only way he knew how. There was such strength in the man, Gwenyth thought, yet there was nothing he could do to heal his wife and return her to the woman she had once been.

"She sleeps now, and sweetly so," the

nurse murmured.

Gwenyth stepped quickly away from the bed. She realized she must look like a ghostly interloper, for she was wearing only her white nightdress, her feet bare, her own hair in wild disarray. She found it difficult to speak, even though the nurse's words had broken the awkward silence in the room.

"I'm sorry. I heard her distress and did not see . . . did not see anyone with her," she whispered.

Rowan continued to stare at her in rigid silence.

"We arrived just after you entered," Tristan said, "but did not interfere."

She was amazed at the harsh quality of Rowan's voice when he spoke, though his words were kind.

"It seems that you soothe her where others fail," he said. "Go to bed, for you must be tired. We are with her now."

Tristan offered her a weak smile as she fled the room, so she was startled to find that he had followed her into the hallway. "M'lady?"

She stopped at her own door, turning back.

"M'lady, please . . ."

"I didn't mean to intrude," she said stiffly.

"I . . ." The man was most evidently at a

loss. He lifted his hands, seeking words. "Please, do nae take unkindly to m'Laird Rowan. Ye must ken . . . she does not know him now. And to watch this . . . his heart breaks."

"I understand," she said.

"Y'er kind, m'lady. The laird fell asleep, while the nurse stepped out for air. And I fear that I, too, slept through Lady Catherine's first cries."

She nodded. Rowan hates me, she thought. Before, I amused him. Now he hates me. He does not want anyone to see pain or weakness in him, and he hates me because now I have seen both.

"Ye did soothe her," Tristan said. "Thank you." He bowed in closing.

"Good night," she told him.

"Good night, sleep well, m'lady."

Rowan damned himself. How often had he ridden into battle, slept upon the ground, ever wary for the slightest sound in the night? He had trained himself to be vigilant; in this land, it was not only the English who were the enemy. When there was no one else to fight, his people went to war with one another, so he had learned never to let down his guard in the night.

But Catherine had cried out, and he had

not heard her. He had not awakened.

Instead, Gwenyth had gone to her.

And the wife who did not know him or his voice had responded to the gentle and soothing touch of a stranger, to the sound of her voice.

He sat at Catherine's side throughout the night. She did not cry out again. She barely seemed to breathe. She was like an angel in the vast bed, a tiny angel.

He owed Gwenyth his deepest gratitude, he thought. Yet something in his heart rebelled; this was his private pain. The world had known Catherine as a great beauty, clever, witty, charming, kind. None should have to see her like this.

When the cock crowed, he rose from her bedside, while she slept on. He felt weary to the bone and the heart. He needed rest, yet he was loath to leave Catherine.

Why had he brought *her* here? The queen's command, he reminded himself dully.

She should have behaved like a normal guest. She should have walked in the courtyard, rested in the comfort of the castle and ridden out to see the beauty of the country. She should not have intruded on his personal life.

He knew he should be grateful for the service she had done Catherine, and yet he hated the very fact that she was here. Perhaps it was because she was too much like the woman Catherine had once been, strong and beautiful, determined . . . compassionate.

He dismissed such a thought from his mind.

She was the queen's lady, and she had lived in France too long. She needed to reaccustom herself to the reality of her own country, to learn that she was not the law and couldn't argue with the new faith of the land.

His wife was dying. He could rage against heaven, but he could not change that.

He was startled when Catherine spoke suddenly, her voice so low, so weak, that he had to return quickly to her side and lower his head to her lips to hear her words.

"The angel . . ." Catherine whispered.

He was at a loss.

"I'm here, my love. What do you need?"

Her eyes opened, huge blue pools dominating her face, and she frowned, staring at him. "The angel," she repeated.

"My love, it's all right. You are not alone. I am here."

"She was here. . . ." Again, the words were so soft that he could barely hear them.

"Catherine, it's me, Rowan, your husband,

who loves you."

She didn't seem to hear him, or if she did, his words meant nothing. "I need her," Catherine said, and her features twisted fretfully.

"Catherine," he said softly, almost desperately, again. "Please, it's me. Rowan."

It was as if she did not hear him.

"She sings a song, and it is sweet and beautiful and keeps away the demons," Catherine whispered.

He held still, barely breathing for a moment, his heart in tatters.

She wanted Gwenyth.

"I will bring you your angel," he told her.

Chapter Six

Almost three weeks later, taken beyond the castle walls and gently cradled in her laird's arms so she could have one last glimpse of the Highlands, Lady Catherine breathed her last.

Rowan had ridden out with Catherine seated before him on his great stallion, and there, atop the tor, she had looked out over the beautiful landscape.

In the end, she was lucid. She whispered to him that she loved this valley, then looked up at Rowan, touched his face and closed her eyes for the final time. She was at peace.

Gwenyth was there, only a few feet away, for Catherine had decided somewhere in the recesses of her mind that she had found in Gwenyth both an angel and a true friend.

There had been nothing for Gwenyth to do but sit at Catherine's side, as bidden. Not that she minded. There was something gratifying about being so needed and able to perform some small service for another human being in pain. There was equally something agonizing in it, finding such a trusting friendship with someone she was destined to lose so quickly.

At the very end, Gwenyth had been pleased to see that Catherine had recognized Rowan and asked him to take her out into the countryside. Annie told Gwenyth that she'd seen such a change before, that, sadly, it often came right before death, a last shining reprieve before moving on to heaven, for surely there was nowhere else that such a sweet lady as Catherine might go.

Rowan spent the weeks leading up to Catherine's death in a cloud of rigid silence. If he had not kept such a cold distance from her, looking through her as if she were not there at all, she would have been unable to feel anything other than a deep sympathy for him, though she knew he did not want anyone's sympathy, most especially hers. He didn't want her there at all, she knew, and tolerated her only because Catherine desired her presence.

None of them had dismounted. Gwenyth was upon her mare, next to Tristan, the Reverend Reginald Keogh, Annie, Catherine's nurse, and several other members of the household. They held a silent vigil behind the laird of Castle Grey and his lady.

Rowan was silent for a long while, and then he turned to them. "It is over," he said simply. He was cradling the body of his wife tenderly, his gaze distant. He had nothing else to say, merely turned his horse and started down the hillside toward his home.

When they returned, Rowan carried Catherine back to her bed, leaving the others to await his word. Even Reverend Keogh was not asked to attend the laird's private prayers for his departed lady; like the others, he awaited his time to serve. Gwenyth could only imagine what demons taunted Rowan while he sat with Catherine. Though he had so often infuriated her, she didn't think he had done Catherine any wrong; he had seen to her care to the best of his ability.

As evening neared, Gwenyth could bear the potent silence of the castle no longer; she went down to the stables and sought out her mare. The stableboy, like all the other servants, wore a look of mourning, but he was quick to help Gwenyth and advise her on a path to take for her ride.

"M'lady, 'tis not always safe for one who does not know our forests," he warned. "Ours is a rough landscape."

"I will not go far," she assured him.

And truly, she did not mean to do so. But she soon found herself in the midst of a striking landscape, cliffs that rose high as if touching the heavens, valleys that were deep and beautiful. She passed tenant farms with workers in the fields, grazing lands so rich with sheep that they appeared as deep pools of white clouds. She reached a cliff traversed by a well-worn path and took it, aware that she was climbing higher and higher, but not entirely aware the sun was falling. From her vantage point, when she looked out, she could see the coast, the setting sun dazzling upon the water. On this day, when Catherine had died, there was no mist, no foul weather and no hint of rain.

Looking out, she could see the ferries returning to the shore. She realized she did hardly know her own home when she stared across the sea right then. Shading her eyes against the dying sun, she thought Islington Isle might be the very large spit to the far right. She could see the red rays strike an edifice there on the rock that made up most of her family's home.

Islington. Her home. She realized that she feared it, dreaded it. She had left when she was just fourteen. She had been schooled in Edinburgh under the care of Mary of Guise for several years, until she was sent to

France when it was decided that Queen Mary must have a new lady-in-waiting, one more aware of the changing conditions in the queen's own realm.

She had been glad to leave. She had grown up with kindly nurses, but they had been under the harsh control of Angus MacLeod. He wasn't a bad man, merely a grim one, and he had always begrudged the decision that she should bear her father's title, though the law would customarily have granted the title and lands to the male heir. Her father's death while fighting for James V had caused the Queen Mother, regent following her husband's death, to decree that the title went to Gwenyth, just as her daughter became the queen at so tender an age.

The rock edifice that seemingly rose straight from the rocks and the water appeared to shimmer for a moment, as if in welcome. Perhaps, she thought, it was not welcome but warning. She gave herself a mental shake. She was as filled with pain as the rest of the household. Such a sad fate never should have struck such a gentle lady as Catherine. Now she was gone, death having claimed her at last. There would be no more suffering and no more fear. And so, despite the beauty of the day, there was now a pall about them all, Gwenyth thought.

The sun fell, leaving the cold to wrap itself around Gwenyth, who realized suddenly that she was atop a dangerous tor in the near blackness of the night.

"Come, girl," she told her mare, keeping all signs of the sudden nervousness she felt from her voice. "It's time to head back."

The mare, despite Gwenyth's best efforts, sensed her unease. As she tried carefully to wend her way back down the path, the mare pranced nervously.

"One does not *prance* on such ground," Gwenyth informed the horse, but to no avail. "And I am not losing my seat again, my love," she announced firmly.

They made it down the first slope and came to a valley. There were no longer sheep everywhere. Where the herders had taken their flocks, she did not know. In the dark, everything about this rugged land looked alike.

She eased her grip on the reins, allowing her mare to take the lead. She heard the cry of an owl as they started back across a field and nearly jumped herself. The mare shied, but still Gwenyth kept her seat.

"Home, girl, home," she said softly, urging her horse forward again.

She rode through gentle fields, without

seeing another human being.

After a few hours, she realized they were getting nowhere, either going in circles, or heading north rather than southeast. She stopped, desperately trying to get a feel for the position of the water, so she could regain her sense of direction. She thought that the breeze, which was making the night ever colder, was coming from the northwest, and having made that determination, she took control of the reins once again.

What had happened to all the farmhouses she had seen earlier? She had not come upon a single one since riding down from the peak. She chastised herself for her foolishness in getting so lost, though she knew that berating herself, whether in silence or aloud, would certainly do her no good.

At last she decided that she should find a copse, which would at least provide a place to sleep, and renew her hunt for a path back to the castle once it was morning. At the far end of the valley she could see a rising thicket of trees outlined in the moonlight, and she thought she could find a sheltered place there, a brook for water, surely, and a lumpy bed of pine needles.

There was little to fear, she assured herself, since she hadn't seen another human being in hours.

Laird Rowan would certainly not notice her absence that night, so she needn't fear she would worry him. And yet . . .

She felt a new sense of despair as she realized that Annie and Liza would certainly notice when she didn't return, and they would set up an alarm. With luck, Tristan would see to it that someone went out in search for her without disturbing Rowan's nightlong watch over his beloved Catherine.

As she headed toward the deeper darkness of the copse, she shivered and chastised herself again, mocking her own foolishness.

Then she saw a glow from somewhere in the trees.

She reined in the mare and narrowed her eyes. She could just make out a campfire burning, and she hesitated, but only briefly. True, the Highlanders were known for being a law unto themselves, but she was convinced that none would hurt her. She was the queen's lady, and she was under the care of one of their own, Laird Rowan of Castle Grey. She urged the mare forward, even when the horse protested, trying to wheel and run.

Later she would rue the fact that she hadn't allowed herself the good sense to follow the mare's instincts.

As she headed toward the light, the darkness suddenly filled with sound, a rustling in the trees before her, then behind her, at her side.

The mare shied, and Gwenyth tried to turn, to run.

But she knew it was too late.

Rowan remained where he had been for hours, seated, his head low, at the side of the bed. He didn't look at Catherine's beautiful features; he knew death had brought a peace to her face that he had not seen for far too long; she looked now as if she merely slept in great comfort.

He wanted to feel agony. He longed for pain. Anything . . .

Anything to banish the heavy burden of guilt.

He gritted his teeth. He had never offered another woman what he had offered her. Once upon a time, she had ignited every breath of passion and loyalty within him. They had laughed; they had loved; they had shared deep discussions on the state of the realm, on horses, even on the improvements that must be made to the castle.

Once upon a time. . . .

But it seemed so long ago now. And far too often since her accident, he had been eager to escape the castle, grateful for his duties because they had taken him away from the cruel specter of what was, compared to that of what had been.

And when he had returned this time . . .

Not only had she not known him, she had longed for the solace of a stranger.

And then, just hours before her death, she had known him and, sensing the approach of her own death, had bade him take her to the tor, that she might see the land and the sky one last time.

He had never offered another soul his love, but he had tarried often enough with other women while she had lived. Whores, strumpets, no one who mattered or could be hurt, no one who even engaged his mind, much less his heart. They had not mattered, had meant nothing. . . .

Yet now, as she lay here, he felt he had betrayed her. He had left home not just for duty, but by choice.

He wanted to punish himself for deserting her, wanted to feel the pain, not the dullness, the cold, that had settled around him.

"Forgive me," he whispered, hands clenched before him. "Catherine, dear God, I pray you can forgive me."

At first he paid no attention to the commotion in the hallway; he knew no one would disturb him. Despite Reverend Keogh's opinion that he needed to allow the body to be preserved, set to rest in a coffin, prepared for services, he knew he would be left alone, that everyone would await the end of his personal mourning.

But finally the to-do grew so loud and so close that he could ignore it no longer, so he stood, frowning, and strode to the door, casting it open.

Tristan was a dozen feet away along the hallway, speaking anxiously — and loudly — to Annie and Liza. Both women were obviously upset, and even Tristan looked deeply concerned.

"What is going on?" Rowan demanded.

The three of them spun around, looking at him with surprise, concern — and dread.

No one answered.

"Tristan? God, man, has a cat got your tongue?"

Tristan cleared his throat. "Laird Rowan, we did nae mean to take ye from y'er lady. We've a bit of a problem here, but I'll deal with it, m'laird, I swear."

Rowan strode down the hall toward them, frowning. "What is this 'bit of a problem'?"

"Lady Gwenyth rode out, my Lord Rowan!" Annie cried, distressed. "And she has not returned."

"She rode out," he repeated blankly.

"Aye."

"Who allowed her to do so?" he demanded, staring at Tristan.

"M'laird, I should have been far more attentive, but . . . she asked no one's permission, she simply left," Tristan explained. He stood tall, ready to accept his master's displeasure.

Oddly enough, Rowan felt no anger for Tristan. He knew Gwenyth far too well. But with her, he was furious. And, strangely, he was glad to be furious, to feel an emotion, to feel . . .

Alive.

"When did she leave?" he demanded.

"A few hours before dusk, I believe," Annie said.

"I'll rally the men. We will find her, I swear it," Tristan assured him.

"I will ride, as well," Rowan said grimly, then paused, inhaling deeply. "Inform the Reverend Keogh that the women may prepare my lady's body, and that we will set a vigil in the hall, so the people may attend to their prayers before her burial."

He turned and strode away to prepare.

He did not have to ride, he knew; his men were capable and could go in search of Gwenyth without his help. But he could not sit still. There were dangers in the darkness, but the little fool was far too self-assured to realize it. He wanted to throttle her. She was his responsibility.

As Catherine's death approached, he had written to the queen, to tell Mary that their travels would take longer, and she had replied to say that she understood the necessity of attending at the deathbed of a loved one. It was his duty, she had said.

Aye, his wife was dead, and it was his duty to pray by her bedside. No one would expect him to shirk that duty for another, and lesser, this night. He did not have to ride.

Then he thought of Gwenyth, alone in the darkness of the Highlands and knew that aye, he did.

"Hello?" Gwenyth whispered aloud, alarmed to hear a quaver in her voice. "Hello?"

It was then that a man leaped from the brush at her side, catching hold of the mare's bridle. The mare shied violently, but the fellow kept his hold.

"Why, 'tis none but a girl, entering the woods alone," he announced in the Gaelic of the Highlands.

Two other men stepped forward to flank her.

"I'm sorry to disturb your evening," Gwenyth said. "I'm Lady MacLeod of Islington. You are probably acquainted with my uncle. I'm traveling under the protection of Laird Rowan Graham, and am a guest at Castle Grey, where there has been a tragic loss. Perhaps you would be so good as to direct me to the proper path, that I might return before the night grows any later?"

"Lady MacLeod?" one of them said, stepping forward. Someone suddenly lit a torch, momentarily blinding her with its sudden light.

She knew she was being studied, and it made her uncomfortable. She hadn't liked the tone taken by the man who had spoken.

"Laird Rowan Graham will be looking for me," she said sharply.

"Really?" The question came from the same man.

She blinked against the light, trying to make him out. He was tall — and very hairy. His beard fell to his chest. He was about fifty, a massive, well-muscled man. There was a younger fellow at his side, also bearded, and so like him that she knew he had to be kin, probably a son. The third man was lighter than the other two, blond where they were dark. She noted quickly that his tartan was of a better quality and that he wore fine shoes, while the other two were clad in boots that showed signs of heavy wear.

It was the young blond man, clean shaven and more slender, who spoke up then. "Lady MacLeod?" he murmured.

" 'Tis a gift," the older man said.

"Will you please help me find my way?" she asked nervously.

"A MacLeod!" the younger, bearded man said.

They all seemed amused, their eyes calculating.

"I am one of the queen's ladies," she said sharply.

"Aye, well, 'tis true the queen has returned," the blond man said.

"Aye, a Catholic," the older man said, and spat.

"And kind," Gwenyth said quickly. "She wishes all her people to worship as they choose."

"Come down, m'lady," the older man said gallantly. "I am Fergus MacIvey. Perhaps ye've heard of me."

She had not.

It didn't matter; he wasn't waiting for her

reply. Without her permission, he reached for her, lifting her from the mare. She didn't protest; he was the size of an ox, and she already knew that she was in trouble here, though she wasn't at all sure why. She was a MacLeod, and that seemed to be a problem. Had there been some dispute between the MacLeods and these men?

Her heart sank. She knew she had to keep her wits about her.

"The queen is indeed a just and kind lady," she said, landing on her feet. "But she is advised by her brother, James Stewart, who can be a hard and punitive man, it is true."

The three exchanged skeptical glances.

"M'Lady," the blond man said, bowing slightly, "I'm Bryce MacIvey, thane of the clan. Perhaps ye've heard of *me*."

She had not heard of him, either, so she simply remained silent.

"This is my kinsman, Fergus's son, Michael," Bryce MacIvey said. "Ye're upon MacIvey lands, y'see."

"M'lord, good men," she said, forcing a smile in acknowledgment, "I'm sorry to be trespassing, and sorry to have disturbed you. If you would just be so good as to direct me back toward Castle Grey . . ."

"We'd not have ye goin' off with no

sustenance to see ye on y'er way, nor would we send ye off into the dark without escort," Bryce said.

"As it seemed Laird Graham allowed," Fergus noted.

"I'm a very competent horsewoman," she said.

"Mayhap, but ye should not be out in the dark alone," Bryce chided her.

She did not like the speculative way he watched her and knew she had to speak very carefully. "Laird Rowan's wife died today," she said softly. "He is in mourning . . . and his temper is both weary and foul."

Her words caused another exchange of glances.

"Come, we'll get ye some ale to slake y'er thirst, meat to settle y'er hunger," Fergus said.

She had no choice; Fergus had her mare's reins, and Bryce had her by the arm, so she allowed them to lead her over to the fire that burned in the night.

She was given a seat upon a rolled tartan before the flames and offered ale in a horn that was surely a relic of someone's Viking ancestor. She accepted the drink politely, realizing that she was, indeed, thirsty, though water would have sufficed much better. The ale was strong and bitter, and she had to force herself not to cough and sputter.

Fergus handed her a small piece of meat; he did not tell her what it was, and she thought she might well be dining on squirrel. She merely thanked him and began to chew. She had been mistaken; the meat was some kind of fowl, and not at all bad.

But once she was politely seated and fed, the three stepped away, and she knew they were discussing her, though they claimed they were trying to determine the best way back to Castle Grey.

By listening carefully, she could hear enough of what they said to send chills racing along her spine.

". . . a MacLeod . . ." That from Bryce.

". . . rich dowry . . ." Fergus.

". . . revenge upon old Angus!" Michael said triumphantly.

"What of the queen's wrath?" Bryce asked.

"Laird Rowan . . . the more deadly," Michael advised.

Pretending to get more comfortable, she slid closer to where they were speaking, the better to hear their conversation.

Fergus began to speak in a heated whisper. "Aye, and what will they do, Bryce, if ye take the lady now, eh? Why not wait for a marriage come the mornin'? That can be no hardship, surely? She be a pretty creature, indeed. She has an alluring beauty."

"What of Laird Rowan?" Michael asked.

"The fool has let her loose. He is deep in mourning and will not even notice her absence until it is too late," Bryce pointed out logically. "And I do not care to wait for morning."

"Possession is indeed the greater part of the law," Fergus admitted.

Gwenyth kept her seat as she listened, pretending she didn't hear them. Panic had made ice of her blood and frozen her limbs, but she knew she dared not let on, not if she wished to have any chance of escaping this band. She was incredulous that they would dare to suggest violence against her in any way, and yet she knew she should not have been. She knew how apt the clans were to battle one another, and how eager to take justice into their own hands.

Clearly, her uncle had done something to make these men enemies to the MacLeods, and equally clearly, they meant for her to pay the price.

And her service to the queen was no protection, because Mary had just returned. She was a foreigner in their minds, and not in control of her country yet. They no doubt knew that if she moved against them, she might incite a revolt among all those who feared her religion and her ties with France.

Bryce MacIvey came strolling to her side, excitement in his eyes now, as well as speculation. She knew her fate had been decided. Tonight she would be the victim of rape, and come the morning, a forced marriage. It would be easy enough for them to find the proper minister. Once the deed was done, she would be trapped, the scorned wife of a laird who had done nothing but use her in revenge and for his own monetary gain. Her lands were far from the richest in Scotland, but they provided revenue just the same.

She had been a fool, such a fool. She could scream forever, and no one would hear her. She didn't even know where she was, other than on MacIvey lands. True, they would face the wrath of Laird Rowan and the queen, but still, once the deed was done, the vows spoken, what could anyone do? She would be tainted goods, and that would be the end of it.

And there was no one here to help her; there was not a chance of rescue. Therefore, she would have to rescue herself.

"Ah, m'lady, how is the pheasant?" Bryce inquired politely.

"A sweet morsel, quite delicious," she

said. "I admit to a terrible hunger and thirst. The ale is fine, as well. I thank you sincerely for seeing to my needs."

"Naturally we, being men of honor, could do no less," Bryce said.

"We think it best to wait for the morning and escort ye home," Fergus said gravely.

"The dark is no time to be ridin'," Michael advised.

"Oh?" she said.

"The land hereabouts is rugged and fierce," Fergus told her. He seemed to be the leader here, though it was his blond kinsman who held the title. He was older, and the most powerful in build.

It was Bryce, however, who would lead her off into the woods. Bryce she needed to somehow best.

She must play innocent, must keep them all off guard. She must allow him to lure her deep into the woods, for getting him alone was her only chance of escape.

Bryce looked at her then and said politely, "The news you bring us is most tragic, that Lady Catherine has left this world at last."

She bowed her head.

"And ye are here with Laird Rowan," he said. There was speculation in his words.

"Aye. At the queen's command, I travel with the man."

There was silence. Were they wondering if the queen had decided that she would make the proper second wife for a man such as Laird Rowan? She found the very idea despicable when his loss was yet so new, but if it would help save her freedom for these men to believe such a thing she was more than willing to support the lie.

"Laird Rowan needs no more power," Fergus muttered, staring at Bryce.

Her heart sank. Perhaps the lie wouldn't help her after all.

What now?

The time had come for a decision. Bryce approached her, extending his hand. "Come, m'lady, and I'll show ye a bit of the sweet forest here. We'll find a place where ye can rest for the night, a place where ye'll be safe as we guard ye through the darkness."

"Thank you," she said, accepting his hand with what she prayed was an expression of innocence and gratitude, and stood, taking her time, dusting off her skirts. She weighed the pressure of Bryce's grip. He was more slender than the others, but hardly without power. Her one hope was to trick him, giving her a chance to inflict a blow that would render him immobile.

He led her some distance away, which told

her that he knew these trails well.

"What about the beasts in the forest?" she whispered, clinging to his arm.

"Ah, ye needn't fear. 'Tis mainly deer here, though we occasionally see a few boar, but they disturb none that do not come after them."

He stopped, and she worried, because they were still too close to the other men.

She let go of him, striding almost blindly along the path, wishing her eyes would accustom themselves to the darkness.

"M'lady, where are ye going?" Bryce demanded, his tone developing a slight edge.

"Just further into the woods," she said.

"But I know these woods and where it is safest to sleep."

"I am a member of the royal court," she said. "I must have my privacy, Laird Mac-Ivey."

"Ye need go no deeper."

"But I must." She didn't dare run, but she quickened her pace.

He fell in behind her, so she hurried all the more. And at last, when she was a good distance from the fire, she began to run.

He caught up with her, grabbing her arm, the vise of his fingers very strong. She stared at him, forcing herself not to fight in any way.

"My Laird?" she said.

Any pretense fell from his features. "This may be sweet and easy, m'lady, or more difficult. The choice be y'ers."

"This . . . ?"

"The MacLeods owe me," he said softly.

"Ye've a feud with Angus?" she demanded, still pretending innocence.

"Aye. Y'er uncle caused a bitter fight that led to the loss of Hawk Isle, taken by y'er own kin, lady. Ye owe me. Ye owe me the income of that land, and of Islington."

"If an injustice has been committed by my uncle, I will rectify it," she said.

"Indeed, you will."

He was done talking and started to pull her to him.

Despite the ice in her veins, she bided her time, listening to her instinct for self-preservation.

Only when he was certain that she was cowed, pliant in his arms . . .

Only then did she strike.

She kneed him ferociously. When he doubled over, she struck him atop his head with her doubled fists, using all her strength. When he fell, screeching in agony, she knew it was time to run again.

She tore through the forest, ruing the fact that Bryce MacIvey was making enough noise to wake the dead as far away as York.

No matter. It was done. And now, if she was caught again, she would be tortured, she was certain. That left escape as her only option.

So, despite the darkness and the unknown trails, she kept moving as quickly as she could. She ran and ran. At last she heard the sound of a brook ahead and made her way there, paused, drank deeply of the cool water, then hesitated.

She was stunned when the sound of rock against rock suddenly split the night and light burst to life in the darkness.

Fergus was there, lit by the glow of a torch.

She backed away, aware that Bryce Mac-Ivey was still somewhere behind her.

"Aye, y'er a MacLeod, all right!" Fergus lashed out furiously as he started toward her, his face a distorted mask of fury.

She turned to run and, to her horror, plowed straight into a body.

Even in the shadows, her heart sank. She had landed in the arms of a fiercely scowling Bryce MacIvey, and Michael was coming up beside him, moving to flank her.

She backed away, wrenching free. She was surrounded on three sides, and still, there was nothing to do but run.

This time Fergus was ready, leaping toward her with speed and fury. Just as he would have grabbed her, he suddenly went still, an odd look on his face.

Then, to her absolute amazement, he fell face forward at her feet.

A voice rang out in the darkness from beyond, harsh and filled with such authority that it seemed as if the very forest went still.

"Touch her again, MacIvey, and I vow upon my late wife's soul, you and your kin will all be dead men!"

CHAPTER SEVEN

Rowan's fury hadn't abated a whit.

Perhaps his anger was something he needed desperately, something he was clinging to because it was vital to feel something . . . *anything.*

His fury was further fueled now by the scene he had come upon.

The MacIveys were a crude and vicious lot, ever ambitious, ready to sell their souls for any improvement to their land or income. Working their hereditary lands with greater care had never occurred to a one of them. They were known to strike up ridiculous feuds, challenging their neighbors.

They were prone to losing.

Thus far, James, acting on behalf of the Crown, had tried to keep some form of peace in the Highlands, but men such as these had done everything possible to undermine his efforts. Not that the Highlanders couldn't feud easily enough on their own. But equally, they tended to be of proud moral character; they had laws unto themselves and, though there had certainly been abductions throughout the ages, rape was something they despised among invaders and did not practice themselves.

Gwenyth had walked right into this. And on this night of all nights! She had gone still, staring at him, heaving for breath, her eyes wide with shock, her hair tumbled about her shoulders. She was indeed a rare beauty, far too tempting for men such as these to have ignored. And there remained the feud with Angus to spur them on. She was a little fool!

"Ye've killed him, Rowan. Ye've killed me man, Fergus!" Bryce raged.

"He's not dead, more's the pity, merely unconscious. I try not to kill men for stupidity. I will report your crimes to the Crown," he said coldly.

"What crimes?" Bryce demanded. "We were trying to help the lady, nothing more. She feared us, and I feared for her in the dark."

"You liar!" Gwenyth exploded.

It looked as if Bryce were about to set his hands on Gwenyth again. Rowan urged his mount just slightly forward, and Bryce apparently thought better of it, though he could not stop himself from speaking.

"She is mistaken."

"She is not," Gwenyth snapped icily.

Bryce's eyes narrowed. "If she thinks something other, it is because she is a witch, one who sought us out, found us somehow in the forest, where she cast the evil eye upon us."

"Good God, what a ridiculous excuse for idiocy!" Rowan thundered.

"What is your anger for? The lady stumbled upon us. Unless, of course . . ." Bryce smiled, a slow and nasty smile. "I hear that your lady is scarcely cold yet, but perhaps you are already planning for the future. Y'er claim has been . . . laid, and thus y'er fury with me," he announced, laughing.

"I should kill you now," Rowan said quietly. "But murder can be so complicated, though I doubt I'd pay much of a price. Still, I would be compelled to kill both Fergus and Michael, as well, and they should not have to die for the folly of following their laird, who ought to know better. You'd best get Fergus to care. He's been given a good thump upon the head with yonder rock. My aim has always been impeccable, as you know."

"Y'er on me land!" Bryce cried, but he

made no move to step forward.

"Which borders my own. You had only to set the lady upon the path yonder, and she would have reached the wall," Rowan said. "Gwenyth, come here now," he said.

She realized then that he wasn't alone. There were a number of horsemen behind him. She obeyed the command without hesitation.

He reached a hand down to her and lifted her up before him on his own mount.

"Wife barely dead," Bryce dared to mutter.

"Because of that fact, I will let you live," Rowan said softly, and yet with more menace and promise than might have been in the loudest shout.

There were no more exchanges as Rowan turned his horse toward home. She saw then that he had been accompanied by Tristan, the guards who had ridden with them from Edinburgh and three more men from Castle Grey. They didn't follow until Rowan had cleared the copse with her, and she realized that Rowan hadn't trusted Bryce and his companions. He had dared to offer his back to them only because of his trust in his own men.

Gwenyth wanted to say something, anything, a thank-you . . . an apology. But when

185

she would have begun, he warned her sharply, "Don't speak, Lady MacLeod."

And so she rode back to the castle before him, painfully aware of him, humiliated, and too shaken to fight against the feeling.

At the castle, Annie and Liza were waiting for their return.

Rowan did not speak to her, just as he had not spoken on the ride, as he set her down in front of Annie.

"See to your lady," he said brusquely.

She turned quickly enough to see his face. It was a stern mask, his eyes cold.

"Thank you," she said stiffly.

"Don't ride out alone again," he returned.

"Wait, please," she said. But he did not.

"My poor, poor dear," Annie crooned, then chastised her. "What were you doing, m'lady? God knows, you must take care. You serve the queen, and you are a lady in your own right. Ah, mistress, that ye can be so sheltered as not to know the minds of men . . ."

Annie didn't even know half of what had happened, Gwenyth thought wearily.

"I'm fine," she murmured uneasily.

Tristan returned quickly from the stables. " 'Twill be a hard day, come the morning," he said, smiling gently at Gwenyth. "No harm done, lady, though there might have been. But ye're safe now, so best ye get some sleep."

"Aye, sleep," Liza, who had stood silently by, watching, said, as she slipped a supportive arm around Gwenyth's waist. "Come, all will be better in the morning."

It wouldn't be better. Gwenyth knew it.

The women had tended to Catherine's body, using spices, vinegar and acqua vitae, so that she might remain beautiful, looking as if she were only sleeping, while she lay in the great hall in the fine wooden coffin that had been so carefully carved for her.

Rowan stood unmoving for most of the day, as the people of his holding came through the castle, saying their prayers, wishing her Godspeed to heaven, where surely such an angel would dwell. The numbness had settled upon him again, except whenever he noticed Gwenyth, who had taken up a position nearby. He felt the same wealth of passionate fury stir within him each time his eyes fell upon her, although he could not fault her behavior that day. She managed to walk a thin line, appearing regal, yet greeting the mourners as if they were all friends, and making certain they were all offered wine or ale as she thanked them for their love for their lady.

Many of the villagers looked at her with curiosity and speculation, and he realized that his own people were wondering just as the MacIveys had if she were not the object of his affection — his mistress.

That thought stirred his wrath to a further degree, despite the fact it was not such a wild stretch of the imagination. She was young; she was beautiful; she was titled. She would make a proper wife for a laird.

Not this laird, he thought angrily, all the more so because he could not deny finding her attractive.

He wanted to send her far from him, for she disturbed him beyond reason.

He tried to tell himself it was only because Catherine had held her so dear, because his wife had wanted Gwenyth's presence, when she had not even known his face.

He needed his distance from her, he thought. The expression of sweet gravity on her perfectly sculpted features as she spoke to those who came through made him long to roar out a denial, to stride out, to find his horse and ride . . .

Ride into oblivion.

Late in the day, Tristan urged him to break his vigil, to eat, but he could not. He knew that Gwenyth was only a few feet away, with nothing to do once they had closed the great hall to the mourners, and that she would overhear him, but he could not bring himself to care.

"Leave me be with my lady through the night," he commanded.

"Me good laird —" Tristan began.

"Leave me be," he repeated.

Tristan knew him well and obeyed. Rowan was only dimly aware when his steward led Gwenyth from the hall.

He did not stand throughout the night but pulled one of the great brocade chairs from the fireplace, set it by the coffin and slept thereon.

No one disturbed him until morning. When Tristan came to check on him, Rowan told him, "Do not leave her alone, Tristan. She wouldn't want to be alone."

"I'll be here, m'laird, watching, until you return." Tristan cleared his throat. "We will bear the Lady Catherine to the chapel for services at ten, if that meets your desire."

Rowan nodded. "Aye," he said, and left.

In his chambers, he felt the keen sense of it being a far different place. He had not slept in here since Catherine had become so ill, sleeping by her side when he was home — or not sleeping at all. His life had changed in the blink of an eye when Catherine had suffered her accident. Until then, he had been a happy man, but he had quickly become a hollow one. He had chosen to give his all to the Crown, even before the queen had returned. Every man needed a passion, and with the loss of Catherine as she had once been, he had made his country his passion.

It was odd; he could scarcely remember when he'd had a wife — a real wife. Still, with her passing, he felt the hollowness all the more.

There was not much that could be said for fairness in life, he thought bitterly. Catherine had been nothing but kind, had looked for nothing but good for all men, yet her fate had been cruel, while idiots, madmen and butchers seemed to live long and well.

He called for a tub and water to bathe, then dressed slowly and with care; it seemed important that he be at his best to afford Catherine her last honors. Finally, when he was clad in his tartan and clan brooches, he hesitated. It was so final, to say the last prayers, but he could tarry no longer.

When he reached the great hall, his men were ready. Catherine's coffin was lifted as tenderly and carefully as if she but slept, and Reverend Keogh stood at the front of the coffin, Rowan's household assembled around him. At Rowan's nod, the reverend began his prayers. The procession moved across the hall and out to the light, and from there to the chapel that flanked the castle walls.

The words said for her soul seemed to blend together. Rowan knew that he didn't think it necessary for any man to ask God to accept Catherine; indeed, if there was a God, she was already in His keeping.

He was grateful that Reverend Keogh was a good man who spoke only the words that were proper for a funeral rite; he made no mention of the world at large, the good or evil therein, or the proper way for any man or woman to worship. He spoke eloquently about Catherine, and when he was done, all present passed by once again, kissing the coffin, or setting wild flowers upon and around it. At last the service was over.

Rowan strode from the chapel, aware that his workmen were already waiting to see that her coffin was set properly in the family crypt, in the niche below the one that held his parents, and in company with those who had come before them.

Somewhere, stonemasons were already preparing a magnificent plaque to cover the tomb that would be her silent memorial now.

He was expected, he knew, to welcome the local thanes and the villagers into his castle once again, but he could not. He left that task to Tristan — and his unwanted guest, Lady Gwenyth — and strode to the stables, mounted his horse and rode out, just as he had earlier longed to do.

He couldn't help but wonder if his restlessness was like that which must have seized Gwenyth two days before. The suggestion angered him, and he did not want to know why.

But he did know, even without any thought at all.

Those who believed he hungered after her were not so far astray in their thoughts.

And that he *could* want her, with Catherine so recently dead, appalled him.

If she were a whore, a loose woman, a courtesan with no reputation to lose, it would be one thing. But she was not. She was a lady born. The queen's lady.

He could not forgive himself for the desire he felt, and it angered him further to remember that Bryce MacIvey had coveted her, had nearly taken her for his own.

He reined in on the high tor where he had brought Catherine to breathe her last.

Gwenyth would be leaving come the morning, or as soon as he could arrange it.

And leaving with orders that she be guarded like a jewel, that no man be allowed to upset or make free with her, no matter what Angus's intentions to control her might be. She needed to be taken away from his own fury, Rowan thought. In fact, she needed to be wedded to a laird in some distant place, where she could be temptation for no other.

He simply wanted her gone.

"Catherine," he said aloud softly, and bowed his head. It had been more than two years since they had visited Catherine's home in England and she had nearly died in the accident, more than two years since his son had been stillborn, a secret he had shared with no one, and Catherine had lost all sense of the world. He lowered his head, glad that at least he had been there with her at the end. Glad that she had known his face one last time, that she had touched him.

Then, after a moment, he said very softly to the heavens, "Forgive me."

Gwenyth was awake, but barely, so she was startled by the tapping at her door so early in the morning.

She had not seen Rowan for several days. The castle was decorated in black cloth, subdued and somber, as was natural for a state of mourning. But Rowan had not remained inside. He had ridden out before the sun each morning and returned late, and none had dared disturb him.

She had been irritated that she was not allowed out at all, but because of the nearly disastrous end to her last foray, she stayed in the castle as bidden.

No, as ordered.

She was not a fool, and she did not want to chance another encounter with men such as the MacIveys, but she was growing restless at the lack of things to do. There was an excellent library in the castle, and so she read, but after so many days, the black drapery and the air of gloom that hung over the castle began to feel suffocating. She, too, mourned Catherine. But she could not know what those who had known her for years — who had loved her, like Rowan — were feeling. She wanted to afford Catherine every honor, every drop of grief, all the respect, that she deserved. But she felt as if she needed air.

She sat up in bed as the gentle tapping came again.

"Yes?" she said.

Her door opened a crack.

"Lady Gwenyth?"

It was Tristan.

"Aye?"

"I'm sorry to disturb you, but Annie asked me to tell you that she is on her way to see to your things."

She frowned. "Oh?"

"Indeed, my lady. Y'er to ride on to the ferry for Islington this morning."

"Laird Rowan intends to leave so soon?"

"Nay, lady. Ye're to ride on with an escort."

"I see," she murmured.

She heard Tristan clear his throat. "When ye've dressed, m'lady, would ye be so kind as to spare me a minute of y'er time?"

A curious smile curved her lips. "Of course."

As soon as the door was closed, she leapt up, washed and dressed quickly for the day. As she struggled with the ties for her stomacher, Annie arrived and, clucking, helped her. "Me job in life is but to serve ye, lady. Call upon me more often."

"I like a bit of privacy, Annie, and you serve me very well, thank you," she murmured. She noticed that Annie was wearing an amused grin, despite the dark air that sat upon the castle.

"What is it?" she asked.

"Oh, I cannae say, m'lady."

"Of course you can — your job in life is to serve me, is it not?"

Annie laughed delightedly. "In this, I cannae!"

"And why is that?"

"Because Tristan would speak with ye."

"Annie?"

"Me lips are sealed on this, m'lady. They must be. 'Tis not me right to speak."

Truly curious, Gwenyth hurried to the great hall. Tristan was there alone, hands folded behind his back as he paced the great room.

"Ah, m'lady."

"Tristan."

He looked around, at the black draped around the castle.

" 'Tis truly not the proper time to speak of such things, but I fear that . . . well, you are to ride to Islington."

"And?" she encouraged.

His cheeks burned bright red.

"Tristan, please, speak your mind."

He came to her, fell upon one knee and took her hand. "M'lady, I ask that you grant me the hand of your maid in marriage."

Her mouth gaped open. "Annie?"

He looked up at her, puzzled. "Nay, lady. Liza Duff. She has enchanted and bewitched me. Nay, nay, I do not mean bewitched, good God, else fools would have her on a pyre again. She has helped me here, these few weeks. She has been such a friend, and I . . . old gnarled fool that I am, believe that she has feelings for me, as well."

She smiled as he looked up at her with such hope and earnest appeal in his eyes. "Tristan, I am not the woman's keeper. You must ask her."

He shook his head gravely. "Ye must give y'er blessing."

"Have you spoken with Rowan?"

"Aye, and he said that I must speak with ye."

Gwenyth's smile deepened. "If it is only my approval that you need, then I give it most freely. If Liza agrees," she added hastily. She would never force anyone to wed, she vowed to herself.

But apparently Liza agreed. She burst in from the corridor that led to the stairs, rushing toward Gwenyth. She looked as if she was about to throw her arms around Gwenyth, then hesitated and almost skidded to a stop. Her face was alive with happiness.

Gwenyth laughed, reaching out to give Liza a hug.

"Bless you, bless you, lady!" Liza said. "Dear God above, I owe you not only my life but so much more in service, and truly, all my days I will serve you when you call upon me, and yet . . . I was all but dead, only to find such tender care with Tristan. I . . ." She paused, swallowing guiltily. "I am sorry to find such happiness myself now, when . . . when there is such sorrow here, and . . . I don't know when we can be duly wed, but —"

"Today," Gwenyth said.

They both stared at her, jaws gaping.

"No grand ceremony, no fancy rites," Gwenyth said. "Liza, if you would remain behind, if you two truly love one another, then I will stand witness. I can swear to you that I will have such a swift service honored by Laird Rowan."

They both remained silent, just staring.

"It will not be legal."

"Queen Mary will make it so. She asked James to ensure that the marriage is recognized by the Church, it there was any question. Where is Reverend Keogh?" Gwenyth asked, then was surprised by a soft cry of delight and turned to see that Annie, too, had entered the hall.

"He is in the chapel, I believe," the older woman said.

"Then we will go there and speak with him," Gwenyth said commandingly, suiting deed to words.

Reverend Keogh was aghast at the idea of

a ceremony without the proper time allotted beforehand, but he agreed to it when Gwenyth explained that she was leaving for her own estates, and that she did not feel right leaving Liza behind unless the marriage had been finalized. As they spoke, she was stunned to see Rowan stride into the chapel, the dark look he always seemed to wear those days upon his face.

"Lady Gwenyth, escort has been arranged. You are to be upon the road within the hour," he said curtly.

She straightened her spine so that she was at her tallest, then spoke softly, but with determination. "I will not leave so quickly. You are aware that Tristan and Liza wish to marry?"

"You would stop them?"

"Good heavens, no, my lord. I would have them marry today."

He frowned so fiercely that she almost stepped back. "The castle is in mourning," he told her.

She nodded. "It is in Catherine's sweet honor that I would have them quietly wed today. Here, now, before God."

"The papers are not drawn," Reverend Keogh murmured.

"You may read the rite, Reverend, and then fill out the proper papers," Gwenyth said, staring at Rowan. She bit her lip, careful to choose the right words to use. "Everyone honored Lady Catherine," she said very softly. "But would it be wrong, in her memory, to leave this man who served her, and you, so long and faithfully, without giving him the wife he loves, the solace that he needs? My Lord Rowan, I beg you. Set aside the grief that plagues you so. Allow this marriage here and now, simply and quietly."

He stared at her, his expression thunderous. She thought that he might actually be about to growl.

"Reverend Keogh?" Rowan said.

"Such haste is not seemly," the reverend said with a sigh. Then he lifted his arms. "And yet, Laird Rowan . . . if these two would be satisfied with the very simple word of God, and you and Lady Gwenyth to stand witness . . ."

"So be it. Do it," Rowan said.

Gwenyth blinked, amazed. His anger didn't seem to have changed in the least, but perhaps he had decided that Tristan deserved happiness for having been the one to serve Catherine most loyally.

More so than himself.

"Do it," he repeated.

They all looked to Reverend Keogh.

"Come to the altar, then," the churchman said.

"Oh!" Annie cried delightedly, clasping her hands together.

"Laird Rowan, you will stand so. You will give the bride freely to Tristan. Lady Gwenyth, here is your position, as witness."

And so Reverend Keogh began his ceremony. He was a God-fearing man, dedicated and gentle, and, he talked for a very long time.

At last Rowan cleared his throat, interrupting him. "Perhaps, Reverend, we could get to the vows?"

"Indeed," Reverend Keogh said, abashed.

And so, with joyous looks upon their faces, Liza and Tristan were wed. They made an odd couple, for she was much younger and thin as a reed, while he was a staunch and solid fellow, his face as weathered as the rocky tor. But the looks on their faces were so beautiful that Gwenyth was not surprised when even Rowan stepped outside himself for a moment to be glad for the pair.

But then he said impatiently, "It is done."

"My Laird Rowan, a moment. We must have the papers duly signed."

Rowan chafed as the reverend went to the room where his table and great Bible were situated, then sat in his hard wooden chair and wrote. At last he called them in. First the bride and groom signed, the bride marking an X, and then Rowan and Gwenyth.

When the reverend opened the great Bible to enter the couple's names, Gwenyth couldn't help but notice that the last entry was Catherine's death — and the one just before that for the stillbirth of the infant Michael William Graham.

"*Now* is it done?" Rowan demanded.

"Aye," Reverend Keogh said.

"Then Lady Gwenyth must be on the road," Rowan said.

His eyes met hers, and she couldn't help but feel a qualm. He looked as if he despised the very sight of her.

She had forced him to ride out to her rescue on the very night of his lady's death.

"I will be gone immediately," she assured him.

He nodded.

She turned to Liza, giving her a hug, and then Tristan. She slipped a delicately carved gold ring that Mary had given her in France from her finger, and pressed it into Liza's hand. "For you. And, Tristan, you have been so kind to me. I believe you admired the roan in our party. He is a gelding, but he is a fine animal. He came with us from France, where he was part of Queen Mary's stables. His name is Andrew, though I know not why. He is yours."

"Bless you, m'lady. Ye gave us gift enough in one another," Tristan said.

Rowan cleared his throat, and Gwenyth thought he sounded angry, but he spoke kindly just the same. "I will grant a homestead to you both."

Perhaps, she thought, he was upset that she had reminded him, with her own gifts, that he needed to offer something to the couple. No matter.

Gwenyth felt a sudden urge to leave that was surely greater than his desire to have her gone. Though she was trying desperately to maintain her own calm demeanor, it was difficult to be so despised. "I will be going now," she said to the assembled company.

He bowed deeply, suddenly. "Good journey, Lady Gwenyth."

She nodded. "God be with you, Laird Rowan."

He turned and hastily exited the chapel. She was sure he would not be in the courtyard to bid her a final goodbye, so she was shocked, a few minutes later, when he was.

She was mounted on her mare, who had been mysteriously returned, with Annie at her side and her escort of ten men at the ready, when he appeared in the courtyard. She had been saying her fondest farewells to Tristan and Liza when she saw him stride from of the castle and realized that his horse was being brought out.

He mounted without a word to her, handed a satchel to one of his men, then moved his massive stallion, Styx, to her side.

"You will not make the ferry by nightfall if we do not ride quickly," he said.

"You . . . are accompanying me?" she inquired.

"As far as the ferry. I fear that the news of your journey may have reached the MacIvey clan, and I am responsible for your welfare until you are in your uncle's care," he informed her.

As Styx moved restlessly, Rowan lifted an arm to their escort and started across the drawbridge.

"Godspeed, my lady!" Liza cried, running alongside the mare.

"May He be with you," Gwenyth returned.

"Oh," Annie said softly, " 'tis so beautiful to see them together."

Tristan was trotting along at his bride's side, and Gwenyth lifted a hand to him. "Thank you," she mouthed.

He shook his head. "Thank *you,* Lady Gwenyth. I am ever in your debt."

Then Liza and Tristan were behind her as her mare picked up speed, cantering behind Styx and the Laird of Lochraven.

The journey to the ferry was no more than a few hours, perhaps, but to Gwenyth, it felt like days. Despite Annie riding behind her, she had never felt quite so alone.

When they reached the shore and the ferry, Rowan dismounted immediately.

Apparently the ferryman had been awaiting them, for he strode forward and said, "Laird Rowan," in unsurprised greeting.

"Brendan, are you set for the lady's journey?"

"Aye, m'laird. I'll see that she arrives safely, and whatever the hour, I'll await the return of y'er men, if that's what ye'd have me do."

"Nay, good man. The men will reside with her until I'm able to return for her myself, that we might continue our journey as commanded by the queen."

Brendan, a rugged-looking man of stout build and imposing height, nodded gravely. " 'Tis best," he agreed.

"The sea, how does she today?"

"A bit rough, but nae so bad. I've seen her far worse, m'laird."

Rowan suddenly stared at Gwenyth, and a reluctantly admiring smile curved his lips.

"I doubt it will be too rough for my lady."

She stiffened in her saddle. "I do not fear the sea, 'tis true," she assured him.

Rowan strode to her side and, as he lifted her down, there was a moment when her eyes met his and she did not see the fierce hatred she had sensed in him before. Indeed, now it seemed that there was speculation there.

She felt the keen power of his hands, breathed the scent of him as he set her on the ground. She was amazed to feel tremors streak through her, and she was eager to be upon her own feet.

"Gavin is now my representative," he told her. "He bears letters to your uncle. You need not fear him."

"I don't fear him. I barely know him," she murmured, blushing. How could he have known that, in a way, she *did* fear Angus?

He was so cold and driven by duty. She didn't mind working — she never had — and Angus believed that they owed it to their tenants, those who worked the land for them, to show that the masters of the house were willing to do the same. No, what scared her was the possibility of what he might consider duty.

Despite the queen's command that she shortly sail for England with Laird Rowan, would her uncle be willing to sell her to the highest bidder in marriage, if it meant the betterment of Islington?

Rowan watched her gravely for a moment, then shrugged. "Still, I have sent letters. He will be aware that you are on the queen's business and that I will come for you in good time."

She realized that she was holding her breath.

He was staring at her, so she let it out softly and tried to speak. At last she managed, "Truly, I am sorry for the burden I have been, for the trouble I have caused."

He actually smiled. "Rue your recklessness, and take care with it. I admit I loathe the MacIveys and was glad to arrive before . . ." His voice trailed off, and his lips tightened as he pointed a finger at her. "No recklessness. Gavin will see to that. In fact, I imagine old Angus will see to it, as well. However, in case there is any question, my letters remind him that he is not free to act as head of the family and, for example, dispose of your hand in marriage. Only the queen has the right to determine your future at the moment."

"Thank you," she murmured, wondering if he were capable of reading her mind.

He stared at her again, and she realized

that it was apparently as difficult for him to speak as it had been for her. "Nay, lady. Thank you."

From around his neck, he took a delicate gold chain and pendant she had not noticed before, then fastened it about her neck. She realized it was an intricate and very beautiful Celtic cross.

"My lady would have dearly loved that you should have this, so I give it to you now in thanks for your care of her," he told her.

She felt the oddest sense of warmth seep into her. "She was gentle, kind and beautiful. And you have my deepest sympathy, Laird Rowan."

He stepped back, his features suddenly harsh again. "Godspeed," he said, and that was the last he said to her before he remounted Styx to watch the party make ready to leave. Before the ferry was even fully loaded, he nodded to Gavin, turned his horse and rode away.

As the ferry started out upon the rocking sea, she looked up to see him watching from atop one of the high tors some distance from the sea.

He might have been a statue, as cold and hard as the stone itself.

Indeed, she thought, he was an extension

of the rugged land, and like that land, he watched impassively as she drew away.

■ ■ ■ ■

PART II

The Queen Triumphant

■ ■ ■ ■

CHAPTER EIGHT

Gwenyth chewed upon a blade of grass as she read Queen Mary's letter.

". . . the difficulty being that Maitland, bless him, though the finest ambassador possible — he served my mother well, you know — is still just that: an ambassador. In consequence, I am eager for the time when you reach England. I see the dilemma that Elizabeth faces, for England sorely fears the hand of a Catholic monarch, yet I cannot sign a treaty that says I cede my rights to the English crown when I am awaiting her legal word that I am her heir. She has stated in public that she sees no one with a clearer right to the English throne than I, but she will not commit to such a belief legally. She claims she will not do so until I sign the treaty, and I cannot sign the treaty until she has so committed."

Gwenyth sighed, looking at the sky. It was so beautiful that day. In fact, she had found her own estates here on Islington to be far more beautiful than she had remembered. Perhaps she had forgotten the power of the sea and the passionate dash of the waves upon the shore. Or the valleys, those slim stretches of green with the sheep so white upon them. Even the ragged, defiant rise of the rocky castle above the earth was dear to her now.

It was not Castle Grey, by any means. There were far more drafts, fewer tapestries, and the fires never quite seemed to warm the bones. But it was a handsome castle, nonetheless, built entirely for defense, yet proud and regal while still well-suited to its purpose.

The master's quarters were hers; Angus had never taken them for his own, even when he had known that she would be gone for years. It wouldn't have been right; it wouldn't have been Godly.

And he was a Godly man.

Church services on Sunday were long, taking up most of the day. No one worked on Sunday. Indeed, even within the castle, they saw to themselves, just as Angus had insisted that while she was here she should go out with the fishermen on their boats, and learn what the shepherds did with their days, as well. Sunday was a day of rest, and Angus ordered the servants to observe it as such.

But in fact, she had not found Angus as much of an ogre as she had remembered. Perhaps it was because she had matured and seen something of the world, so she was no longer a child to be easily intimidated by him. He was stern — he reminded her of John Knox — but he had been gentle when she had arrived. He had greeted her almost lovingly — at least by his standards. He had offered no embrace, but there had been a smile and even kind words noting that he was proud of her, that he'd heard from Laird James that she had remained a Protestant despite the queen's papist ways, and that she had conducted herself at court with grace and intelligence.

He had read the letters from Rowan — including one that Rowan had carried from the queen — with a grim expression. She knew that Mary had informed him that her future would remain in royal hands, but she knew not what Rowan's letters had contained, other than the few points he had mentioned and, from her uncle's reaction, that he had recounted at least some of what had happened the night she encountered Laird Bryce MacIvey.

The giveaway had been her uncle's cry of fury as he had informed her that if a Mac-

Ivey so much as made landfall upon Islington, he would consider the man guilty of far more than trespass and see to it that he was conducted to Edinburgh for trial.

Gwenyth had to admit she was actually touched by his fierce determination to protect her. Almost.

"Such a man to pretend to greatness," Angus swore, his salt-and-pepper beard shaking as he enunciated each word. "When you are wed, it will be for the better of land and crown, a laird of my choosing, with the blessing of the queen. Ye'll not be sold so cheaply, ever!"

Sold.

What a word. Had he meant to use it?

"I thank you," she murmured, "for your vehemence on my behalf."

"Indeed," Angus agreed, and he was pleased, she realized.

She was glad to have pleased him, and she didn't mind continuing to do so.

She had enjoyed the rough waters and hard work of the fishermen — who had, she was certain, curtailed their language when she was upon their boats. And accompanying the shepherds, as she was doing today, was certainly not vile, either. She was able to relax, as she did now, with the rich scent of grass and earth around her, the sky above her, beautiful and ever changing, and read her recent correspondence from the queen.

And yet . . .

The queen's letter made her long for a return to Edinburgh. Mary wrote to her as if she knew everything that was happening at Holyrood, as if they had never parted, but Gwenyth was beginning to feel the distance. Months had now passed. A year had come and gone since she had first left Edinburgh. She had once believed that by this time, even with a long sojourn in London, she would have returned to Mary and her court. But though Laird Rowan's official time of mourning had certainly come to an end, he had never come to Islington for her. She knew from Mary's letters that the situation at home had caused her to order Rowan to return to court — without her. The plan remained, however, for Gwenyth to travel to London to meet with the Queen of England. But there was never a specific mention of when.

She returned to the missive.

"Ah, that you were here. The nobles in Scotland are such a quarrelsome group, ever at one another's throats. I do thank God for my half brother, James. His advice is all that keeps me sane at times. There was a rumor that Aaron, the son of Chatelheraults, intended to abduct me, as he was so in love. James Hepburn, Earl of Bothwell, is feuding with the Hamiltons, and this is of a far more serious nature. Bothwell wanted revenge upon Aaron Hamilton for some slight, and he broke into the house of a certain Alison, known to be a paramour of Aaron's, and I'm quite disgusted to say that force was used. Thankfully, my brother was near, as there was nearly a riot in Edinburgh, and I had to have both men arrested. What shall I do with these Scottish nobles? They have a far greater power than the nobility in France, but I have sworn that I will not play one house against another, and that I will be just in all things. But I am the queen, and I *will* be respected, though it is difficult to practice wisdom, even mercy, and maintain the respect due this office. Scotland is lovely in so many ways, but it is not the refined and well-governed country I knew so well."

Gwenyth winced at that. There was little more to the queen's letter than a promise of her care and concern, so Gwenyth decided to destroy it on the spot, lest someone unscrupulous read the queen's comment regarding her people. She immediately tore it to shreds, letting the bits of paper fly in the breeze.

She rose, stretching, noting idly that her hair, which she had worn loose today, was now decorated by long stems of grass. It mattered little here, where no one was assessing her apparel. She was casually clad in a linen shift, a wool dress and her cloak. She couldn't help but think of being at court, where skirts lay over petticoats that lay over fine linen, where choosing which jewels to wear was a major decision every day. Mary, despite the excellence and richness of her long hair, had dozens of wigs and hairpieces, and dressing her could take far more than an hour. Mary loved clothing, jewels and pageantry, and when she was in the queen's company, Gwenyth found such display to be fun, as well. But here . . .

Here the lairds and ladies were one with their people, and life was simple.

As she stood there, waving to the shepherds who had gathered to dine on their midday meal of cheese on bread, she heard the sound of horse's hooves and spun around quickly, shielding her eyes from the sun.

She did not know the man who was riding toward her, but she didn't fear his arrival. Angus had at his service, always, twenty well-trained men-at-arms, and additionally there were the ten men, headed by Gavin, who had remained at the behest of Laird Rowan. She could roam this isle at will with no fear of any evil. And she had enjoyed exploring all the caves, beaches, nooks and crannies and tree limbs that had enchanted her as a child.

She had so dreaded coming here, but nothing had been so terrible as she had imagined. The only source of upset was the man who, against her conscious will, continually haunted her dreams.

There was a cold truth to life, though. She was of too fine a family to be considered a proper bride for a MacIvey, but Laird Rowan was of too fine a stock to consider her for marriage.

Mary herself had warned her not to fall in love with him. He was of royal blood and nothing more than a remote memory, she reminded herself as the horseman drew nearer.

"My lady!" The man spoke with a decided English accent. He seemed surprised, however, when he saw her.

She thought with amusement that he would not have expected to find the lady of the land in the grass, barefoot. "I am Lady MacLeod, aye," she said, waiting.

He wore a feathered hat, which he doffed as he dismounted from his horse and approached her. She knew that he was studying her with interest, despite the passive expression he attempted to wear. "I am Geoffrey Egan, sent by Queen Mary," he told her.

She frowned in worry. "The queen is well?" she asked anxiously.

"Indeed," he said hastily. "I am here because she has urged that you move on to England with all speed."

Gwenyth felt a slight tremor in her heart. She was to move on alone.

"I see," she murmured, though she didn't see at all.

"If I may offer my horse, we can return to the castle, my lady, and all will be explained as you make ready." He cleared his throat. "I have already spoken with your uncle, and your woman is even now seeing to your belongings."

Gwenyth smiled. "I have my own mount," she assured him.

Her long stay on the isle had made her very good friends with the wayward mare who had deposited her on the ground before the boar at Holyrood. She let out a soft whistle, no doubt shocking the messenger. But the mare, Chloe, instantly appeared from over the next hillock, obediently trotting straight to Gwenyth, who was sure that her visitor was equally shocked that the mare wore no saddle, and that Gwenyth instantly and yet modestly mounted astride.

"Are you ready, Geoffrey?" she inquired.

"Indeed, at your leisure, my lady."

She kneed the mare, delighted with the instant burst of speed, and was quick to put the no-doubt disapproving messenger far behind. She was amused as she dismounted in the courtyard, filled with chickens and other beasts, and tossed the reins to one of the stable hands with a quick smile and a thank-you.

The messenger arrived at last, huffing and puffing. "My lady —"

"Come into the hall," she told him, walking ahead.

But when she scampered up the outer stone stairs and straight into the castle's cold and barren great hall, she was quickly brought up short. Angus was there, along with Gavin, a few of the other men-at-arms, and a man she had not been expecting at all.

Rowan.

She was sure that her cheeks were instantly suffused with scarlet. She no doubt looked like a farmhand herself — or worse. She might well have given the impression of being a less than virtuous maid who had just spent a few hours tumbling in the hay with a stableboy.

She stood dead still on her bare feet — eyes far too wide, she was certain.

Rowan was anything but mussed or tumbled. Tartaned, his insignia brooch in place at his shoulder, his hat at a perfect angle atop his head, boots shined to a high gloss, face a bit leaner but still as ruggedly attractive as she remembered, he might have stepped straight from the queen's presence.

She felt the sweep of his eyes over her costume, saw the arch of his brow, the twist of wry amusement that lifted his lips.

Angus, tall, lean, grizzled and a bastion of dignity, stood by his side.

"My lady." Rowan swept his hat from his head, offering a deep and courtly bow. Such a display was certainly a mockery at this moment.

"My Laird Rowan," she murmured, her eyes moving quickly to her uncle's. "I was not aware of the impending honor of your arrival at our poor isle," she murmured.

"Oh, I'm sorry. Geoffrey was to have informed you."

Geoffrey chose that moment to come panting into the hall. "I'm so sorry. She . . .

the Lady Gwenyth got . . . quite ahead of me."

"Ever forward into the fray?" Rowan said.

Was there a rebuke in his words?

She forced a smile, wishing that she couldn't feel one particularly large piece of grass tickling just above her brow. "On this isle, there is never a fray. In fact, with my uncle's good men and those you placed at our disposal, I dare say heaven itself could be no safer a place."

Perhaps she shouldn't have mentioned heaven. Something in his eyes hardened.

To her surprise, Angus instantly rose to her defense. "Lady Gwenyth is aware that men and women serve their laird with far greater fervor when those who govern it know it as they do," he said. "I had asked her to accompany our shepherds into the fields today."

She flashed him a grateful smile, and he smiled in return. It was a shock, but a pleasant one.

Whatever other errors she might have made, she had definitely earned her uncle's approval during her time here.

"Perhaps," Rowan said, "but I believe that the lady will need a bit of time to prepare to travel in appropriate style."

"Really?" She could not stop herself from

arching a brow in response. "This is a wild country, as well you know, Laird Rowan. I am quite capable of riding it in any style."

"You may, of course, suit yourself," he told her. "But then the queen, I am afraid, who is so fond of dress and pageantry, may well be disappointed."

"The queen?" she murmured.

"Aye."

She frowned, studying him. "Are we on our way to England?"

"In a roundabout manner. Mary has determined that the time is right to visit her Highlands so . . ."

Gwenyth turned to Angus. "Uncle, perhaps you would be so good as to see to a meal for our guests. I will be ready shortly to ride."

So saying, she hurried up the stairs to the rooms. She intended to get ready quickly; she did not want Rowan here long, did not want him judging her home.

Not when she had come to love it here so much herself.

Angus frowned, staring at Rowan over a tankard of ale. "The queen has a dispute with Lord Huntly?" He shook his head. "The man is a Catholic now, is he? He has ever changed with the wind, whatever is necessary to improve his estates. He is all but king himself, nearly as strong a power on the mainland as the queen herself. But what is the argument? One would have thought he would have ingratiated himself with her — a Catholic monarch."

Rowan took a deep breath, trying to think how best to explain the situation quickly. "The queen has made it clear that she does not wish to impose her religion upon her people, only practice it herself in peace, as she would have others do. She does not take sides. John Gordon, the son of George Gordon, fourth earl of Huntly, seriously wounded Lord Ogilvie in a duel, and now Lord Huntly has refused to turn over his son for justice, acting as if his Catholicism somehow exempts him from justice. In addition, it's being said that he considers his son to be the proper bridegroom for the queen, and that, too, displeases Her Majesty. The queen had originally intended a journey north to enjoy the country and to hunt, but now her intent has taken a new direction."

Angus MacLeod shook his head. " 'Tis a dangerous journey. Lord Huntly can call forth thousands of men."

Rowan looked up at the sound of footsteps and stood, politics no longer of interest in this moment, because Gwenyth had reappeared.

She was now properly attired for a journey, her bodice fitted, her hat jaunty and her skirt a rich green velvet drapery. Her hair was contained in a neat coil beneath the hat, and she was the picture of propriety. In fact, she was . . .

Stunning. A feast for the eyes and the senses.

But no more so than when she had first entered only a few minutes ago, cheeks flushed, feet bare, sweeping smoothly into the room, as if borne on air.

He found himself thinking that she was a witch. She walked into a room and heads turned. She looked at a man, and something in his muscles tightened. She . . .

She was so like Catherine in so many ways, so not like Catherine in others. She was swift to argue, so passionate for whatever cause she chose. She had a streak of stubbornness as wide as the country, and a quick wit that she didn't mind using against the slightest hint of criticism.

No, not a witch; he did not believe in the foolishness that so many learned men of his day saw as God's truth. She was simply young, beautiful, and possessed of a charm that lured and seduced. And she had somehow, from the moment they had met, decided to be his enemy.

While he. . . .

And yet there was still something he could not bear. Something that had to do with the agony in his heart when Catherine had turned from him.

Rowan stood and straightened, looking at her, though he directed his words to Angus. "The queen intends to bestow the title of Earl of Moray on her brother, Laird James. Laird Huntly has been behaving as if the lands and revenues of Moray are his own, and now the queen means to wrest them from him."

Angus, noting Gwenyth's entrance, rose as well, but as he did, he groaned, lowering his head. "More war," he whispered.

"Let us pray not. Perhaps she and Huntly will come to an understanding."

Angus arched a skeptical brow. Then he frowned. "I cannot allow my niece to accompany you on this journey. It is not safe."

Gwenyth rushed forward. "Uncle Angus, please. The queen has asked for my presence. And were it not safe, do you think the queen herself would be traveling? If there is any threat, she can summon thousands of archers and men-at-arms. She is," Gwenyth reminded Angus, "the queen."

Angus sighed.

"I am commended with your niece's safety, Angus," Rowan said. "You must know, sir, that my men and I would lie down and die before allowing any harm to befall her."

Angus was still frowning as he turned to Gwenyth. "You will heed every word spoken by Laird Rowan?"

She hesitated noticeably.

"Gwenyth?" Angus persisted.

"Until the queen commands otherwise," she said.

Rowan lowered his head, smiling. She might be the lady here, but Angus had long ruled the land, and she knew she needed his support in any matter relating to her future when she was within his sphere of influence.

"Indeed, Gwenyth?" Rowan queried politely.

She stared at him with tremendous dignity and very cold eyes. "I would never seek to be any burden upon you, my Laird of Lochraven."

"What is your interest in this?" Angus asked him sharply.

"To serve the Crown," Rowan said wearily. "I do not fear the earl of Huntly. My holdings are far too strong for him to attempt to extend his feud to me. I have admired the queen's determination not to fall to his wild suggestion that she create territories where the Catholics might hold sway. She has honored her country's decisions. I can find no fault with her. She is intelligent, witty and ready to take the advice of learned and able men, such as her brother."

"Then," said Angus, "there is nothing left but that you take your leave."

Gwenyth lowered her head. Rowan knew it was lest her uncle should see the excitement in her eyes.

"I took the liberty of sending Geoffrey to see that the stableboys outfit your mare with a proper saddle, my lady," Rowan informed her.

"How very kind of you," she murmured. "That will indeed save us time, and I know that you would reach the mainland while there's still light."

When they stepped outside, he saw her smile as she bade her uncle a tender goodbye. And then they were on horseback, riding swiftly for the ferry.

The seas were rough, as they so frequently were. She did not seem to notice. She stood at the wooden rail, her expression thoughtful as she looked back at her home.

"You're sorry to leave?" he inquired, having thought it best to keep his distance, yet finding himself unable to do so.

"Naturally."

"Perhaps I could explain to the queen —"

"I'm more anxious to see the queen," she quickly interrupted.

"Ah."

"You have seen her . . . since I have seen you," she remarked.

"At her bidding," he said.

She turned away from him, studying the sea again. He realized that she was disturbed that the queen had not sent for her before this.

"I'm sure Mary wanted you to enjoy time and peace at home," he offered sympathetically, then decided that sympathy — which might seem like pity — was not something anyone should offer the Lady of Islington.

"Indeed, some of us *can* find peace," she told him.

He straightened and walked away, then was startled when she ran after him, setting a hand upon his arm. When he looked down at her, he felt a tremor shake him. Her eyes were so wide, liquid.

"I am so sorry."

He nodded and moved away, but as he did, he found himself worrying anew. He loved his country dearly, but it seemed destined for bloodshed. And he did not

231

want Gwenyth to be a part of it, because he feared that even if he were to lie down and die for her, it might not be enough to keep her safe.

They rode hard, and there was little chance for conversation as they hastened to cover ground during the daylight hours and were exhausted by nightfall.

It was best that way, Gwenyth decided. She shared a few words with Annie when they rested, and he spent his time with his men. She could often hear them speaking, sometimes tensely and sometimes with laughter.

They caught up with Queen Mary and her party at Aberdeen, a town in the sway of Lord Huntly. The queen was lodged in one of the manses of Sir Victor D'Eau, a man of mixed Scottish and French descent. They arrived while she was meeting with Lady Gordon, Countess of Huntly, in a parlor just beyond the great hall.

The doors had not been closed. Perhaps neither woman cared whether they were overheard, or perhaps it had been purposely arranged so, with both women seeing an audience as beneficial, whatever transpired.

The countess was a woman of great vigor and had aged far better than her lord, who had gown quite corpulent with age. She was attractive and well-dressed, and a multitude of her attendants were waiting in the hall as she could be heard pleading with the queen.

Mary, it seemed, was adamant. She was appalled by the scandal attending the duel, and deeply upset because she cared about Ogilvie, as well.

"Your son, dear countess, must turn himself in," Mary said gravely.

"I beg you, do not judge him too harshly," the countess urged.

Mary's tone softened. "He must turn himself in," she repeated. "I promise you, he will not come to harm. But the law must be obeyed."

There was silence. Then the countess agreed with a soft sigh. "I will see to it," she promised.

Words of farewell were exchanged, and then the countess swept into the crowded hallway, lifting a hand for her women.

She was quickly followed out by the queen, causing everyone to dip low in a curtsy. Mary didn't seem to notice. Her eyes came alight with pleasure at the sight of Gwenyth.

"My little Highlander!" she cried. "Oh, Gwenyth, you have reached me so quickly." She gave Gwenyth a fierce hug, then looked beyond her. "Laird Rowan, with what speed you have achieved your goal. I am ever so pleased."

Despite the queen's words and his pretense of pleasure at her greeting, Gwenyth thought Rowan appeared disturbed. Then she realized why. Everyone in the room was watching them.

"Little Highlander . . ." Lady Gordon, Countess of Huntly, repeated, then turned back to the queen, leaving her ladies to stand silently behind her. "Why, it's Lady MacLeod of Islington, is it not?"

"Indeed. Lady Gwenyth, I present Lady Gordon, Countess of Huntly. Countess, Lady MacLeod," the queen said.

Lady Gordon took a very long look at Gwenyth while murmuring some pleasantry. Then she noted Rowan's presence. "Ah, the Laird of the Far Isles," she said.

"Countess," he replied, bowing his head in acknowledgment.

"I can only imagine that you've traveled with a host of Highland devils," she said teasingly, but Gwenyth knew the words were seriously meant as the countess attempted to gauge the manpower Rowan had brought with him.

"That, my dear lady, from the princess of the Highlands herself," he replied politely and in kind.

Lady Gordon laughed uneasily, and Gwenyth saw that Mary was watching the exchange carefully.

"Well, we are indeed a breed apart from the Lowlanders," the countess agreed.

A law apart, Gwenyth thought.

"But the hour grows late," the countess went on, "And our good Queen Mary has had a long day. I will take my ladies and depart. No doubt we will meet again very soon. My queen . . ." She offered another curtsy, then took Mary's hand and kissed it. "Thank you," she said sincerely.

"Your Grace," Rowan murmured quickly, "surely you've men at your command, quite close. Pray tell me so."

Mary laughed, but the sound was weary. "Oh, aye, my fine Laird Rowan. I'd not trust the lady — nor her husband — without a strong body of armed men at my back. Now tell me, how many are in your company?"

He shook his head. "Thirty. Thirty fine men, adept with swords and arrows, knowledgeable about cannon and firepower . . . but beware, for this is Gordon territory."

"Your men are a welcome addition, though I do not travel lightly." She smiled then. "Oh, it is so good to see you both."

As she spoke, James Stewart entered, looking anxiously at the queen.

"She has agreed that her son must turn himself in," Mary said.

James nodded grimly.

"James is recently married, you know," Mary informed Gwenyth.

"My deepest congratulations, my Lord James," Gwenyth said.

He nodded. "Thank you, my lady." He turned his attention to Rowan. "Well? What did you see along the way?"

"I wish I could assure you that there no forces would rise against the queen, but I cannot," he said bluntly. "I saw no sign of a large army massing, but that does not mean that the Gordons and their kin cannot raise one quickly."

"I don't know yet if we can control the Gordons as allies, or if their power must be crushed," Mary said.

James lifted his hands, shaking his head. "The countess relies on witches and familiars to advise her."

"Witches?" Gwenyth laughed aloud. "Oh, dear. I can't —"

She broke off, realizing that both Mary and James were staring at her.

"You mustn't underestimate the powers of such harridans," he told her.

She looked at Mary, who nodded sadly in

agreement.

"But . . . you can't believe that . . . that . . ."

"I think that the countess would gladly call up the aid of demons," James said, and he meant it.

"Brother, I've a greater fear at the moment," Mary said.

"What is that?" James asked.

Rowan shrugged, then looked at Mary and answered for her. "I fear the power of the Gordon clan. There has been talk of abducting the queen. Remember, John Gordon is a handsome young fellow. I believe he may well feel he has quite enough charm to . . . woo the queen, even if he has to force her hand first. You are in grave danger here, Mary."

She smiled, nodding. "I know. I will not fall into any traps, I promise. And John Gordon will soon be in prison in Edinburgh."

"Aye," Rowan said, but he sounded doubtful.

"You are still disturbed?" Mary asked.

"It seemed to me that despite her pretense of amicability, Lady Gordon was laying plots even as she spoke. I do not think she would be averse to kidnapping Your Grace, or the Lady Gwenyth."

"Me?" Gwenyth said in astonishment.

"If one cannot have gold, one is often

happy with silver," the queen murmured.

"And there is something else you must keep in mind," Rowan reminded her.

"And that is?" Mary inquired.

"I know that you don't intend to send John Gordon to trial immediately, nor was his offense such that he would lose his head or face the hangman's noose," Rowan said.

"Go on," Mary urged.

"If he escapes, he'll be dangerous indeed," Rowan said.

CHAPTER NINE

The days that followed were a strange combination of celebration and danger.

They moved warily through the Highlands, though in Rowan's assessment, there were enough men in the queen's service to protect her against anything other than an all-out assault, and as it seemed she was welcomed by most, he didn't see an imminent danger to her person.

When they neared Strathbogie, Mary conferred long with her brother, Ambassador Maitland and Rowan himself. He was glad when she decided to bypass the Gordon stronghold there and continue on to Darnaway Castle. It was not Holyrood, but it had a large hall, and it was there that Mary made the public announcement that her brother had been named the Earl of Moray.

From there they traveled on to Inverness, and it was there that trouble erupted.

News came that, just as Rowan had feared, John Gordon had escaped his imprisonment in Edinburgh. He had gathered a troop of a thousand men and was now hurrying after their party. Another Gordon, Alexander, refused them entrance to Inverness Castle, though it was a royal holding and in Gordon hands only because Lord Huntly was sheriff of Inverness.

Such a refusal was simple treason. It could not be excused under any circumstance.

As they camped on the land before the castle and the queen weighed her options, word came from Lord Huntly that the gates were to be opened to allow the queen entrance.

"The wily old goat has heard that the Highlanders are ready to rise for their queen in the face of such an insult," James said.

Rowan couldn't argue that. He had seen the people cheer Mary in the streets. Even so . . . "Armed men enter first," he warned.

Mary despised violence, but when James informed her that the captain of the castle must be hanged, the queen paled but could not disagree, and the man was hanged over the battlements without delay.

At their first meal in the great hall, Mary rose, lifting her glass to her supporters at the long table. "To the Highlands. We must dress as these valiant folk. Laird Rowan, you're close enough in appearance. The rest of us must take to our clan tartans."

Rowan looked around the table at the queen's ladies, at her close advisors, at the men-at-arms invited to the great table, and wondered what was to become of them all.

The queen had made no final decision as to what was to become of Lord Huntly. The man was not a fool. He moved constantly from one of his holdings to the next, always ahead of the queen, while his son and his men harried the queen's party. Rowan had been wary and on alert for so long that he was exhausted and feared whatever time the queen might spend beyond the fortifications of the castle.

Gwenyth, surrounded by the queen's Marys, seemed light and happy. She lowered her head to listen to words spoken by Mary Fleming, and her smile was radiant. The queen's ladies were all pleasingly attractive, but none shone like the Lady Gwenyth. He forced his attention to James Stewart, who was drawing invisible maps of the country-side with his finger upon the table.

"All Huntly land," James said, his expression serious as he shook his head. "Although I have seldom seen the queen merrier. She seems to love the Highlands and is calm in the face of the ever-present danger offered by Huntly." He set his tankard down hard. "She has never fallen to his coy suggestions that she have a Catholic stronghold here in the north, but neither does she relish her duty of seeing that he is ousted from his position."

Rowan held silent. James Stewart was an ambitious man himself, and Rowan wondered if Mary truly understood people, even now. She had to move against Huntly, and she knew it. But he wondered if she was aware what a serious mistake it would be to cast all the power with the Protestant lords, her brother at the head of them.

"Rowan?" James said, and pointed at the invisible map. "What do you think?"

"If I were Huntly . . . here, when we leave to cross the Spey . . . therein lies the danger, and we know that John Gordon is following us with a thousand men, at least."

"We will be fiercely on guard," James said.

"What, not a singer among you?" the queen demanded, drawing their attention as she laughed with the musicians who had just entered, bearing their various instruments. "We all love to sing, but Gwenyth is our star. Come, my dear. These men know all the lovely Highland ballads, and you, dear friend, know them all, as well."

The queen dragged Gwenyth forward as the musicians began to play.

She had a beautiful voice, Rowan thought, and rose, just as the others at the table began to do so, ready to dance at the queen's behest.

He had to leave, he thought, as she sang just as she had sung to Catherine, night after night, before his wife had died.

He caught her eyes across the crowded hall, and when she looked back, he knew it was in apology. She had but obeyed the queen's command, he knew, but still, he could not stay and quickly exited the great hall.

They crossed the Spey without incident, though they knew John Gordon and his troops were watching from the woods.

Perhaps they made no move, though they saw the vulnerability of the party as it crossed the river, because they were aware they were being watched in return. Perhaps John Gordon knew that despite the army he had acquired, he didn't yet have enough strength to attack the queen.

When they reached the castle at Find, the queen ordered that it be surrendered, but she was not obeyed, and the men advised her that it could not be taken without cannon. And so they passed by.

On the return to Aberdeen, she was joyously greeted. And it was there that she sighed and gave in to James, allowing him to send for weapons, cannon and men. In the days that followed, emissaries carried messages between Huntly and the queen, she making demands, he countering them.

As Rowan sat to breakfast with James and Mary one morning, one of the queen's spies arrived. The man was exhausted, and when the queen stood to greet him, Rowan and James followed suit.

"The countess was angry when you denied her a meeting here, Your Grace. She rode out to meet her husband. I heard her crying in despair. She said her witches assured her that he would lie dead by the tollbooth by nightfall, not a mark on his body. They plan to attack, and she is convinced he will die."

"Where and when will the attack come?" Mary demanded.

The spy hung his head. "I don't know. I had to run away with what I had. My presence was noted, and I feared I would not be able to get back with what little I knew if I did not quickly slip away."

"You did right, and I thank you for your service. You will be rewarded."

Rowan turned to James. "He will take up

a position on the Hill of Fare, right above the field of Corrichie."

"What makes you so certain?" James asked.

"He has it in his mind that any of the Highlanders fighting for the queen will desert, that he will take the day."

"And *will* they desert?" the queen asked softly.

Rowan turned to her. "I don't believe so. You have given them no cause. And you . . ." He hesitated, afraid to create a bloodbath, then told himself that the battle would be fought, so better a bloodbath for the enemy than for the queen and their party. "Strike him here. He will be trapped, and I'm quite certain he will not see it," Rowan said, explaining with lines on the floor as he spoke. "If he's forced down the hill, he will be caught in a swamp. There will be no escape."

"You are certain that the landscape sits so?" James said.

"I know the Highlands like the back of my hand, Lord James."

"But you can't be certain he will choose the position you have indicated."

"It is the only one he *can* take. He will believe he has the high ground, and that he will hold it."

The queen looked saddened as she looked at the two of them. "Then so be it. We will be ready," she said, and looked intently at Rowan. "I pray you are correct in your prediction of his position."

The queen had taken to spending the mornings in council with her brother, and sometimes with Rowan and Maitland, as well, so Gwenyth was startled when Mary burst into her room, where she had been reading to pass the time.

"The insolence . . . the treason!" the queen cried.

Gwenyth struggled quickly to her feet, staring at her monarch.

"The word has come. Huntly indeed intends to attack. His wife's witches have said he will be triumphant, so says our spy. Witches! A pox on them all. They practice their evil craft illegally, and it is almost impossible to bring them to justice."

Gwenyth was silent; she still found it difficult to believe that someone as well-educated as the queen could believe in the power of witchcraft.

The queen continued. "Thank God we avoided some of Huntly's holdings. It is almost unbelievable, but the man actually intends to abduct me, to force me into marriage with his son. It's . . . despicable." She shook her head. "It's treason."

"He will not succeed," Gwenyth said, trying to calm Mary before she became so upset that she made herself ill.

"This would not have happened in France," Mary said.

"I fear that men are avaricious everywhere," Gwenyth said. "They always want more than what they have."

The queen sank down on Gwenyth's bed. "I will have to do battle against one of the few Catholic lords in this country. May God forgive me."

Gwenyth weighed her words carefully. "You are the queen. You must rule your country. You must preserve Scotland, no matter what it takes."

"I must," Mary agreed, distraught. She gripped Gwenyth's hand suddenly. "Laird Rowan is confident he knows Huntly's plan of battle, but what if he is wrong? What if we fall?"

"We will not."

Mary stood and began pacing again. "If only I knew for certain . . ."

Gwenyth watched her tortured pacing. "What of your spy?"

"He can get no closer. I have other men out there, but . . ."

"Someone will find the truth. Huntly has held power here these many years," Gwenyth told her, "and yet so many of your good Highlanders are in awe of their beautiful young queen — they will honor and support you."

The queen stopped. "The townspeople will know something. Servants know everything, and they tend to whisper," she said.

"That's true," Gwenyth agreed. Then she frowned, afraid that an idea had been born in the queen's head.

"We must go out among them," Mary announced.

Gwenyth's heart sank. She had been right. "Mary, they will recognize you. They'll bow down, but they won't talk."

The queen shook her head, growing excited. "We will go in disguise. Like washerwomen, like fishwives . . . servants, seeking the markets."

Gwenyth bit her lip, surveying her monarch. "Your Grace, you cannot hide in a crowd."

"Why not?"

"You're far too tall."

Mary hesitated. "I will go out as a man."

"It's still too dangerous."

Mary began to pace again. "We must win. The gall of Huntly — and his wretched son!

John Gordon is of the opinion he is so powerful and fetching a young man that I will be delighted to make him king and obey in his shadow. They think that I am so fickle a queen that I will forget the will of my people, that because of my religious beliefs I will turn on those who do not believe as I do. They will attack *me*."

"Mary, you have the finest men at your service."

"And I would not lose them, Gwenyth. But what if things do not go as Laird Rowan expects? We will go out in the streets, as servants, and we will hear what gossip circulates there."

Gwenyth shook her head. "No. You cannot, Mary. Not as a man or a woman." She took a deep breath. "I'll go. I'll take some of your hairpieces and have Annie dress me in the proper garb. She and I will walk the shops and the green, and find out what is being said among the people. Besides, my lady, I need not feign the accent that will let me blend with the people here."

Mary frowned, watching her. "I would not put you in danger."

"Yet you would put yourself in danger!" Gwenyth laughed softly. "You are gold, Your Grace. I am but silver."

Mary smiled at that. "You will stay near

the manor. And you will return the minute you have heard anything about the battle."

"Aye, Your Grace."

"This mission must be completely secret. You must take care. What if you are recognized as one of my ladies?"

"I will not be recognized," Gwenyth assured her.

Gwenyth was able to prove her point an hour later when she entered the hall in Annie's clothing, cotton stuffing filling out her blouse and skirt beneath her jacket. She wore poor, oversized work boots, a dark hairpiece, and a woolen shawl over everything. She had used charcoal on her cheeks and around her eyes to give herself the look of someone who had been working over a fire all day.

When she and Annie entered the queen's chambers, the queen did not recognize her. "Annie, where is your lady?" Mary demanded. "And who is this you have brought before me? Does she work here in the manor?"

Gwenyth burst out laughing, and Mary gasped, then laughed, as well. "Indeed, you've proven your point."

"I will take no chances, Your Grace," Gwenyth assured her. "We will shop the stalls and hear what we may."

Mary hesitated, then nodded. "We have to be certain," she said. "But if you're not back before nightfall, I'll have the guard out after you."

"We will be back," Gwenyth assured her.

As they left the queen's chamber, Gwenyth nearly froze when James, Maitland and Rowan walked by. But none of them noticed her. James and Maitland didn't pay them any heed; Rowan merely offered a nod and a slight smile to Annie.

As soon as the men had passed by, Gwenyth grabbed Annie's hand and went running down the hall, trying not to laugh. Annie freed herself from Gwenyth's hold, turning to berate her. " 'Tis a fool's errand we're upon, I tell ye, a fool's errand."

"Oh, hush, Annie. Please. I'm but playacting for a matter of a few hours."

They strode past the queen's guard, who had been stationed around the manor when she had bowed to her brother's decision that they must be on high alert at all times.

"The city is filled with the queen's forces," Annie noted.

"Aye, she has her best archers, her finest military minds . . ."

Annie let out a breath. "Then 'tis good enough, I suppose, to protect fools against fools' errands."

"The fish market," Gwenyth said.

Annie eyed her warily, and they walked on. "At least ye've the right accent for it."

They walked the streets, huddled together like a pair of servants who had long attended to the same master. Gwenyth knew that Aberdeen was small enough that many people would know one another, and yet it was large enough that visitors might roam the markets unremarked.

As they perused the stalls, they were greeted by the squawking of chickens, the aroma of fish and the cries of the hawkers peddling everything from woolens and needles to cooking utensils. A toy maker dangled a puppet before them, and they thanked him for the entertainment but moved on. At each stall, they pretended to be weighing the merchandise against the coins in their purses. At length they paused before a vendor selling cups of ale cheap.

Annie lifted her nose at the place and gave the vendor a long speech on the amount of dirt he was allowing into his ale, complaining that she didn't like imbibing Aberdeen dust. And as she argued her point, Gwenyth at last heard two maids nearby whispering about Huntly and his planned attack.

"It may well be now that he sets himself up as king here," one girl, a tiny but work-worn redhead, whispered, giggling.

"Aye, an' that will make the countess a happy woman — and a queen," the second maid, a pretty young lass with brown hair, agreed.

" 'Tis also said they mean to take the queen an' marry her off to their son. Then the whole of the country will be under Huntly rule," the redhead whispered, looking nervously around.

"All the better for us," Gwenyth chimed in beneath her breath, yet loud enough for the two women to hear.

Annie, bless her, kept up her chastisement of the vendor, giving Gwenyth ample opportunity to join in with the maids.

The redhead giggled again. "What do I care, who is king, who is queen? I work the whole day long, no matter who rules."

The dark-haired girl was more serious. She sniffed. "Ach, we may find our lot far worse if the laird fails and the queen takes revenge."

"And would Laird Huntly fail?" Gwenyth asked as if such a thing were impossible.

"Never," the redhead agreed.

"We'd best be going," the brunette urged her companion. "So many to feed, with the men climbing to the heights."

"Camping upon the Hill o' Fare soon

enough," the redhead said.

The brunette elbowed her. "Come, it's time to go."

"Or the countess will be showin' her wrath," the redhead agreed.

They hurried on, nodding farewell to Gwenyth, who grabbed Annie by the arm, almost causing her to spill the cup of ale she had finally agreed to purchase.

"We can go back."

"Back?" Annie said.

"Aye, now!"

They started back to the manor, no longer strolling the aisles and pretending to judge the merchandise for cost and quality. In her haste, Gwenyth began to stride quickly, deep in thought.

Annie pulled her back. "Ye can't go racin' through the place," she warned.

Gwenyth turned back to Annie, who had been huffing and puffing behind her, and started walking again. With her eyes still on the older woman, she plowed into the muscular body of a man. Startled, she looked up and was instantly filled with unease.

She had walked straight into Bryce Mac-Ivey.

She held her breath, wondering what he was doing there in Aberdeen, since she knew he was one of the Protestant lairds. Perhaps that didn't matter. Perhaps he and his men had chosen to fight for Laird Huntly against the queen.

To her great relief, he looked down with disdain, clearly not recognizing her. "Stupid woman, get out of the way," he commanded.

She readily complied.

Apparently her face betrayed her rush of fear, because Annie demanded, "What? Who was that?"

"Bryce MacIvey," Gwenyth said, shuddering.

Annie gasped. "The clan that borders Laird Rowan's lands?"

"Aye."

"He might have known ye."

Gwenyth looked at her, shaking her head. "Didn't you see how he pushed me aside? He has no interest in servant girls."

"Let's hurry on," Annie urged.

But Gwenyth paused then, thoughtfully watching the man as he strode away, into the crowd. Then he stopped, as if in confusion, and looked back.

She stared into his eyes, and he frowned before hurrying away again.

"He's come to fight against the queen," Gwenyth said.

"Perhaps he's come to fight *for* her," Annie suggested.

Gwenyth shook her head. "He's dangerous, and he hates Laird Rowan. He desperately wants to increase his holdings, and he cannot not do so while Rowan supports the queen and the queen bows to his judgment."

"Then we must return to the manor and tell all we know," Annie said.

"We don't know enough," Gwenyth protested. "Laird Bryce's presence changes everything."

"We know enough," Annie insisted.

"All right," Gwenyth agreed softly.

They were on a quiet street nearing the manor when Gwenyth heard hoofbeats behind her. She started to turn, only to find herself swept up by the rider. Bryce MacIvey. A scream tore from her throat, which gave no pause to the horseman. Despite the thunder of the horse's hooves and her own state of danger, she was aware that Annie had also been snatched. She continued to scream loudly, praying that they could attract attention before being carried too far away.

Her heart thundered as she tried to think. Had he taken her because he knew who she was? Or only because she had aroused his suspicion, watching him as she had done?

The horse was moving with such speed that she knew she would be badly injured, perhaps die, if she fought so hard that she fell to the roadside.

And so, with a man she despised holding her tightly upon his mount, she had no choice but to cling to the horse and wait to see what fate would bring.

It had been easy, with the buildup of arms on both sides, for Rowan to keep himself busy and not spend time dwelling on the woman who had come to haunt his every moment, waking or sleeping. But today, knowing that an attack was imminent, Rowan found himself disturbed when he didn't see Gwenyth among the queen's women.

When he asked Mary about her favorite's absence, she was vague. "She went to the market, I believe."

He remained worried. Aberdeen had seemed to welcome the queen — despite Huntly. Still, that any of the queen's ladies might be blithely walking about was a concern. Rowan knew too well how fickle the minds of the Highlanders could be, especially as now, when caught between loyalty to a new young queen, and the laird they had known and honored for years.

When he also couldn't find Annie busy at any task within the manor, he found himself growing more concerned. At last, he made up his mind that he was going to take a walk to the market and find her. He was irritated as he stepped out; there were now more than a thousand of the queen's men finding shelter in the fields, forests, halls and houses in the area. There were drills to be carried out and formations to be determined. His own cavalry awaited his command, and yet here he was, on a fool's errand.

Outside the manor, he found Gavin speaking with one of the queen's guard, awaiting his orders. But when Gavin lifted his brows, awaiting a military summons, Rowan shook his head and said only, "Join me. I need to find the Lady of Islington."

"I saw her maid, not an hour ago," Gavin told him.

Rowan frowned. "Where?"

"Heading with another servant toward the market."

"Did this servant dwarf Annie?" Rowan inquired.

"Aye, indeed."

"It was Gwenyth," Rowan said with annoyance. "What in God's name is she about?"

Gavin laughed. "It was not the Lady

Gwenyth. She had to be a kitchen maid. She was all sooty, dark haired — and quite corpulent."

Rowan shook his head. "Trust me, my friend. It was Gwenyth. And I want to find her before she gets herself into some new trouble."

Even as he spoke, he heard screams coming from the direction of the market. He looked at Gavin. "Get the horses," he told him brusquely.

He was amazed when the troop of horsemen — six of them, two bearing screaming women — passed by the very manor itself, with all the queen's guard in attendance. When the guards would have sprung to life, Rowan stopped them. "It may well be a trap, intended to mow down many of the queen's finest before the battle. Inform Laird James that I am following the mob into the forest beyond. Tell him to take care, to avoid the obvious route, but to come after us."

Gavin arrived with the horses and looked questioningly at Rowan. "So we will ride into this trap?"

"Nay, Gavin. We will take the old Roman road through the trees, while these fellows will be tempting the queen's men upon the established trail."

Gavin nodded gravely. "Those were Mac-Ivey colors, worn by the horsemen."

"Bryce MacIvey in the lead," Rowan said in agreement.

"They will know the old roads, as well."

The jolting, brutal ride lasted a good thirty minutes, carrying them far from the queen's manor — and the great host of men arriving to fight on her behalf.

When they came to a halt at last, in a small clearing deep in the forest, Gwenyth was dismayed to realize that there had been no pursuit, though they had been taken from beneath the very nose of the manor and its guards

Of course, who among the queen's guards would desert his post to ride to the rescue of two servants, servants no one would even have realized were in the queen's employ?

She found herself crudely dropped to the ground and let out no sound, but she heard Annie's bellow of protest at her rough fall. Gwenyth sprang to her feet, quickly adjusting her mantle and the woolen scarf atop her head, knowing full well it was more important than ever to maintain her disguise.

As Bryce MacIvey stared at her then, she realized that he did not in fact know who she was — only that he felt he *should* know.

"What manner of idiocy is this?" Annie railed from behind her. "What fool laird has decided that servants of the Highlands are to be abducted and abused?"

Bryce spun on Annie, approaching her with menace. "Ye are no Highlander, woman. I can hear it in y'er voice."

"She's me dear auntie!" Gwenyth cried out in old Gaelic. That drew Bryce's attention back to her, and she thought quickly before speaking again. First she spat on the ground, as if in disdain of him, even if he was a landed laird. "Me auntie is in the queen's service. I live in the woods outside Aberdeen, with me mum. But the queen does not allow for her servants to be ill treated. They'll be comin' fer ye, that they'll be!"

"Let them," he said.

Then she knew. The woods were surely crawling with his men. He had expected, even intended, to be followed. He must have had it in his head he would gain favor with Laird Huntly if he winnowed down the queen's troops.

Perhaps it was not so strange that no one had followed. The queen's guard must have seen through his ruse.

She pointed a finger at him and spoke

sternly. "When the queen wins this battle, m'laird, ye'll hang. Mark me words, ye'll hang."

He scowled fiercely. "What? Do ye be some witch, casting out predictions?"

"No witch, m'laird," she said. "No witch, be I — just none other than a loyal Scot."

Bryce let out a sound of disgust and thrust her toward his men. "Keep a careful watch," he ordered them. "As for this one . . . she's young enough. Do with her what ye will. Then . . . well, we'll see. Like as not Laird Huntly will see that she hangs."

As she was thrown forward, the woolen scarf around her head was loosened. She had lost too many of her hair pins during the reckless ride, and now the hairpieces she had borrowed from the queen began to fall away.

"She sheds!" cried a man.

"She's filthy," added another.

"What whore is not?" Bryce MacIvey demanded. "Clean her up, if ye choose. There's a brook through yonder trees."

Fergus MacIvey came riding through the group of men. "What foolishness is this, Bryce? We mustn't play with the queen's refuse. We must stay on guard."

He dismounted and, coming through the crowd, grabbed hold of Gwenyth. She lowered her head, knowing it was best not to fight him. She was desperate to maintain her disguise. But he lifted her chin, despite her pretended subjugation.

He stared at her in stunned silence, searching her eyes, and then he started to laugh. "Bryce, y'haven't the eyes of a blind mole," he announced.

Bryce MacIvey didn't appreciate the laughter, even from a kinsman. "Fergus, guard y'er tongue!" he roared.

"Take a look at y'er *servant* girl, me lad," Fergus said.

Bryce MacIvey strode over, wrenching her from Fergus's grasp. He slipped his hand into her hair, jerking away the last of the hairpieces, bringing tears to her eyes and an involuntary cry from her lips as he did so.

Then he, too, started to laugh.

"Already," he said to his men, "we have bested the queen." His eyes narrowed, and he pulled Gwenyth closer. "And you, little witch, have lost indeed. There is no great Highland laird with his men to stop me now."

CHAPTER TEN

Gavin crawled back down the tree.

"There's a goodly number of men. It appears that Laird MacIvey has brought the whole body of his kin. Say . . . fifty-odd fellows, hiding in the woods."

Rowan considered the odds. They weren't good. But even as Gavin had taken to the height of an old oak to survey their options, he had watched as Bryce MacIvey had discovered the treasure he held.

Now he saw Annie step forward indignantly. "Touch her and the queen will see that y'er disburdened of all that ye hold. How dare ye put your faith in a man such as Laird Huntly, one who has wavered time and again in his own beliefs? Supporting the Covenant of the Protestants one minute, proclaiming Catholicism his true religion the next. Agreeing to his son's arrest one minute, joining him at arms the next?"

"Shut up, old woman," Bryce commanded, his eyes still on Gwenyth.

"She's not an old woman," Gwenyth protested. Rowan had to admit, she was not easily cowed. "I swear, Laird Bryce, if you touch me, you will die. That is both a promise and a prophecy."

"A self-proclaimed witch, are you?" Bryce taunted.

"You will die," she repeated.

"I think we'll consummate the union afore the ceremony," Bryce informed her.

"You are seeking death!" she seethed.

"Oh? I am surrounded by my men. What oracle has assured ye that I'll die?" he taunted.

"A firm belief in God," she informed him.

He moved to touch her face, and she reacted with a blow across his cheek that resounded throughout the forest.

Rowan winced, then felt a hand upon his shoulder. Gavin.

"You'll do her no good dead," Gavin informed him wisely.

And he would not. What they needed was time. A troop of the queen's guard would soon join them.

"Time . . . we need to play for time," Rowan said.

"They don't know me," Gavin reminded

him. He looked at Rowan, a question in his eyes.

"All right," Rowan said at last.

Gavin grinned. "I've no costume, no disguise . . . but I will prove myself a fine enough actor. Just you wait and see."

It had been a mistake, striking the man. Even if she were the most able swordsman in the country, she could not best the number of men at Bryce's disposal. Nor did she have a sword.

Gwenyth saw that Annie was ready to jump to her defense again, and she was afraid that she was asking only for torture and punishment for them both. And so, as Bryce started to respond and all his men seemed to take a step closer, she spoke quickly. "Stop!"

To her amazement, they all paused.

"Laird Bryce, what you desire is my estate, and that is something you'll acquire only through marriage. You're under the belief that you can perpetrate a rape, and then I'll be forced to marry you. You are mistaken. If you wish to have my lands, then you must make me believe that you are desirable enough to marry."

A slow smile curved his lips. "You are quite unbelievable."

Fergus stepped toward him. "She is playing ye, Bryce. Ye cannae trust her."

There was a sudden thrashing in the trees. Everyone spun to face the sound, and Gwenyth's eyes widened as a man strolled into the small clearing. He was wearing only his hose, breeches and dirty white linen shirt, along with what seemed to be half the forest, leaves in his hair and covering his clothing.

He walked with a strange lurch and came to a stop in the middle of the company, looking around. "Why, 'tis a celebration right here in the heart o' the wood. Welcome, good gentlemen." He sketched a low bow. "Ye've entered me realm. I am Pan o' the Forest. Welcome, welcome, especially if ye've brought some good ale."

Gavin!

This meant that Rowan was not far behind.

" 'Tis a lunatic," Bryce said with disgust. "Get him gone."

"Gone?" Gavin protested. " 'Tis me abode ye've entered. *Ye* be gone."

"Do something with him," Bryce demanded of his men.

"Leave him be," Gwenyth said. "Cause injury to one of God's poor creatures and you'll not be a man I would marry."

Fergus strode forward, hands on his hips as he accosted her. "My, we're a fine piece of work, m'lady, are we not? A marriage can — and will — be forced."

"And it will mean nothing, nothing at all, if it is not blessed by the queen," she assured him.

"Or the king," Fergus said smugly.

"You are far more a lunatic than that poor man there," Gwenyth said with a pleasant smile. "Do you think it will be so easy? John Gordon must win the day, and I do not believe he can prevail against the queen's forces. I think you will hang, my good man." She raised her voice, looking around at the men who filled the clearing, some on horseback and others afoot. "And those in your company, if all is lost, will hang, as well."

Rowan had to smile grimly, despite the circumstances, as Bryce's men moved back *en masse,* if only half a foot or so.

"Don't let the queen's *spy* unnerve ye from y'er cause!" Fergus cried out. " 'Tis fear alone that can vanquish ye, men." He looked at Bryce, working himself into a rage. "Take her, take her now, and be done with it. She's playing ye for a fool, lad. Be a man!"

Fergus's taunt sent Bryce into action. He wrenched Gwenyth toward him, but she was no easy opponent. She lashed out, and Rowan heard Bryce's roar of pain, as the man stumbled back from her again.

It might be the only real chance he had, Rowan knew, and he made his decision with split-second timing.

He drew an arrow, strung his bow, and let the arrow fly.

Bryce was struck dead center in the chest.

He did not even recognize his own death at first, only stood, staring at Gwenyth in shock for a moment, and then, at last, he fell.

"We are surrounded!" someone cried out in fear.

And the troops began to break, horses bolting, men crying out.

"Stay!" Fergus raged, rushing to Bryce's side. He saw immediately that his kinsman was dead, and he rose, staring at Gwenyth in such a rage that Rowan could hold his position no longer. He kneed Styx and went crashing through the forest. The bow and arrow were no longer useful; he drew his sword.

When Fergus strode forward, heedless of repercussion, ready to strangle Gwenyth, she was prepared. She ducked his hold and raced across the clearing, heading for the protection of the trees. Just as she reached them, Rowan burst into the clearing, his sword swinging.

Fergus shouted a fierce order, for not every man had deserted. It seemed there were suddenly men everywhere, some running into the fray in loyal defense of the clan, others running away in pursuit of self-survival.

Rowan's initial aim had been to battle Fergus, but he was diverted from that cause by the onrush of soldiers. Gavin, meanwhile, dropped his pretense of insanity and hurried to Bryce's fallen body, then unsheathed the dead man's sword.

Bryce's men were little match for the training Rowan and Gavin had received from the masters at both the Scottish court and as guests of the English queen. MacIvey's forces began to fall around them.

"Rowan!" came a cry.

It was Gwenyth. A man was rushing him from the rear.

Weaponless, she had nonetheless found a clump of dirt to throw the enemy's way. With his attacker temporarily blinded, her warning and missile gave Rowan time to turn to face the attack.

In seconds they heard the arrival of the queen's men, a multitude of horsemen, thrashing hard and furiously through the forest. At that point, it was a matter of mere minutes before the skirmish was ended.

When he had faced his last enemy, Rowan dismounted and approached Gwenyth, trying to contain his anger.

"You fool! You risked your life, Annie's, Gavin's and mine," he informed her coldly.

She stiffened, staring at him, dignified and *regal,* despite the soot on her face and the total dishevelment of her person.

"I am on the queen's business," she informed him.

He felt his jaw lock. It was difficult to argue against such a statement, so he turned away.

"You were not asked to risk your life!" she called after him.

He straightened his back and did not turn to face her again but strode back to Styx. She was on the queen's business, was she? Then the queen's personal guard could see that she was safely returned to her mistress.

Besides, he did not want her to see how he was shaking.

The skirmish in the field was nothing compared to what lay ahead. Rowan didn't have time to worry about what transpired between Gwenyth and the queen; it was imperative that he take command of his own troops, for the real battle was at hand.

In addition, he admitted to himself that he was furious with the queen, and therefore, he knew he had to avoid her. He was astounded that she had so mistrusted his advice that she had apparently needed to have his words verified. And he was horrified that she would let one of her ladies wander into danger rather than rely on the men who were honor bound to serve her with their lives.

He took control of his own forces, under the general command of Laird James and Laird Lindsay, along with Kirkcaldy of the Grange and Cockburn of Ormiston. The queen now had in her service one hundred and twenty harquebusiers and a number of cannon.

The day began with the queen's men firing upon Huntly's numbers upon the hill. They were sorely ravaged by the cannons and the harquebus fire, and began to fall. When the command was given, the cavalry rode in hard, followed by the infantry. The battle became hand to hand.

But the Highlanders never deserted the queen, as Huntly had surely prayed. In the midst of the fighting, as Huntly's troops grew ever thinner, mowed down or slipping away, the remaining men were forced into the swamp, as Rowan had foretold.

He was riding with Laird James when Huntly, Sir John and one of Huntly's younger sons, Adam, were caught and brought before them. As Laird James rode forward to face Huntly, the man stared back. Then, without a word, he tumbled from his horse. Laird James cried out, seeking to know what mockery the great earl was up to, then discovered that the man had died.

Sir John leapt down from his own mount and rushed to his father's side. He was not allowed his grief, for he and his young brother were quickly seized, and Laird Huntly's body was tossed over the haunches of a horse and taken from the scene.

It was over. The swamp was a gruesome arena of dead men, body parts and blood. And the queen's forces, with the support of the countryside, stood triumphant.

At the manor, Gwenyth paced her quarters restlessly. Mary had ridden out to address her troops before sending them off to fight, but Gwenyth had not been allowed to attend her. She was deeply dismayed and had argued the point, but apparently the queen regretted her decision to send Gwenyth out to spy and was horrified at the danger she

273

had cast her lady into. At first Gwenyth had been certain that Rowan had brought such a grievance before Mary, but then she discovered that he had not seen the queen at all; he had gone to lead his own troops.

Throughout the day, Annie came at intervals to report on what was happening.

Gwenyth could not help but ask about Laird Rowan.

"I've heard naught of him, but the queen's forces hae prevailed throughout the day, m'lady."

As the day faded, Annie returned, filled with news of the victory. "The queen is gloating, radiant. It was a massacre, so they say. And hear this! Laird Huntly died in his saddle, not a mark upon him." Annie paused to laugh. "It was just as Lady Huntly's witches said it would be — he has been brought to the tollbooth at Aberdeen, and there he will lie through the night, not a mark upon him. His heart gave out, I imagine, at the loss. He knew his noble head would fly. I don't know what vengeance the queen will take upon his clan, but this much is sure — the Gordons will no longer defy Queen Mary and keep the nor'east and the Highlands from her rule."

"What of Laird Rowan?" Gwenyth asked.

"I know not, m'lady. I have still heard no word."

When Annie was gone, Gwenyth returned to her pacing. She had obeyed the queen throughout the long day; she had remained in her chambers, safe from danger. But now the battle was over, the day won, and she longed to know that Rowan was all right and to see him. She wasn't certain why. He had been so angry with her, when he'd had no right. They were both servants of the queen. She owed him no explanation.

No matter. She had to see him.

Rowan felt weary, bathed in blood.

He had chosen to leave his quarters in the manor, and that night he took over one of the smaller hunting lodges just beyond the town, in the forest where the MacIveys had thought to make a stand and win the approval of Huntly. It was now peopled with his own men, the men of Lochraven.

The people had rallied behind the queen, and he'd been surprised to find himself something of a hero to the townsfolk. The servants in the lodge were pleased to have him. The lodge itself was, and had been, a royal holding and not beneath the Huntlys, so perhaps it was natural that those who made their livelihood there were pleased with the outcome of the battle.

They had been merry while preparing the meal he shared with his men, despite the vast amount of labor it entailed. And when he chose a chamber within the lodge, the stableboys and valet were quick to bring him a massive tub, and pot after pot of boiling water, though the steward was afraid that he would wash away all the natural defenses he needed against the "agues tha' migh' be takin' a body" after such exertion as the battle.

Rowan, amused, assured the man that he had enough defense within his body, covered with blood and mud or no.

So it was in the wee hours of the night that he at last lay in the great wooden tub, the room darkened and in sweet shadow, the only light rising from the embers of the fire in the hearth. The steam was rising around him, and he welcomed the feeling of cleanliness and the heat that relaxed his muscles. Laying his head back upon the broad wooden rim, he closed his eyes and let out a sigh, enjoying the sweet sensation of heat and steam. He should be jubilant. They had won. But he was still disturbed.

Mary was proving to be a good queen, but she had also shown that she could act recklessly under duress.

What monarch in history had not? he chided himself.

Was it only because of Gwenyth that he felt so angry? Would he have felt so betrayed had it been one of the queen's other ladies? None among them might have so easily blended with the people here; perhaps Gwenyth *had* been the best choice.

He realized he was disturbed, as well, because, as yet, they had not found Fergus MacIvey among the dead. The man was dangerous, and it frightened Rowan to think he might still be out there, hatching his plans of revenge, now that the MacIveys would be stripped of their holdings. Clan loyalty was everything in the Highlands, and if Fergus were alive, he would not let the matter rest.

He froze suddenly, muscles going rigid. He'd heard the slightest noise, and it wasn't the snap of a log in the hearth.

Someone was in his chamber.

He opened his eyes to mere slits without otherwise moving. He couldn't believe that his men were anything less than entirely vigilant, but . . .

A hooded figure was tiptoeing toward the tub. It paused a few feet away, then came closer. Someone come to murder him in his bath? A Huntly loyal, with access to the royal domain, ready to sacrifice all for his death?

His hand shot out, and he heard a startled, feminine cry as his fingers closed around a woman's wrist. He sat up, ready to fight.

"Stop, please! It's me!"

The woolen hood fell back, and as she jerked in response to his sudden attack, the cloak slipped to the floor.

To his amazement, his nocturnal visitor was Lady Gwenyth MacLeod. She was wearing a nightgown and a rich velvet robe, the gown in softest white, the robe a brilliant shade of crimson, richly embroidered. Her hair was loose, her face scrubbed clean, and she looked as innocent as an angel and as sensual as Lilith herself.

With gritted teeth, he tossed her wrist from his hold, staring at her with suspicion and unconcealed anger. "You just took your life in your hands again, you little fool!" he informed her. "What in God's name are you doing here, slinking around my bedchamber?" he demanded.

She rubbed her wrist, backing away, her eyes managing a look of both apology and defiance, all in one. "I am not slinking," she protested.

"You came tiptoeing up to a man in his bath. What reaction did you expect?" he demanded.

"I came to beg pardon, and to explain," she said indignantly.

"And no one informed you I was not available to be seen?" he inquired.

A flush covered her cheeks.

"As if it were not idiotic enough to leave the manor and come here dressed like that, you didn't seek a proper entry, did you?" he inquired.

She hesitated, then shrugged. "I was afraid you would refuse to see me. I entered through the kitchens. . . . I brought towels," she told him, sweeping an arm toward the trunk at the entry, where she had dropped the linens.

He scowled. The heat from the bath had relaxed him; now there was another sense of heat tearing through him and every muscle in his body was tense again.

"Fine. You're brought towels. That will certainly atone for risking four lives. Would you leave now, please?"

She stared at him, myriad emotions passing swiftly through her eyes, and then she turned to go.

He didn't know what he was thinking.

Or perhaps he wasn't thinking at all.

He sprang out of the tub, catching her before she could reach the door and turning her toward him. Once again, her eyes met his, and for a moment, just for a moment, all her defiance, all her anger, was gone. There was something there as naked as his flesh, something lost and pleading, something that spoke of the time they'd spent in each other's company.

And something else was there, too.

A silent admission that there had always been more between them than the battle, that he had been wrong to blame her for being who and what she was, that she had been wrong to blame him for his honesty. He opened his mouth; he meant to say something. But he didn't.

Instead he drew her to him, pulling her against his wet and naked flesh, and looked long into her eyes, then kissed her lips. He had not intended such a thing; indeed, he had fought against it for what felt like forever. Then he felt her fingers sliding up the dampness of his chest, curving over the muscles of his shoulders, tentatively moving into the wetness of his hair, drawing him closer.

Her mouth returned the slow, simmering passion of his own, and then it erupted. She was sweet, tasting of mint, and of a longing and hunger to know more of him. He trembled there, holding her and feeling, beneath the velvet and linen, the heat of her body, the perfection of her form, the way it melded to his own. He'd not been drinking; there was no excuse for the heady insanity that leapt into his being, his mind, his soul.

He lifted her closer against him and moved to the massive four-poster, but he did not lay her gently down but fell heavily with her to the mattress. Her fingers grew swiftly confident, coursing along his shoulder, his arm, his back. He drew his lips from hers and met her eyes again, and they offered neither protest nor explanation. She moved against him, and he kissed her again, swiftly growing ravenous to taste more and more of the sweetness of her mouth as her lips parted and her tongue parried his.

The velvet robe had come open. He found her throat, the flesh of her breasts, his hand moving over the thin linen gown. She moved against him, fingers taut now in his hair, the writhing of her body stoking the sure madness of fire in him. He felt her lips upon his shoulders, the instinctive play of her tongue. He moved still further against her, lips moist fire against her, until he wanted more than he could have with the fabric in the way.

In the glow of the fire, he rose. He met her eyes, as enigmatic as the shadows, as he stripped both velvet and cotton from her, and lay down again to cradle her against him, flesh to flesh. Once more he caressed her with the liquid flame of his lips, stroking his hands over the smoothness of her flesh, cherishing the heated, vital feel of it. It occurred to him that they could both be damned for this indiscretion, she, the queen's lady and he, her sworn protector. But damnation would be a worthwhile price to pay for this moment, when the world seemed right, when his senses and soul seemed to be filled after years of emptiness, when it felt as if he had found the very essence that had been missing from his existence and now made him soar.

She gasped and arched against his touch, and as her fingers and lips played over him, he lost himself in the scent of her, the slight brush of her fingers, the exquisite and agonizing touch of her tongue. She moved her body against the length of him, her hair trailing like silk over his skin, arousing, exciting. He knew she was fragile, that he must take care, and yet, as they loved one another with lips and touch, he knew the rising thunder of an exultant passion, and as the minutes of tenderness slipped by, his strength and ardor grew. With her beneath him, he slid against her, lips finding every inch of her, paying the most evocative attention to her breasts until small gasps escaped her, then moving lower to caress her midriff and belly. He eased himself along her length, tending then to her ankles, calves and upward along her inner thigh . . .

And then to the heart of her sex.

She clutched his back, raked her fingers through his hair. He felt the touch of her fingertips sliding along his back, not caressing, but holding on, feverish . . . intense. Felt the startled jolt and shift of her body, the expulsion of her breath, as she gasped and cried out. . . .

He rose above her, met her eyes, took her lips again . . . kissed her as he adjusted his body over hers, then slid smoothly into her, mindful to move slowly and with great care, despite the lightning tearing through his own veins.

She never cried out then, but she clung to him as he eased the thrust and glide of his hips, drawing her surely into the rhythm he set, and when he felt her rock and shudder beneath him, he allowed all the power he had held in abeyance to flood free. Her arms wound around him tightly as she all but melted into him.

And then she moved . . .

Moved in a way that brought sheer pleasure and madness leaping through him, his limbs, his sex. Time was gone; fire and shadows were gone. The world was pure darkness and sheer, shocking light. She was no longer fragile, she was a whirl of fever and passion, sliding against him, rubbing the length of his body, sheathing his sex.

He fought the explosion of climax, longing for her to know it first. And then, just when he thought he would die of the blaze consuming him, she shuddered, strained, went limp, and he allowed himself the rocket fire of a shuddering, volatile explosion within her. Again, again, the tremors racked through him, and then, even then, she held him, was one with him, trembling, clinging. . . .

A long while later, he eased to his side next to her. Her eyes were closed now, and she quickly found a place against his shoulder, her head resting upon his chest.

He sought desperately for the right words to say. And as he did so, he admitted to himself at last why he had felt such anger for her, why he had needed so desperately to be away from her.

It was easy to bed a whore.

It was hard to love.

She had, all unintentionally, beckoned and beguiled him from the moment he had seen her. When he'd had no right to feel such fascination, she had seduced him blithely from the beginning, and it had been no fault of her own.

He had not been able to bear his own disloyalty to Catherine, because while she had lived, he owed her his love.

She didn't speak, and the right words continued to escape him. Even though he was compelled and attracted, he was not at all certain he could say what he felt, and so he resorted to irony.

"Far better than towels," he said.

At that, she moved, contentment turning swiftly to fury. She started to rise, but he held on to her, at which point he discovered to his amazement that she was well-versed in Gaelic curses. "Let me up!" she demanded.

He pulled her close instead, trying not to laugh. Her eyes could change so quickly. Right now they were the color of the hottest fire — almost demonic against the shadows.

"No. Stay," he urged, his voice soft, the power in his arms more than matching her own.

"Not if you intend to mock me again," she said, and he had to try very hard not to smile, her words were so prim and dignified despite the fact that she was lying naked on his bed.

"I would not dream of mocking you."

"Listen to your voice! You mock me by telling me that you would not mock me."

She was still straining against him, features so beautiful in the firelight, hair like a cloak of crimson and gold. He did laugh then, which further infuriated her, but he rolled, pinning her to the bed, so she had no chance of escape.

"I swear I'm not mocking you. And if you came to offer an apology, I assure you, I have never had pardon begged of me so magnificently."

"I swear, if you don't stop —"

"Stop what? I don't know what words to say to you. Am I glad that you are here? Aye. Am I incredulous that you arrived as you did . . . that you gave to me as you did? Indeed. You want the truth? All of it? I thought you a rare beauty the first time I saw your face. I thought you a treasure indeed fit to serve a queen. Was I afraid of you? Beyond all doubt."

She relaxed slightly beneath him, puzzled then, and still wary. "Afraid of me? Perhaps that is the worst mockery, my Laird Rowan."

She grew still, and he shook his head, gently easing his fingers into her hair, marveling again at the sight of her. "Nay, lass, believe that I feared you."

"Why?"

"Because I wanted . . . this. I wanted you so much, when it was so wrong."

Her lashes fell, thick and radiant, over her eyes. "It is still wrong," she whispered.

He winced. "Nay. For I have truly mourned my wife. And I loathed myself long enough for wanting you — aye, hating you, even, that I could not be what Catherine needed when she died. Hating myself more. I could forgive myself many things, but not betraying her with my heart."

She stared at him, searching his eyes, as if she was as tormented in her own soul as he was in his.

"If you would seek my remorse that you came here, I fear I cannot give it," he told her.

"I was wrong," she said softly, and a rueful smile played upon her lips, though her eyes remained grave. Her words came as a bare whisper. "I could not allow such an admission, even in my heart, but I came here . . . for this."

He needed nothing else.

He kissed her again.

And made love to her again. She was even more adventurous, and just as passionate, as beautiful, arousing and exciting. If he had a lifetime, he thought briefly, he would never have enough of her, never tire of the sweet, provocative scent of her flesh, the taste of her lips. . . .

But later, as she lay awake, staring at the ceiling, he feared that regret was slipping into her heart and cradled her against him. "What?" he whispered. He didn't add the words that whispered in his mind: What, *my love?*

Did he love her? Aye. He loved her as he had loved Catherine. Loved her because she was like Catherine, kind and eager that life should be good, that none should be hurt.

And he loved her because she was nothing like Catherine. She was quick to passion, quick to throw herself into danger at the behest of or for the sake of another. She was a fighter, such a fighter, and she would never admit defeat, even with her dying breath.

"I . . ." She turned to him. "I should not have come."

"Yes, you should have."

Very gravely, she shook her head. "You don't understand. The queen is the most chaste of women. And her maids . . . yes, they all love to sing and dance, love costume and pageantry and flirting. But they are . . .

they are good."

"You're very good," he told her, and he bit his lip, knowing the words could mean many things.

"This makes me. . . . a . . ."

"No. It's all right. I will make an offer of marriage."

He was stunned when she shook her head vehemently.

"No?" he inquired in shock. He had known that, one day, whether for mutual benefit following long negotiation, or perhaps even through liking, he would marry again. He needed an heir, and for an heir, he needed the proper woman.

He certainly hadn't imagined he would propose — to anyone — so soon. And he certainly hadn't imagined that a woman with a *lesser* holding than his own would turn him down, especially after coming in her nightclothes to his chamber.

"I cannot marry without the queen's permission."

"You think she will not allow you to marry me?" He was indignant.

That, at last, brought a smile to her lips. "I came here of my own free will and desire," she said very softly. "You do not have to feel compelled to marry me."

"I must marry again, no matter what," he

told her.

She stiffened. Wrong words again.

"But you are not compelled to marry me, nor must I marry you, m'laird," she said firmly, and rolled out from under him, ready to rise.

He gently caught her arm. "Where are you going?"

"I have to return. I am one of the queen's ladies. If she awakes, if she feels that she needs me and I am not there, she will worry. And send guards out."

He smiled. She was so grave. Today had been a tremendous victory for the queen. Mary had not just won a battle, she had won her Highlanders. Tonight, if ever, she would sleep well and deeply.

"Not yet," he told her.

"I cannot stay."

"Just a little while longer."

For once, she was easily convinced.

CHAPTER ELEVEN

She loved him.

She had loved him for so long that she did not even know when it had begun.

And in that, she understood what it was the queen longed for so deeply. A marriage that would suit the state — and more. One that could offer her the radiance, the ecstasy, that Gwenyth had found that night. To love, to be in love, to be loved in return. . . .

She fell suddenly back to earth. He had offered to marry her. He had never said that he loved her.

Gwenyth spent the next morning in a haze. She could talk about it to no one, of course. Not even Annie, who had helped her slip out, and who had found out the name of the dairymaid who worked in the kitchen at the lodge, the sweet girl she had impersonated when she slipped in.

Annie was certain her pure and chaste charge had gone — fully dressed — to explain to Laird Rowan that she had gone out in disguise only to prevent the queen from doing so. Gwenyth wasn't at all sure how she had managed to keep a straight face as she told Annie that they had *talked* things out very politely, but somehow she had done so.

Then she had helped the queen to dress in her finery and attended to her when she went to the castle and addressed her people. The queen was clearly elated at her victory and their support, but was also very serious, making certain her people knew the importance of what had taken place, that she wished no ill to anyone, that all she craved was prosperity and happiness for *all* her people, no matter how they chose to worship, and a Scotland that was respected by the world.

Gwenyth had done this while trying not to look over at Rowan, who stood with Laird James and the other military advisors, no sign upon his features that something so . . . unusual had happened in the night. Or perhaps it was not so unusual for him.

But she . . . she was *different.*

She was changed entirely.

That night, when they continued to celebrate in the hall, she managed to convince the queen that the Highlanders would be far more entertained if they were invited to sing and dance. But when the queen agreed and invited everyone to take the floor, Gwenyth was asked first by the Laird James, and she felt as if her heart would tear apart when she saw Rowan with Mary Livingstone. In time, however, she was in his arms, and then she was afraid again she would give herself away.

"How was your day?" she asked, as they drew together, but they moved apart in the steps of the dance before he could reply.

When they came together again, he smiled and said, "I had a lovely day, m'lady. But not near so lovely as my night."

She felt her cheeks flood with color. "You mustn't say such things."

"Every man should speak the truth."

They drew apart.

They came together.

"We need to speak to the queen," he said gravely.

"She has been jubilant throughout the day," she replied. "But I must repeat — you are not compelled to marry me."

"I give the offer freely."

Something tugged painfully in her heart. Aye, he offered. It was the right thing to do. And she was insane if she did not accept.

But . . . she wanted to be loved, not just

desired. She wanted to be craved as a wife, not given the title because she was entertaining between the sheets and, given his position, it was necessary that he marry again.

They drew apart, and when the music brought them together again, she said only, "Perhaps."

"Oh?" he arched a brow in amusement.

"Time will tell," she told him.

The music came to an end, followed by a burst of applause. Rowan smiled at her, but then, to Gwenyth's surprise, the queen summoned him. He bowed deeply and went to do her bidding.

Gwenyth escaped the floor, hurrying back to her seat on the dais, not wanting to dance with any other man. But the Laird James sat down beside her and let out a sigh. "My sister, the queen, can be reckless," he said.

She looked at him. He waved a hand dismissively. "My dear, I know full well you were sent out on a ridiculous mission the other day."

"But . . . I was able to ascertain where Laird Huntly meant to gather his troops. Though I was unable to return with that information," she admitted.

James looked ahead, brooding. "She would have gone herself."

Gwenyth merely nodded in reply, though

she had no idea whether he had turned back to her and saw her response or not.

"She intends still that you should travel to London."

"Aye." Had she meant it as a question or a statement? She did not know.

"The succession is very important," James said.

"Of course." Was it so very important, though? Gwenyth wondered. Wasn't it enough to rule one nation?

But looking at James, she thought sadly that even the best of men always seemed to want more.

And how did she know that Rowan wasn't the same? In his heart, did he crave another English heiress, someone to balance out the richness of his Scottish holdings?

"Take care — take the gravest care — in your dealings with Queen Elizabeth," James warned her gravely.

"Of course," she said again.

"You are not an ambassador."

"No, my Laird James, I am not. Nor did I ask that I be sent. Mary said that I should go."

James nodded, rubbing a finger along the stem of his goblet. "I am not against the undertaking. Laird Rowan is one of her favorites and will no doubt keep you safe so long as it is in his power to do so. I am just warning you to take care."

"Of course, Laird James."

He rose then. A few minutes later, flushed, and followed by several of the ladies of the court, Mary returned to the table. "How I love to dance," she said.

Gwenyth stood at the queen's approach, as protocol dictated, and smiled. "Indeed, and you do so extremely well," she said. It was not flattery; Mary truly was an excellent dancer.

"So do you, my Highland poppet." The queen lifted her chalice in toast. "To my Lady Gwenyth, ever loyal and brave. Tonight we say goodbye to our dear friend once again. Tomorrow she heads south to visit my dear friend and cousin, Elizabeth of England." She spoke gaily. Around her, her courtiers applauded in approval.

Gwenyth bobbed a curtsy, once again wishing that the queen would not take her so by surprise. She had known she was going, just not so soon.

No matter what she had said, she longed to marry Rowan. To be his wife. But now....

Rowan returned to the dais with Laird Lindsay.

"My Laird Rowan, I have just informed my Lady Gwenyth of what I discussed with you only a few minutes ago: that you will begin your travels tomorrow. I ask you to convey my deepest love and respect to my cousin. And you will, of course, protect my Lady Gwenyth."

Rowan bowed handsomely to her. "It shall be as you command, my queen. And I serve you, as ever, with my life."

Around them, there was applause and cheers. Gwenyth met Rowan's eyes, and she knew she should have been happy. He was handsome, one of the finest warriors in the country but also a well-educated man. He was pleased with his assignment. Pleased to be her protector.

But she wanted so much more. And this meant a long journey. A long time before they could even approach the queen.

Queen Mary set her chalice down. "Tonight, I bid you all rest well. I thank you again for your support, and I pray God watch over Scotland. Gwenyth . . . will you tend me this last night?"

It wasn't a question. It was the queen's command.

"At your pleasure, Your Grace," Gwenyth said and, with a slight nod to the company, she hurried after the queen.

In the bedchamber Mary had chosen, the queen whirled around, clapping her hands together. "I am still on fire with victory. The people love me," she said, beaming.

Gwenyth agreed. "So they proved."

She stood behind Mary, finding the pins that held the headpiece in place, removing them and starting on the queen's own lustrous dark hair. She hesitated, wondering how to broach the subject of her own marriage. Or even if she should.

"Your Grace —"

"There is one thing that I now must have," Mary murmured.

"Your Grace —"

"A husband. It is such a dilemma. But. . . ." She let out a long breath and turned to Gwenyth, clasping her hands. "Thus far, all has gone well. But . . . I cannot rely on my brother forever. I feel that I am ruling alone, and I don't want to be Elizabeth. I don't want to be an unwed, barren queen."

Gwenyth stared at her, opened her mouth to speak, then closed it again.

"I can think about nothing other than the fact that I need to make a proper choice — and that I must be acknowledged by Elizabeth."

She turned around so that Gwenyth could help her from the stiff collar she was wearing. Gwenyth had long tended the queen, and knew all the proper care of her clothing and accessories.

"Marriage," Gwenyth murmured. "It is something I've wondered about myself."

Mary lifted a hand. "Dear Gwenyth. You mustn't consider such a step at this moment. You know that I will see to it that you are properly wed when the time is right, but that time is not now. You must get to know Elizabeth and, with Laird Rowan's help, win her to my side. Maitland and others have advised me that she loves Laird Rowan. And why not? My dear cousin, the fierce spinster, has never pretended that she is not thoroughly amused and entertained by handsome men — she simply chooses not to allow any of them to share her power. When you return . . . perhaps. In time. And it will not be so long, I promise, my dear, dear, Gwenyth."

She spun around. Gwenyth barely let go of a hook in time to keep from ripping the queen's brocade bodice.

"I will not be Elizabeth! Now, my dear, off to bed with you. Laird Rowan has been given orders for the morning. The death of his dear wife delayed this journey far longer than I had anticipated. Do you know how long I have ruled now? And now I am triumphant! Such a victory will be sweet on his lips when he sees the English queen."

Gwenyth nodded. "I will do everything in my power to further your cause, my queen."

Mary was satisfied. She began removing her heavy skirt, quite capable of taking care of herself when she chose.

"I am the only proper heir to the English throne. Elizabeth must be made to see that although I am fiercely Catholic and love my religion, I am no threat to the English Church. Of course, the English will be furious if I seek a Catholic husband . . . they would prefer a man with English blood. But . . . should the English turn on us, as they are so wont to do, then we would need the power of a foreign king." She broke off. "I repeat myself, I fear. You must go and get some rest. I am eager for you to reach Queen Elizabeth and to report back to me."

"Aye, Your Grace," Gwenyth replied.

"Come, hug me warmly and let me bid you the best goodbye."

Mary was emotional. She was also determined. She said goodbye with a warm embrace, then shooed Gwenyth from the room.

In her own quarters, Gwenyth discovered that Annie had been informed they would be leaving in the morning. Her night dress was set out, a riding ensemble set apart for the morning and her trunks were packed.

Annie rushed in from her small adjoining room, clapping her hands. "London!" she said excitedly. "Ah, m'lady, how magnificent to meet yet another queen."

Gwenyth nodded. "Aye, to meet another queen," she said, and tried to sound cheerful. At that moment, she wished she knew no royalty at all, that her father still lived and that she had simply met Rowan as any woman might meet a man.

She was a fool. She'd known all her life that duty came above all else, not just for the queen but for herself. Duty would always outrank love. The queen, in fact, had warned her. *Don't fall in love with him.*

But the queen was related to Rowan! Surely she would understand, when the time was right; she would give her consent, and all would be well. Oddly, all Gwenyth could feel was a sense of foreboding.

Rowan had known the long weeks of travel would be difficult. Roads in Scotland quickly became impassable with snow or rain, and they were traveling with a large party: Gwenyth, Annie and ten men, Gavin among them. He was a favorite of Gwenyth, easily making her laugh as he himself could not.

She was also enamored of his performance on the day when he had played a lunatic to stall for time in the forest. He was young, closer to her age than Rowan's, and he was a fine musician, proficient with a lute.

Sitting one evening around a campfire, since it had been decided that they would sleep in the woods rather than ride hard and in darkness searching for an estate or a town, he watched as Gwenyth complimented Gavin on his performance. "You were excellent, so convincing."

"My lady, you are a true mistress of disguise. My performance was but paltry in return."

Gwenyth was admired by all his men. Whereas he had been angry at the risk she had taken that day, they were deeply admiring.

They didn't argue along the road, he thought, but neither did they ride together. He kept his distance from her, for being with her was too painful. He had tried to speak with the queen, but she had wanted to talk about nothing except the English throne, her difficult situation and her orders for him once he reached England.

"She was quite incredible, was she not?"

Gavin demanded from his seat before the fire, breaking into Rowan's morose thoughts.

"If one can call a fool incredible," Rowan replied.

Gwenyth gasped. "Mary threatened to go out herself," she informed him.

"Some sense might have been talked into the queen," he said, arms folded across his chest as he leaned against a tree.

She lifted her head, smiling, refusing to be offended. "Playacting, my good Laird Rowan, is an excellent strategy."

He nodded. "I shall remember that, my lady."

She, too, nodded quickly, then looked away. She tried hard never to give away a hint of what had transpired between them, he noticed. He didn't believe it was a matter of shame but rather that they both conducted their lives according to the queen's will. And they both knew that she considered their trip to England crucial to the future of her realm and her rule.

"Gavin, play something will you?" Gwenyth asked.

"Indeed I will, and I know just the piece," he assured her, and began.

Early one morning,

As the day was dawning,
I met a fair lady
Far along the way.
And so wooed her,
And so I kissed her,
And then so again,
I went along my way.
And when I came again,
She sped me on my way,
Singing ever so softly,
Please, for you will leave me,
Please don't deceive me
How could you use
A poor maiden so?

Gwenyth and Annie applauded, as did the rest of the men, who teased Gavin for being a musician and far too attractive, though their words were all in good fun.

Rowan would never have said he was jealous of the young man, exactly, but he often envied him his easy ways.

"Sing with me," Gavin asked Gwenyth then, and so she did, their voices melding beautifully under the rich canopy of the forest.

"Best get some sleep," Rowan advised when they were done. The women found a comfortable place beneath a spreading tree, and five men slept, while the other five took first watch.

Morning came, with the softest nip in the air. Everyone washed quickly and drank at the brook that bubbled through the trees nearby, and on their way to the next town, they found a farmer who was happy to make them a filling breakfast of bacon, bread, fish and eggs.

They traveled south through the Highlands, down to the border country, and finally reached Yorkshire, where Rowan made the decision not to enter the great walled city. They bypassed the city and traveled on until late at night — despite the fact that Annie allowed her grumbling to be heard.

"A fine lady, the queen's lady, travels in this party, and we might have stopped at a fine castle and been welcomed there — even if this be England," she said.

"You'll like the castle where we're stopping, Annie," Rowan assured her, riding back to disarm her with a grin. "Won't she, Gavin?"

Gavin solemnly agreed. "It's a fine place, Annie. I promise you."

At last they came to a great walled fortification. Gavin had ridden ahead then, and the drawbridge was already down, providing safe passage above the moat. Within the walls, a stone castle rose several stories into the night sky. Outside the walls, the countryside they'd been riding through was lush and fertile, and there were numerous cottages. When they reined in, Gwenyth looked at Rowan with weary but curious eyes.

"Where are we?" she asked.

"It is called Dell," he told her.

"I see," she murmured, though she did not.

"It is mine," he told her.

"Yours?"

"A gift from the Queen of England. I hold it through no one," he added quickly, thinking she might surmise he had gained the estate through his marriage to Catherine. "I accomplished a small service once for Queen Elizabeth, and therefore, I am Lord of Dell."

"I see," she repeated, and this time her smile was dazzling.

They were greeted by his steward, an amiable man named Martin, a corpulent and cheerful fellow who was delighted that his lord had returned to his English land and quickly had a very fine meal prepared. The men joined them for the late supper, and there was much discussion about the storage of crops and the maintenance of the castle, so Gwenyth excused herself as quickly as she could.

Rowan had seen to it that Gwenyth was given the chamber kept in preparedness at all times for the ambassadors and nobles who often stopped here on their journeys to the north and south. The bed was vast, the mattress firm and not at all lumpy. The hearth was huge, the fire warm.

Shortly after he saw Gwenyth leave, Rowan excused himself, knowing his men might well enjoy his hospitality long into the night.

This time, he came upon Gwenyth in the bath. He slipped silently into the room, where she was resting her head on the rim of the tub, appreciating the hot water after their long ride.

"Ah, m'lady Gwenyth. I've brought towels," he said.

"Annie is on her way back," she advised him gravely when he entered. "She thinks that I must have some warmed wine, if I'm to sleep well."

"We'll bolt the door."

"And how will I explain that?"

"Simply say that you're already half-asleep."

"You don't believe she'll suspect some . . . danger?" Gwenyth teased.

"Do you want me to leave?" he queried.

"Nay, m'laird, never!" she protested. "But perhaps you should hide in the wardrobe."

"My dear Lady Gwenyth, it is far beneath my dignity to hide in a wardrobe," he replied.

As he spoke, there was a tapping on the door, and Annie's anxious voice sounded softly. "M'lady? Are you all right? I thought I heard voices," she said. "Should I send for the guards?"

Rowan turned and opened the door, despite Gwenyth's gasp.

Annie stood in the hall, her jaw dropping. Afraid she would also drop the tray with the pitcher of wine and chalice, Rowan quickly rescued it.

"Please, dear woman, I'm quite afraid some small spider might drop into your mouth. Close it, and do come in," Rowan told her, setting the tray on a trunk.

Annie snapped her jaw shut and entered the bedchamber. She stared from Rowan, still resplendently handsome in the formal attire he had donned for dinner, to her mistress.

Gwenyth was afraid that the maid who had tended her so lovingly and so well for so long now was going to voice her sternest disapproval. She was equally afraid that their affair might be given away. Instead, to her astonishment, Annie grinned, and then she began to laugh outright.

"Well, well. So ye've both finally realized what all the rest of us have long seen," she said.

Gwenyth frowned.

"Oh, nay, y'er not suspected of *this,*" Annie said, still laughing. But then her laughter faded, and she set her hands on her hips and stared at Rowan. "This is nae a round-heeled maid to satisfy yer fancy — m'laird."

Rowan leaned against the wall, amused. "Nay?" he inquired.

"Nay," she echoed a fierce frown.

Rowan gave her his deepest, most charming smile. "Annie, I have promised the lady I will wed her. Thus far, she has refused me."

"What?" Annie's jaw dropped again.

"I have my reasons," Gwenyth said.

"Well, not a one of them can be good enough," Annie said with complete certainty.

Gwenyth did not have a chance to tell Annie any of her reasons, because Rowan stepped in and informed her maid, "The queen would allow no conversation about my second marriage until her own domestic situation is settled. She was quite fierce on that score. But, Annie, I am a man of my word. I am quite aware that Lady Gwenyth is no lightskirt."

Annie stared at Gwenyth. "Ye will marry the laird, m'lady," she said sternly.

Gwenyth had to laugh, then looked at Rowan. "We needn't wait for the queen. Annie says that we must marry."

"Don't ye go mocking me," the older woman said sternly.

"Never, Annie," Rowan said solemnly. "I give you my most solemn vow that I will marry your mistress."

He was serious, Gwenyth knew. Wrong reasons, right reasons. At that moment, it didn't matter. He was there. He had made a vow. And he would never give his word lightly.

Annie was shaking her head as she started from the room. "Don't ye be mindin' me. I'm off — minding me own business." Then she paused and turned back. "There be a bolt on that door. I suggest ye use it."

"It is my castle," Rowan reminded her politely.

"Mayhap," Annie sniffed, but happily. "I still say, bolt the door."

"Thank you. I stand well-advised," Rowan said.

He bolted the door as soon as Annie was gone. He set down the wine, walked to the tub and reached down, then, soap and all, pulled Gwenyth into his arms. If he had been ardent before, he was doubly so now. If she had longed for him before, it was with an ever-greater desperation now.

Now she knew what it was to feel the power of his muscles, the sleek ripple of his flesh beneath her fingers. Now she knew that his kiss would make her feel as if she had never really lived before.

It mattered not to either of them that she soaked his fine clothing through, for even as he took her from the tub, he had begun to cast it all aside.

She never knew where it went, only that she was touching him, unafraid to explore. She was half-maddened in her desire to stroke him, feel the vital contraction of his muscles and bask in the feel of her flesh against his. She cupped his hand in her palm, her lips upon his throat as she savored the drumbeat of his pulse. She was learning to play, to tease and taunt, and the taste of his flesh beneath her tongue was purely erotic. She could not be close enough to him, and as she pressed herself against him, she did so with the sole intent of feeling some part of his flesh along every inch of hers. She caressed him with her fingers, trailing them along his body as he had trailed his along hers. She was not so experienced a lover yet that she was not hesitant at times, but his ardent whispers urged her along, drove her to new heights. She grew bolder, feeling his hands always upon her, yet he let her play and experiment first, and she could tell from his response that she was instinctively learning all that was most seductive. She dared to let her fingers dance upon his erection, followed by a harder touch, a liquid caress. She savored the hoarse cry of surprise and pleasure that issued from his lips, the fierce ardor with which he grasped her to him, the trembling power with which his arms held her when he made love to her, when he was one with her, and it seemed the world itself shook with the wild ferocity of their passion.

He did not leave her in the night but lay by her side and held her.

When the morning's light broke gently through the arrow slits, she woke and was immediately aware that he had already wakened and still lay by her side, leaning on one elbow, watching her. "When you grow to be a very old woman, m'lady, you will still be a beauty."

She laughed, her brow furrowing. "M'laird, when I grow to be a very old woman, I will be quite wrinkled."

"The soul never ages," he told her. "Did you know that?"

"Are you saying I have a beautiful soul?" she queried.

"Aye, that I am," he said gravely. "But this morning, when I woke, it was your face, I must admit, that I noticed. That, and perhaps the way the sun's rays fell upon the length of your back . . . perhaps even how it made your hair catch fire."

"My hair will turn gray," she told him.

"It will. But no matter how you age, you will have beauty in your face, in your eyes and smile."

She wondered if it was possible to be any happier as she curled closer to him and said, "You will be a very striking old man."

"Muscles do not remain strong forever, and flesh sags. I will be stooped and possibly bald," he told her.

"Ah, but you, too, will always have your face."

"Not so delicate as yours, I fear."

"I don't believe such a strong chin will ever go weak. And your eyes . . . even if the color begins to fade, they are so deep a blue that they are nearly black. They will always be fierce," she said gravely.

He gently stroked her cheek with his knuckles. "And to think you had little good to say about me once."

"Mary is a good queen," she told him earnestly.

"Aye, she has proven so," he agreed.

"You still do not sound certain."

"Twenty years from now, I shall be certain," he said, and he threw off the covers, then held himself poised above her. "My lady, you serve her well in her chambers — may we keep her out of ours?"

He waited for no answer. The morning had come, but he did not intend to forget the night.

At last he lay beside her again, cradling her to him, surprising her with his passion when he spoke.

"If only we could remain right here."

"If we remained here," she reminded him, "we would not reach Elizabeth. We could not convey to her the respect in which Mary holds a man's choice of religion. We could not make her understand that Mary is her proper heir, deserving of recognition."

His fingers threaded through hers. "We could not return to the queen and gain her consent for our marriage," he said flatly.

Gwenyth rolled to him, rising up on her elbow, seeking his eyes. "Rowan, I swear . . . I'd not trap any man into marriage."

"Well, you were certainly bold," he said

softly, and with affection, "but I do believe that I did the trapping."

"I suppose that's what you *must* believe," she teased.

"It is the truth, and therefore what I believe."

He pulled her close again, and kissed her long and tenderly. But when that kiss threatened to become more, he drew away with regret. "There is nothing I would like more than to remain here," he said with a sigh, his eyes still tender. "But we have to ride. We are still only in the north of England."

He turned away then and rose, but he leaned down to press a kiss to her forehead before he picked up his strewn clothing, dressed, and at the door bid her rise.

"Breakfast, then the road," he told her.

"Aye, I shall move," she promised him as he closed the door in his wake.

The sheets still held a hint of his scent, so she remained where she lay, hugging her feather pillow.

It seemed impossible to be so happy.

She would never leave him, she vowed.

And surely, whether he said so or not, surely he loved her. Would do so always.

CHAPTER TWELVE

London.

The city seemed huge.

Gwenyth reminded herself that she was quite accustomed to Paris, and London was not so different, merely very . . .

English.

Rowan's townhouse was near to Hampton Court, just down the river. A handsome barge sat out back, which could quickly bring them to an audience with the queen.

Although she had known that Catherine was English, Gwenyth had not realized just how welcomingly Rowan was received in his wife's country. As they moved about the city, they constantly met people who knew him and were glad to see him back in England, and who stared at her with ill-concealed curiosity.

Rowan took her to Westminster Cathedral so she might see the coronation church of the English royalty, and they were received, as well, by the warden at the Tower of London. At home, she was given her own wing, which included a parlor just behind the bedroom, with access to the floor above, where Annie had her room. Rowan's master's quarters included a room with a massive oak writing desk and chairs for his accountant and other business attendants.

Their first days in London seemed almost magical. They rowed upon the Thames, walked in the parks and visited the markets. He did so as her escort, and in public, they were entirely circumspect.

The nights, however, were hers.

At last the day came when they received a letter from Queen Elizabeth. She had set aside an evening to spend time with her "dearest Laird Rowan," and professed herself anxious for all and any messages from her "dearest cousin, Mary of Scotland."

"She sounds most genuine in her affection," Gwenyth told Rowan.

He arched a brow at her, amused. "Don't rely on 'beloved cousin' for victory," he warned her. "Elizabeth is a crafty queen. And she is careful always," he added.

The steward of this house was a cheerful old fellow named Thomas, and Thomas — if he noticed the closeness of Laird Rowan and Lady Gwenyth — was careful not to comment upon it. Rowan had assured her that he had employed the penniless old soldier for his ability to keep a strict confidence, and he didn't seem at all alarmed by anything said or done in the man's presence, but for the sake of Gwenyth's honor, he was circumspect.

Thomas had brought the queen's letter to his master's quarters, and Rowan, though not completely dressed, had crossed the hall to Gwenyth's realm. She hadn't risen, but rather enjoyed the services of Annie and Thomas here; each morning, one or the other of them brought her a tray of coffee and pastries. She had never had coffee before, though Rowan told her it was a popular drink in Constantinople. It was far less popular in London, though, and most of the country had never so much as heard of it. But years before, when Rowan had been a lad, the elder laird had taken his young son on a long voyage that took them to the Continent and even to the East, where he had developed a taste for the bitter beverage. "All things can be obtained, my lady," Thomas had assured her, "when you know the right merchants. And, of course, can afford the price."

She didn't really understand all of

Rowan's holding, nor did she really care about his property or wealth. With all her heart, she simply loved the man.

She couldn't, however, regret the fact that he could afford coffee. She loved it, especially when Thomas served it with rich cream and sugar, another commodity that was not always easy to purchase.

That morning, she had just set the tray aside when Rowan came in to show her Queen Elizabeth's letter. He'd handed it to her, and she had marveled at the fact that it had been handwritten and closed with the queen's seal. It had offered such a familiar tone of friendship.

"It sounds as if you know Queen Elizabeth better than Queen Mary," she told him a little primly.

He laughed. "I happened to be in England and was able to support the queen when things were not going in her direction."

"Oh?"

He sighed, stretching out upon the sheets of the bed he had left not long ago. "Now it seems that Elizabeth sits so comfortably upon her throne, while Mary is still gaining the support of her people, but it has not always been so easy for Elizabeth. Believe me, she understands Mary's dilemma well. And while there are others besides Mary with claims to the English throne, there are none so viable. And I believe that is Elizabeth's personal opinion, as well."

"Then she should simply sign her name to that," Gwenyth said, moving closer to his side.

He smiled. "Nothing is ever so easy and you know why. Mary has yet to sign the Treaty of Edinburgh."

"She can't sign the Treaty of Edinburgh, because as it is currently written, she would be giving away her claim to the throne of England."

"There's more," Rowan said with a shrug, smiling and slipping his arm around her. "Think of it this way — Elizabeth came to the throne at the age of twenty-five, young and beautiful. She was, beyond a doubt, the most outstanding marriage prize to be had."

"But she has turned down all those who have requested her hand."

"She has said many times that if she marries, it will be as queen."

"And that means?"

He gently touched a lock of her hair, smoothing it back from her face. "It means that she loves to be loved — she is still a striking woman in a man's world. She will not marry a Catholic prince and give power to any other country over her own, and she will not marry an English noble, because she will not give power to one family over another. If she marries, she intends to keep her title in reality, as well as in name. She will rule and no other. She has learned, however, the difficulties of being both a queen and a woman, with a woman's heart. Robert Dudley was one of her favorites, and many thought they were far too intimate, especially since Dudley had a wife. His wife died — her death was deemed an accident, but many believe it was suicide, that she was distraught over her husband's assumed infidelity with the queen. But she held her head high throughout the scandal, and she has made it clear that she will not marry Dudley. Indeed, there's been rumor that she's offered him as a potential bridegroom for Mary."

Gwenyth gasped. She was indignant. "Queen Elizabeth would suggest such a man, her . . . *discard,* to our queen?"

Rowan laughed, pulling her toward him. "Such pride! But, indeed, I am quite certain that Mary would never accept Elizabeth's discard, as you call the man. Actually, Elizabeth has a sense of humor and thinks that perhaps she should have married Dudley, as long as she had his promise that he would then marry the Queen of Scots if she should die. By marrying two queens, the man would have double the chance of fathering at least one royal heir."

Gwenyth studied him carefully. "She does not sound like such a virginal queen."

He shook his head. "Who ever knows what goes on in the heart or mind of another? But there was a scandal when she lived with her stepmother, Catherine Parr, and Somerset. The man would have loved to take her as his bride, rather than her father's widow. He tried too many times to climb too high, and he lost his head upon the scaffold. It is dangerous to be noble with royal aspirations."

She hesitated, studying him. "If rumor holds true . . ." she teased.

"It isn't rumor, m'lady, it is fact. My mother was the child of King James V of Scotland, recognized and loved, as he recognized his other children."

"And you have no royal aspirations?"

"I value my head, thank you. My claim would come behind more than a dozen others. And," he added, "my love is for Scotland. My own land. My own life."

The last was gently spoken, and his smile was tender.

She smiled, then regretfully rolled away from him and rose. "I have to dress, and carefully, my good laird."

Rowan shrugged and rose, as well.

"You will enjoy taking the barge down the river," he said, then left her.

They attended the queen at Hampton Court, and were invited into the Withdrawing Chambers, the queen's personal rooms, rather than the more public Privy Chamber or the Presence Chamber, where many were welcomed. One of the queen's retainers showed them into her presence. She wasn't in her bedroom but a parlor suite, with the bedroom just beyond. A small table was set for dinner; a servant was there to offer them wine or ale when they arrived; and the queen appeared from her bedchamber as they entered. Rowan bowed deeply, and Gwenyth knew that protocol demanded she sink into a low curtsy and await the queen's summons to rise, which she did.

Elizabeth was in her early thirties, and Gwenyth couldn't help but judge her quickly. She was fairly tall, her own height, nowhere near as statuesque as Mary. She had well-coifed golden hair with a touch of red, and dark eyes. She was decked in a gown of silk with a doublet in velvet, and her crown sat comfortably atop her head. She was not a great beauty, but she was certainly attractive.

"Ah, my dear Laird Rowan," Elizabeth greeted him, waving him near that she might bestow a kiss upon each of his cheeks. Her hands upon his shoulders, she stood back to survey him, then nodded, as if in approval of what she saw. There was a spark of mischief in her eyes.

"And," she murmured and turned, beckoning to Gwenyth, "my *dear* cousin's maiden, the Lady of Islington."

Gwenyth bowed her head low in acquiescence.

"Well, child, let me see you," Elizabeth said, and Gwenyth looked into the eyes of the English queen.

"You're tall."

"Not so tall," Gwenyth said.

Elizabeth laughed, pleased. "Careful — I'd say you're an inch above my own height, and I like to believe that I am tall."

"You *are* tall, Your Grace," Gwenyth said dutifully, bringing a smile of deep amusement to Elizabeth's face.

"You spent a year in France, I believe, so I have ordered a French wine in hopes that you will like it," Elizabeth told her.

"You are very kind."

"Actually, I am intrigued," Elizabeth said, but instead of elaborating, she turned to Rowan then. "I am so sorry for your loss," she told him. "Some time has passed, and I hope you are doing well."

"Aye, well enough, thank you."

"You were involved, I imagine, in your queen's battle with Huntly."

"Aye."

"A matter nicely solved. I was interested to hear all that transpired, and pleased to know that my cousin feels as I do on the matter of religion. Men do, and will, continue to die over their protestations of faith, though I try to minimize their opportunities."

"I swear, Your Grace," Gwenyth said earnestly, "Queen Mary does not intend to interfere with the Church of Scotland in any way."

Elizabeth looked at her. "Very well said. Of course, I had heard all about you. Mary has sent you as her most ardent enthusiast, and you are somehow to convince me that my good cousin is, as she claims, a proper heir to my throne."

Gwenyth felt her cheeks growing flushed. "She is indeed all that she claims," she said very softly.

"But I am not dead yet," the queen said, amused. "And do you know what I have decided, dear Rowan?"

He was wearing a half smile; the queen's

attitude apparently amused him.

"What is that, Your Grace?"

"I don't need to name an heir to this throne. I have decided that I am quite unwilling to die."

"I don't think any of us intends to die, especially not so young," Gwenyth offered.

"Ah! The lady called me young. Well, I can see already that we shall be dear friends," Elizabeth said, and seeming even more amused. "Rowan, be off for a bit. My ladies will all be quite happy to see you, I'm certain," she added wryly.

Rowan stood, watching her without moving toward the door.

Elizabeth made a waving motion with her hand. "Rowan, do go on. I wish to speak to this delightful creature alone."

"As you wish," he said at last and, having no choice, left them alone.

Elizabeth wandered to the large chair in the center of the room, indicating a divan across from it. "You may sit." As Gwenyth did so, Elizabeth said, "Go on. Tell me of the wonders of your queen."

"She means to be a good queen, to be fair and just in all things. You don't know how it broke her heart to battle Huntly, a Catholic laird, but the kingdom, and the people, are most important in her heart. She would dearly love to ratify the Treaty of Edinburgh, but she feels that she cannot. She was grateful when you gave her safe conduct to Scotland, though it came when we had long sailed. She wishes nothing other than to be, in truth, your dearest cousin, your friend in all things."

"She will not be my friend," Elizabeth said sharply, "if she continues to negotiate any possible marriage contract with Don Carlos of Spain."

Gwenyth answered carefully, for there might still be secret negotiations taking place with Spain, even if she hadn't been entrusted with that information. "Mary is very aware that, like yourself, she must marry for her country."

"Is she?"

"She was promised to Francis as a child, and she befriended him as a child. She was a loyal and tender wife to him in every way."

"Easy — when you are Queen of France," Elizabeth offered.

"Not so easy. He died slowly, and she never left his side," Gwenyth said.

"Ah, she is kindhearted."

"Very."

"Passionate?"

"Of course, especially when good government is involved."

Queen Elizabeth leaned forward slightly. "And in all else?"

"She . . . is kind to her friends. She loathes violence. She is well educated, and she loves her books, horses and hounds."

"I hear she is an excellent hunter."

"She is."

Elizabeth smiled, apparently having sensed something in Gwenyth's tone. "And you are not?"

"I am not fond of the hunt."

"You are honest, at least."

"Queen Mary is very honest."

"That, my dear, is not always an asset for a queen. She is lucky, though."

"Oh?"

"If all her subjects remain so earnestly assured of her goodness, she will have a long and prosperous reign," Elizabeth said.

"Would you consider acknowledging her as your heir?" Gwenyth asked hopefully.

Elizabeth leaned back. "No."

Troubled, surprised by the queen's bluntness, Gwenyth fell silent.

"I can't," Elizabeth said, smiling to take the sting out of the words. "I am not yet so firm upon my own throne that I can afford to make choices that may imperil my own rule. Perhaps, in time, I can do as your queen requests, but for now, I can't honor a

Catholic princess. You must realize that. I will not acknowledge her, but neither will I acknowledge any other. I have said before that I consider her to have the clearest right to the throne at my death. But right does not always mean power. And even when power is granted to someone, it doesn't mean they were the right party to have it. Now, I am sure you have been charged to spend time at my Court. You are to speak highly of your queen daily, until I have had her name all but etched inside my mind, because I hear it daily from all sides. Therefore, you will most certainly spend time here, with my lords and ladies, and in my presence. You must see how we do things in England." She rose, ready to pace, and waved a hand that Gwenyth should remain seated, which left her feeling uncomfortably small. The queen stopped, staring at Gwenyth. "I believe I will live a long life. I will not fall prey to any man, because I have learned that caring too deeply creates havoc. I will be a queen in all things. England may one day take a husband, for the people clamour for an heir, but Elizabeth will not marry for passion. Perhaps, when I am completely convinced that your queen offers me no threat . . . but it is a waiting game we play. I can wait."

"Queen Mary has been a wife, and she will surely marry again," Gwenyth said. "She intends to leave an heir for Scotland."

Elizabeth smiled. "The woods are far too full of royalty now, so many would-be heirs to the throne. Perhaps the Scottish queen will make a choice that pleases me. Then we shall see."

She strode to the door that separated them from the outer chamber. When she opened it, Gwenyth saw that Rowan had obediently joined in a laughing discussion with several of Elizabeth's ladies. She couldn't help but feel a deep pang of jealousy, though she would not allow herself to show her feelings. If queens could be so cold, perhaps a lesser noble could be, as well.

"Rowan, we shall dine now," Elizabeth said.

"Your Grace," he acknowledged, and with a nod to the group, he returned to the room.

"He is very popular here," Elizabeth said to Gwenyth. "But then, you must see his excellent points. Tall, a well-built swordsman, extremely well-educated and well-traveled. Charming. A full head of hair. Strong teeth."

"He is not a horse, Your Grace," Gwenyth found herself saying. And then, of course, she was horrified at herself for having rebuked the English queen.

But Elizabeth only smiled. "Ah, a backbone. Thank God."

Rowan was followed into the room by what appeared to be a stream of servants, all carrying trays, and those trays all in silver. Gwenyth didn't believe that Elizabeth was attempting to impress her with English wealth; this was simply the way the queen dined when she held a private audience.

Elizabeth took the seat at the head of the table, then Gwenyth sat, followed by Rowan.

"A good solid English roast, Laird Rowan, though your Scottish cattle offer up tasty cuts. And there is fish, as well. Lady Islington, the onions are particularly sweet, and the greens are quite delicious. I hope you will enjoy the meal."

"In your presence, Your Grace, I would enjoy any meal," Gwenyth said.

"Rowan, she is quite a talented diplomat," Elizabeth said, then, holding a morsel of meat near her mouth, she paused. "Were you with Rowan, my dear, when Catherine breathed her last?"

"She was in my care, aye," Rowan said.

"Ah," the queen murmured.

"Mary had intended that Gwenyth travel south much earlier than has occurred," he said. "As it happened, I stayed at Castle

Grey for some time, and my lady traveled on to her ancestral home."

"Were you sharing a bed at the time?" the queen asked bluntly.

Gwenyth gasped.

The question obviously didn't shock Rowan. He looked at the queen calmly. "Nay," he said flatly.

Elizabeth nodded thoughtfully. "Yet some time has now passed," she pointed out.

Gwenyth wanted nothing more than to escape the table, the room and the queen's presence.

"Dear child, if you don't want people to know," Elizabeth said, "you will have to find a way *not* to follow the man's every movement with your eyes."

"I intend to ask for her hand," Rowan said.

Elizabeth smiled. "A love match. How charming."

After all the queen's words, Gwenyth was startled to hear something of envy in her voice.

"You could make a very advantageous marriage, you know, Rowan," Elizabeth said. "She is a beauty, your queen's own dear servant, but . . . Islington?"

"*She* is sitting right here," Gwenyth said, stunned that her sudden anger allowed her to speak.

"I am the queen. If I wish to speak as if you were not here, you must not notice," Elizabeth said, and there was amusement in her voice.

"Madam," Rowan said, "there are serious matters of state to dis—"

"Yes, and I am quite bored by all of them at this moment. I am far more interested in the two of you. Rowan, the Countess Mathilda is newly widowed. She is young, as well, and brings with her vast, rich lands. I have heard that she has mentioned a longing to speak with me about you as a possible new husband."

Gwenyth was stunned to see Rowan smile and shake his head slightly. "Your Grace, I hold English lands of you, and gratefully so. But I am a servant of the Scottish queen, and not to be bartered for a foreign country."

Gwenyth thought that Elizabeth would surely explode, and she did.

With laughter.

"Don't you want greater power, more and more land?" she demanded of Rowan.

"The thing about land . . ." he said thoughtfully. "Like a crown, one must always scramble to keep it. I am blessed. I have fine properties as it is. I have Catherine's inheritance, and it was Lady Gwenyth my wife turned to at the end, Gwenyth who watched over her lovingly when she did not even know my name. There was nothing between us then, and there has certainly been no shame in the behavior of the Lady of Islington. With *my* monarch's permission, I intend to marry the lady."

"Bravo!" Elizabeth told him.

He turned to Gwenyth then, "Believe in her temper, her anger and her demands. But she loves to bait a man, as well."

"I am sitting right here," Elizabeth said. "And I am the queen." Then she laughed, and Gwenyth was surprised when Elizabeth set a hand upon her own. "I am glad you gave comfort to Lady Catherine. She was a great beauty and a wonderful friend. You would have cared for her dearly, had you known her in better times."

"I came to care for her dearly as it was," Gwenyth said.

Elizabeth looked at Rowan. "I am well pleased. The lady is both lovely and well-spoken. Send for your things. I would have you both reside at court for a time. I believe I would enjoy a game of tennis tomorrow. Lord Rowan, you will be my partner. Lady Gwenyth, you will play with Lord Dudley. I think it's time I favored Lord Rowan above a few of the other nobility who are grown far too confident these days."

"As you wish," Rowan said.

"You do play tennis, Lady Gwenyth?" Elizabeth asked.

"Of course. Queen Mary is quite good at the sport. She loves to be out in the fresh air. Her gardens at Holyrood are lovely."

"I shall pray that you commend me to her so highly," Elizabeth said.

Gwenyth was silent.

"You are supposed to answer with an assurance that you can think of nothing but the most brilliant and marvelous words where I am concerned," Elizabeth said.

"I will certainly convey that you are exceedingly clever," Gwenyth said.

Elizabeth laughed. "And that is all?"

"I will tell her that you are every inch a queen."

"She is a quite a treasure, Rowan. I shall pray for the two of you, for life is never as simple as we would have it be. Now, Lady Islington, dinner is over and it is your turn to retire. There are matters I would discuss with Rowan."

When they were alone, Elizabeth looked at him gravely. "Events are in an uproar in your homeland yet again, Rowan," she said.

He frowned. Matters in the Highlands had

seemed quiet enough when they left, and he had assumed that he would hear any news quickly if the situation changed, for there were fresh horses kept at numerous stops along the long road from London to Edinburgh, so that riders could swiftly carry correspondence from one court to another.

"There was a man in Mary's party from the moment she left France for Scottish soil. A Frenchman, most avidly in love with his queen. He was sometimes with the Court and sometimes traveling on his own. It seems that he has been executed."

Convincing her French retainers and her Scottish court to speak as one had often been a difficulty for the queen, exacerbated by the fact that the Scots themselves had so many different agendas, sought such different rewards, and gave such different advice.

"What has happened?" he asked.

"Perhaps I should tell you all that I know has transpired since you left the queen's side. Sir John Gordon was tried for treason."

"Naturally," Rowan said. "Many in the Huntly party admitted there was a plan that our good queen should be abducted and forced into marriage with the fellow. He escaped justice, and he raised arms against her."

Elizabeth sat back in her great chair,

delicate hands upon the upholstered arms. "I loathe an execution myself. Mary was in attendance when the Frenchman died. He cried out that he was ready to die for his great love for his queen. Apparently the execution was a sadly botched affair." She stared at Rowan. "It is exceedingly difficult to find an executioner who does not make a blundering mess of the process. So many people do not realize the tremendous kindness my father showed my mother when he sent to France so an excellent swordsman could do the grisly deed."

Rowan made no reply. Elizabeth was clearly deep in thought, and he did not care to tread upon the images that were occupying her mind.

"I barely knew my mother," she told him. "I had my own household at the time of her death, though I was but a toddling child. But there is something about blood, I suppose, because the stories I hear often tear at my heart. If you were to listen to my sister Mary's lords, she was a witch, a strumpet. If you listen to those who surrounded her at her death, she was innocent of all save her ability to continue to enthrall my father — and produce the son she left behind. She died well — all men say so. She was careful to beg my father's pardon at her death. It's amazing, is it not, that men and women go to their deaths begging pardon of those who wronged them — and paying the executioner well, so the torment will not be prolonged."

"I have seen those whose faith in the hereafter is so strong that they truly believe their travails on earth mean nothing," he told her.

She shook her head. "So many die so brutally — over the wording in the book meant to honor our most gentle Savior. But enough reminiscing. To return to my tale, at the Frenchman's death, Mary was so distraught that she took to her bed for several days. She was very ill."

Rowan asked quickly, "She is well now?"

"Well enough. Such emotion. Indeed, I've known illness, and I've known horror. But a queen cannot allow her emotions to rule her so completely. There has been more, you see. This courtier, a fellow name Pierre de Chatelard, apparently went a bit mad. He burst into the queen's chambers not once, but twice. The first was forgiven. On the second evening, Mary was quite distraught, screaming that her brother James, Earl of Moray, must run the man through with his sword. Moray acted with greater calm than the queen. The fellow was duly arrested, tried and executed."

Elizabeth was watching him; she was a very shrewd woman, he knew, one who read as much from the reactions of others as she did from their words.

"I can only say that I have ridden at her side, served her, sat in council with her, and I will swear by all that is holy that she is as chaste as a maiden never married, that she never encouraged the man in any way."

Elizabeth shrugged. "I do not think that she is me," she said.

"Your Grace, no one is you," he said simply.

"And you are smirking, despite your best resolve not to, Laird Rowan. My point here is that Mary must have a husband."

"Laird James Stewart is a fine advisor for her."

"He is her illegitimate half brother. He cannot take the place of a king consort."

"Like you, she intends to marry with grave care. Surely, Your Grace, you know yourself that men will do foolish things for love — especially love for a queen."

"Love for a crown," she said sharply.

"A crown is certainly a lovely treasure set before the eyes — but I think you are not a woman who lacks confidence in her own abilities."

"Flattery, Laird Rowan."

He shook his head. "I certainly try not to insult with my speech, but there is danger inherent in the fact that both you and Queen Mary are young and very attractive."

She laughed suddenly. "You have heard, certainly, how I teased her advisor, Maitland. Poor fellow, I did quite torture him, trying so hard to make him say that one of us was prettier than the other — I even tried to make him say that I was the taller. Alas, I failed in that."

"Maitland is a good man and a fine ambassador in Queen Mary's service," he said.

"You speak carefully, but you don't lie," Elizabeth mused. "And you are one of those Scots in a difficult position indeed, with loyalties to both England and your own beloved home. I tell you, Laird Rowan, there is truly nothing I love so much as peace. I seek good government and peace, which together bring prosperity. So know this," she said, her expression suddenly intense. "I will never accept a Catholic marriage that binds Mary to a foreign house. I will first accept the threat of war with Scotland and France, Sweden or Spain. If she wishes to remain in my good graces, she will take serious care with her plans for marriage."

"Your Grace," he said, puzzled, "I had thought that both my Lady Gwenyth and I — and Maitland, in his many discussions with you — had thoroughly convinced you that Mary intends most firmly to take the greatest care with her marriage. She knows that she is queen. She would not risk war among her own noblemen by her marriage, nor war with you, her much-loved cousin. Believe me, she knows the grave seriousness of her every move."

Elizabeth sat back. "I have no doubt that my cousin is kind, earnest and passionate, and that she intends to do the best she can with the power she wields. Whether she can prove herself worthy of navigating difficult emotional waters is something that frightens me."

He lowered his head. Word of Elizabeth's own temper tantrums had certainly spread.

"I am quick to anger, but I do not fall apart," she said, as if reading his thoughts.

"Queen Mary will not fall apart."

"Then I pray that we shall remain *dearest cousins,*" Elizabeth said.

"We all pray it will be so."

Elizabeth lifted a hand and grinned. "You know, of course, that I did not see you here alone *only* so that rumor would arise?"

"Perhaps not 'only,' but certainly I am

here at least in part so that your courtiers may whisper that you have shown me favor, and therefore they will not whisper about you and Dudley."

"Ah, but do you know that I gave Dudley the title Earl of Leicester that he might be a man of greater importance and riches, a more juicy tidbit for your queen?" she asked.

He hesitated. "Mary is very proud," he said at last.

"As a queen should be," Elizabeth said. "We shall see what the future holds."

She *would* see, he knew. Elizabeth was known for sitting back to watch and wait whenever she faced a difficult decision. That way, others were at fault when ventures went wrong.

"Whatever lies before us, I am delighted in your company, Rowan."

"Your Grace, you know I always enjoy an audience with such a powerful — and beautiful — young queen."

"You will cause much jealousy," she said, grinning.

"If that is your wish, I will do my best to oblige."

"Tell me, will the new love of your life be suspicious? Truly, Rowan, the lady impressed me. She will not veer from honoring Mary. And when I suggested that there might have been an affair between the two of you before Catherine's death, she was quite honestly horrified. You will face that rumor, of course."

"She is my love and my life," he said softly. "And no, I don't believe that she will suspect any evil — of either of us."

Elizabeth laughed. "If only you were a good English subject."

"None of us can help our birth, Your Grace."

"Ever the statesman. Go now, before the hour grows any later. I will enjoy forcing you both to remain with my court for some time."

He bowed deeply and left her, but he found one of the guards of the wardrobe, an elevated house valet, waiting outside the door to escort him to his chambers, where his possessions awaited him. When the queen *wished,* events occurred quickly.

Rowan wasn't pleased that they were moving into Hampton Court Palace; he would have preferred being in his own house on the river. The days that had passed while they had awaited the queen's pleasure had been ideal. But he knew Elizabeth. Even had he protested in any way, he still would have done what she wanted, and she would have found new ways to torment him, besides.

She considered him as much a friend as she could consider any man, he knew. And she had sincerely liked Gwenyth. She could be vain, but she also enjoyed having attractive women around her — just as long as none shone so brightly as she. But more than that, he knew that the queen dealt with so much flattery and cajolery that she was enjoying Gwenyth's honesty.

She was also amused by their affair. Very amused, it seemed, for when she had commanded them to leave his townhouse on the river, she had been playing at her own games, as well. He was somewhat familiar with the vast halls of Hampton Court, and he was quite familiar with the room he had been assigned. It had a false door built into the wall next to the mantel, one that led to the room next door.

To Gwenyth's room.

Perhaps Good Queen Bess had a more romantic heart than her familiars suspected, despite her own stern determination on how she intended to live.

Nor were they the only guests. The queen's court — with all her noble office holders, ladies, accountants, council, officials, servants and servants' servants —

numbered nearly fifteen hundred souls, many of them housed here at the palace. Rowan knew that several hundred dined in the great hall at night. The Court was larger than many a village among his holdings. But that was of no consequence now, he thought, his mind returning to the possibilities the night offered.

Gwenyth did not know that the rooms connected.

Thomas and Annie had brought their travel cases and dutifully moved them in while he and Gwenyth had still been at dinner with the queen. He knew that their servants were now housed elsewhere in the vast tangle of chambers and rooms, leaving him free to open the door to Gwenyth's room and explore.

In the dim fire glow, he could see that her brushes and hair accessories were laid out on a dressing table, and that the wardrobe — the door ever so slightly ajar — held her clothes, everything neatly arranged for her use.

Gwenyth herself was asleep. He could imagine her ritual, the removal of all the paraphernalia she wore, which was exchanged for her more comfortable nightclothes, the time spent at the dressing table, brushing out her hair. Now she lay in the bed — that glorious hair strewn around her on the pillow, catching the firelight — looking like an angel.

As he slipped in beside her, she awoke and started to scream, so he quickly clamped his hand over her mouth.

"Good God, would you have me executed for an assault in the night?" he whispered to her.

Her eyes, wide in the firelight, met his and softened. He felt her lips curve into a smile beneath his palm as she slipped arms around him. "Never," she whispered as he removed his hand.

She asked him no questions about his private time with Elizabeth, only found his mouth with her own, then used her tongue to create an instantly simmering fire upon his lips, within his mouth.

In seconds, they were wildly entwined.

She was the love of his life, and surely that could only be a good thing. No evil lay between them, only the future, which promised to stretch out before them brilliantly, as brilliantly as the fires that raged between them.

Her arms were so fierce, her lips so passionate. And the way she moved. . . .

It did not matter if they lay together in the woods of Scotland, a townhouse upon the Thames or in the quarters thoughtfully meted out to noble lovers at Court.

He held her tightly, when passion was spent. Held her as if . . .

As if he feared to lose her.

There was no reason for the fear, he told himself, but still he lay awake long into the night, pondering the strange haunting doubts in his own mind.

It was only at dawn that he left her, and he did so with the deepest regret.

They would be together again by night, he chastised himself as he forced himself to leave. She slept on, her hair a golden sunray on the pillows, face exquisite.

And still he was afraid, with no way to explain his fear.

CHAPTER THIRTEEN

Tennis was always fun, Gwenyth thought, and the grounds at Hampton Court were beautiful.

Robert Dudley was an exceedingly handsome man, tall and well versed in courtly manner. She wondered, however, if he was not stretching even his excessive charm and luck, for he strove to be close to Elizabeth at every turn.

Gwenyth noticed, too, that the queen seemed to enjoy tormenting those who thought they could sway her. She would laugh and be kind to Dudley one minute, then turn to Rowan the next. She enjoyed creating a certain jealousy among her courtiers. That, Gwenyth realized, and making certain that none would think himself too favored, too grand.

Elizabeth would indeed hold on to her own power.

When Dudley missed a ball that should

have been an easy volley, Elizabeth accused him of attempting to let her win. Gwenyth, however, had no intention of allowing anyone to win easily. Losing by pretending to lack even the simplest skills did not seem like a way to flatter the English queen, nor like something that would be appreciated.

She was, in addition, Mary of Scotland's representative here. She owed it to her queen to represent both her rule and her country well, so she played for all she was worth, forcing Dudley to throw himself into the game.

At one point she crashed into him as they both went after the ball, and he eyed her speculatively — and appreciatively, she thought, stepping hurriedly away.

Here was a man who had flirted so outrageously with the queen that she had been touched by scandal. Then, whether in jest or with serious thought, the English queen had suggested him as a marriage partner for the Scottish queen. And now was he attempting a flirtation with her, as well?

She decided that she was not particularly fond of court life. And though she certainly could never tell Elizabeth so, she thought that Mary's court was by far the more virtuous.

"Take care," Dudley warned her, catching

her arm and offering her a broad smile. "Elizabeth does not like to lose."

"Neither do I," she told him meaningfully.

"She is the queen," he said.

"But I serve another — who is also a queen," she told him.

"My future bride?" he taunted.

"I sincerely doubt it," she told him.

"Let's finish playing!" the queen called sharply, and they went back to the game.

At last, and thanks to Dudley's fawning determination, the game was lost.

It was true that Elizabeth was in high spirits, but when she shared her exuberance and joy, it was with her partner, Laird Rowan, and not Robert Dudley.

Gwenyth, longing for nothing more than to be quit of royal company at that point, managed to excuse herself, feigning a sore ankle, and made her way back through the long and confusing corridors of the palace and at last to her room, Annie was there, humming as she tended to her mistress's clothing.

"Are ye all right?" Annie asked, noticing the feigned limp Gwenyth had thought it wise to maintain, lest she be seen.

"I'm quite fine, merely aggravated. Such games they play here."

"You love tennis," Annie said.

"Never mind."

"Ah, you lost."

"I don't care that I lost," Gwenyth protested, then hesitated. "On the one hand, this English queen seems so intelligent and judicious, even kind. But she places far too much importance on games that can have no significance for her. I just wish that we were home."

"I thought that you were fascinated by London."

"I was. Annie, what are the chances that you could arrange for a bath for me now?"

The older woman went off in search of a tub and hot water to fill it, and soon she was helping Gwenyth from her clothing, clucking over the condition of her corset, the whalebone bent and misshapen, and bemoaning the emptiness of Gwenyth's purse while they were in England.

Gwenyth didn't care, merely submerged herself in the water, leaned back, closed her eyes and pretended to sleep, hoping that Annie would let her be.

When her maid finally left, Gwenyth opened her eyes and let her thoughts wander, wondering why she felt so irritated by the day's events. And then she knew.

She didn't trust Elizabeth.

There was no doubt that the woman was

a clever and effective queen. But equally, there was no doubt that she would readily use whatever lesser human beings were at her disposal to further her own ends.

Rowan didn't like Robert Dudley.

He never had, and he never would.

Dudley's father had lost his head for involving himself in royal intrigue, but that didn't seem to stop Dudley from daring a great deal. He was a tall, well-built man, and he seemed to think extremely highly of his own charms, something Elizabeth had certainly allowed.

Watching Dudley with Gwenyth across the court had not endeared the man to him in any way. He knew Dudley's mind. He was the queen's favorite, but there was no one who could swear that the queen had ever been genuinely intimate with the man, who considered himself free to indulge in petty affairs, while still maintaining his absolute devotion to his queen. Even if Elizabeth now teased him with the thought of a marriage to Mary of Scotland, Dudley would consider the queen's lady a succulent temptation and his by right. Too many men with a certain degree of rank and power felt they were allowed such indiscretions. But small though her lands and property might be,

Gwenyth was a Scottish noble in her own right and not a prize for Dudley or others of his ilk to claim.

And Rowan was not beyond jealousy.

Despite her completely cordial and proper manner, he knew Gwenyth well and had seen that she was clearly seething when she left the tennis court. But he could not follow her at first, for Elizabeth demanded that he accompany her to the hall, and while they walked, she casually told him that she had given leave for Lord and Lady Lennox — previously stripped of their Scottish lands — to return to Scotland and reclaim their holdings. Watching her, Rowan was curious — and wary — for they were the parents of Henry Stewart, Lord Darnley.

"Are you putting the son forward as a possible king consort for Mary?" he asked. He knew Darnley and liked him less than Dudley. At least Dudley made no pretense that he was anything other than a lascivious and ambitious man.

Darnley was but a boy, glorious and golden to look upon. He could hunt, dance and play the lute. He was also selfish and overly indulged. Rowan couldn't imagine him ever having to fight in battle, being able to rouse people to his cause or make a stand.

"No. I am allowing Lord and Lady Lennox to return to Scotland because it has been too long that they have been punished for old infractions." She shook her head. "I don't think that such a marriage would please me at all. Henry Stewart is a cousin of mine, as well. He has claims to both the English throne and the Scottish. I would not like to see the pair together. It is one thing for my nearest kin to seek the throne upon my demise, quite another to think they might want to grasp it while I live and breathe. I thought that you should know," she told him.

"I see." He bowed to her. "I thank you for so candidly sharing your thoughts."

"See that they are relayed, just as I spoke them," she told him. "I'm arranging for you to meet with Mary's fine Mr. Maitland, along with my own ambassador, Throgmorton." She linked arms with him. "They think I don't know that Maitland is secretly negotiating with Spain regarding Don Carlos as a contender for the Scottish crown."

He pulled back, staring at her. "Your Grace, it is public knowledge that you continue to entertain yourself with marriage negotiations with suitors from many places."

She smiled. "There is power in negotiation."

"I see. You wave the great carrot of England before the mules of the Continent, secure in the belief that you can quickly form an alliance should you need one."

"I can protect myself from my cousin's French connections and perhaps stir old animosities, if it becomes necessary," she told him.

"I will see that Queen Mary is duly warned. May I take my leave?"

Walking with the queen, looking around, he saw no sign of Robert Dudley, and misgiving filled him.

Elizabeth nodded regally. "We will see you and the Lady Gwenyth at dinner this evening."

"Aye, dear queen, as you wish."

"I do love those words — *as I wish.*"

"You are queen."

"But it wasn't always so. You know, of course, that I entered the Tower once through Traitor's Gate. I know, as few do, how lightly crowns sit upon royal heads. But I intend to keep my crown, and my head, at all costs. You may take your leave, Lord Rowan."

He was anxious to do so and strode quickly through the long halls of the court, nodding to acquaintances and even old friends but never stopping, so anxious was he to reach Gwenyth's chamber.

When he neared her room at last, he started to breathe a sigh of relief. But as he drew closer, he saw that her door was ajar and saw the figure of a man.

Someone was there!

His long strides became a run. He reached the door just before it could be closed against him and threw it open with a thunderous shove. Inside, he found a scene to send his temper soaring.

Gwenyth was in the bath, fingers tightly gripping the wooden rim. And Robert Dudley was there, on his way to the tub, but he stopped short at Rowan's arrival.

Rowan drew the knife at his calf, eyes narrowed.

Dudley, who was unarmed, drew back.

"Good God, Graham, what is in your head? I have merely come to see to Lady Gwenyth's ankle!" he exclaimed.

Rowan wasn't sure what he said, only that without thinking he swore in the ancient Gaelic tongue of his father. Whatever his words, his meaning was clear enough to Dudley, who backed even further away.

"Cause harm to me, Rowan, and Queen Elizabeth will have your head."

"When you were intent upon the rape of a lady within her court?" Rowan countered, seething.

Dudley pretended shock. His jaw set; his eyes became hooded. "Do you know my position, Laird Rowan?"

"Do you know mine?"

"I see that you are ready to wield a knife against an unarmed man."

To Rowan's distress, Dudley's words galvanized Gwenyth into action. She had been watching the confrontation, wide-eyed, but now she grabbed the linen towel that awaited her, drew it around herself and leapt toward him. "Rowan, you must drop the knife!"

He did so, casting it across the room toward the hearth.

"Let there be no weapons," he said in a deadly tone.

"Let there be no fight!" Gwenyth pleaded.

Rowan stared at her, certain his eyes were glazed with the fury that constricted his muscles.

"Let there be no fight," she pleaded again.

He didn't know if Dudley was right about his favor with Queen Elizabeth being so great that any lie he voiced to her would be believed. Elizabeth was far from stupid. But she would always have her way — even if that meant forgiving the gravest offense because she had a greater goal in mind.

God, how he loathed Dudley at that moment. He longed to strangle the man with his bare hands. But if he did so, he would hang.

And if he were to hang . . .

Gwenyth's life would be in grave danger.

"Rowan," she whispered, then walked away from him, her back sleek and bare, glistening from the heat and steam of the tub. She held her towel more tightly to her, walked up to Dudley and struck him hard across the face.

Dudley, shocked, rubbed his chin.

"You are the queen's favorite, not mine," she assured him. "And if you ever think to surprise me again, I promise you, you will not need to fear death at Laird Rowan's hands, because I will kill you myself. In Scotland we are not trained just to charm, we are trained, even lasses, to preserve our lives against foreign assault."

Dudley was far more stunned by her assault than he had been by any of Rowan's threats. Even so, Rowan felt the need to reinforce her words. "If you go near her again, Dudley, I *will* kill you," he promised.

Dudley laughed then, but it was a sham, there was no humor in him then. "I didn't know, Laird Rowan, that the lady was your mistress."

"My relationship with the lady is not your

concern. She is one of Mary of Scotland's ladies-in-waiting, and as such, she should command your respect."

Dudley looked at Gwenyth. "You are seeking power in the wrong place. Laird Rowan is from a bastard branch of the royal family."

"I am not seeking power, Dudley. In fact, the more I see of power, the less I crave it. Now get out."

"What if I were to tell you that Queen Elizabeth sanctioned my visit here?" Dudley asked softly.

"I would call you a liar," Rowan told him. But his heart sank. Could Elizabeth be that duplicitous? "Get out," he said, echoing Gwenyth's words.

"Good lords, sweet lady! What on earth goes on here?" came a sudden demand.

Rowan spun around. The queen, followed by a number of her courtiers, was at the door. Whatever she was truly thinking was hidden by the tremendous shock on her face.

Dudley answered quickly. "We've both come to see that the Lady Gwenyth is quite all right, after she injured her foot this afternoon."

"Someone do be kind enough to offer the poor child a robe," Elizabeth said sharply.

One of her ladies, the homely but very sweet Lady Erskine, raced past the rigid men. She found Gwenyth's favorite velvet robe and wrapped it around her shoulders.

"I'm sure, my lords, that you meant the lady well. What else dare I think?" Elizabeth said. "But I suspect she would like her privacy, so perhaps you will leave her. *Now.*"

Dudley bowed to her deeply. "Indeed, my dearest queen. I meant to seek an audience with you immediately. There are pressing matters at hand."

Rowan didn't speak, only stared at Elizabeth, and was stunned when her eyes fell and it seemed that there was a slight flush upon her cheeks.

"Laird Rowan, you appear distressed. I am certain your good man Thomas has seen to it that there is a fine wine in your chambers. I suggest that you take your rest, as you are surely weary from the day. Dudley, you will accompany me."

Having been given no choice, Rowan strode down the hall to his door and, with a bow to the queen, entered the room and closed his door.

He waited, ready to explode, listening to her voice and Dudley's as they moved down the hall and out of earshot.

He was about to burst through the connecting door when Gwenyth did so first. Towel gone, she raced naked and shaking into his arms.

"She is horrible!" Gwenyth cried. "She made all that happen. She did it on purpose. She will not make any commitment to the man, yet she wants him at her beck and call, and she would offer up anyone to amuse him so that he stayed her patient dog."

"Shh, it's all right. It won't happen again," he told her tensely, privately recalling the expression on the queen's face. He didn't think she had manipulated that scene; she had been too genuinely appalled by what she saw. Still, this was probably not the time to convince Gwenyth of that.

She pulled away from him, her eyes huge. "Nay, don't say such a thing to me. You look as if you will go out and kill him . . . and then . . . oh, Rowan!" She threw herself back into his arms, still shaking.

Well, there it was. He longed to kill Dudley, but he could not. What promise *could* he make to her?

"I swear," he vowed aloud, "that I will never let him near you again."

"It would be better if . . . if . . ."

He lifted her chin, knowing she was thinking that it would be better if Dudley were dead.

"Don't even say it," he whispered, smoothing the damp hair back from her face. He suddenly found himself on his knees before her naked, trembling form and took her hand. "I swear, Gwenyth, that I will guard you with my life against all evil." He looked up at her. "That I will love you until my last breath."

She gasped softly then fell to her knees before him. His hands cupped her head, her eyes searched his with a shimmering of tears, and then her lips were on his. She kissed him with a sweet and aching tenderness that flooded his soul, as well as his senses.

He lifted her from the floor and into his arms, and laid her with infinite tenderness upon the great canopied bed, then stretched out beside her, and his whispers bathed her flesh with the softest breath while his words were impassioned steel. "By my honor, I vow that I will love you, come what may, through all the days of my life. With every drop of blood in my veins, with every fiber of my flesh, bone and being . . ."

"Rowan," she cried softly, and again her lips found his. When she had finished kissing him there, she proceeded to bathe his shoulders with the exquisite sweep of her teeth and tongue, as her hands, so delicate, so enticing, moved over the length of him. In his heart he felt a passion that needed to be sworn physically, just as he had sworn his devotion with words, and he caught her fiercely, rolling her beneath him. With volatile, rising passion, he made love to her in the most carnal manner, seducing, enticing, with the moist searing of his tongue, the stroking of his hands, fingers, lips. There had never been a time when he had made love to anyone so violently, so intently, so tenderly, all in one. The body, no matter what its fire, could not impart all that he meant with his soul. He would never grow tired of her; she enchanted him anew every time she rose to meet his desire, and in the end they both lay gasping, heaving, trembling . . . and locked with one another, arms and legs, his erection easing in her body. He did not want to pull away; he did not want to be parted from her.

"We're leaving," he said softly. "Tonight."

"Rowan, we cannot. We have been sent here by one queen and are the invited guests of another."

"By virtue of my holdings in England, I have rights," he told her vehemently.

She pulled away at last, stroking his face, a smile upon her lips. "Rowan! We spend so much time praying that her passions do not rule our queen. We must not take leave of this place in anger and without permission. I believe Elizabeth respects you very much. Speak with her again. We can't become her enemies."

Lying rigidly, he thought he did not care. Then he sighed at last. "I will summon Annie. You will not stay alone."

"Summon Annie, and beg an interview, alone, with Elizabeth. She wanted to create a stir. That I believe. But though I don't know her, the more I think upon it, I do not think she intended these events. I cannot believe she would cause an incident between two countries over something so . . ." She paused, biting her lip, shaking her head, "So trivial as one man coveting another's mistress."

He drew away from her, his frown rigid, his features taut. "Have you listened to nothing I have said?"

She smiled. "On the contrary, I have savored and trembled with every word. But to Dudley, if he knew anything, it was only that you are the great Laird Rowan, while I am a lady with far lesser holdings. You once married a great heiress, and I am hardly that. I am here as Queen Mary's champion, and that does not make me a great prize."

"There is no greater prize," he said

hoarsely.

"I fear I am sleeping, that I will wake up, and this will all have been a dream," she told him.

He cradled her against him. "It is no dream." Quite suddenly he stood. "Stay in here until you hear Annie in the connecting chamber." He dressed quickly as he spoke, choosing his Highland regalia.

He left her, after first assuring himself that the hall was empty. At the end of it, he found Thomas, and he ordered the man to find Annie, and said that he expected both of them to stay by their chambers, watching over Lady Gwenyth. Thomas gravely and quickly obeyed, and Rowan went in search of the queen.

Despite Rowan's demand that she remain in his chamber, Gwenyth dared to return to her own room and begin dressing, slipping into a linen sheath and then awaiting Annie to help her with the stays, petticoats and grand array she intended to wear for the night. She would never allow herself, as Queen Mary's lady, to appear any less stylish than the women of Elizabeth's Court. She was angry, feeling terribly betrayed and, despite her insistence to Rowan a few minutes ago, not at all sure what had happened. Had Elizabeth released Rowan from her presence just in time to prevent a rape? Had it been a warning to Dudley that she would always pull the strings?

She didn't know. She knew only that she missed her home more with each passing moment.

"God rot all the offspring that can be traced back to that wretched Henry VII," she said aloud, then froze, because Rowan was the grandson of James V of Scotland, the grandson of Henry VII of England. "The wretched legal offspring," she muttered then. "And God rot Queen Elizabeth especially," she added, feeling that would suffice for the moment.

Annie arrived at last. "Good heavens, but ye are in a state this afternoon, m'lass," Annie tsked.

"Court life does not agree with me," Gwenyth said.

"I think 'tis wondrous here," Annie said.

Gwenyth stared fiercely at her maid. "Enough," she groaned in aggravation. "Come make me regal enough for this assembly. I just don't like being . . . manipulated," Gwenyth murmured.

"Welcome to the masses," Annie said drily.

Gwenyth drew away. "Am I difficult?"

Annie paused, her hands on her hips, then

shook her head. "Y'er the Lady of Islington. I'm a servant. Y'er beneath the queens, and I am a pawn. And that be the world."

"A queen should never foolishly risk a pawn."

"Ah, but if a sacrifice is needed, surely it should be a pawn."

Gwenyth laughed suddenly. "I never knew you loved chess."

"It will come right, m'lady. I believe it will," Annie said gently.

Gwenyth turned around, letting Annie finish dressing her. The maid was setting the last pin into Gwenyth's hair when there was a tap at the door.

Gwenyth started.

" 'Tis a knock and nae a death sentence," Annie said, striding to the door.

It was Rowan. He appeared exceptionally tall, shoulders broad beneath his tartan mantle. And he was smiling, wearing that wicked look of rueful amusement that had once so irritated her and now seemed to slip around her heart.

"We've an appointment," he told her.

"An appointment?" she queried.

"Come." He stretched out a hand to her.

She joined him slowly and suspiciously. He laughed. "You'll like this plan — at least, I think you will. Are you coming, Annie?"

"Me? The likes of me?" Annie said, aghast.

"Aye, Annie, come along."

Warily, Annie followed. They found Thomas, straight and very correct, waiting for them in the hall. "If I may, good woman?" he said, and offered Annie his arm.

"Good heavens, what is this nonsense?" Annie asked.

"No nonsense. You'll see," Rowan assured her gravely. "I need you, Annie, to perform a service for the Lady Gwenyth and me."

"A service, m'laird?"

He laughed and started down the hall, and beneath his breath, Gwenyth realized, he was humming. His eyes lit up each time they fell on her. She acknowledged, looking at him, that nothing in her life had ever meant as much to her as this man, that she had never known such happiness as she had known in his arms. She had never realized the true depth of love until she had met him.

"Where are we going?" she queried softly.

"You'll see soon enough."

They seemed to walk the halls forever. And then, Gwenyth realized, they had come to the chapel.

He opened the door, urging her in. There was a single occupant in the room, a black-clad minister with a white collar waiting at the altar.

"Come in here, my lady," the minister said, beckoning. "And you, good man, good woman," he continued, addressing Thomas and Annie. "No doubt this could have been accomplished with much more style and decorum, but . . . as it stands, I am a bit nervous, having no real blessing but rather the impatient nod of the sovereign that I may do this. I haven't the leisure of the entire night."

Gwenyth stared at Rowan.

He smiled. "My dearest Lady Gwenyth, for such a lovely creature, you're looking a bit like a fish. Do close your mouth. Reverend Ormsby, you may begin."

"But . . . ?" Gwenyth said, still uncomprehending.

"Good heavens, my love." Rowan fell down upon one knee, taking her hand. "My dearest Lady Gwenyth MacLeod of Islington, will you do me the tremendous honor of becoming my wife?"

Tears stung her eyes. "But will this be legal?" she whispered.

"Before the eyes of God, no matter what prince of earth may not approve, I am pledging my heart to you."

"Will the couple please come before me?" the minister said, clearing his throat.

"That's us," Rowan told her.

"Oh, dear God," she choked, touching his face.

"Well?" he said. "Will you vow to be my wife?"

"With all my heart!"

He stood and drew her forward to stand before the altar, and the minister began to speak, though she barely heard his words.

At one point there was a sound from the rear of the chapel. Gwenyth turned to see that it came from Queen Elizabeth and Robert Dudley. Dudley appeared to have been dragged there. Elizabeth had set her hand upon his arm in a possessive manner. Oddly enough, the English queen had a very benign expression on her face and smiled at Gwenyth.

In the midst of her euphoria, Gwenyth knew that, once again, the Queen of England was playing her cards with room for a bluff. Undoubtedly Rowan had her permission for this hasty and secretive marriage to which she would not stand as official witness, though she would be a witness all the same, so that, when she chose, she could defend them . . .

Or back away.

Suddenly Gwenyth heard Rowan speak, words strong and sure as he promised to love her, honor her . . . she wasn't sure what else was said, for she still felt as if she were living in a dream.

The chapel was bare. There wasn't a flower to brighten the occasion. There were no players, no music. Yet she couldn't have been anywhere on earth more magical than the whitewashed chapel with its simple ornamentation. She could scarcely believe the woman she had been hating for treating her so lightly was standing there, the most powerful person in the country, granting their union.

Most of all, she couldn't believe that Rowan was by her side, and that he loved her. That he was taking her as his wife.

The room was spinning, but she fought it.

When it was her turn to say her vows, her voice quivered. She could not stop it. Her feelings were sure and true, but there was such a tremor in her voice. . . .

It was certainly the most beautiful ceremony that had ever been, a beauty accomplished by the perfection of Rowan's vows alone.

And then Reverend Ormsby pronounced them man and wife.

"Do kiss your bride, Lord Rowan," he said.

And he kissed her. A kiss like so many others . . .

A kiss so different.

Remarkably, unbelievably, miraculously . . . she was his wife.

CHAPTER FOURTEEN

It was a time when all the world seemed right, so right that there were moments when Gwenyth could not help but feel a twinge of guilt. She was living beneath a foreign queen and in a foreign land, but she had never been happier.

Christmas came and went. A miraculously happy time.

And still, they resided in London.

Easter came. Another joyous occasion, although Gwenyth was well aware it would be much different if she were in Edinburgh, at Mary's Court. Here, too, there was pageantry, but of a far more muted kind than would be found at Mary's behest.

On Good Friday, they atoned. On Easter Sunday, they celebrated.

And a new season began.

But Gwenyth knew they had not been given the distant blessing of a woman such as Elizabeth without giving something in return, and she wondered what price they would have to pay — and when. But most of the time she put such fears out of her mind, and living was nothing but sheer joy, days and nights completely at their leisure, royal outings to be taken if they so chose, and endless time alone. Sometimes it was the magnitude of her happiness that actually frightened Gwenyth, knowing, as she did, the fate of Catherine Grey, who'd had her marriage declared null and void by her monarch, and who still resided in the Tower, while her husband was kept in other quarters, her two babes well-tended but illegitimate. But whether Elizabeth was a legal witness to their marriage or not, she had approved it. Gwenyth could only pray that Mary was eager to placate Elizabeth, and that there would be no difficulty when they returned to Scotland and presented their queen with the fact of their marriage. She was convinced of Mary's kindness, as she reiterated to Elizabeth, never forgetting her duty in the English capital.

She loved Rowan with all her heart; she was his wife. And there were moments when she knew she had achieved a happiness that few ever knew on earth, and she held that fact closely to her heart whenever she grew afraid.

There were many letters from Scotland, those Gwenyth received from Mary encouraging her in her ways, for Elizabeth had written to Mary to say that her "kind sister of Scottish soil" was doing much to endear her to the woman she had yet to meet. But Rowan, on the other hand, often received letters from Laird James Stewart, Earl of Moray, and James Stewart was not so pleased.

For Henry Stewart, Lord Darnley, had made his way to Scotland.

At first he had been one among many courtiers to amuse Mary, being a bit over her height and a man trained to be a perfect companion. He could hunt, play games, meander through a garden and was adept at one of Mary's favorite pursuits: dancing.

Then the man fell ill.

And when he fell ill, Queen Mary of Scotland fell in love.

They had been in London many happy months, living in Rowan's townhouse after receiving the queen's blessing to leave Hampton Court Palace, when Rowan received word that he was to return to Scotland.

Gwenyth was in the company of Queen Elizabeth, involved in a game of croquet that included the Spanish ambassador, when she learned that their idyll was over.

Maitland, Queen Mary's kindly envoy, approached and went through all the necessary greetings, complimenting Queen Elizabeth and her party. And then he said, "Lady Gwenyth, I have just left your husband. He is preparing for his journey."

"His journey?"

It seemed that her heart sank in her chest. Maitland had said *his* journey, not *their* journey.

"Laird Rowan is called immediately before our good queen's presence. You, m'lady, are to remain here."

She longed to shout, to disavow his words.

Elizabeth struck her ball with her mallet. "It will be best now if you are here," she said firmly.

There was an edge to Elizabeth's voice. Something had happened that Elizabeth did not like, and Gwenyth could only surmise that it had to do with Henry Stewart.

Elizabeth stared at her then. "You will send a letter, of course, to your dear Mary. You will make her understand that I am totally opposed to this marriage."

Gwenyth was angry, but she concealed her emotions. Obviously Queen Elizabeth and Maitland had information that she did not.

Had Mary of Scotland decided that she

would indeed marry Darnley?

Perhaps she shouldn't have been so surprised, but she knew Mary well. She had thought that Mary would never take a mere *subject* as her husband. Mary had a firm belief in her rights as queen. She had spoken about marrying for the benefit of the state and not for herself.

"Has . . . Queen Mary announced that she will wed Henry Stewart?" Gwenyth asked.

Again Queen Elizabeth whacked her ball. Hard.

Elizabeth was angry indeed.

But the English queen was complex. Why had she allowed Henry Stewart to return to Scotland if she had not meant for him to be a suitor for her "dearest cousin"? Had she been testing Mary's loyalty to her? Hoping to dangle temptation before her eyes, then deny it?

Elizabeth turned to her. "She seeks the approval of the princes of the Christian world. Since Lord Darnley has a tendency to listen to the great Protestant speakers and then attend Mass, the royalty of many countries will agree that it is a suitable marriage." She hit her ball so hard that it left the lawn entirely. "*I*, however, do not approve it."

"I should ride with my Lord Rowan and see Queen Mary," Gwenyth said.

"Rowan is going to attempt to mend the rift between Queen Mary and her brother, James Stewart. You are to stay here."

"But —"

"I have not ordered that it be so. The direct command has come from Mary, who is certain that you can somehow change my heart on this matter."

"I don't believe that I can do so!" Gwenyth said.

Elizabeth shrugged, looking away. She was a complete enigma. "Rowan will be back soon enough," she said.

That night Gwenyth returned to the town-house and ran to him, throwing her arms around him, clinging to him.

"My love, it's just a small parting," he told her.

Despite his words, she shivered.

A small parting.

She was tempted to tell him that they could defy their own queen, that he could give up his lands in Scotland, that she would willingly do the same.

But she knew that she could not. Rowan loved Scotland, as she did herself. He felt, she knew, that he might be able to bring peace between Lord James and his sister.

"When do you leave?"

"In the morning."

"We have tonight," she said simply.

And that was it. They had the night.

One night.

Gwenyth treasured, savored, every minute, every second, they lay together. She knew that in the days to come, she would need to close her eyes, remember every brush of his fingers, every whisper that left his lips, every nuance of his form and feeling.

There were moments of extreme passion, and moments of the utmost tenderness. They did not sleep through the long hours of the night, and in the time that they lay awake, they assured one another that their parting would be brief. But words were only words, and no matter how fervently they were spoken, Gwenyth couldn't escape her fear.

And yet, she knew, they could love so fiercely only because they were who they were. Were Rowan forced to repudiate his sense of love and duty for his country, she would destroy the very essence that made him the man he was.

She was not so sure about herself. She had served Mary with all her loyalty and trust. But she was afraid that when she returned, she would no longer know the woman to whom she had given so much faith and support.

At the first light of dawn, he pulled her into his arms. He made love to her one last time with a fierce ardor, with agonizing tenderness, gentle, volatile, cradling her in his arms as if welcoming her into his soul. She clung to him in return and dared to close her eyes.

Despite her deepest desire to hold him to the last, sleep overcame her.

When she opened her eyes again, he was gone.

■ ■ ■ ■

PART III

Passion and Defeat

■ ■ ■ ■

CHAPTER FIFTEEN

James Stewart was in a rage.

He was not at Court; he had used every excuse *not* to make appearances when commanded to do so.

"I despair," he told Rowan. "My sister arrived here with the best of heart, soul and intentions. She cared for the country. She charmed the people, earned their respect. Now . . . it is as if she has forgotten all her training regarding politics and government. She has simply gone mad."

Rowan held silent, a heavy dread upon his heart. It was more than sad to see Mary and her half brother so torn apart. It was deadly.

He didn't need to reply. James continued without pause, gesturing as he spoke. "The fellow was raised in England and is all but a servant of Elizabeth. His mother thinks she has a right to the crown of England, and if she marries her pretty lad of a son to Mary of Scotland, the entire family will become all the more puffed up."

"Elizabeth has stated unequivocally that she will not bless such a union," Rowan told James.

James shook his head. "Go to Mary, see for yourself. She has quite lost her mind. Her wedding is planned."

"And you don't intend to be there?" Rowan asked.

"Nay, I do not!" James said forcefully. "She would hand the country over to the boy's parents, the Earl and Countess of Lennox, and I tell you, the lairds here will not accept it."

"But they may, in time," Rowan told him. "If an heir to the kingdom is produced from the marriage, the people will rally to Mary, whether they are fond of her choice of husband or not."

"She has already styled him as king, though the parliament or privy council must approve," James stated irritably.

"There has to be peace between you two," Rowan said. "There must be — or there will be further civil strife."

"I will not see my sister hand over our father's realm," he said flatly. "You must go to her and take my letters."

And so it was that Rowan arrived in Edinburgh in time for Queen Mary's wedding to Henry Stewart, Lord Darnley.

There had been changes at the queen's court, he saw. She had a new secretary, an Italian man named Riccio, and though her dear Marys were still all in attendance, there were several new young Frenchwomen and a few young Scottish women of high birth.

He was not even invited to see the queen before the wedding, which was to take place the following day in the chapel at Holyrood, though James's letters were at least taken to her.

The queen did not wear the traditional white but was dressed in black, with a great black hood, elegant and becoming certainly, but a clear announcement that she came into the marriage as a widow, the dowager queen of France. She exchanged her vows with Henry Stewart, and, as he watched, Rowan was deeply dismayed at the spectacle. He'd thought he had come to know Mary. She was passionate, strong-minded, and possessed of the deep belief that she had been born to be queen, that it was her right to rule. How could that woman have fallen in love with such a shallow manipulator?

He told himself that he had no right to judge. He even imagined, with a certain amusement, that Mary might well have first fallen head over heels in love with Darnley simply because the man was an inch or so taller than she was. He was golden and lean and, according to all reports, extremely adept at hunting and dancing, two of Queen Mary's greatest loves.

But there was something about the man that was unsettling. He was too golden. Too young. He lacked the strong character that the Scottish people would have adored and embraced in a king.

Soon after the ceremony, the queen abandoned her widow's elegant black as the feasting and celebration began, and at last Rowan was able to speak with her when he led her out to the dance floor.

Mary was euphoric. She didn't begin with questions about matters of state. Rather, she said, "Oh, Laird Rowan, is he not the perfect prince?"

He didn't want to lie to Mary. "It's certainly wonderful to see you so happy, Your Grace."

A strange look contorted her features. "She is envious, that is all," she said.

"Your Grace?"

"Elizabeth. It is because she will not choose a husband for herself, and she cannot accept that another monarch might do so and still fulfill her obligations. Tell me, how is Gwenyth doing? Well, I believe. Maitland has told me that my cousin finds her fascinating and honest. I must have Gwenyth with her, continuing to support me, especially if my dear husband and I quickly conceive an heir. Then the line of sucession *must* be drawn in my direction."

He lowered his head, understanding the ambition of royals, yet not understanding why it could not be enough to rule Scotland.

"She will, in her own loyal way, sway Elizabeth where others might not," Mary said calmly.

"You have yet to meet Elizabeth," he said warily.

"Yes — because she continually finds a reason why we should not."

"Your Grace, there are serious matters that I must discuss with you."

"In time. Here is the crux of your return. Will my brother beg my pardon?"

"Your brother loves you," he said.

"My brother loves power," she said, and stopped dancing to the music she so loved and stepped back, staring at him. "You will return to James. You will convince him that I will not turn from my husband. He will beg my pardon or he will be outlawed."

"I will go to him with your words," he

said. "Your Grace, I would like to request that you call my Lady Gwenyth back to your service."

Her eyes widened. "Are you mad? She is dearly needed where she is. Of all my ladies, Scots by birth or no, she is best suited to be there as my representative."

"I have married her, Your Grace," he said softly.

He was astounded by the fury in the queen's eyes. "Does everyone seek to defy me now? I care not what trivial games you played together on your journey, you are not married! I will not have it! How dare you bow to Elizabeth and seek her sanction, rather than mine!"

He was stunned. "Your Grace, you must now know to what lengths passion can drive a man or a woman. I beg you —"

"You have offended me, Laird Rowan," she said icily. "And you will not disturb my celebration further by impressing upon me the disloyalty of my subjects. Go to my brother. Perhaps you can learn to repent together!"

With that, she walked from the dance floor and slipped immediately into the arms of her new boy-husband. Rowan stared after her, still shocked by her anger.

He watched her as she walked with the

golden boy-king into the center of the room, and shook his head. This marriage was not destined to be what the queen dreamed, but there was no one here who would dare tell her so or to whom she would listen in any case. Henry Stewart was tall; she would never see that his height did not give him either wisdom or strength.

As he rode from Edinburgh, he told himself that Mary's reign would survive because it had to. She had been only an infant when her father had died, but her mother, Mary of Guise, had been an excellent regent, despite her religion, despite the English, despite the constantly feuding nobles.

Then, after the death of the Scottish dowager queen, James Stewart had ably and cautiously kept the government in good form.

But now . . .

An heir.

The Queen of Scotland needed an heir.

Once that was achieved, so much would be forgiven. And perhaps there would even be an agreement with Elizabeth, who continued to play at marriage negotiations and use them to her own benefit. He didn't believe, however, that Elizabeth meant to accept any offer that might compromise her rule. Unlike Mary.

In time, though, Mary would see reason. Surely.

At the moment, however, he was certainly in disgrace.

So be it. He did love Scotland, but he had learned that he could live happily as a man, as a *husband.*

He rode to find James Stewart where the man waited at his own estates.

Waited and, Rowan feared, plotted.

Gwenyth despaired as she read the letter she had received from Mary Fleming, who had succumbed to the advances of Maitland and agreed to be his wife. Gwenyth couldn't help but feel a sense of resentment at first — the queen was so willing to be kind to others, yet she had been so unwilling to discuss the idea of *her* possible marriage.

But it was because of Maitland that she was able to receive the letter, and she devoured it eagerly.

Not one of us approved of Darnley, and we are still horrified, so you must, of course, burn this letter once you've read it lest it fall into evil hands. Gwenyth, you can't imagine how we see this man

— and how the queen sees him. It is sheer insanity. In his speech he is grumbling and as selfish as a child. He thinks he is greatly deserving, that the nobles will all bow down before him. He can't see that most loathe him and his scrambling parents, and that they fear the Lennox power in Scotland.

I love our good Queen Mary as do you, but I fear this marriage. Please don't think I am anything less than loyal; I pray that it may all end well despite the signs.

I don't understand what happened; the queen wouldn't speak about it. But she argued with Laird Rowan — right on the dance floor in the midst of her marriage celebrations! Be warned; she is of such a temper that she defies even those she loves and admires when there is any threat of disrespect to Lord Darnley. She is still convinced that you will have more power with Elizabeth than a hundred men who speak of nothing but state. I miss you, Gwen, as do we all. Take the gravest care with all that you say and do; we are in dangerous times.

Setting the letter down, Gwenyth stared at the fire burning low in the hearth of the master's chambers at the town house.

She had received a letter from Rowan earlier, and he had described the wedding, but he had left out any mention of his own argument with the queen. He had told her only that the rift between the queen and her brother, Laird James Stewart, was widening, and that he was a futile messenger, going from one to the other, praying for peace.

Gwenyth rose, distracted.

Her days were not miserable. Annie was with her, and Thomas was a capable and gentle man, taking care that all went well.

She was not a member of Elizabeth's court, and she preferred to keep her distance. Each time she was summoned to attend Elizabeth, she was careful to remember her role as Mary's subject. She did not harp upon the subject of her own queen, but she *was* careful to take advantage of every opportunity to mention her talents, her morality, her steadfastness, all her strengths as Queen of Scotland and potential heiress to the English crown. Elizabeth, however, seemed to be baiting her. When she needed amusement, she called upon Gwenyth for games of cat and mouse.

And to be honest, since Mary's marriage to Darnley, their conversations had become very difficult. Elizabeth was most emphatically enraged, and her temper was such that it was difficult to broach the simple truth: *she* had been the one to bless the return of the Lennox household to Scotland. *She* had all but ordered Henry Stewart, Lord Darnley, north, to her cousin's court.

There were times when Gwenyth wondered if Elizabeth didn't long to be happy, as it seemed the Scottish queen was happy. She had probably dangled young Lord Darnley out there as a temptation, just to see what would happen, assuming he would entertain Mary, but Mary would consider herself far too royal to marry a mere subject.

There was a knock at the door, and her heart leapt. It was foolish, she knew, but she prayed each time someone arrived that Rowan had returned. He would never knock at his own door, of course, a thought that allowed her to smile, even though she felt a bitter disappointment in her heart at the realization.

Thomas entered after knocking and said, "My lady, the queen requests your presence."

"I see. For what occasion?" Did the queen want her attendance at a dinner? Was she interested in a game of some sort?

"She has news to impart to you."

"I see," Gwenyth said, and stared at

Thomas, hoping that he knew something.

But he shook his head and said, "I don't know what has happened, my lady."

"Thank you. Well, then, I will get ready to go to court."

As she rode Rowan's barge down the Thames, she tried to count the days he had been gone. It seemed as if it had been forever. She wanted so desperately to see him again. She knew, and she understood, that there would be times when they had to be parted; he had been serving Scotland far too long to forget his love of his country now.

And fate had put her in a like position, though she still, in her heart, resented the fact it had been so easy for Mary to send her away.

When she arrived at court, she was quickly met by Maitland, who looked at her sadly.

"What is going on?" she whispered to him anxiously.

"More trouble, I fear. God save our queen, but her temper is something of late."

She didn't have to ask him which queen; Maitland was loyal to Mary.

One of Elizabeth's personal servants met them outside the queen's chamber. There Maitland stopped. "She has asked to speak with you alone," he said.

Worried, Gwenyth found herself escorted in. Elizabeth was actually in bed. She looked worn and impatient.

"Your Grace. You're not well," Gwenyth said with concern.

Elizabeth waved a hand in the air. "An ague, and exhaustion. I'm not so ill, I promise you. I refuse to die, you know."

Gwenyth lowered her head, smiling.

"Ah, you mustn't laugh, my dear lady. I mean it. All this fuss over my crown when I die . . . I shall simply live, and that is all."

"I pray that you do so for as long as a woman may," Gwenyth told her.

Again, Elizabeth smiled. "I believe you mean it," she murmured. She eyed Gwenyth then with a gentle expression. "Well, there is nothing to do but tell you what I have heard, and through reliable sources, and what I intend to do. First, I am sending you to the Tower."

Gwenyth gasped, so stunned she nearly fell.

"Do sit," Elizabeth said drily. "I am having you incarcerated as a show of my anger."

"Your anger?" Gwenyth breathed.

"With my cousin over this wretched Darnley affair. They were duly wed, and now they are off making an unseemly effort at creating an heir — thus twisting my arm ever further."

Gwenyth hesitated. "She told me once, when we first came to Scotland, that she found him fascinating. Very handsome. And that was only because he had been sent to give her his condolences at the death of Francis. Please . . . you must understand. She truly wants to please you, I believe. But she doesn't know you. And she . . . she is very passionate."

"So I hear," Elizabeth murmured.

"I mean to convey that she is a woman with a tremendous heart, a woman who needs and desires the proper husband."

"My point. He is not the proper husband."

"She is in love."

"Something you understand all too well."

"Aye."

"That," Elizabeth said very softly, "is the truth of why I'm sending you to the Tower."

"I admit, I am confused," Gwenyth said.

There was a sparkle in Elizabeth's eye. "It will only be for a short time."

"I am certainly grateful to hear that," Gwenyth said fervently.

"Mary, Queen of Scots, has stated that you are not legally married. She is furious with Laird Rowan, despite his efforts to bring about peace between Mary and her barons. She has outlawed her brother, James

Stewart, and Laird Rowan with him. James has been appealing to me for asylum. I, of course, will have to keep my eye on events. I do not believe in usurping a proper monarch, but many of the nobles feel as James Stewart does, that Mary is no longer fit to rule, that she has given in completely to the whims of her new husband and no longer seeks the sage and learned advice of those who would consider the well-being of the whole of Scotland, not only their own quest for personal gain."

Gwenyth had remained standing though her limbs felt weak. She had heard only the first words Elizabeth had spoken.

She had no legal marriage.

"Mary has also written, demanding your return."

Gwenyth exhaled. "I see. But . . . I'm going to the Tower?"

"Because, my dear, I have decided to befriend you. You have offered me nothing but complete honesty, and it is a travesty that Mary is seeking some petty vengeance against you while she dallies in her foolish passion."

"I'm sure . . . I'm sure that Queen Mary will rise to the occasion," Gwenyth managed to whisper.

She couldn't believe that her queen had

turned from her so completely, and yet she knew that Elizabeth was not lying.

"Well, you will understand then why I am sending you to the Tower. Since the Queen of Scotland refuses to recognize your marriage and your husband is outlawed for his friendship with James Stewart, being my guest for the time being will be best for your health — and that of the health of the child you are carrying."

Gwenyth lowered her eyes, feeling more and more as if the world were slipping away from her. She had only recently realized that what Elizabeth had said was true.

They were expecting a child.

It should have been the happiest occasion in the world.

It *was* the happiest occasion.

But she desperately longed to have her child's father with her, and she couldn't help but be furious that Mary, whom she had served so loyally, had turned a blind eye to her happiness. And it was difficult to imagine, as well, that Mary — who had once turned so trustingly and correctly to her half brother James — now not only repudiated him but also, apparently, any man who was his friend.

"The Tower is not so terrible a place, though it has witnessed a great deal of horror. I have been a guest there myself, you know," Elizabeth said. "You will have complete freedom within the walls," she added.

"Thank you," Gwenyth murmured.

"I won't have you arrested until tomorrow," Elizabeth told her.

"Annie may come with me?"

"Naturally."

Laird Maitland was waiting for her outside of the queen's private quarters.

"I'm going to the Tower," she told him flatly.

He nodded. "I believe it will be best, for now."

Gwenyth looked at him with a frown. "Why would Mary do this to me?" she asked.

He looked away. "Elizabeth is sending you to the Tower, not Mary."

"Mary has made Rowan an outcast and declared our marriage void in the eyes of Scotland. What has happened? She needed me so much, relied on me. And now I am . . . disposable!"

"Ah, lass, let things simmer down a bit. It's hard to imagine that she will not make peace with her brother. But you have to understand, Laird James is all but threatening a rebellion. I believe that he has asked Elizabeth for aid."

"Will she fight Mary?"

Maitland shook his head. "I have had long discussions with her envoy, Lord Throgmorton. Long discussions. Elizabeth is insistent that Mary's right as queen be protected. If she were not, she would jeopardize her own position, you see."

"She would not fight even for the cause of Protestantism?"

Maitland laughed with little amusement. "Mary claims that she has no grudge against the Church of Scotland but will not see the Catholics in Scotland persecuted. James claims that his sister is growing too fond of her Catholic cause. Quite frankly, at this point, it is a power struggle and nothing more. But many of the barons of Scotland — whether they dare speak with Laird James now or not — loathe Darnley and his rule. Then again, many of them will loathe any man who rises when they do not."

"What will come of all this?" Gwenyth asked worriedly.

"Let's pray for peace. In the meantime, it will appear that you are Queen Mary's loyal subject, so loyal that you will gladly sit in the Tower of London for her. In the meantime," he added softly, "you will have your child. Discreetly. When the time is right, do not fear, the Queen of Scotland will bless your marriage. You need have no fear for yourself or the babe. Just be patient."

"I don't even know where Rowan is."

"Nor do I, at this moment. But do not fear. I believe in my heart that all will be well. If we didn't have faith, we couldn't continue on each day, could we?"

"Each day seems an eternity," Gwenyth said.

"But we fight each day." His eyes twinkled. "Some fight with swords, and some fight with words. I will serve the queen. My queen. And I will have faith and pray for the best. As must you."

"But Rowan —"

"Rowan knows how to manage in this world."

"You are declared an outlaw as well, you know," James fumed furiously to Rowan. James was packing his bags, getting ready to flee across the border.

Rowan had never intended to go to war against the queen, but James had been willing to take a stand against his younger half sister. But Mary had gained something in Scotland they had once fervently hoped for: the love of the people. Riding into Edinburgh while his sister and her new bridegroom traveled north to visit her lands,

James had not found the support he needed to force a showdown that would keep Henry Stewart and his ambitious family from rising any higher.

Now word had come that Mary, having been told about his defiance of her rule, had ordered his arrest. A series of secret communications between James and Elizabeth had ensued, leading to this planned flight. Rowan was sorry the Scottish laird did not know the English queen as he did.

Elizabeth was a master of double-talk. She had promised Laird James nothing, though she had not refused him.

As ever, she would watch which way the wind blew.

Rowan had heard that he had been declared an outlaw, as well, but he didn't believe Mary meant her threats against him; he had done nothing but try to ease her every waking moment. He had been the messenger she had requested time and time again. He did not seek power, only the well-being of his nation.

Admittedly, he resented the queen, and with good reason, but he had not betrayed her, had never said a word against her. Even in her fierce denial of his marriage, he had not turned on her in any way.

"There has to be a way to solve this,"

Rowan told James.

"There is. I'm going over the border," James told him. Rowan was not surprised. He had found James deep in the Lowland stronghold of Laird MacConaugh, a staunch Protestant lord who held lands so close to England that he could come and go at will.

"I will ride south and seek an audience with Elizabeth. You must ride with me. You can hasten such an event."

"James, we must break this stalemate. There must be peace between you and your sister. You are the very heart of Scotland to many people. To many nobles —"

"Our nobles are as fickle as the wind."

"And the wind changes," Rowan agreed wearily. "You have to understand. I must stay and try to make the queen see reason."

"She is too infatuated with that ridiculous fop to see reason," James said.

"Aye." Rowan hesitated. "But her infatuation will end."

James hesitated. "Stay, then. Tell her that I felt I had to leave, that I feared for my life, because she has come so thoroughly under the domination of her husband and his family. But, my friend, unless she quickly sees the fault in Lord Darnley . . . there is little hope for real peace in Scotland."

"I love Scotland. I want it to be a country

of peace, a place where I may at long last raise a family. Where my sons may grow up proud."

James smiled grimly. "Perhaps, then, you should travel with me. And visit your illegal bride."

"Don't you think I'm anxious to return to her?" Rowan asked, shaking his head. "I have to make my peace with Mary first."

"Godspeed, then," James told him.

That night, as Rowan neared Edinburgh, riding alone on Styx, he saw a party of twenty horsemen riding forward to greet him.

To his amazement, one of them, a man he had never seen before, rode ahead of the others, challenging him. "Laird Rowan Graham, Earl of Lochraven?"

"Aye. I've come to wait for the return of Queen Mary," he said. "I seek an audience, on behalf of Laird James Stewart and the health of the realm."

"You are under arrest, m'laird."

"I am under arrest?" he repeated.

"For high treason."

"You jest."

"I do not," the man said. Then he swallowed uneasily, his Adam's apple bobbing. He lowered his voice when he spoke again.

"Would that I were jesting, Laird Rowan," he said. "God, would that I were." He looked nervous, uneasy.

"Who are you, man?" Rowan demanded.

"Sir Alan Miller."

"Your accent is English."

"I am in the service of . . . Lord Darnley." He lowered his head. "Your arrest has been charged to me."

And he was most unhappy about that fact, Rowan knew.

He looked at the rest of the men who had come to take him into custody. He didn't recognize any of them. They were not the warriors who had defended Scotland through the years. This was a group that had gained power through Dudley or his father, the earl of Lennox. They were not an impressive group. Styx was a far finer mount than any of those ridden by these men. He sincerely doubted that any of them knew a thing about swordplay.

He could run. . . .

He did not want to fight. He didn't fear for his own life, only that he would be forced to kill too many men, and he did not want to have murder added to the charges against him. The queen might well have him tried for treason, but there were far too many lairds of honesty and sobriety to see

405

him convicted.

"If it is the queen's pleasure that I should be under arrest, then I submit to your authority, good sirs," he said.

Alan Miller let out an audible sigh. "You will be taken to Edinburgh Castle, and there held, until trial."

"At your leisure, Sir Alan."

The man rode closer to him. "I must take your sword and your knife."

Rowan handed over his weapons. It was cold, but the young fellow was sweating profusely. His hands shook as he took the sword.

Rowan set his own hand on the younger man's arm. "You don't need to fear me. I am coming of my own will."

Alan Miller looked at him, swallowed, then nodded. "God protect you, sir," he said quietly.

"Shall we?" Rowan said.

And so he returned to Edinburgh and the queen's service, he thought bitterly.

CHAPTER SIXTEEN

Word regarding Rowan's incarceration in Edinburgh reached Gwenyth in a cruel way.

She knew her time of confinement was approaching soon, but beneath a great cloak, her condition was scarcely noticeable. She had trusted few people with the truth of her pregnancy, due to the strangeness of her situation. She had never known that such an about-face could occur, that she could be so "loved" by the queen she served that she could only find safety by being imprisoned by another.

After the first anxious, torturous months, she had learned there was nothing to do but practice patience and find activities to keep her occupied. The only word she had at first came from Mary herself — who bade her to remember obedience and ordered her to continue to keep reminding the English queen at every opportunity that the fate of England rested on recognizing Mary as her heir. Mary wrote to her that she was a good and beloved friend. She didn't mention a word about Rowan or her marriage.

The four Marys kept up with letters to her, as well, but they tended to be very chatty, and offered no real information. She wondered if they were afraid their correspondence might be read.

Time passed so slowly, and she received no word at all from Rowan, which disturbed her greatly. But she had to make the time pass, and, despite her own sick fervor and worry, she couldn't allow herself to fall ill.

She had the babe to think about. And when she felt too sorry for herself, she unwaveringly ordered herself not to die in childbirth. She intended to make nothing easy for those who were tormenting her — which, she sadly admitted to herself, meant Mary of Scotland. In her own letters she took great care with her words, going back and forth daily on whether or not to pour out her heart to the queen, to appeal to the woman who was so madly in love with Darnley that she should have been the first one to understand similar feelings in a loyal subject.

But she hesitated, afraid to speak freely to Mary after what Elizabeth told her and after learning more and more about the situation from Maitland. Mary was no longer the woman she had known; Darnley had changed her.

So Gwenyth sought to pass the time well, walking in the courtyard, tending to her mind, her spirit and her health. She knew that Mary of Scotland passed many a government council meeting by sewing or embroidering, but those were arts that, sadly, she had not mastered herself. Instead she kept a journal. Her life as a prisoner wasn't entirely wretched. She was being held in the Beauchamp Tower of the great fortification, and she was free to attend services in the White Tower on Sundays, and free to roam the halls there. The wardens had begun to display arms from throughout the centuries in the Tower, and she could roam at will and study the various forms of defense, and the ways they had changed over the years. There was an excellent library, and she was welcome to make free use of the books.

Elizabeth was not at all a cruel jailer; she even sent for Gwenyth upon occasion, though she did so in secret. As time passed, she grew less and less prone to discuss Mary Stuart and her husband. Gwenyth knew, however, that Elizabeth did not wish her ill.

Then, as Gwenyth walked the Tower

grounds with Annie one day, she walked straight into another of the "guests."

She hadn't known Margaret Douglas, Countess of Lennox and the mother of Lord Darnley; she hadn't even known the woman was back in England until she had heard, through gossip, that the woman was in the Tower, as well, arrested on the queen's order due to her son's marriage, which Elizabeth had not sanctioned.

Margaret Douglas was a woman with her own connection to the throne of England. Her mother had been Margaret Tudor, Queen Mary's grandmother, through Margaret Tudor's second marriage to a Scottish earl. She was still a grandchild of Henry VII, and therefore had her own place in the line of succession.

These days, she was certainly feeling extremely bitter about her "cousin" Elizabeth's ill treatment of her. Slim, agile, still attractive, with a strong face and a stronger stance, she strode toward Gwenyth with long and furious steps.

They had never met, but Gwenyth instantly realized who she must be and would have greeted her politely, but she was given no chance.

Lady Margaret Douglas raised a finger and pointed it at her. "You! They say the

410

queen writes more letters on your behalf than any other. But that cannot be true. I am Henry's mother! I have royal blood in my veins, while you . . . you are whore to that wretched man who spurned his righteous queen and took up with the likes of James Stewart, the ungrateful bastard child of the king who was my half brother's child. Wretched little witch, you must have the queen enchanted. But trust me, you will rot in hell, just as he rots in Edinburgh Castle now. They will proclaim him a traitor, and he will die a traitor's death!"

The maid who was walking with the countess quickly set a hand upon the woman's arm, while Annie stepped in front of Gwenyth like a bulldog, as if expecting the other woman to attempt physical violence. One of the castle guards came rushing forward, as well.

The countess had evidently not lost her mind entirely, even if she dared much because of her Tudor blood. She satisfied herself by spitting on the ground at Gwenyth's feet and walking away.

"M'lady!" Annie said, turning to her.

Gwenyth knew she had gone pale. No one had told her that Rowan was being held in Edinburgh. That he had been accused of *treason.*

"I'm fine," she told Annie, and stared at her maid, "Why didn't you tell me? You had to know. Someone out there had to know!"

Annie's face betrayed her. She had known. Just as Queen Elizabeth had known.

"You can't be upset, my dear, dear lass," Annie insisted. "Think of the babe . . ." She trailed off, staring at Gwenyth, who stared back at her, a crooked grin of pain and irony upon her lips.

"The babe?" she said, as if in question. "The babe is coming."

Gwenyth actually welcomed the pain of childbirth; it kept her from worrying so frantically about the fate of her baby's father.

Treason.

It was a dire accusation. Men and women were executed for such a crime. He might die never knowing his child. In fact, she thought wildly, she didn't even know if he had been told that she was expecting.

Then, when her child was born, when he gave out a lusty wail and Annie announced that she had a beautiful and healthy son, she forgot even the father as she cradled her infant with awe.

He had come with a full head of hair and blue eyes. Ten fingers, ten toes. She counted.

He was miraculous. He was so perfect. He was . . . *hers.*

And Rowan's.

She forced herself to banish fear from her mind for just a moment and lay in pure wonderment, watching him greet his new life, adoring him when he cried, falling in love with him all over again as he suckled. She wouldn't let Annie take him away until the midwife insisted that she must have some rest, and even then, it was only due to the hefty brandy she was given that she was able to sleep.

When she awoke, she cried out, and Annie saw to it that the babe was brought instantly to her side. Once again she counted his fingers and toes, stared into the grave little eyes that seemed to return her stare, and lay amazed.

It was only later that worry slipped back into her mind with a vengeance.

What if his father was about to lose his head, or hang by the neck? Worse, Scottish traitors sometimes had to face the horrible fate of being drawn and quartered. . . .

When she cried aloud, Annie hushed her with a stern warning. "You'll make the babe sick. You'll not be able to nurse him yourself, if you ruin your milk by growing so upset."

Gwenyth didn't know if such a thing was

possible, but she dared not ignore the warning, so she tried to reassure herself by insisting that they could not execute Rowan. They could not possibly believe him a traitor.

But she knew that they could. How many had died near the very place where she had birthed her child? Tyburn tree sat just beyond these walls. Thousands had died there. Thousands who were surely innocent of the charges they had faced.

This was England, but Scotland, her beloved Scotland, could be just as cruel. Laws and lands were only as just as those who ruled them, and Mary — this Mary — was not the even-handed queen she once had been.

Thomas came to see the babe, and as he tenderly held the child, he, like Annie, tried to reassure her.

"The Queen of Scots will not dare harm Laird Rowan. She continually postpones his trial, knowing that far too many nobles will rally to her brother's side if she raises a hand against a man who has been known as nothing but fair, who has never done anything other than fight for Scotland. You'll see, m'lady. The lad's father will be fine."

"Thomas, you have to tell me. What was his crime? Did he take up arms against the queen?"

"No, he did not. He was arrested merely for his association with James. The people are for him. He might have run, might have fought, but he did not. He trusted in his queen. She will not execute him. He has never grasped for power, has refused to kill when there was no battle. Neither the nobles nor the people would stomach his execution, and the queen well knows that."

"You told me none of this," Gwenyth said accusingly.

"There seemed no reason, my lady," Thomas said. "We didn't want you upset. It could have been dangerous for the babe."

"He needs a proper name," Annie reminded her. "We must all think of a perfect name for a perfect child."

"Rowan, for his father," Gwenyth said.

"Ah, perhaps, just perhaps, it's not my decision . . . but my laird's father was called Daniel. Perhaps Daniel Rowan," Thomas suggested.

Gwenyth said the name aloud. "Daniel Rowan Graham."

"You must do as you wish," Thomas said.

"Daniel Rowan Graham," Gwenyth repeated. "That is his name. And he must be baptized here, and quickly, as well as quietly."

Both Thomas and Annie were silent for a moment, knowing it was sadly true that the child should be baptized quickly. Infants died easily, and none would have a child depart to the next life without being duly baptized.

Arrangements were quickly made. As they had stood to witness her wedding, Gwenyth knew none but these two must stand as her son's godparents.

"Ah, dear lady, you need finer folk than us to be godparents to this child," Thomas told her. "You need godparents with power and riches —"

"No," she informed him bitterly, for those with power and riches had seemed to turn on her. "I will have you, who love him, stand for him before God."

Thomas and Annie looked at one another, and it was agreed.

Daniel was but a few days old, a beautiful, sound, lusty baby, when he was brought to the chapel and duly baptized. The ceremony was performed by Ormsby, the same minister who had spoken her wedding rite, and she was pleased.

At the last minute they were startled by a noise at the back of the chapel. When Gwenyth turned, afraid — and instantly

416

ready to do battle for the life of her infant son — she saw that Elizabeth had come. "Proceed," Gwenyth told Ormsby, unsure what the queen's advent presaged.

In the end, the Queen of England did not partake in the ceremony in any way, but she was there, just as she had been for Gwenyth's marriage to Rowan.

And when the baptism had ended, Elizabeth told Gwenyth that a small supper had been set up in the Beauchamp Tower, and she would speak with her there.

As they sat together over the meal, Elizabeth did not touch the babe, but she admired him. Gwenyth wondered if she looked at the child and perhaps wondered what it would be like to have such a son herself, an heir to the English crown. But there was something in her stance and resolve that told Gwenyth she was determined to manage her world alone in her lifetime. As she watched her cousin's difficulties across the border, no doubt Elizabeth realized anew that she was a female ruler in a man's world. She was tenacious, and she didn't mean to allow anyone to dispute her claims, her decision on a mate. Therefore, there would be no mate.

Beside the cradle, which had belonged originally to the first Daniel Graham and had been brought from the town house, Elizabeth handed Gwenyth a rolled parchment, complete with the royal seal.

"Thank you," Gwenyth murmured, curious at the gift, too well-mannered to open it then.

Elizabeth smiled. "It's a land grant. A tract in Yorkshire. Safe behind well-established English lines, close enough to your native Scotland. It is his —" she said, nodding toward the baby "— and his alone. He is the newly created Lord of Allenshire." She inhaled. "I think it best *not* to announce his birth now. But, due to the service and pleasant company of both his parents, I am delighted to offer him my protection."

Gwenyth was silent, feeling both gratitude and a chill sweep over her. His father might have perished already. She herself might never be able to return home.

But Daniel had a royal protector.

She went down on one knee, taking Elizabeth's hand. "From the bottom of my heart, I thank you for your gift."

"You're welcome. I seldom meet people who are completely honest with me — especially while serving another." She smiled suddenly. "I have a better gift for you, I believe."

"There can be no better gift than Your

418

Majesty's protection," Gwenyth said.

Elizabeth was amused. "But there is. My dear cousin Mary is said to be giving birth soon. She has sent a letter, begging that I give you leave to go to her. I have written to her in reply, suggesting that she release those prisoners she herself holds unjustly." She lowered her voice. "The gift I grant you is time with your child. It is my strong suggestion that you *not* take him to Scotland with you. You must convince the queen to give her blessing to your marriage first. You don't want this babe proclaimed a bastard."

Gwenyth gritted her teeth, lowering her head. The world seemed to spin. She suddenly knew what it was like to be more than willing to die for another. She would fight until her last breath for her child — even if that meant leaving him in England while she went north, there to fight for herself and her husband.

"You have given me such tremendous gifts," Gwenyth said to Elizabeth. "I am beyond grateful, and I cannot possibly repay them."

"Your gift to me in return, Lady Gwenyth, will be for you to maintain your honesty and ethics. Royal personages, flattered day and night, appreciate words of truth. Now, there is someone who will come to see the child later this week, a rather sad and embittered fellow himself."

"Who?"

"James Stewart, Earl of Moray, who has come to my country seeking sanctuary. I cannot, will not, give him arms or a blessing to fight the rightful Scottish sovereign, Mary, even if his cause is mine and in my heart I believe it to be right."

The world seemed to sway in truth. James Stewart was here. His cause abandoned as he fled. She knew that he dared not return to Scotland now. And Rowan had been accused of supporting his rebellion!

"Thank you," she managed.

Elizabeth studied her. "I wish I could say that all will be well, but I'm afraid that I have lived through far too much to lie. I *can* tell you that I believe you will always do what's right, and that, surely, God will bless you."

Would God do so?

Put not thy faith in princes. . . .

She had to be strong. She had to believe.

James came at the end of the week. He was exceptionally joyful, given the fact that he was by nature dour and undemonstrative.

He had always been a good friend to Rowan, though, and to the queen. It was

420

sad that they should have had such a terrible falling out.

"When did you last see my Laird Rowan?" she asked him anxiously.

James told her when they had last met, in the Borders. "I think that, in time, his faith will prove justified," James assured her. "The Lennoxes fear his power, but then . . . Lady Lennox is here, is she not?" he asked with wry humor. Then he studied the child again. "Well, he is a mite, no more. Very fine head of hair. His father's hair, so it seems." He looked at her. "And the blood of a king flows in his veins, as well."

"Something that doesn't please me, I'm afraid," Gwenyth told him.

"Oh?"

"It seems to me that the children of kings are ever fearful of what the other children of kings may want."

James looked at her. "I would never have sought to hurt my sister. I only hoped to stop the tyrannical sway of the idiot she wed and keep his family from sheer lunacy, and the power-hungry barons from destroying my country in their thirst for control."

Gwenyth was silent as she wondered whether Mary knew and believed that her brother would never have harmed her, and she shivered.

She was surprised when James set a fatherly arm around her shoulders. "Mary will not execute Rowan," he said, apparently having discerned her thoughts. "You know how she feels about violence."

"Aye."

"Take comfort in that," James advised. "You've been summoned back to her side. Indeed, you have seen the way Mary writes. She has begged for your return. Though she does not know it, she needs you to bring some sense into her life."

"She must be so angry with Rowan to have imprisoned him."

"Go to her first as her friend, only then can you speak to her on Rowan's behalf."

"I'll try to remember all that you have said, and all that I have learned, being so often in your company."

James smiled, pleased. "You will leave soon. Godspeed."

She thanked him, assuring him that, somehow, he and Mary would find peace, too, though in truth, she wondered. Feared.

There was simply so little peace to be found when considering the lives of those of royal blood.

Gwenyth stayed a month more, quietly, in the Tower.

She was torn the entire time. She could not leave her babe when he was so young, yet she dared not tarry longer, even though every report that came from Scotland assured her that the queen was meeting with Rowan. She was resolute on putting off a trial, urging him to declare his absolute loyalty to her crown and her king.

Hearing some of the reports, Gwenyth secretly damned him.

Swear whatever she wants, she urged him silently. Save yourself.

But she knew Rowan, and he would opt for care, consideration and the truth. He would never swear an oath that he did not mean. And it wasn't that he didn't wholeheartedly serve his queen. He would simply refuse to pledge himself to Darnley or damn James Stewart, and that would be that.

Finally, the day came when she felt she had to leave her son in the care of Thomas, Annie and the nurse.

"Ye're beautiful," Annie said. "With the figure of a lass again, so quickly. Ach, at times, ye don't look old enough to be the mother of this fine child." There were tears in the older woman's eyes, a sign of her genuine sadness that she wouldn't be going to Scotland with her mistress, but Gwenyth had told her that she trusted no one other than his godparents to look after Daniel.

Gwenyth cried, holding Daniel, then kissing Thomas and Annie goodbye.

She had been given an English escort; they would see her to the Borders, where she would be met by a company of Scottish soldiers, who would lead her safely on to Edinburgh.

When she left the Tower itself, alone and by barge, she looked back.

Lady Margaret Douglas was on the lawn. Still imprisoned. She must have known that Mary had demanded Gwenyth's return and not her own. A chill fell over Gwenyth as the woman cried out, "Witch! Go on, harlot! She lets you leave, and not me, for you are a traitor to Queen Mary. Don't think they do not beg for my release. Mary has written endless letters on my behalf. She pleads with Elizabeth to release me. I am held unjustly. But you . . . you bring your spells and enchantments before the queen and now the king, *my son!* I know it's you — you who have caused the strife. They turn on my son because of witches like you. God will have his way. You will die, harlot witch, and the fires of hell will destroy you!"

The woman was insane, Gwenyth thought, driven mad because she'd plotted and planned to get her son married to the Queen of Scotland, but she was paying a price.

No, she wasn't insane, and that was what was most frightening. She was simply furious. She was being a mother, protecting her child.

She had no right to treat Gwenyth so cruelly, but that didn't matter. At some point, somehow, Gwenyth would have to find away to forgive the woman, even be friend her, for she was Mary of Scotland's mother-in-law, and Gwenyth was the queen's lady.

Gwenyth found herself praying that Elizabeth kept Margaret imprisoned in the Tower for a very long time.

Rowan's imprisonment was not without comfort, but for a man of action, it was exceedingly frustrating, for he was held to his room in the castle. There he spent endless days pacing, finding ways to release his pent-up energy, doing what he could to work his muscles. He was well taken care of, and he did not believe that Mary wished him ill. In her mind, he had conspired with James, and James had thoroughly drawn her wrath. She had lifted him up, given him titles and land, and he had shown her the worst possible ingratitude. Mary's greatest fault lay in her frankness; she was not a person for whom intrigue came easily. Rowan had learned he was not yet facing a trial because evidence of his treason was still being studied.

In early spring, Mary came to visit him, and she was not the same woman he had faced only months earlier.

He had heard that she was pregnant. In December, the rumors had begun, though it had been whispered that the queen was merely ill. Then news came that she was expecting, and that, he knew, was a moment of sheer joy for all of Scotland. Should Mary have died without issue, there might well have been anarchy. James was illegitimate, as were many other possible contenders for the crown. Darnley would be a candidate, but one so hated it would be almost impossible for him to rule, despite his Lennox associations.

She did not, however, appear to be an ecstatic mother-to-be when she came to the castle to speak with him, her "traitorous" subject. She came with a number of attendants, including her wizened new favorite, the musician and now her secretary, Riccio.

Rowan stiffened, knowing that not only

James but many of her nobles — even those loyal to her and her marriage — loathed the man. Only recently had the queen come to depend so desperately on him, and Rowan knew in his heart it was another mistake on her part.

Her husband, however, was not with her.

Rowan rose hastily, paying her the honor due her. "Leave us," she told the others. The warder hesitated, as if Rowan had been a bloodthirsty murderer rather than a loyal subject who had submitted to this degradation rather than create any possible conflict. He would have been resentful, had the queen not said impatiently, "Leave me. Good God, the man is my nephew. He will not harm me."

Everyone disappeared down the corridor, and the warder, still wary, closed the door at last.

"My deepest congratulations," Rowan said, nodding toward her swelling belly.

She arched a brow. "In this, at least, my marriage is a success."

He held his tongue; whatever she had just said, Mary did not wish to hear anyone preaching to her about her choice of husband. "I'm sure, Your Grace, that you will always do as you see fit. And Scotland will be grateful for an heir."

"The heir has not yet breathed his first," she pointed out.

"There is no reason for you to fear. You are young and have the strength of . . . of a queen," he said softly.

"I am sorry to do this to you," she told him.

"I believe that you are."

"But you have betrayed me."

"Never."

"You will not call James the traitor that he is."

"I never lifted arms against you."

"No," she said, and there was a petulant tone in her voice when she went on. "You were busy seducing one of my ladies."

"I love her, Your Grace."

"That is ridiculous."

"I beg your pardon?"

She waved a hand in the air, brushing him aside as she sat and turned away. He remained standing. "Only a fool believes in love."

She looked at him suddenly, her huge, dark eyes wide and haunted. "I have married Henry, married him before God. I have lifted him up. And he is a fool. A very pretty fool, but a fool nonetheless."

"He is your child's father."

"A pity," she said bitterly.

He kept silent, knowing there was nothing he could say that would not be a mistake.

"I have made this bed . . ." she murmured.

He knelt down before her, taking her hands, searching her face. "Mary, you are my queen. Scotland's queen. You entered into a marriage you deeply desired. You . . . chose to lift Darnley up as your . . . more than your consort."

She offered him a wry smile. "A Scottish parliament will never grant him the title of king in his own right. I see that now, and I see why. He cares nothing for government. He is vain and selfish. He wants only to hunt and gamble and drink . . . and spend his nights whoring, I imagine. What have I done?" she whispered.

"Mary, you have been a good queen. You must remain a good queen. You are the sovereign. If any at your side demand that you go against your own better judgment, deny them. Be the Queen Mary your subjects love, and don't let any man take that from you."

She nodded, offering him a slight smile. "I can't let you go, you know."

"I have never offered you harm. I have never offered you anything but my loyalty."

"I believe you."

"Then . . . ?"

"I can't let you go. I brought charges against you. Now they must be disproved."

"How do you suggest that I disprove your charges?"

"Publicly deny James. Call him the traitor that he is."

He lowered his head. "Mary, you have just said that —"

"That I married a weak-willed, spineless, debauched husband?"

He arched a brow to her, as always keeping silent rather than agreeing with such remarks.

She shook her head. "James played me falsely, acting as if the nobles would entertain such an alliance, then standing firmly against it. Elizabeth is quite right in the games she plays. She knows there is no man she can marry who her subjects will accept without going to war. It is truly not fair that queens must suffer this idiocy while kings do not. But the point is that James did not know enough about Henry to loathe him, he was simply furious with the shift of power."

"Perhaps he was insulted that his advice meant nothing once you met Darnley."

She shook her head sadly. "What has come between us . . . it is bitter. Because Henry's mother was such good friends with

Mary Tudor, because of my Catholicism . . . he thought that he could raise the Protestants against me. I have done nothing!"

"Mary, I beg you, reconsider your stance on Laird James. You two have been too close for you to let this divide go on forever."

She looked at him very seriously. "I should prize you deeply, but . . . you stand so hard on his behalf."

"But I don't stand against you."

She rose suddenly, walking across the room. "You do know that I was absolutely furious with Lord Bothwell. Then he escaped imprisonment here, and now he has wheedled his way back into my good graces."

He smiled. "Are you suggesting that I escape?"

"Would a queen suggest such a thing? Never!" she proclaimed. But then she leaned down by him where he remained upon one knee and planted a kiss on his cheek. "I needed to see you," she said. "I know that I can trust you, that you will not repeat my words. Good day, Laird of Lochraven."

She went out the door, and he did not hear the locks snick in her wake. Still, he waited, waited until the moon rose high over the castle walls.

The door was not locked.

He slipped out to the hallway. There was no guard. He strode to the winding stairs that led from the tower where he'd been incarcerated to the winding turret stairs that led straight to the yard. He kept close to the building as he stepped out into the night. A quick look up showed him that there were guards atop the parapets.

A movement in the night warned him that someone was near. He held dead still, waiting. He had no intention of doing murder now.

Someone moved furtively near him. He waited, taking great care, then shot out in the dark when the figure was almost upon him, catching the fellow unawares, his arm around the man's torso and his free hand clamped over the man's mouth.

"Don't betray me. I don't wish to hurt you."

A soft mumbling came in response. Still keeping the greatest care to constrain the man and see his face, he turned him, and a smile sprang to his lips.

It was Gavin.

Rowan released his hold and said in relief, "Gavin."

"My Lord, come. We need to hurry. I do not entirely know what is happening, but the queen's lapdog, that little whelp of a man Riccio, suggested that I come tonight with a hay wagon and a monk's cloak."

Riccio?

The mention of the man's name was not reassuring, but he had heard that the queen trusted him in all things, and so long as the man did the queen's bidding, not that of the nominal king . . .

"Where is the cloak?"

"Here, on the ground. I dropped it when I thought you were a guard near, intent on slitting my throat."

"I'm sorry. I thought *you* were a guard."

"Well, here we are, and I suggest that we hurry."

Gavin stooped quickly to retrieve the lost bundle of coarse brown wool. Rowan immediately slipped the cloak over his head and around his shoulders, pulling the hood low.

"This way," Gavin said softly.

Rowan bent his head as if in deep prayer, and clasped his hands together before him. They passed by a number of people busy at their assigned tasks, even so late in the night. A silversmith was rolling up his tarp, a tinker closing the cover over his basket of needles and small wares.

"The wagon is yonder," Gavin said.

They did not walk too fast, nor did they go too slow. As they reached the hay-strewn vehicle, Rowan saw that it was pulled by a single white horse. It was one of his own from the stables at Castle Grey, an older but reliable warhorse, Ajax. He was still capable of picking up speed, once they had cleared the gates.

"Best you hide yourself in the hay, my Laird Rowan."

"I think not. I think we're safer if I sit at your side."

"Oh? And what do you know of being a monk?"

"Not much, my good man. But neither do I care to be skewered if a guard chooses to thrust his weapon into the hay, searching for contraband."

"Ah," Gavin murmured. "Hop up."

And so they both sat atop the driver's plank on the poor wagon, and Rowan took up the reins. They crossed the courtyard and came to the gate, where the guard looked at them curiously. As Rowan had expected he might, he held a long pike.

"Where are ye off to, this hour o' the night?" he demanded.

"The priory atop the hill. I have been summoned by a woman of the queen's own true faith," Rowan replied.

The guard scowled but didn't insist on seeing Rowan's face. Rather, he moved to the back of the wagon and began thrusting his weapon into the hay, just as Rowan had feared.

"True faith indeed," he muttered beneath his breath. "Pass."

Rowan didn't reply, only flicked the reins, and Ajax obediently moved forward.

Rowan forced himself to keep the horse at a slow gait while they made their way from the city and past the most heavily populated area, but as soon as they entered the woods beyond the fields, he again flicked the reins, urging Ajax to go faster.

They had nearly reached the farmhouse that Gavin had told him was their goal when he knew they were being followed. He quickly drove the wagon off the road, into the trees.

"How many?" Gavin asked tensely.

He listened. "Two, no more."

Gavin drew a knife from one of the leather sheaves at his calf and quickly handed it over. "I dared bring no larger weapons," he apologized.

"It doesn't matter. We have to catch these men and bind them. I cannot kill them."

Gavin looked at him as if he had gone mad. "They will come with swords, m'laird.

Do we die here tonight?"

"Nay, we take grave care."

He rid himself of the cumbersome cloak and cowl, and glanced around, glad of the darkness. "There," he told Gavin, pointing across the road. Then he turned to quickly catch a branch and shinny up an old oak.

Gavin had scarcely found his own position before the horsemen came trotting down the road. Indeed, they were castle guards.

"He'll have headed north, to his Highland fortress!" one said, not even bothering to lower his voice.

"Aye, and that's why there's just two of us sent off in a vain chase southward," the second fellow complained.

They were both armed with swords, but neither was prepared for attack. Rowan motioned to Gavin, and, as one, like spiders in the dark, they fell silently from the trees.

The men were easily taken down from their mounts. They struggled for their swords, but both were breathless and stunned. The fellow Rowan had taken was corpulent, puffing, easily disarmed. While the younger man might have given Gavin a bit of a struggle, he did not have the chance, for Rowan stepped from the puffing fellow to the other, seizing his sword from his belt even as he scrambled for it. He set the point at the man's throat.

"Gavin, strip the good man's horse of its bridle. We have need of the reins."

"The animal will head back to the castle," Gavin pointed out.

"It can't be helped," Rowan said softly.

Gavin did as bidden, then returned with the leather reins to be used to truss the guards.

"They know ye're out, traitor," the younger one dared to say.

"So they do," Rowan responded calmly.

When he went to tie up the heavier, older guard, the man cringed. "Good God, man, just sit still. I have no intention of harming you," Rowan said impatiently. Even so, the man watched him warily.

"Traitor," the first man muttered again.

"Nay, the man is no traitor. We'd be dead if he were," the older one said.

"But —"

"Ye have me gratitude fer me life," the older guard said.

Rowan nodded as he finished securing the man. "It's a busy enough road. Help will be along by daybreak."

"Can ye pull us over by the trees?" the older man asked. "It would be a hard lot if we were to survive the . . ." He paused.

There hadn't really been a fight. "If ye chose not to kill us and we were to be trampled to death upon the first light."

"Aye, that we can do," Rowan assured him.

When they were about to leave and had moved out of earshot of the prisoners, he took a good look at the remaining horse, which they had tethered to a tree, then turned to Gavin. "You don't happen to have Styx stashed away somewhere, do you?" he asked.

Gavin grinned. "Nay, and we must return the wagon at yonder farm. Truly, the queen didn't wish to harm you. Styx was returned to Castle Grey soon after you were taken, but I think you'll find he's closer than that now."

"That is a mercy."

"We must quit Scotland, you know," Gavin said somberly.

"We'll leave the wagon here and take this horse. And we'll go quickly now, even if the majority of the queen's men are headed toward the Highlands."

And so they rode together on the remaining mount until they came to the farmstead, where an anxious man awaited them. Rowan told him where he might find his wagon, and warned him to go quickly, while there was still darkness and before the guards could be discovered.

"You'll find that the horse we've left for you, Ajax, is a fine one. Gavin, we've a gold piece for this fine man, haven't we?"

"Indeed."

"See that my horse is well when I return," Rowan said.

"I'll feed the good fella apples aplenty from me own hand," the farmer promised.

They mounted, both on their fresh horses, and Rowan was deeply pleased to be reunited with Styx, then headed out quickly, not wishing to bring any danger to the farmer.

"To London?" Gavin said.

"Aye."

Rowan had never intended any other course of action; his one driving thought each day, all that had kept him alive, was his eagerness to see Gwenyth again. Even so, when Gavin had spoken, his heart had given an unexpected jolt. Leave Scotland, and not as an ambassador traveling south.

In exile.

"There is no other course of action," Gavin said.

"I know."

Gavin smiled at him. "There is one bright spot, my lord."

"My lady wife."

"And more," Gavin said, still grinning. "Your son."

His jaw dropped; he felt it but could not control it. At last he managed to speak, albeit in a croaked whisper. "What?"

"I have it from Maitland, my lord. It is no rumor, though the birth was kept very quiet. You have a son, now several months old, hale and hearty. Daniel Rowan, your lady christened the lad."

CHAPTER SEVENTEEN

Gwenyth arrived in Edinburgh at the end of a long day's ride, and Mary Fleming was the first to greet her, riding astride outside the castle walls.

"Gwenyth!"

The Scottish guard of ten men, fine fellows who had met up with her at the Borders and taken over the task of escort from their English counterparts, allowed them the time to greet one another. The lady's maid sent by Elizabeth herself, a young girl from Stirling who would go onward to her father's home, was equally discreet, holding back out of earshot.

Gwenyth thought she would fall from her beloved Chloe, Mary Fleming gave her such a fierce hug from the saddle. When they pulled apart, Mary said, "There's so much to be told. We'll get you to Holyrood, and I will bring you up-to-date on the most recent affairs."

"Laird Rowan, do you know of his fate?" Gwenyth asked anxiously.

"He escaped. All believe that the queen intended him to do so. Yesterday, there was a session of parliament, and she demanded that a bill of attainder be drawn up against the lairds in rebellion, yet she chose not to have his name mentioned, though he is still banned from the country."

"He escaped?" Gwenyth repeated dully.

Surely it could not be true and God so cruel that she had been allowed to reach Edinburgh, so close to seeing his face again, only to find him gone.

"Aye. There is word that he is over the border, perhaps with Laird James at Newcastle." Mary Fleming appeared very sad and grave and set a hand comfortingly on Gwenyth's shoulder. "He is safe. Guards went after him, but he managed to leave them trussed up on the road. They spoke highly of him, and now his reputation with his peers and the people grows. No one believes that the queen ever wished him harm. She is just in such a temper about the rebellion, and —"

"Let us get to Holyrood. Away from prying eyes and ears."

At last they reached the palace and the room that had long ago been assigned her, where she sat upon the bed and listened to Mary Fleming.

"You have been gone so very long. We've missed you, Gwenyth. Sometimes it seemed that you could say things we could not. We are all Scots, but we came here with so much that was French. Mary often had more faith in your words. Of course, once she had such faith in James, her brother, as well. The trouble all began with Lord Darnley. And now . . . while the queen awaits the birth of her child, he is out drinking each night, and God knows what other diversions he seeks. I believe there is a conspiracy all around us."

"Against the queen?"

"Perhaps. It is so hard to tell truth from fiction. I know only that certain lairds remain furious about Darnley. They whisper that he has become far too much a Catholic monarch. The lairds despise him, and there is a rumor that some are suggesting he be given more power — so that our good queen may lose her rights and a Protestant monarch can be set in her place. Always, everywhere, secrets are whispered behind our backs. I fear for Mary."

"But . . . she is about to have a child. She will produce an heir for Scotland, and she will . . . she will win over the people and the lairds."

"I hope you are right. Now you must get ready. The queen is planning a small supper party in her rooms tonight. She knows that you are here, and she is delighted."

"Will Laird Darnley be at this supper?"

"Do you jest?" Mary Fleming said drily. "No. Laird Darnley — or King Henry, as he calls himself and as the queen honors him — will be out drinking and carousing, as is his way. His chamber lies just beneath the queen's, but he rarely comes up the privy staircase that connects them."

When Mary left her, Gwenyth lay upon her bed for a long while, heartsick that she would not see Rowan, yet also grateful that he was out of harm's way. She was bitter, however, that she had come to Scotland from England just when he had left Scotland for England.

At last she rose and, with the help of a castle maid, dressed. Shortly thereafter, a tap on her door from one of the queen's chamber servants alerted her that the time had come for supper.

Mary's personal quarters were in the northwest tower of the palace and consisted of four rooms: a presence chamber that led to her bedchamber, and beyond her bedchamber, two smaller — though far from small — rooms that could also be reached via the privy staircase into the bedchamber. As Mary entered the queen's bedroom, heading for the supper room beyond, she heard the soft sound of the queen's voice and she noted the stairway that now led to her husband's, the *king's,* chambers.

Then she forgot the past, for Mary saw her, even in the midst of her company, and hurried through the supper room to greet her. Gwenyth forgot that she was angry with the queen, so concerned was she to see how much Mary had changed. The laughter that had once lurked constantly in her eyes had dimmed, and her features were gaunt. She seemed to have aged greatly.

"My dearest Gwenyth," Mary said and held her tenderly, as if she meant the words.

"Your Grace." Gwenyth dipped low with all propriety.

Then the queen swept her inside. "You know your friends, my dear Marys, of course. And you no doubt recall Jean, Lady Argyll and Robert Stewart."

Of course, Gwenyth thought. Jean was the queen's illegitimate half sister, and Robert was her illegitimate half brother. Robert had evidently not fallen from favor along with James.

The queen went on with the introductions. "This is my page, Anthony Standen, Arthur Erskine, my equerry . . . and David Riccio, my musician and my most estimable secretary." She turned to the others. "This is Lady Gwenyth, freed at last from the hold of my cousin Elizabeth."

They all greeted her. She had met Anthony and Arthur before, and they were true men who served the queen well. Jean had never been anything but a loving and supporting friend to Mary, and Robert, too, seemed to have her best interests at heart. The Marys were always her loving servants. At least in the night's company, the queen had surrounded herself with those whose loyalty could not be questioned. Except for David Riccio, Gwenyth thought, whose true character was a mystery to her.

As the meal progressed, Gwenyth noted that, although David Riccio might have been as ugly as a toad, he was a clever man with a dulcet voice. He had the ability to make the queen laugh, something that, Gwenyth thought, she clearly did not do often of late.

The little man grinned at her. "Welcome home," he said. "I still know so little about this vast and wild land, though I have been here these many years. Such passions and tempers here, such *life.*"

Gwenyth smiled, about to answer him, when they were disrupted by a loud noise from the bedroom area. Looking to the door of the supper room, Gwenyth saw that Lord Darnley had entered.

She understood Mary's waning affection. The man was young, yet he managed to look old and dissolute. "The king arrives!" he announced.

The others rose. Mary did not. "Henry, how lovely of you to take the time to join us," she said.

He smiled, and even from a distance, he smelled as if he had all but bathed in a keg of ale. Walking into the room, he tilted to one side.

A second man made an appearance from the direction of the staircase. It was Patrick, Lord Ruthven. Gwenyth knew him, but still, she was amazed to see him. He had been ill, she knew, something Mary Fleming had told her earlier. Indeed, he looked as if he were still ill, and he sounded delirious when he began to speak.

"Let it please Your Majesty," he said, offering Mary a sweeping bow that all but tumbled him from his feet. "May it please Your Majesty that yon man, David Riccio, has stayed far too long in your presence, in your bedroom."

"Have you gone mad?" Mary demanded furiously, looking from Ruthven to her husband. "David is here at my most royal request," she announced firmly, then looked at Darnley. "This can only be due to your ridiculous machinations."

"Blame not your good lord, my queen," Ruthven insisted. "Riccio has bewitched you. You don't realize that people talk, that they say you make a cuckold of your good husband."

"I am with child!" the queen roared, still disbelieving all that she saw. "I play cards and I listen to music, while my dear sainted husband plays at other games."

Mary's fury was so great that Gwenyth was afraid that she would soon burst into tears and fall into a state of emotional distress that would harm both her and her child.

Suddenly, the room began to fill with more men. Gwenyth didn't know all of them, but she recognized George Gordon, the younger, Thomas Scott and Andrew Ker.

"If you've an argument with David Riccio, then he will appear before parliament," Mary said evenly.

But her words had no effect. Gwenyth

could see immediately that, whatever they might later claim, these men had come to do violence.

David Riccio, too, had realized that something dire was afoot, for he leapt from his chair as if to run, but there was nowhere to go. He headed toward the massive window, behind the queen's back.

Gwenyth stepped back just as the rush of men overturned the table. Someone managed to hold on to a single candle as the others were extinguished, the threat of fire fading and the only light in the room now coming from the fireplace, and the one remaining candle.

David Riccio cried out in a confused mixture of French and Italian, "Justice, justice! Madam, I pray you, save my life!"

The men had pistols and daggers, and a terrified Riccio literally grabbed the queen's skirts, trying to hide behind them.

Gwenyth sprang to life, grabbing Mary Fleming's hand. "Help! We need help here! Do they mean to murder Riccio?"

"Or the queen, as well!" Mary Fleming cried.

The men had Riccio, wrenching his fingers from the queen's skirts and dragging him, kicking and screaming, through the supper room and into the bedchamber.

"Justizia, Justizia, sauvez ma vie!"

Gwenyth heard the sounds of David Riccio being thrown down the privy stairway, and she cried furiously, "Help! Help! To the queen! The queen's life is in danger!"

Suddenly the room became a sea of confusion; Mary's own servants arrived in panic, bearing brooms and dust mops, whatever weapons they had found. Members of the Douglas clan had apparently been about in the castle, and they rushed in next, followed by the queen's guard, brandishing real weapons.

There were shouts, furious accusations — and a bloody battle ensued.

Gwenyth and the queen's ladies tried hard to form a protective barrier around Mary, but Ruthven had dared to set his pistol against her stomach while his fellows had wrestled Riccio from her presence.

In the end, the rebels were left in control.

David Riccio, the tiny Italian, lay dead, a bloody pulp almost unrecognizable as human, so many dagger wounds had torn into his small frame. When word of his death reached her, Mary cried. But then, she responded with courage as she looked at those who had taken over the palace of Holyrood.

"I am ill," she announced. "I carry the

heir to Scotland. You will leave me be with my ladies to attend me and let me rest."

The men looked awkwardly at one another, then decided to obey Mary and left.

But they were all still in dreadful danger, Gwenyth knew. As most of the rebels drifted from the room and Mary took to her bed, Gwenyth found a renewed sense of love and loyalty for the queen.

As Gwenyth helped her into her bed, Mary whispered, "We will yet find vengeance. Pay heed to every whisper and word our captors speak. Listen for every nuance. We will escape."

The queen's eyes were alight with fire and she leaned heavily on Gwenyth's arm, feigning distress in hopes that those rebels still in the room would leave. She cried out, as if in pain, and at last was left with only her ladies and her supporters.

"Come close," Mary whispered to Gwenyth, and together they began to plot.

Rowan arrived in London on a strangely beautiful day. The weather was disarmingly mild as he made his way to the town house. He had not even reached the door when Thomas and Annie came running down the steps, almost embarrassing him by the ardor with which they greeted him.

There was a great deal that he needed to know; but, having reached the house at last, he had only one thought. "My lady?"

He saw the confused expressions on their faces.

"She . . . has gone at last to Edinburgh," Thomas said.

"Sweet Jesus!" Rowan cried.

"But the babe, Daniel, dwells here, safely with us, at her command," Annie assured him.

And so it was that, as he bitterly rued the freakish accident of fate that had sent them in opposite directions, he was brought to see his son.

"My God," he breathed in awe. The child slept, but he had to awaken him. His son gave a tremendous shiver when Rowan picked him up and then let out a cry of indignation. But then he stared at his father. His eyes were wide, very blue. He had blond curls, and Rowan found himself amazed, touched as he had never been before, and shaking himself as he sat down to hold his child.

Hours later, he at last returned his son to the young woman charged to nurse him and, with Gavin at his side, rode to request an audience with Queen Elizabeth.

He was startled when he was immediately

granted an audience in her privy chamber.

"I will tell you, first, that your bold escape is being quite romanticized across the countryside," she said in amusement.

He shrugged. "My escape was not so bold. I was helped, and from an unexpected quarter."

"So I imagine. I think that we sovereigns, with the strength of our blood, are loath to bring harm to others." She turned away from him, thoughtful. "I know that my sister, Mary Tudor, cried for hours when her highest advisors and council demanded that she execute Lady Jane Grey. There is no pain such as that we face too often, fighting those closest to us . . . who threaten to become us."

"You still have yet to meet Mary of Scotland," he reminded her.

"Her situation is dire, I am told."

He exhaled. "I believe that she rues her marriage, Your Grace."

"You know nothing of what has transpired, do you?" she asked gently.

His heart fell. "My Lady Gwenyth?"

"I should have kept her here."

His heart seemed to reverse itself and leapt into his throat.

"She is well, so comes the news, but word is very confused."

"I beg of you, tell me all of it."

"Indeed, I must," Elizabeth said gravely.

Gwenyth moved about the palace the next morning, silently and as unobtrusively as possible, though the rebels had taken such strong control that they didn't mind the ladies moving about, ostensibly serving the needs of their queen.

She learned that Father Black, a Catholic priest, had fallen prey to the murderers, as well, but that the Lairds Huntly and Bothwell, also intended victims, had managed to escape. Then she ducked into a doorway, listening as two of Ruthven's followers stood guard, and laughed and joked about their easy success.

"I hear the queen will be taken to Stirling, there to be held 'til the babe is born. No doubt she will be happy enough," said one.

"Oh, aye, with her music and embroidery . . . and she can tend her child and hunt in the fields while the good king rules the country." He laughed as he spoke.

"Darnley? Already he shows signs of remorse and wavering — and fear," said the first man.

"He'll not rule the country. Those lairds with something between their ears will do so in his name."

"The queen could well die from this ill treatment," the first man said.

"If so, Darnley has royal blood enough. He'll be a decent figurehead. And God knows, he loves fornication enough to quickly produce an heir elsewhere."

Armed with her knowledge, Gwenyth returned to the queen's side where, joined by several of the others, including Lady Huntly, who was now in the queen's service, she explained what she knew of the plot.

"I have to escape," the queen said. "I must. And then those who honor me must call up the countryside, and we will ride back into Edinburgh in triumph."

"Escape first," Lady Huntly whispered.

Gwenyth was silent, worried. The attack on the queen had been part of a well-planned and very dangerous conspiracy. She did not think they would be easily defeated.

"Gwenyth?" Queen Mary said.

Gwenyth blinked, having become lost in her thoughts.

"You must pay heed," Lady Huntly warned her.

Gwenyth did. She argued firmly against any notion of the queen attempting escape via a bedsheet ladder, pointing out that not only did her condition make it impossible, she would be seen from the rooms above or in an adjacent tower, or noticed by a guard below. "Someone must be convinced to help us, someone from within the fold of conspirators," she said.

The queen, with remarkable bravado, spoke up. "I know exactly who," she said bitterly.

In the morning, Darnley returned to his wife's room. The ladies instantly departed to the chamber beyond, but one of the Marys stayed with her ear to the hallway door to listen for sounds of approaching danger, while the others eavesdropped, ears to the wall.

Henry Stewart, Lord Darnley, was nearly in tears. He spoke in choked words about his distress. "Mary, there was not to have been murder," he said.

Gwenyth couldn't see the queen, yet she knew to what proportion Mary's hatred for her husband had grown; none of this could have happened without his participation. But the queen's words were gentle as she said that she forgave him. Then she talked about the possibility that he might find himself a prisoner, as well, and apparently she convinced him that they were both being used terribly and in an ungodly manner by certain overly ambitious lords who were eager to achieve power.

Later in the day, when Darnley led in the lairds who had so hideously attacked her, she spoke as compellingly as she had with her husband, assuring them all that they would be pardoned.

At that point, word came that James Stewart had arrived at Holyrood.

"My brother is here?" the queen demanded, evidently pleased.

Gwenyth was not so sanguine. James had, after all, attempted to rise against her. But it seemed that Mary was remembering only that James had been there to help her when she had first come to Scotland, so young and with so little knowledge of affairs in her country.

But when she saw James and threw herself into his arms, declaring that none of the horrors could have occurred had he been with her, he had stern words for her. Though Gwenyth could not hear, she watched Mary's face, and saw her fury and her indignation rise.

Then, removing the focus from affairs of state, she screamed out in sudden pain that she had gone into labor and begged that a midwife be sent for, which was quickly done.

Mary requested that the room be cleared of everyone but her ladies, and as soon as the others were gone, she stopped her playacting and carefully outlined their options.

That night, the escape was put into action.

At midnight Darnley came, and together, he and the queen slipped down the privy staircase by which the murderers had gained entrance to her supper party. Her French servants had been warned earlier of the escape, and they escorted her secretly through the hallways.

Gwenyth was on guard at the castle door when the queen and Darnley quit Holyrood, and she quickly led them past the cemetery beside the Abbey. There was a painful moment when the queen stopped beside a freshly dug grave — Riccio's, Gwenyth was certain — and Darnley paled, then began an apology to the queen.

"Shh," Gwenyth warned. "You must away now, no time for regrets, Your Grace."

Outside the abbey, others, forewarned, were waiting. Mary mounted behind Erskine, and there was a horse for Darnley, as well as one for Gwenyth.

The ride through the night began, their plan being to reach Dunbar Castle. Gwenyth understood ever more deeply why the queen had come to so loathe her husband. He was in terror, now that he had turned back to her, that they would be caught by the rebels he had just betrayed, and he brutally urged the horses on.

"Have pity, my husband, for my condition," the queen pleaded.

"If that babe dies, we can have others," he replied carelessly. "Come on!"

They rode hard for five long hours and finally reached Dunbar. There, at last, the queen was able to rest.

Gwenyth, too, fell into bed, exhausted, but she couldn't sleep. She dozed and awoke repeatedly through the night. But even in her dreams, she could hear Lord Darnley, Henry Stewart, self-imagined King of Scotland. *If that babe dies, we can have others.*

Nay, if that babe died . . .

He would never be a royal father. Not even for country or duty would Mary ever allow the man near her again.

She came fully awake, and she wept. She longed for her own child, and for the comforting arms of his father, a man who did not falter or waver, who would never rise in rebellion, then cry and beg for reprieve.

She lay there, shaking, aching, knowing a greater loneliness than she had ever imagined possible.

Mary had escaped. Already Laird Gordon, the pardoned eldest son of the Lord Gordon who had done battle against the queen, and James Hepburn, Laird Bothwell, were already out rousing the countryside, without even having paused to sleep.

They were triumphant, and she should be grateful. They might have all died in the frenzy of the attack or been captured and killed in the escape. And she *was* grateful, she told herself. It was just that she was also . . .

Lonely.

Bothwell and Huntly fulfilled their duty to their queen with admirable speed.

They gathered a force of eight thousand men within a matter of days, although the queen's own proclamation, asking that the inhabitants of the area surrounding Dunbar Castle meet her at Haddington with eight days' provisions, certainly helped swell the numbers.

At the end of March, Mary, heavy with child, rode at the head of the troops, Darnley at her side, a very unhappy man. They heard, even as they rode, that the rebel leaders had deserted Edinburgh, aware that they had been betrayed by Darnley and in fear for their own lives.

As she had promised, Mary entered Edinburgh victoriously.

Gwenyth was relieved that Mary was not forced into battle, and that, even though the rebels deserved to be executed for murder, most of them had fled.

She was equally pleased — though rumor persisted that his name had been signed to a pact among the conspirators — that the events had somehow brought about Mary's determination to forgive her brother James.

And if James was forgiven, Gwenyth thought, then clearly the queen would have to pardon Rowan, as well.

She had not received so much as a letter from him in so long now that there were times when she was afraid she would not know him. Then she would be flooded with anguish, certain that she could never forget him, so deeply did she love him.

Their first days after returning to Edinburgh were filled with both emotion and activity.

One of Mary's first passions was to see that David Riccio was dug up from his impromptu grave and given a proper Catholic funeral. The next was the matter of dealing with her nobles, rewarding those who had so staunchly stood for her, punishing those who had betrayed her. Several of the underlings of the conspirators were arrested and condemned to death.

In addition, Mary was deeply worried about the birth of her child.

"It breaks my heart that my babe will enter a world in turmoil," she said, pacing her room.

"That is why you are kind to Laird Darnley?" Mary Fleming whispered. "So your babe will know at least *some* harmony in life?"

"There will be no question of anything awry between us until after the child is born. There will be no question, ever, that my child is legitimate, the heir to the throne," Mary said, though her absolute loathing for her husband was clearly apparent in her face.

But Gwenyth knew her well. Mary would play the part of the good wife until the child was born. Gwenyth understood, the queen's absolute love for her unborn child and the protective instinct she was feeling. And she meant to speak to the queen as soon as possible regarding Rowan and her own sweet babe, Daniel.

Her chance came a few days later. Mary, having at last reconciled with James Stewart, Argyle, Huntly and many others, felt she had regained control of her world. And when she sat at last, satisfied, daring to take some time alone to work on the tiny garments she was sewing for her child, Gwenyth at last managed to speak to her.

"What of Laird Rowan?"

To her amazement, the queen stared at her with bitter eyes. "What of him?"

"Well, you have taken Laird James back into your confidence . . ."

Mary rose. "Speak not to me about that man. My trials and tribulations began in earnest the minute he was freed. I was a fool!"

Gwenyth gasped and rose, both stunned and dismayed. "Mary! How can you speak against him so? He escaped to England. He —"

"How do I know that? I was merciful and urged his escape, and then murder was done in my very chamber." Mary's eyes narrowed. "Don't be a fool. I have learned a great deal about men, and I warned you once not to fall in love with him."

They were alone. And Gwenyth was so furious and heartsick that she dared speak her mind clearly. "You warned me . . . and then you fell head over heels in love with a man such as Darnley!"

"I am the queen. I had to have a proper

husband."

"But he was *not* proper. Elizabeth —"

"Elizabeth is conniving, double-faced, and — evil! She sent him here. She planned for him to ingratiate himself, for me to marry him, so she could then force an outcry to deny me my right to the English crown!"

Gwenyth took a deep breath, trying to understand all that the queen had been through. She had clearly learned a great deal about duplicity during the length of her reign. Still . . . "Mary, I am his wife."

The queen rose, her eyes and her features icy. "You are not his wife. You are a Scottish subject. *My* subject. And I have declared that your marriage is null and void, do you understand? You are not wed to that traitor. I will see that he remains banished, in England, for the rest of his life — or else he will face the block!"

"Mary!"

"Do you understand me?"

"Nay, I'll never understand you. You have no proof that he was involved in any treachery against you."

"Darnley has told me that he was."

Gwenyth gasped. "You would listen to Laird Darnley?"

"He confessed a great deal."

"He cast out names to save himself. Mary,

have you lost your senses? Rowan always despised Darnley!"

"Indeed, and so did others despise Henry, but they were willing to use him as a puppet against me. They forgot that a man they could so easily manipulate could be manipulated in return."

"He's lying."

"There is nothing so bitter as being betrayed by one you have come to love," the queen said.

"Rowan never betrayed you!"

"Gwenyth, listen to me. Darnley is a pathetic creature, but I am in power again, and he is afraid. He gave me Rowan's name. Rowan was a part of this conspiracy, don't you understand?"

"I will never believe it."

"Then you are a fool. A worse fool than I have ever been," Mary assured her.

"I have a child with him."

Mary stared at her, stunned. For a moment it seemed that she might bend, soften, but too much that was ill had been done against her. "Then you have a bastard," she said coldly.

Gwenyth clenched her fists, staring at Mary. "I love him. In the eyes of God, he is my husband and the father of my child. And if you so bitterly loathe my husband, I can no longer, in good conscience, serve you."

Mary looked as if she had been slapped. "So you would betray me, too."

"Never."

"I will see that you do not have to serve me, then."

"I can find my own way out of Scotland."

Mary shook her head. "I am to let you go — to join with him in a country where I am despised? God knows, Elizabeth never sends help or sympathy from England. I have my spies, you know. She might have denied James an army against me, but she certainly funded him when he needed money. You will not go back to England, my Lady Gwenyth."

"Will you imprison me in Edinburgh Castle, then?" Gwenyth demanded, a touch of contempt in her voice.

"Not in Edinburgh Castle," the queen said softly, and turned her back on Gwenyth.

"Leave me."

"Your Grace, I am begging you one more time to consider —"

"Leave me. Now."

Heartsick, Gwenyth returned to her room, where she passed the time pacing, wondering what would happen now.

She did not have to ponder long.

There was a knock on her door. Guards

— the same guards who had so recently seen to her safe arrival — were in the hall.

Their leader looked at her and sighed, deeply, wearily. "Ye are to come with us, my lady."

"Where?"

"We cannae say."

"I am a prisoner?"

"Aye, lady. I say so with my deepest sorrow."

"What manner of clothing shall I bring?" she demanded.

"We ride north," the man said.

"I will be ready shortly," she assured him.

She did not even have Annie near her, she thought. She was far away from her precious babe and being taken farther still.

Worse, Rowan had been branded a traitor again — and this time the queen believed it.

She longed to throw herself on the bed and cry, to rant aloud hatred for the queen.

Except that she didn't hate Mary, though she was furious with her for her refusal to see the truth. And furious with herself for having been blind to danger.

She packed her own possessions quickly. When she was done, she opened her door and pointed out her belongings to the guard, then asked that she be allowed to see the queen.

Mary granted her an audience, and Gwenyth saw immediately that the queen, too, had been crying. Mary took her into her arms.

"Dear God, Mary, I would never betray you," Gwenyth whispered.

The queen stepped back. "And that is why I will keep you from all temptation," she whispered back.

"What?" Gwenyth asked, confused.

"Sadly, I do know what it is to love and feel the passion that you do. I was blinded by something that glittered before me, but its beauty was superficial, and now I am paying the price."

"You know Rowan." Gwenyth hesitated. "You know him well." She almost mentioned that he was of her blood, but she did not. Darnley, too, was of her blood, and the tie to Henry VII did nothing to make him a commendable man.

"Aye," the queen said gravely, and shook her head. "I know him. I had great faith in him. And I pray God that he may somehow find a way to prove that Henry, Lord Darnley, my husband, has lied to me."

Again Gwenyth paused. "He is the one who betrayed you," she said. "Why would you believe him now?"

"Because he fears me now. He betrayed me, and then turned on those with whom he betrayed me. I am his only hope. Gwenyth, there will be an inquiry. But as for now . . . I will love you both. I will keep you safe."

"Mary —"

"Take her," she said softly to the guards who waited at the door.

Tears streamed down Mary's face, but events had hardened her, and she did not relent.

CHAPTER EIGHTEEN

"I would suggest, Lord Rowan, that you simply stay in England," Elizabeth said, when she had finished telling Rowan of the events in Scotland.

Rowan looked at Elizabeth and shook his head. "You know that I cannot."

"Your country is a hotbed of traitors, and it seems there is no rhyme or reason as to those who have been pardoned — and those who have not," Elizabeth said. "Queen Mary writes letters as if she is a secretary herself, long passionate letters. She wants you to be innocent, she dares not believe it." Elizabeth shook her head. "I have it from reliable sources that there truly was a plot. Mary's dear Maitland never signed the agreement between the lords, but I believe he knew of it. Not that there is anything on paper that admits the lords meant to commit murder, but they did sign a Protestant agreement to wrest Mary Stuart from the control of David Riccio and to place the crown matrimonial on the head of Darnley. Now Mary has taken James Stewart, Earl of Moray, back to her side, though there are indications that he was connected to the plot. Your precious land is in deep trouble, Rowan."

"But there, Your Majesty, is the truth of the matter. It *is* my precious land. And Gwenyth is there."

"Mary has forced a legal issue and said that in Scotland, you are not married. And no one knows where she has ordered Lady Gwenyth held."

"I will find her."

"You will lose your head."

"I must take the risk."

Elizabeth sat back, studying him. She seemed both curious and amused. "Take a long look at the situation, please. The Scottish lairds are ever at one another's throats. When one man is lifted, the rest of his peers turn on him like a pack of angry dogs."

"Is that so different anywhere?" Rowan asked her.

Elizabeth's smile deepened. "We are not so quick to violence here. I have more power than Mary," she said. "I can, and do, imprison those I suspect may be against me. I watch, I listen, and at times I give pardon. I fear for you, Rowan. You are an honest man among thieves."

He could not stop himself from pondering aloud. "I don't understand. I scarcely know Darnley, and what I know, I do not like. Still, I have done nothing to the man. Why would the queen have turned on me?"

"She arranged for you to escape, and immediately thereafter violence was done to her. You provide a convenient scapegoat for any who are guilty. You have never altered your position, in that you have supported James and her barons. I know you believe a united and strong Scotland must be at peace in itself, but I fear that Mary has set upon a course of action that has ensured that will never happen. Yes, from all I have been told, she has come to despise Darnley. But she will support him now. She has no choice. She will not ask for an annulment or a divorce."

"Because of her child," Rowan said bitterly.

Elizabeth nodded. "Because of the heir, she will outwardly support Darnley in many matters. Until her child is born, she will take no action that will cast any doubt on the paternity of her babe, so it is born legitimate. Therefore, I suggest you use caution. Wait until the babe is born. Then you will see. Soon after, I predict, Darnley will fall from grace."

"I fear for Gwenyth in the meantime," he said quietly.

"I envy you both, you know," Elizabeth said.

"Envy?"

"Circumstances have been unjust, and yet . . . in both of you, I see such deep commitment. Perhaps your faith and the depth of your love will save you in the end. Or perhaps they will bring about your demise. Or, as happens so frequently in this world, perhaps time and hardship will make enemies of you, and all that is tender and romantic will end in bitterness."

"That I will not allow," he said.

"Don't behave as recklessly as your kind are so quick to do."

He couldn't help but inquire. "My kind?"

"Highlanders," she told him, but she did so with a smile. "I am only advising you, of course. In the end, you will do what you will do."

The news reached Gwenyth at the beginning of July that Queen Mary had been delivered of a baby boy, healthy and fine in every way, though the queen's labor had been long and hard.

She wrote Mary a long letter, describing her happiness at the event, but in reality she was miserable, wondering if she was doomed to spend her life as a prisoner. She spent long, agonized hours wishing that she dared send to London and ask Annie and Thomas to come north with Daniel, but since so many terrible events had taken place, she was afraid to do so. Daniel was safe where he was, and she had to be content with that.

As in the Tower, she was not kept harshly, only at the rather bleak and fortified holding of James Hepburn, Laird Bothwell, newly elevated because he had been instrumental in the queen's escape from Edinburgh. She spent a great deal of time writing letters to the queen, and to her own family and friends, but though they were duly taken from her, she doubted they were ever sent on.

She was allowed visitors, at least, and Angus MacLeod came to see her soon after she learned about the birth of the royal child. Angus had begged her to bow to the queen's fury over her marriage and drop her claim as Rowan's wife. She was astonished that her uncle could be so fickle, as she knew he had admired Rowan.

"The queen can strip you — and Laird

Rowan — of every holding," he told her gravely. "Thus far, she has been content to await her child. But now the babe is born, and we cannot know what she will do." Angus shook his head. "Love. What is love?" he said to her wearily. "Marriages are contracts that bind families, secure alliances. Ye know that, child."

"I've seen what wonders they do," she told him drily.

He hesitated. "The queen is using yer name upon occasion, ye should know."

"Pardon?"

"She is offering ye as a prize to many a man who will support her."

"I am not so rich as to be a prize worth winning!" she exclaimed.

"She has suggested that other holdings, seized from the rebels, will be granted to your new laird husband, once ye have one." Angus walked to the hearth, shaking his head. "A marriage contract is a marriage contract. Sixty-year-old widows have been wed to twenty-year-old men. Oft, a bride in her teens is given to a fellow so ancient, he is like the walking dead. That is the way of the world. But to a fellow seeking to plant his seed in the future of the world, a young bride is desirous. And beauty is not a detriment."

"She cannot marry me off without my consent. And I do not believe she would do it."

"You still love your Mary so dearly, don't ye?" he said.

"I am bitter, of course. But I watched her change. I watched her arrive with hope, with love for Scotland, with the confidence that she would be a good queen, one who would unite her country. I know she is misled right now, but I also know that, eventually, she will see the truth."

"I pray that ye are not blind, lass," he said gently. "But as ye have this belief, I will remain quietly at Islington, far from politics, and do me best fer ye." He was silent for a moment. "And fer Daniel, whatever may fall."

She wondered how she had ever found Angus to be stiff and cold. Since she had come back from France, she had discovered that he had been nothing but honorable and constant. And she told him so, hugging him tightly, perhaps embarrassing him a bit, until it was time for him to leave.

She continued her letter campaign, writing to Mary, to Annie and Thomas, and to Rowan, though she knew that none of her letters would reach him.

Very few letters made their way back to

her. She did receive letters from one person: Queen Mary.

One letter informed her that Mary suggested she consider marriage to Donald Hathaway, newly created Laird of Strathern. The queen was full of enthusiasm, describing Donald as young, hale and vigorous.

Gwenyth threw the letter down with fury, but there was more on the page, so she picked it back up.

Understand I do this with all love; word from reliable sources states that Laird Rowan, in complete disregard of his duties in his own country, has wed Elisia Stratfield, daughter of an earl, and is now fully in the service of the Queen of England.

Gwenyth refused to believe what she had read. Still, she allowed herself an hour's fury and tears. And then . . . despair.

As the year waned, she was stunned when an escort arrived, sent by Mary, who desired that she be returned to court just after the Christmas season. She was still so hurt and angry that she longed to refuse, but in the face of the queen's wishes and a half-dozen able-bodied men, she had little choice.

And she did not intend to spend her life in the queen's protective custody.

Even if the news of Rowan's betrayal were true.

"There," Gavin said, pointing.

From his position atop the tor, Rowan could see the arrival of the queen's men through the trees. Gwenyth, in a handsome cloak that draped over her mare's hindquarters, rode behind the leader of the party, a maid behind her, with five armed guards at the back.

"I see," Rowan murmured.

"It is madness to attack," Gavin said. "We are surrounded by the earl of Bothwell's minions, and ye've taken such grave care never to harm another man fer doing his duty."

"True." Rowan watched the party moving along the road. He itched to attack, to do battle, to win or lose. But two factors weighed heavily upon him. He didn't want to kill. And neither did he want to risk the lives of his own men, ten fellows who had stuck with him through thick and thin.

He knew his arrival in Scotland had not gone unnoticed. But despite the royal ban against him, he had been greeted with love and honor by the people of Scotland.

Friends, those who had kept silent and far from court, had allowed them to stay and rest; in markets and farm towns along the way, the tenants and craftsmen had known him but kept their peace.

Here, they were surrounded by the forces of a man who was ambitious beyond imagination, and high in the favor of the queen.

"We will not attack, but we will follow," Rowan said.

They did, keeping a discreet distance from the party ahead of them.

Gavin, not nearly so recognizable as Rowan, rode ahead as a scout. Toward nightfall, he returned to Rowan's position in the woods.

"They have stopped for the night at Elwood Manse," Gavin told him.

"I have never been there," Rowan said.

Gavin grinned. "I have."

Elwood Manse was not a fortification of any kind; rather, it was the residence of the Reverend Hepburn, a Bothwell cousin.

It was a handsome, rambling dwelling. Sheep and chickens moved about the front lawn, and the great house was surrounded by charming, thatched-roof cottages.

The Reverend Hepburn had obviously been alerted to their arrival; he was waiting outside his dwelling, ready to meet her. He was a stout man with a full head of iron-gray hair, and everything about him seemed as stern and rigid as his coloring.

The queen's men were lodged in surrounding abodes, while Gwenyth's maid was given quarters in the attic, and Gwenyth discovered that she herself was to dine with the reverend and be accommodated in the manse itself.

Reverend Hepburn was a courteous man, but he was also determined to preach. As she was served a fine fish dinner, he talked about the state of the country. "We are deeply gladdened by — I daresay we are *rejoicing* over — the birth of our dear Mary's heir, which will bring us all to greater glory. But we will all need to do our part to see that peace is at hand for all Scotsmen."

"Of course," she murmured, all the while wondering what he was going on about.

"That means that we will all bow in obedience to the queen," he said firmly, amazing her when he pointed at her sternly with his fork. "We are all duty-bound, my lady. Fantasy plays no part in the reality of life. Traitors will not be tolerated."

She knew that she should just hold her peace and be done with the meal as soon as possible, but she could not. "If you are referring to Laird Rowan, he is no traitor. Nor do I believe that, in her heart, Mary thinks so. She has not had his lands seized, reverend."

The man's eyes narrowed. "So you would be like the wretched folk who do not see the truth. They cry his name in the streets," he said with disgust.

"And he will be vindicated."

"The queen will be avenged." The man smiled. "If he is seen in this area, I promise you, the queen will be given a quick and easy solution to the problem he represents. We will deliver his body unto her."

"She has never condoned murder. Are you mad?"

"Any man must fight to preserve his house and lands."

She stood, utterly disgusted with him, and knew she could bear no more conversation. "I have had a tiring journey today. I beg your pardon. I will retire."

He stood, as well, and she knew he intended to force the issue. She moved too quickly, however, seeking the bedroom she had been assigned on the ground floor in the east wing of the house.

The maid she had been assigned in her imprisonment, a young girl named Audrey, came to her, but she politely bade the girl to leave her alone. She didn't know Audrey well, and felt she could not find help or comfort in her presence. She longed to have Annie with her again, but could not deny the fact that Annie needed to be with Daniel.

The one benefit to Reverend Hepburn was his irony; he had sent a rough wooden tub to the room with hot water — a silent rebuke that she should bathe away her sins.

Alone with her thoughts, she alternated between anger and despair. The world, she thought, was a madhouse, filled with lies and rumors, liars and ambitious climbers, eager for nothing but to assuage their own greed.

At length — certain she had steamed away more than a few sins, even if not those the reverend felt plagued her — she stepped from the tub, donned the softness of her linen nightgown and lay in bed, eager for sleep.

It was not so easy.

It seemed that the Reverend Hepburn had decided she would be able to atone for a few more sins if he provided her with the hardest, lumpiest mattress available.

She wondered if she would indeed be guilty of a sin if, in her heart, she damned the man to hell.

The Manse was in a gentle valley, and even by the dim light of a weak moon, it was beautiful, epitomizing the true magic of the land Rowan had always loved so dearly.

They came on foot, leaving their horses in the surrounding forest with one man to hold guard over their mounts. The manse was quiet. And unguarded.

Rowan was certain the queen's escort did not expect any trouble. Their duty was to deliver one of the queen's ladies to her side. They had no reason to expect trouble, and so it was easy enough for Rowan and his men to study the house, to find entry.

Gavin, as ever, was at his right hand when they entered through a parlor window, followed by several minutes of trial and error.

Rowan found the room where the reverend himself slept; the man snored with the energy and volume of a thunderstorm. He closed the door, then continued down the hall. There were bolts inside all the doors, and he prayed that Gwenyth had not thought she was in danger, that she had not shot the bolt.

And, at last, he found the place where she slept and breathed a silent thanks to God when the door opened easily at his touch.

Time slipped away as he watched her in the moonlight. He had left her, so long ago now, sleeping as she did now, hair free and strewn across her pillow like golden fire in the light of the dying embers in the hearth. She looked like an angel and a siren in one, clad in white, yet that sheer white fabric was clinging to the curves of her body, hinting at the lithe perfection beneath.

He stood in the doorway for several long seconds, then silently closed the door, trusting Gavin to stand guard in the hall. Still, he took time to slide the bolt.

Then he walked over to her, and sat by her side. He saw the dampness gleaming on her cheeks, and realized that she must have fallen asleep in tears. He steeled himself for a moment; he had heard a great deal about her impending marriage to one of the queen's newest favorites since arriving in Scotland.

But then, he had also heard that he was married himself, and that was surely as absurd a rumor as could be found. He had to wonder if she'd had the strength of mind, the faith, to know that there were those who enjoyed discrediting others — while finding favor for themselves — and were quick to create lies.

She opened her eyes.

He was ready to quickly clamp a hand over her mouth lest she cry out. But she didn't. She only stared at him. "I am dreaming," she whispered.

He choked back a cry of emotion and bent down, lips hovering just over hers. "Then let me dream with you," he whispered.

Later, he knew he should have spoken further, that there were so many things that needed to be said between them. But their emotions were too strong. His lips touched hers, and thoughts and words were lost in the trembling sweep of passion. They had been apart forever, it seemed, and yet, in her lips, in the eager and hungry return of his touch, he sensed the world becoming right. He lay down beside her, hands sliding over her linen gown, feeling the wonder and heat of her form. She turned into him, fitting herself against him, and their lips remained welded together as he stroked and held her, closer and closer. Her hands were on him, as well, reveling in the freedom to stroke bare flesh, and in her touch he rose to a maddened fever, heedless of time, of place, of life itself. Their lips parted at last, but only so their fevered kisses could fall elsewhere.

Urgency ripped through him with a cruel violence at the feel of her breasts beneath his fingers and lips. The gentle play of her hands and tongue upon his rising passion was unbearable. At last, in the tangle of half-discarded clothing, they came together wildly. She moved against him, an arc of flame and a writhing force, a feast for the hunger of his senses so volatile that his excitement raged wildly, out of control, leaving only the smallest space for reason somewhere within. Yet somehow that reason, rooted in pride and sexual desire and caring, won out, and he held back, urging her still further, until it seemed the world around them exploded.

He was so satisfied and replete that he did not hear the tapping at the window at first. It was Gwenyth who burst up to a sitting position and stared at him in the firelight, alarm in her eyes.

"Rowan!"

He heard the urgency of Gavin's cry.

He rose, quickly adjusting his clothing. He had left Gavin in the hallway, not outside the window.

"There is a great commotion. The queen's men are rising, gathering their weapons."

Even as Gavin spoke, there was a pounding at the door.

Gwenyth was up, staring at him. "Get out of here," she whispered urgently.

"You must come with me."

To his amazement, she stepped back, and he saw the torment in her eyes. "No."

"Aye!"

"Lady Gwenyth?" someone called from the corridor.

"Get out," she ordered him, shoving at his chest. "Get out. I . . . I am to be married. Now get away, you idiot. Would you lose your head upon the block or hang like a commoner? Get out!"

He gritted his teeth. He had no idea what had given the game away and caused such a fury in the night.

"You are coming with me."

"If you touch me again, I swear I will scream, and you will watch your men die painful deaths before dying ignominiously yourself," she warned. "Now go."

"Lady Gwenyth?" The call from the hallway was louder this time.

"Go. You are an outlaw. You have betrayed the queen, and I despise you," she said coldly. "I will marry a proper laird, legally, and you will remain my enemy."

He couldn't have been more stunned if she had slapped him.

And then she walked toward the door, ready to open it as she called, "I am here. You have woken me from my sleep. Pray give me a moment to don my robe."

He longed to spin her around, rage against her, proclaim that she was his wife and he had never been a traitor. But then he heard Gavin cry out and realized that one of the queen's guardsmen had come upon his devoted friend.

And so he leapt out the window, though he still thought to avoid murder, and only gave the attacker a firm knock upon the head, allowing Gavin to rise, unhurt.

"What in God's name has happened?" he asked as he steadied Gavin on his feet, leaving the other fellow prone beneath the window.

"People are rising to arms," Gavin said. "I was still in the house when the messenger arrived and roused the family. Henry Stewart, Laird Darnley . . ."

"Aye?"

"He has been murdered," Gavin said.

Rowan was gone, and Gwenyth hastily flung on her robe, so shaken that she could barely dislodge the bolt.

"Open your door, Lady! You are in grave danger!"

The bolt gave, and she stepped back.

Reverend Hepburn, his sword in hand, nearly crashed into her anyway. He looked anxiously around the room.

"What has happened?" she cried.

"God knows what is going on now. The entire country is in an uproar. Fear stalks the land tonight. Darnley is murdered, and everyone suspects everyone else of the crime."

She let out a stunned breath, chills crawling over her flesh. "The . . . the queen?" she demanded.

"She was not with her husband. She is safe."

His eyes narrowed as he examined the room more closely. Just then one of the queen's men came striding in from the hall.

"Lady Gwenyth is in danger. I know not what faction could wish her ill, but there was a fellow at her window, and when one of my men would have taken him down, another attacked him."

"What do you know of this?" Reverend Hepburn demanded.

She shook her head, feigning fear. "Am I safe now?" she cried, as if in despair.

"Calm yourself, my dearest lady," the captain of her escort said. "We will surround the house. We will give you privacy to dress and then —"

"You caught no one? You don't know who was seeking to harm me?" she cried, mimicking fear.

He hung his head slightly. "No, my lady. They were like wraiths. They disappeared into the woods."

"How many men were lost?" she whispered.

"None, though one man has quite a headache."

"We must leave for Edinburgh at first light, I beg you," she said.

"Aye, lady," the captain of the guard agreed, and walked away.

Reverend Hepburn stared at her distrustfully, there was no charge that he could bring against her. All he had was suspicion, so she bade him good-night.

"Don't bolt your door again. We must be able to get to you if the danger returns."

Gwenyth agreed to leave the door unlocked, yet begged that a man be stationed at her outer window.

He agreed, and then, at last, he left her. Shaking, she closed the door and walked stumblingly back toward the bed. It had seemed so brutally hard, but it had cradled such magic. And yet, already she began to wonder if she had been dreaming.

Nay, for life itself seemed the greater nightmare now.

Rowan had come, and he had escaped,

but she knew she had broken his heart in order to convince him to leave.

The people were roused in his favor, she knew.

And now Mary's consort was dead. Murdered.

Ice seemed to fill Gwenyth's veins as she wondered what import his death would have. She should have felt terrible sorrow; she should have been worried about the queen, about the state of the realm.

But instead she was afraid only for one man. Rowan.

And she was afraid for herself. Would he ever understand just how terrified she had been for his life? Or would he believe that she, like the queen, had betrayed him?

She didn't cry. And she didn't sleep.

She only sat there through the night, numb and shaking.

When Gwenyth arrived at court, she was taken instantly to the queen. Mary looked calm; she did not appear to have given way to hysterical tears. She, too, seemed to be numb.

"Dearest Gwenyth!" she cried, rising as Gwenyth dipped low in her curtsy. Then the queen drew Gwenyth to her in a fierce hug, as if there had been no harsh words between them.

And Gwenyth held her in return.

"Murder," the queen whispered. "My life is plagued by murder."

Gwenyth didn't dispute the fact. As they had ridden hard for Edinburgh, more and more news had reached them. There had been some kind of plot to do with gunpowder, and an explosion. Laird Darnley — who had been ill and resting at the queen's house at Kirk O'Field, planning to return to Holyrood the following day — would rightly have died in the explosion. But he had not. He had been found outside the abode.

Strangled.

It was certainly an irony. The queen had grown to despise her husband. She had tolerated the man, while letting her displeasure with him be known, only for the sake of world-wide recognition that James, her babe, had been born indisputably legal.

"It might have been me! I might have been with him. I had to attend a masque, else I might have been there with Henry."

It was true. No matter how hard Mary tried to be both strong and fair, she had made enemies. And the ever-fickle lairds were changing once again. After all, Scotland now had a male heir, duly proclaimed the child of Mary and Henry. Legal and accepted — and only a few months old.

Now Darnley was dead.

They were indeed living in dangerous times.

Rowan remained in the Highlands, though not staying in his own domain, lest he bring down the wrath of the powers surrounding the queen upon those he loved. It was easy enough for him to find support there, and due to family loyalty, his location would be protected. For the moment, he and his men had taken up residence with the Mac-Gregors of High Tierney, a place with a barren rock fortress and many farms. They were surrounded by hills catacombed with caves in which many a Scottish noble had found refuge throughout the centuries.

Now, having climbed the rugged outcropping of high hillside lands that rose over the sea, he sat atop a tor, brooding. The wind was wicked, but he barely felt the force of it. In the distance, snow covered the mountains, but beneath him, the earth was green. He chewed upon a blade of grass, knowing that he should have been planning an appeal to the queen, because whatever message he sent must be very carefully worded.

But the thoughts that should have ruled

his mind did not.

She risked my arrest, he thought in fury. Risked my men.

He could not believe it. But he had been there. He had no choice but to believe it.

She had said she intended to marry the man the queen had chosen for her.

One voice warned him about the fickleness of women. Another reminded him of how passionately they had made love, and told him that she had acted as she had out of fear, and in his defense.

They hadn't talked before he fell into her bed, and that was a mistake. Yet maybe what they had shared was more meaningful than any words.

Then again, maybe it had just been the meeting of two sexual beings long starved of contact.

He rejected that thought. He'd had his days of seeking simple physical pleasure when Catherine had become so ill, when he had longed for something that meant nothing, that hadn't tainted his love for his wife. What he and Gwenyth had shared in that bed was far more than mere physical pleasure.

He gritted his teeth, standing to face the whipping wind.

For the moment, he would bide his time.

Every day, he gained greater and greater respect here, though he wasn't sure why. He might have been named a conspirator by the queen's consort and damned by the queen, but he was becoming a folk hero nonetheless. He had refrained from murder, he thought wryly, though he had been accused of it.

He turned his thoughts at last to the best way to approach Queen Mary.

She would be in official mourning for forty days. In that time, Gwenyth would be at her side, and nothing that wasn't of immediate importance would be decided.

And then . . . God alone knew in what direction the wind would blow.

CHAPTER NINETEEN

The days that followed Darnley's death were strange indeed, Gwenyth thought. There were long periods of silence and genuine grief, as well as the inevitable state visits. And the accusations.

The Countess of Lennox had been released, and she was in a state of mourning and rage.

The Count of Lennox was demanding that James Hepburn, Laird Bothwell, be tried.

Laird James Stewart, Earl of Moray, had hastened to London, anxious that Elizabeth know he had nothing to do with the evil deed.

And somehow, in the midst of everything, Mary had come to the realization she had not been a target but that instead her lairds had conspired to see her husband had been killed. He had not been murdered because she was unhappy in her marriage. He had been murdered because her factious barons had wanted him gone from the scene of power.

Despite the aid that James Hepburn, Laird Bothwell, had earlier provided her, Mary saw to it that he was brought to trial soon after her official period of mourning for Darnley was ended with a solemn Mass of Requiem.

Lennox was not able to attend the trial, having been waylaid in England. Ever a gossip and troublemaker, he had been held at bay. Gwenyth learned later that Queen Elizabeth had sent a messenger requesting the trial be delayed. Mary either did not receive the message or did not care that the messenger had come.

Though the judges themselves noted in writing that it was considered common knowledge throughout the city that James Hepburn had been guilty of conspiracy in the grisly deed, there was no one to swear witness against him, so Bothwell went free after trial, boasting as he rode through the streets of Edinburgh.

The queen did not seem to care one way or the other about the outcome of the trial. She continued as she had been, most often displaying a calm face before her people, going about the business of government, and yet in private she sometimes gave way to feelings of loss and depression, and cried. Afterward she was quiet, as if still in a state of shock.

Mary Fleming, who had married Maitland — who had been in disgrace himself, since the queen had believed him to have been involved in Riccio's death, but since found pardon — tried in vain to speak with the queen. Still, it was through Mary Fleming that Gwenyth learned much of what was going on around their tight inner circle.

"The barons are in a fury, a frenzy of activity, and I don't believe the queen realizes the danger in what is happening," she told Gwenyth in private. "The problem is that she is too good, wanting to see only goodness in those around her." She lowered her voice, looking anxiously toward the queen's bedroom, where Mary rested. "She can't see the depths of evil and ambition in men. Lennox has raised a group against Bothwell already. The factions are becoming more roiled and angry." She hesitated, looking at Gwenyth. "You should know this, but I beg of you, don't speak on his behalf as yet. It's said that, while the barons fought fiercely among themselves in council, they all proclaimed the innocence of Laird Rowan. And Mary roused herself at last and said that *in her eyes* he was pardoned. As there are no official charges against him, I believe he is a free man, no matter who speaks against him. But understand this, Gwenyth. Bothwell was angry when he heard that Rowan was cleared. He may be honored and adored by the country, and even forgiven by the queen, but he remains in danger."

Gwenyth exhaled, wide-eyed with hope as she stared at Mary Fleming. "God knows the hours I have spent praying, but . . . can he be pardoned for what he did not do?"

"It's an acknowledgment that he did nothing, I believe."

Gwenyth hesitated. "What of the rumors regarding his English marriage?"

Mary shook her head sadly. "Not even my husband knows the truth of it. During his last audience with Elizabeth, she did not tell him the rumors were false, nor did she say that they were true. Gwenyth, you must have patience and faith. The queen has not suggested again that you should marry Donald, and he is a part of Laird Bothwell's retinue. So, you see, she is not a fool at all. She is careful about any shift of power."

Gwenyth hesitated but opted to trust her friend, and told Mary Fleming what had happened when she had been on Bothwell land. Both kept their attention warily on the queen's door.

"So . . . you claimed against him to preserve his life?" Mary Fleming said. Her cheeks were flushed, though Gwenyth had certainly shared none of the details of the encounter.

"But will he know that?" Gwenyth asked.

"In his heart, certainly!" Mary Fleming said, ever the romantic at heart.

The queen called out for them then. When they rushed to her side, she looked so weary and ill that it was no surprise when she said, "I would leave the city. I must see some of the country . . . a different place from Edinburgh. There is too much strife here."

Mary had not been well, but she had insisted on going secretly to Stirling, where her son lived, for it was thought that Stirling was safe. Gwenyth did not mind Stirling; it was a beautiful place, with graceful hills and dales. It was also a place of national pride for all Scots, for it had been at Stirling Bridge that William Wallace had so thoroughly defeated the English. The castle was fine, comfortable and well fortified.

And she had been there last with Rowan.

She held silent about Rowan, as Mary Fleming had warned her, grateful that it proved to be true that Rowan's name was on the lips of the people, and spoken always with respect.

Mary, however, continued frail and ill, often swooning when disturbing matters were broached to her. She was happy only in the presence of her child, and in that, Gwenyth felt her own heart break. The world was cruel indeed.

Her own child would not know her by now. She missed him as she might a limb, an essential part of her being, like breathing, like the beat of her heart.

But she dared not see him until his rights in the world were guaranteed. And it was not without deep resentment that she served the queen while Mary tended to and played with her own infant.

But Mary was not at all the passionate and confident woman who had first come to Scotland. Those who loved her feared she had suffered a breakdown of sorts, and worried continually. She had acted with such extreme courage and cleverness after the murder of Riccio, had made quick decisions and extricated herself from a life-threatening position.

But now she remained listless, and she was so ill when they started their return journey to Edinburgh that they had to stop along the way at Linlithgow and spend a night at the beautiful palace where she had been born, overlooking the glory of the lake.

They were a small party: the queen, her ladies, and Lairds Huntly, Maitland and Melville, along with a small guard, and they were met at the Bridge of Almond, a mere six miles from Edinburgh, by a huge force of over eight hundred men, armed, mounted and unmistakably dangerous. Bothwell rode straight to the queen's side and warned her that terrible danger awaited her in Edinburgh, so she must accompany him to a place of safety.

There was dissension; Maitland, in particular, was wary of the man and his news, but Mary lifted a hand and declared that she did not mean to be the cause of more dispute. If Laird Bothwell thought there would be greater safety in escorting them all to the castle at Dunbar — which she had given into his keeping just a year earlier — then they would attend him.

In the circumstances, Gwenyth didn't see how the queen could have responded any other way. Bothwell had an army with him. The queen was guarded by only thirty men.

By nightfall they were in Dunbar Castle, the gates were closed, and hundreds of men were ready to fight against anyone who might come to challenge them for possession of the queen. They quickly learned that there had been no danger to the queen in Edinburgh. She had been kidnapped.

She was kept with the Laird Bothwell and away from her friends for days. Even within Dunbar, there were rumors that the queen and Bothwell had planned the abduction together. But when rumors circulated that Mary had agreed to a seduction, as well, Gwenyth knew them to be a lie. Mary had always adhered to a strict standard of morality.

When Gwenyth saw the queen again, she found Mary to be as listless as ever. There was certainly no joy in her voice when she told her ladies, "I have agreed to marry Lord Bothwell."

"But he is married!" Gwenyth said in shock.

Mary didn't rise to anger, only lifted a hand. "See the strength and power he has? He has abducted a *queen* in the middle of her country. He is arranging a divorce." She looked away, her eyes vacant. "Jean married him because it seemed a good alliance. She will not mind the marriage being set aside. Perhaps an annulment will be arranged. But it will be a Protestant wedding."

At Dunbar, the queen's loyal retinue was

aghast, but they were powerless.

Mary Fleming and Gwenyth spoke late into the night, as they were sharing a room. "It is as if she is transfixed," Mary said. "He raped her, and she is not in a strong enough state to protest. She is lost as I have never seen her before. They are saying such terrible things, that she was sleeping with him before Darnley's death. But they're wrong. Remember when she first fell so madly in love with Darnley? Then, she was passionately involved. I do not see her behaving that way at all about Bothwell."

"It's madness. The country will be up in arms."

"Aye," Mary Fleming agreed gravely.

"This . . . this can't be," Gwenyth murmured,

"But it is."

At last, with Bothwell riding at the queen's side, they returned to Edinburgh. The guns were fired in honor of the queen, but it seemed, even to those who loved her, that Bothwell was in charge.

With unseemly haste, Bothwell's marriage was dissolved.

Twelve days later, Mary and Bothwell were married, in a Protestant ceremony, as sure a sign as there could be to those who knew Mary well that she was changed. The

Mary who had first come to Scotland would never have set her God and her faith aside.

Even as they exchanged their vows, the people of Edinburgh began to protest. There were cries in the streets, shouts of "Only wantons marry in the month of May!" and "Marry in May, regret it for aye," Scottish dialect for "forever."

Gwenyth was certain Mary found no happiness in the days that followed. She was gentle and cultured, and Bothwell could be brutal and cruel. The queen had once admired him for his power, but he was a jealous man, and now she often excused herself from the company around her, and Gwenyth knew it was because the man too often drove her to tears.

By the end of the month, it was apparent that there would be bloodshed in the land before long.

And in all that time, Gwenyth had not seen Rowan, nor heard from him, or even of him.

Just weeks into the marriage, Bothwell, Mary and their retinues moved to the castle at Borthwick, but they had barely settled there before the castle was surrounded by insurgents. Bothwell left the castle by night to gather supporters, leaving Mary behind to defend it, though he knew that the castle could not withstand a siege.

Gwenyth helped Mary dress as a man, and she did the same, darkening her face with soot, wearing the clothes of a worker. By night, they departed.

As they neared Castle Black, where they hoped to take refuge, they paused, hearing a cry in the night. It was a messenger sent from the Wauchope family, neighbors and supporters of Bothwell.

When the horseman reached them, Mary was ready to fall.

"Is it the queen?" the man asked anxiously, and he dismounted quickly, looking at Gwenyth.

"Aye. You must take her, and quickly. She is about to faint," Gwenyth advised him.

"What of you, m'lady?"

"I will be fine walking, if you will but set me upon the right road."

Gwenyth watched as the fellow gallantly set the queen atop his horse, then mounted behind her. He looked back anxiously at Gwenyth, then along the road on which they had been traveling.

"Go quickly," Gwenyth ordered him.

"I will come back for you."

"I thank you, and God bless you," she told him.

He was quickly gone, and Gwenyth was

grateful the queen was in good hands, but she found herself sorely afraid, alone along the trail. She walked with speed, suddenly aware of every whisper of wind, of the sighing of the trees and the snap of every branch.

Night, she told herself, nothing but the noises of the night. There might be boars in the forest and other fearsome creatures, but there were no creations as frightening as ambitious men.

There was a sudden loud crack to her left. It was no forest sound, and she started to run.

And then it seemed that the woods came alive. There were men everywhere.

"The queen!" someone shouted.

"We have found her!" came another shout.

"Don't be daft, it isn't the queen. She hasn't the height."

She ran, but it didn't matter that her heart pounded, or that her legs burned. They were everywhere, and she could only pray that Mary had made it safely through the forest before their arrival.

At last, no matter how she zigged and zagged, seeking to disappear through the trees, she was caught, slammed to the earth and held there by a man's foot planted upon her chest.

Her cap had fallen, and now her hair spilled free on the ground. She could do nothing other than stare up at her captor in defiance. To her horror, she knew the man. It had been a very long time since she had seen him, but she hadn't forgotten him.

Nor had he forgotten her.

"Why, 'tis the Lady of Islington, Gwenyth MacLeod," he said.

The man above her was broadly built, his face heavily bearded. It was none other than Fergus MacIvey, he who had tormented her so long ago, on the day she had ridden out from Castle Grey.

Rowan had come to her rescue then.

He would not come now.

It was what Rowan feared, always, deepest in his heart.

Civil war.

Queen Mary had been rescued and brought to Castle Black. There, she had met with her husband and, with him, had made her way back to Dunbar, where Bothwell had left her, riding out again to gather more supporters.

In the end, Mary had been betrayed.

Laird Balfour had urged her to return to Edinburgh, where she would find greater protection. When she left the defense of

Dunbar, she had several hundred supporters, as did the rebels. Rowan was certain
that Mary had not been afraid; she would
have believed in the love of her people, and
expected to be reunited with Bothwell on
the field of battle.

The armies faced each other eight miles
outside Edinburgh, and many of the lairds
Mary had so trusted abandoned her cause.
Mary, with Bothwell, was at the head of her
own defenses, with her new husband. Balfour, too, stood with them.

Lairds Morton and Home led the rebel
cavalry; the lairds of Atholl, Mar, Glencairn,
Lindsay and Ruthven led the opposing
troops.

Rowan was not on the battlefield; he had
already returned to Castle Grey, where he
had taken stock of his own men-at-arms,
preparing for whatever course of action he
decided to take. He was anxious to reach
the capital, anxious to find Gwenyth now
that it seemed he had officially been pardoned, but he had learned through bitter
experience that he had to take care. Especially now. The country had gone insane following Bothwell's abduction of Mary, and
then his marriage to her. Rowan wrote to
London, to Thomas and Annie, and to Elizabeth. He asked the Queen of England to

provide safe escort for the two faithful servants to bring Daniel to Lochraven.

In the end, no major battle occurred. Mary's supporters simply began to shrink away, so she, ever convinced of the underlying decency of her subjects, stopped the bloodshed by demanding that Bothwell be given safe conduct. She herself offered to return to Edinburgh, there to face all inquiries.

But she was not treated like a queen. The lairds feared her, and Rowan knew why. They were crying out against the murder of Darnley — but many of them had taken part in it and feared to be accused, should the queen gain the ear of the populace. And so Mary wasn't allowed to stay in Edinburgh but was taken to a Douglas holding for incarceration.

Rowan himself had not believed the lairds meant harm to their queen, but as the dire news continued to arrive, his fears grew, and he rode to Edinburgh, where he met with Maitland. He hadn't believed that the man had been involved in the original revolt against the queen, but when Maitland couldn't face him at first when they spoke, Rowan realized the man was indeed guilty.

"No wonder we have been vanquished time and time again throughout history,"

Rowan told him. "We can't even be loyal to one another."

"Rowan, please, I feel badly enough," Maitland told him. "Do you know the years I have served Queen Mary? Far longer than her stay here. I am sick at how she suffers, but you must understand. Even her French ministers pleaded with her to abandon Bothwell when she had the chance, but she would not do so."

"Let me speak with her."

Maitland hesitated. "The lairds will demand that Bothwell pay for the death of Darnley. The rumormongers were right. The evil deed was his."

"Then let Bothwell pay, not the queen."

"The lairds wish for the queen to abdicate and pass the crown to her son."

"So that they can rule."

Maitland was quiet for a moment. "She turned on you, Laird Rowan. She had you imprisoned. She had your marriage declared null and void."

"She is the queen, and my name was cleared."

"You are probably the only man who is trusted by both sides. Morton, Glencairn and Home are the men responsible for the queen's warrant. They'll give you leave to see her."

Rowan met with the rebel lairds. He knew that he had but one chance to save Mary. He had to convince her to turn her back on Bothwell.

He was amazed when he reached her. She had been rudely captured and ill-used, and her prison could not be a happy one. She had none of her ladies with her, imprisoned as she was in the home of James Stewart's mother, Lady Margaret Douglas.

Lady Margaret resented the fact that her son's illegitimacy had been held against him. She was firmly of the opinion that the throne should have been his, not Mary's.

However, she had offered no real cruelty to Mary, who, when he saw her at last, rose gallantly to the occasion of his visit, though she was pale and gaunt. "Rowan!" she greeted him with her natural affection, then told him with a smile, "You know, I totally absolved you of all sins long before this charade began. Now here I am, begging *your* forgiveness."

He took her hands, kneeling before her and seeing a slight sheen of tears in her eyes. "I have always served you to the best of my ability."

"I know. I have been deceived so many times." She drew him to his feet, smiling. "I have put my trust far too often in the wrong men."

He took a deep breath. "That is why I'm here."

"Ah, yes, I know why you are here. Everyone trusts you. I have fallen on the harshest of times, while you are lauded throughout the country. I cannot even suggest that you find Bothwell and join with him on my behalf, for he has been detained in the north."

"My queen, you must allow the marriage to be dissolved. There will be no reconciliation with your lairds if you do not."

"I cannot," she said softly.

"You must," he urged.

"I cannot, and I will not," Mary said, and her answer was surprisingly firm. "I am with child, and I will not allow any child of mine to be born illegitimate.

His heart sank. He knew he would not dissuade her.

"So . . . they allow so little news to reach me here. How does your lady? Have you sent for your own babe as yet?"

"What?"

She smiled. "Never have I seen a woman so fierce in defense of someone she loves. Surely, you have reconciled whatever differences I caused with Gwenyth?"

"I had thought she was still in your service, held with your other ladies."

Mary frowned deeply. "I last saw her as I escaped to Castle Black."

It seemed that every muscle in his body turned to water. "You have not seen her?" he asked in disbelief.

"Or heard aught of her, Rowan. If she was captured . . . surely none would offer her harm."

He could say nothing on behalf of Scotland at that moment, for he very much feared that Mary's assessment of her people was dangerously wrong.

He bowed, shaking. "Forgive me, Your Grace, but I must go. I have to find her."

Once she had dreamed. Now she had only nightmares.

She could not have been captured by a man who despised her more. When the good fighting men around Fergus MacIvey and Michael, brother of the slain Bryce and now Laird, would not allow her to be treated too roughly, Fergus found a new method of revenge.

It started with her fury and her fear.

As men shouted that Mary was a whore and a murderer, she damned them all. "The queen has never been anything but moral and good. You have no right to speak of her so. God will not forgive you this mockery and cruelty."

"God has turned his back on ye, whore of Satan," Fergus told her. He had the eyes of a true maniac, and his words were filled with a chilling glee. "God and man both. The whole country knows yer great protector has taken an English wife, and even he — especially he — has turned his back on ye."

Was it true?

Did it matter?

In Rowan's eyes, *she* had turned away from *him*.

She tried not to think about Rowan, tried not to long for the time when happiness was all around her, and it had seemed that it could never be ripped away.

At first she was treated well enough, taken to the home of a Sir Edmund Baxter and confined there. She was guilty of crimes against Scotland, she was told, because she had been helping the queen to escape. Fergus and his men left, and that in itself was a relief.

She was there for several weeks when, from the room where she was confined, she heard men talking excitedly in the parlor. The queen was imprisoned; she had given herself up rather than cause bloodshed, but she had not been returned to Edinburgh. Instead, she had been taken to a Douglas holding.

It was after that news arrived when Fergus MacIvey returned.

When he dared to return, she thought.

And he did so with another man, a man she had nearly forgotten.

Reverend David Donahue.

Even when she was brought before Donahue, she didn't fear for her life. It wasn't until he lifted a finger, pointing at her, that she realized the true severity of her position.

"Witch!" he cried. "Aye, I knew from the moment I saw her. She spoke for the Catholic whore then, as she does now."

"She bewitched Bryce MacIvey and killed him," Fergus said. "Then she bewitched the Laird Rowan and now pretends to be his wife."

"You are an idiot!" Gwenyth cried. "How can you believe such idiocy?"

She saw their faces. They believed. Or they hated her, and so they wanted to believe. In the end, it was the same thing.

"Bring her to the kirk. Now," Donahue commanded.

Fergus MacIvey and Laird Michael looked

eager to drag her, but she disdained to give them that satisfaction.

"I will walk wherever you will have me go. If it is to the kirk, so much the better. I have nothing to fear from God."

Her words infuriated them further, but they did not lay a hand on her.

When she walked from the house, though, her heart sank. The path was lined with people, men in armor, women, children, farmers, craftworkers. Pitchforks were raised against her, and a rotten tomato was even thrown her way.

"Whore witch of a whore queen!" someone shouted.

She stopped walking. "A good and decent queen ever," she calmly defended Mary.

Another tomato flew her way. She ignored it. If she stopped walking too long, Fergus would set a hand on her, she knew, so with her chin held high, she kept going.

When she came to the kirk, there was another reverend there. He stared at her as she arrived, and she knew that he'd been expecting her.

"I am Reverend Martin, official witch-finder, child, and you will confess your sins," he told her.

She looked around. There were hundreds of people there. They had all been told that the queen had been instrumental in the murder of her husband, Laird Darnley, and that she was a whore who had slept with the man who had committed the murder.

They were all ready to believe that Gwenyth, who had served her, was a witch.

She was shoved rudely inside by Fergus's hand at her back. Four women were waiting for her there. Four strong farm women. She gritted her teeth, holding very still as they seized her. Instinctively, she tried to cling to her clothing. It was no use. In a moment, she heard fabric ripping, and then one of them cried out, "There! 'Tis the mark, the devil's own mark!"

Reverend Martin stood over her, a knife in his hand. She thought that he meant to end her life then and there. She didn't struggle, knowing it would only please them if she did.

"She doesn't cry out, doesn't deny. It is indeed the mark of Satan," he agreed, then wrenched her around, jerking her up by the hair. "Confess!"

She grasped for her clothing, for decency, and stared at him. "Shall I confess to loving a good and moral woman who wanted nothing more than to govern well? Aye, that I confess."

"You have made a pact with the devil," he

said sternly.

She looked around and saw the fear and hatred in the faces of those surrounding her. There had been hundreds of men in the village, all of them now fired up by the call for revolution against a woman they believed guilty of murder. She had served that woman, and so she was guilty, no matter what she said.

"I am God's creature," she whispered.

Reverend Martin's hand cracked hard against her face. She tasted blood. "Do you care nothing for your immortal soul?" he demanded.

She was silent.

He shrugged, smiling slowly. "I have at my disposal, for I never travel without the tools of my trade, many ways to save you from the ultimate fires of hell."

She held her head high but continued silent.

Once again his hand shot out. Her ears rang; it felt as if her head had split. When she would have fallen, he caught her.

"What? What?" he said loudly, leaning down as if listening, though she had said nothing. Then he allowed her to slip to the floor, everything around her blackening, but she was conscious long enough to hear his triumphant claim.

"She has confessed! The witch has confessed!"

And she knew, as well, that she heard the laughter of Fergus MacIvey.

CHAPTER TWENTY

Mary of Scotland had last seen Gwenyth on the road to Castle Black, so Rowan first rode there, and he rode hard. His personal forces, well-trained in his long absence by Tristan's careful hand, numbered in the hundreds, but to move quickly, he rode only with Gavin, Brendan and his customary ten men.

At Castle Black, he met with the lad who had rescued Queen Mary from the road. He hadn't known Gwenyth's identity, though he had known she was one of the queen's ladies.

He was heartsick at the losses sustained by the queen, but he was eager to help Rowan. "The rebels were hot on the tail of our dear queen that night. I tried to go back to help the lady, as I had promised, but the woods were full of men, and I could find her nowhere."

Rowan felt ill, knowing she had been taken

by someone under the confederacy of the barons, and he was no closer to knowing who, specifically, had captured her. The man from Castle Black seemed at a loss on that topic, but then one of his fellows stepped forward.

"They were a mixed group, that I know, fer I was ordered to backtrack and spy. There were Highlanders among the group, I know, for I remember thinking it curious that they moved on to the southeast, rather than heading toward their homes."

And so they rode southeast. Rowan tried to use reason, rather than let a growing and frantic fear seize control of him. He ordered his men to dress as weary travelers, and they split up to roam the countryside, stopping at farm houses, villages and towns.

At last, at a public house, they joined with a group drinking in a pub. Rowan cast a glowering glance at Gavin when he appeared about to rise to fight at an insult to the queen.

"I hear," Rowan said casually, "that one of her ladies was seized, as well, but none of them know of her in Edinburgh."

An older man lifted his ale, shaking his head. "I know of her, and a sad story it is. She was seized on the road but stood loyal to her queen. There were some of the Mac-

Ivey clan among the group, and seems there was some grudge." He shook his head, lowering his voice. "Madness! They brought in a witch-finder, claiming that the woman's witchery had brought about the murder of one of their clansmen, the laird that was."

Rowan fought desperately to maintain a sense of calm. "They condemned one of the queen's ladies as a witch?"

The old fellow nodded. "It would nae ha' happened here. We're quiet folk, and we have sense in the heads upon our shoulders. But there is no help fer it. There's laws against witchcraft."

"Where is she now?" Rowan asked, aware of the husky tenor in his voice as he prayed silently that she was not dead.

"I hear they've taken her to one of the old fortifications near the border."

Not far. He had time. He would have to send for his men. Like it or not, he would be going to war, forced to kill the hapless fools who followed such men as the Mac-Iveys.

The old man looked at him, face tightening in sorrow. "She's to die tomorrow."

Startled by the news, Rowan stood, nearly knocking over the table.

"Rowan, no." Gavin's warning came too late.

But the old man was the only one who heard the cry. A strange smile lifted his lips. "Ye're the Laird of Lochraven, are ye not, man?" he asked softly. He nodded sagely, not needing an answer. "Unless ye're riding with a host of hundreds, ye cannae stop it by force."

Rowan wanted to protest, but he knew the old man was right.

"I am Finnan Clough," the old man said. "I can offer ye little. But ye need nae fear me."

Rowan thought rapidly. "Is there a chemist here?"

"Aye, there is. And I can find ye anything ye need, but —"

"I need a drug. A good chemist will know. It slows the heart and the lungs. It makes one appear to be dead."

The fellow laughed suddenly.

"What?"

"I know the drug. I am ever on the lookout fer its effects meself — I am the gravedigger at the kirk here, ye see."

"The gravedigger?" Rowan said.

"Aye."

"You, good man, can help me far more than you might imagine. I have a plan," Rowan said.

Both Gavin and old Finnan listened.

" 'Tis risky. If they discover yer ruse, ye'll die with yer lady," Finnan said when Rowan had finished speaking.

"I have nothing left but the risk," Rowan told him.

They found lodging at the public house, and there, at the crack of dawn, Rowan garbed himself in his best tartan, dirk at hand in case of need, knives at both calves, sword in the sheath at his waist. His men were dressed with equal grandeur, and they led an extra horse that carried "supplies" bound in a blanket.

He was sickened to see the air of frivolity about the town when they arrived. People were out on the streets, farmers, milkmaids, good wives, men-at-arms. Out on a hill, a scaffold and stake had been prepared, and Rowan imagined that the faggots around it were half green. The fire would take longer to catch in full, prolonging the accused's agony.

His presence was noted by many, his colors too obvious to pass unnoticed. He was glad, for he had meant for his identity to be known.

He went straight to the kirk, where he found Reverends Miller and Donahue at prayer. He did not see any of the MacIvey clan, and of that he was glad. He was certain they did not mean to arrive until it was time for the fire.

He startled the ministers as he entered the kirk with all the noise he could muster.

Both men rose, and Donahue gasped softly. "Rowan, Laird of Lochraven," he said in surprise.

Reverend Martin strode toward him. "There will be justice seen here today, m'laird. Whatever past fancy you might have shared, I'm sorry. The lady must die."

"Indeed, she must," Rowan said, his words flat and cold. "I have my own reasons to despise her wickedness."

Reverend Donahue heaved a sigh of relief, while Reverend Martin appeared greatly pleased.

"I wish to see her. I want her to know that I am here to witness her death."

The two men looked at one another uneasily.

"I wish to see her before you take her out in public. I wish to stop her — if there is anything damning, any lie, she might try to utter it at the stake."

"Ah," Donahue said knowingly. "But the time is now."

"Then you will take me quickly," Rowan said.

"I will escort you to her cell," Reverend Martin told him. "Come with me, good laird."

And so it was that the man easily walked him from the kirk to the stark remnants of the fortification. There was little left for it still to be termed a castle, but there was a roof, and the men within were armed as they sat about at cards and other games. There were twenty of them.

Quite a lot to guard one slender girl, he thought.

One of the jailers joined them, carrying something at his side. A black cowl, Rowan thought.

He was to be the executioner.

They walked down a flight of steps, and it was then that he saw Gwenyth at last.

His heart leapt and thundered. Her beautiful hair was in such sad disarray. Her clothing was torn and ragged, muddied, and she was far too thin. But in her dishevelment, she seemed to have a greater dignity than ever before.

The reverend spoke as they walked. "Thus let it be with all evil. Those who embrace the devil will be burned at the stake until dead. In fire, there is purification, and the root of ungodliness will be ashes cast to the wind."

Rowan found himself pushing ahead of the reverend, but the man continued to speak.

"Take care, reverend," she said softly. "I stand condemned, and if I speak now before the crowd, I will say that I am guilty of nothing. I will not confess to a lie before the crowd, else my Father in Heaven would abandon me. I go to my death, and on to Heaven, because the good Lord knows I am innocent, and that you are using His name to rid yourselves of a political enemy. It is *you,* I fear, who will long rot in hell."

"Blasphemy!" Rowan shouted. She had been staring at him so defiantly, even as she spoke to the reverend. But his cry had stunned her, he knew.

Rowan nodded toward the guard who would stand as executioner, and the door to her cell was thrown open. There was no choice in this; he caught her cruelly by the arm and spun her around. His fingers tore into her hair, forcing her eyes to his as he spoke again. "She must not be allowed to speak before any crowd. She knows her soul is bound for hell, and she will try only to drag others down into Satan's rancid hole along with her," Rowan said, his voice rough with hatred and conviction. "Trust me, for I know too well the witchery of her enchantment."

He held her so that their faces could not be seen by the men watching them, held her so that he could slip the vial from his sleeve, and force it toward her lips. He dropped his voice to a whispered plea. "Drink this. Now," he commanded.

She looked at him. Stared at him with such contempt and hatred in her eyes that he had to grit his teeth to maintain control. "For the love of God, drink this now," he said, and forced the vial to her lips.

Then, the light in her eyes began to fade as the drug took hold.

"She's Satan's bitch!" he cried. "She seeks to make a mockery of us all."

She was almost unconscious; she was sinking against him. He wrapped his hands around her throat.

"Bastard," she managed to whisper hoarsely.

He raised his voice again. "I shall meet you in hell, lady!" he cried.

Her eyes closed, but he kept his hands around her throat and pretended to choke the life from her.

"Stop! You'll kill her," the reverend said, annoyed.

Rowan froze. He tried not to let her fall

too hard, but he had to drop her to maintain the charade. "She is dead," he said, as her body slumped to the cold stone floor.

"You would cheat the fire?" Reverend Martin raged.

Rowan spun around in equal fury. "You are a fool! You don't know what manner of words she might have found at the stake. Would you have had this execution turn on you?" He reached down, picking Gwenyth up from the floor. She hung limp in his arms.

He fought hard not to caress her, shake her, assure himself that she did indeed live, so truly dead did she seem. He pulled his magnificent furred mantle from his shoulders and swept it around her, covering her face. He had to hurry; his timing had to be perfect.

"No one need know that they have been cheated," he announced, rising with his burden. "Reverend, lead the way."

They returned to the main floor of the ruined fortification and walked out into the sunlight. As they did so, Gavin and Rowan's men came riding straight toward them.

"So she is dead, then?" Gavin asked, as if deeply satisfied. But as he spoke, the men circled their horses around Rowan.

"The people are waiting," Reverend Martin said, annoyed.

"Let them wait. I'll not waste a good mantle in the fire," Rowan said irritably. "Give me a blanket, Gavin. We cannot let the spectators see her face, lest they realize death has already claimed her."

They moved quickly and with practiced agility. Rowan made a show of letting his mantle sweep through the air as he replaced it with a coarse woolen blanket.

Ignoring the others behind him, Rowan strode quickly to the scaffold. The crowd, aware that the time of execution was here, hurried to the site.

To Rowan's unease, the guard given the role of executioner leapt atop the scaffold and helped him secure the body.

"Light it, quickly, before someone protests that they cannot see her face," Rowan demanded.

"Aye," the fellow agreed, looking around as if suddenly aware that there might be a protest, and that he could bear the brunt of it.

The fire was quickly lit, the green faggots creating such a black and heavy smoke that those nearest began to cough.

"Wait!" the reverend shouted furiously. "I did not say the words —"

"Behold! A witch burns, a punishment

justly deserved by those who would embrace Satan!" Rowan called. Even as he spoke, he saw a group of horsemen thunder up the hill. Fergus MacIvey, the young Laird Michael at his side, was in the lead.

"Rowan of Lochraven!" Fergus shouted, astonished and uneasy. He reined in his horse; the animal did not like the smoke and fire, and reared high. "You will not stop this!"

Rowan arched a brow. "Stop it? I brought the lady to the flames." He dared not linger then, so he looked at the man with contempt. "It is done," he said briefly, then walked back past the crowd. Only Gavin awaited him, holding Styx's reins. Gavin leapt atop his mount as the rancid odor of burning flesh filled the air.

Rowan looked back to see Fergus and Michael MacIvey staring at the fire.

"Ye can't kill 'em," Gavin warned him. "Not here, not now."

"Aye."

He kneed Styx, and he and Gavin rode down the hill and quickly through the town. They rode hard until they reached the village, where Finnan awaited them with the chemist.

"Bring her to the bedroom," the chemist,

a slender man named Samuel MacHeath, said.

Despite the fact that they seemed to have found an oasis where the folk were honest and fair-minded, Rowan was careful to keep Gwenyth covered until they had climbed the stairs and closed the door behind them.

"Does she live? Before God, tell me that she lives," he said to the man.

The chemist checked Gwenyth's pulse, leaned his ear to her chest, and slowly smiled. He rose. "Aye. She'll sleep some fair time, perhaps as much as three days. But she lives."

Finnan, who had come with them, let out a deep sigh of pleasure. "Ah, now, but good old Amie McGee would be a proud woman to have done something so fine as to use her lifeless body to save the likes of a poor, maligned lady."

"Amy will never know my gratitude," Rowan murmured.

"Say a few prayers fer her soul, good Laird Rowan."

"That I will," he assured the man.

"We should ride as far from here as possible," Gavin warned Rowan.

"Aye." Rowan turned to the two men who had helped them, pressing gold coins, ironically minted with the queen's likeness, into their hands.

"Now, I dinnae say we needed money to do what was godly," Finnan said.

"Nay, good man, you did not. But favor me by taking so small a token of what I have, when you have given me back all that matters."

Finnan grinned. "Ah, a warrior *and* a poet."

With that, Rowan lifted the precious bundle of his wife close to him. This time she was covered gently with a linen sheet. When he hurried back down the stairs, the horses had been watered, his men had mounted, and they were ready to ride.

It was an hour later that the MacIveys caught up to them.

"Graham!" came a roar across the trail.

Rowan turned Styx. Fergus MacIvey, his sword drawn, was ready to ride against him.

"You have played some trick on us, and you will not ride away so easily."

"Careful," Gavin warned Rowan.

But Rowan could no longer take such care. He paused to hand the light burden of his wife to Gavin, then roared out a battle cry of fury.

He raced across the plain of grass. Fergus sped toward him, his sword glinting in the sunlight.

In the center of the field, they met. Their swords clashed, yet neither man was unhorsed. They parried, blow for blow.

Then, with a shuddering impact, Rowan managed to unseat Fergus. He leapt down from Styx, kicking the man's dropped sword to him.

Fergus grabbed the weapon, leaping to his feet, let out a cry of hatred and surged forward. His emotions had gotten the better of him. Rowan had only to shift his weight and let the man rush him. As Fergus tried to make a direct strike through his heart, Rowan stepped aside and brought his sword down on the man's neck.

As Fergus fell, Gavin cried out a warning.

Rowan turned to see that Michael Mac-Ivey had meant to drive his sword into Rowan's back while his uncle had kept his attention.

There was no time to think, no chance to consider whether the man should live or die. Rowan was forced to spin, and as he moved, he caught the man through the stomach, sending him crashing backward.

Rowan stood above the fallen man.

Michael's eyes were open, and a trickle of blood oozed from his lips, and he was dead, an expression of shock frozen upon his face.

Rowan quickly looked up, anxious to see

which of the MacIveys' forces would come for him next. But they had gone, deserting when it appeared they could not win.

It was Brendan who came to his side then. "Laird Rowan, it's over. Let's take yer lady home."

"Aye," Rowan said. "Home."

Gwenyth awoke slowly, feeling as if she had been submerged in a deep, black cave. She was aware of little things first.

A hint of light.

Something soft beneath her.

The scent of clean linen.

But she had died! Surely Heaven could not have the scent and feel of earth!

She tried to open her eyes more fully. She was no longer in rags but a clean, snowy-white gown.

Upon a snowy, sweet-smelling bed.

For a moment the world seemed to be a white mist, and she blinked to clear her vision.

There were two smiling faces staring intently at her. She blinked again.

Annie!

And Liza Duff.

"Oh, sweet Jesus, she has awakened!" Annie cried. Then she leaned forward, her ample bosom nearly crushing Gwenyth as she hugged her, tears streaming down her face.

"It's true. Laird Rowan, Laird Rowan!" Liza cried.

And then he was there, features taut and golden hair blazing, eyes a miraculous blue fire.

"My lady!"

"Rowan?" she said incredulously.

"Aye, my love," he said, and sat at her side. His fingers brushed hers, and then she was tenderly in his arms, as he held her as if she were as fragile as glass.

"It can't be," she whispered, and he pulled away. She looked at him, stunned, lost, afraid that this was but some dying dream. But the linen was real; the heat of his hold was real.

"She's wakened? Thank God, our lady is with us again," came another voice. Gavin.

"Saints be praised!"

Gwenyth looked beyond Rowan and saw that Thomas was there, as well.

Rowan spoke quickly. "We had to substitute a . . . well, a corpse for you, my love, on the stake, but there was no time to talk to you before. You had to appear dead, so I drugged you. I am so sorry to have hurt you in any way."

She blinked, throwing her arms around

him again. "But I am condemned by law!" she told him.

"That is a situation that is being righted even now."

"The MacIveys will never let it be," she said, drawing back again to look at him.

"The MacIveys are no more," he said in a low, hard tone.

"But . . ."

He let out a deep sigh. "Mary has abdicated the throne in favor of her son — by force, I imagine, but it is done. She made provision first that our marriage be declared legal in Scotland, and that Daniel is our legal issue. James, acting as regent, has signed his name to the documents, as well."

She gasped. Such sweet news, though mixed with such a sad addendum.

And yet, at that moment, all she could do was thank God she was alive.

She drew Rowan tightly to her. "Oh, Rowan, I never meant to hurt you in any way. I was afraid . . . and I'd heard . . ."

He pulled away from her, smoothing her hair back, touching her cheek with such tenderness that she was afraid she would faint, and lose out on this sheer joy and wonder.

"I never entertained the idea of another wife, my love. And I know that you cried out against me only to force me to leave."

This happiness was surely more than she could bear.

And then . . .

"My lady," Gavin said, clearing his throat. "There is someone who wishes to see you — if you are strong enough."

She realized, as Gavin walked to the bed, that he wasn't alone.

She stared in amazement at the small human being he carried. A boy with brilliant blue eyes and sun-gold hair.

He looked at her, his eyes wary but curious.

"Mama?" he said.

"He walks now, too," Rowan told her, reaching for the boy and setting him on the bed between them.

Gwenyth stared at her son, the child who shouldn't have known her, who couldn't know her, but who watched her with such curious expectation.

"Daniel," she breathed. Then she looked from him to Rowan and suddenly burst into tears.

"My love, my love," Rowan said, and she struggled for control, anxious not to make Daniel cry.

"I . . ."

"It's all right," he said. "Everything will

be all right," he vowed, and then he smiled. "Because I will never leave you again. Ever. I have served my country, and we both served the queen we love, with all that was in us. But now I have discovered that the Scotland that I love is here on my own land and in my heart, that I cannot change other men, and I certainly can't change the world. So . . . I will always do what I can to speak for the queen, to create peace and reason. But I will never leave you again."

She stroked Daniel's hair, meeting Rowan's eyes, and smiled, though her own eyes remained damp. "And I will love you forever," she breathed. "And ever."

Fate was kind to them.

Even the great preacher Knox was furious when he found out that decisions of the soul were being tried and judged on a political basis.

The Reverend Miller and the Reverend Donahue were arrested to stand trial. The poets of the day wrote beautiful stories about Laird Rowan's rescue of his lady wife, and their status was assured in Scotland, their home secure.

Queen Mary miscarried, and the fierce maternal instinct that had made her proclaim for Bothwell was gone, but the people

— her people, who had so loved their beautiful queen — could not forgive what they believed to be her complicity in a murder perpetuated so that she could marry her lover.

She escaped her captivity from the Douglas stronghold, helped by several members of the family, and fled to England.

Rowan and Gwenyth traveled many times to see her throughout the years of her incarceration by her cousin, gratified to find that Elizabeth — though refusing to see her cousin — also for many years refused her lords' urging when they suggested that Mary was a threat against the state and should be executed. There was still the possibility of a Catholic uprising, and Elizabeth was too wise to incite it.

As the years passed, Daniel was joined by Ian, Mark, Ewan, Haven, Mary and Elizabeth. Gwenyth's children were with her when Rowan, every bit the great knight as when she had met him, when she and Mary had both been such young women, came to her with word of Mary of Scotland's death. He tried to break the news to her gently, told her that Mary had been surrounded by those she loved when she had walked to the scaffold, that no one there, not her enemies, not Elizabeth's servants, could say that she died with anything other than the greatest composure and dignity. She had offered her love to those around her, and she had assured them all that she knew she would find her place in Heaven with her God, and that she was weary and ready to rest.

The threats and the pressure had grown too many and too great. Queen Elizabeth had felt forced to give in.

Headstrong, passionate, determined to be the best ruler she could be, prey to plots around her, still seeking the best in men, Mary, beautiful, vivacious, tempestuous Mary, Queen of Scots, had ended her days with grace and elegance.

No matter how Rowan tried to ease the blow, Gwenyth was heartsick. She cried for days on end. She needed time alone. Rowan gave her that time. He was busy, the threat of war with England looming on the horizon. Mary's people might have turned against her when she had needed them, but they didn't intend to tolerate her death now. But James, her son, now grown, lived with the dream that had been bred into him: that of the joint thrones of Scotland and England. He could have led the country to war, but he did not.

Several weeks after the queen's death, Gwenyth rose from her chair when the family had ended supper and walked around behind her husband, slipping an arm around him, pressing a kiss against his cheek. "I need you so tonight," she whispered.

Rowan rose a little too quickly.

"Good heavens," Daniel said lightly, shaking his head.

"What on earth does that mean?" Marcy — as their Mary was called — demanded.

Daniel, fully a man then, laughed and looked at his parents, then apologized. "I'm so sorry. But you two have been married these many, many, many —"

"Aye, Daniel, move it on," Rowan said.

"Well, it is almost embarrassing," Ian put in.

"What are you talking about?" Marcy persisted.

"It means we're seeking a name for a new baby," Daniel said with a soft groan.

"Daniel, it is a problem we will just have to deal with," Rowan said firmly, and winked at Gwenyth. Then, because he couldn't help himself, he swept his protesting wife off her feet and, ignoring their handsome brood of children, carried her laughing all the way up the stairs.